SHADOW ZONE

STORM CYCLE

"A pulse-pounding adventure intricate enough to satisfy tech-savvy geeks and hard-core adrenaline junkies alike."
—*Booklist*

"Enormously exciting . . . escapist thrills of the highest order."
—*RT Book Club*

"With the authors' trademark research, fast-paced action, and charismatic characters, *Storm Cycle* will blow you away."
—*The Oklahoman*

"Breathtaking."
—*Star-News* (Wilmington, NC)

SILENT THUNDER

"Bestseller Johansen and her Edgar-winning son, Roy, collaborate on their first thriller with entertaining results."
—*Publishers Weekly*

"Gripping."
—*Booklist*

"[In *Silent Thunder*] . . . you'll be rewarded with a bumpy roller-coaster ride as you try to separate the good guys from the bad."
—*Rocky Mountain News*

CLOSE YOUR EYES

IRIS JOHANSEN
and
ROY JOHANSEN

St. Martin's Paperbacks

This is a work of fiction. All of the characters, organizations, and events portrayed in this novel are either products of the author's imagination or are used fictitiously.

CLOSE YOUR EYES

Copyright © 2012 by Johansen Publishing LLLP, and Roy Johansen.
"With Open Eyes" copyright © 2012 by Johansen Publishing LLLP, and Roy Johansen.
Excerpt from *Taking Eve* copyright © 2013 by Johansen Publishing LLLP.

For information address St. Martin's Press, 175 Fifth Avenue, New York, NY 10010.

Library of Congress Catalog Card Number: 2012007561

ISBN: 978-1-250-01041-4

Printed in the United States of America

St. Martin's Press hardcover edition / July 2012
St. Martin's Paperbacks edition / February 2013

St. Martin's Paperbacks are published by St. Martin's Press, 175 Fifth Avenue, New York, NY 10010.

10 9 8 7 6 5 4 3 2 1

For Sherry Tillinger

Who made the world a brighter and more loving place

PROLOGUE

It wasn't just her imagination.

Stephanie Marsh looked back as she walked through the second level of the parking garage for Gold's Gym. She wasn't alone.

She had been aware of distant footsteps attempting to fall in time with her own, but she had told herself that they were just echoes reverberating off the empty garage's concrete walls.

No such luck. There was definitely someone in the shadows behind her.

Or was he in front of her?

Stay calm, she told herself. It wasn't as if she were one of the gym's perfect tens who were weirdo magnets in their skimpy, formfitting workout wear.

But since when did a psycho need a reason to attack a woman at 10 P.M. in an empty parking garage?

She was okay, she told herself. Everything would be fine. As long as those security cameras were—

Her heart jumped into her throat.

Shit. The cameras were in place, but the reassuring red glow of their power lights were nowhere to be seen.

She did not break stride as she reached into her purse and gripped the rubber case of her mobile phone. She raised the phone and stared in disbelief at its illuminated screen.

NO CARRIER.

She was accustomed to losing her signal, but not her entire freaking phone company.

This couldn't be happening.

"Need help, young lady?"

A man stepped from the shadows in front of her. He wore dark tennis shoes, khakis, a T-shirt, and a pullover sweater similar to the one her grandfather wore. The man was probably over sixty, and his entire face crinkled as he smiled.

He looked like a nice man, but she knew better than to lower her guard. Jeffrey Dahmer might have looked like a hell of a nice guy.

She kept walking. "No problem. Have a good night."

"You, too." He smiled again. "The Portland Street exit is closed. You'll have to go out on Wesleyan."

She nodded and walked faster. This wasn't news. The Portland Street exit was always closed after eight.

Just a few more yards to her car . . .

The man held a map of some kind. "Could you help me out with this? I've been wandering around this cocka-mamie garage for ten minutes trying to find a—"

She made a wide arc around him as she neared her car. "I'm sorry, I'm in a hurry."

He took a step closer. And then another. "If you'll just take a look at this . . ."

The map fell away, revealing a glint of steel.

Pain.

She shuddered, unable to move.

The man now stood next to her. He shook his head as

he slowly pulled the blade from her abdomen. "I'm sorry," he whispered. "You don't deserve this."

She stared at him in disbelief, trying to reconcile the kind, regretful face with the horrible thing that was happening to her. She was falling, the floor of the parking garage rising up to meet her. She scarcely felt the impact. Her insides felt like cold concrete, hardening and making it impossible for her to move.

Or breathe. She tried to scream, but there were only gurgling sounds in the back of her throat.

The man wiped his bloody knife with a bandana. "Shh. It will be over soon, Stephanie."

He knew who she was.

Then it hit her.

They had found out.

"Schuyler." She pushed out the word.

"Just relax."

"Tell Schuyler . . ." Darkness crept over her, from the back of her neck, over her skull, taking away thought, taking away everything that she was.

She had to say it. Gotta get this out . . .

"Yes, dear?" he asked gently.

Her eyes fluttered as she summoned the last bit of energy her body would ever give her.

"Tell Schuyler I said . . . to go to hell."

CHAPTER 1

Kendra Michaels pulled the strap over her head and adjusted her guitar in front of her. "We're going to do something different today, Jimmy."

"No!"

She ignored the outburst. Twelve-year-old Jimmy Matthews hated any variation in his routine, but she was determined to coax him, ever so slightly, from his comfort zone. "Look at me, okay?"

Jimmy looked up at her, his dark eyes glittering with defiance. He was autistic, and it had taken weeks for him to feel comfortable enough to make eye contact with her. She'd regarded that as a major victory. She knew there were other breakthroughs to come, if only she could unlock the secrets of that bewildering yet fascinating mind of his.

She held his gaze. "Jimmy, remember when I had you put your hand on my guitar last week? When I told you to feel the music?"

He nodded.

"You liked that, didn't you?"

He shrugged.

"You *could* feel it, couldn't you? I saw you tapping your fingers and moving your feet."

He thought for a moment. "I felt it all over."

"I know. And I thought to myself, this guy has rhythm. You know what that means, don't you? It means you can feel the beat. You can feel it in your bones . . . and in your soul."

He looked away again. "I want to sing. I always sing."

"And you're a really good singer. And you can keep singing, but I want you to do something else."

She turned and walked across her small studio. It was a carpeted, octagonal-shaped room with a whiteboard, a piano, several colorful music-themed posters, and a large mirrored panel at the far end. "Come here, I want to show you something."

Jimmy hesitated.

She smiled luminously at him. "I promise that you're going to like this, honey. Don't you trust me?"

He didn't answer, then nodded jerkily. "I . . . trust you."

Her heart melted. Another victory.

"That means a lot to me, Jimmy." She gripped the corner of a white tarp and pulled it away to reveal a percussion kit.

His eyes widened. "Drums!"

"Do you like it?"

He bit his lip. "Why should I like it? I don't know how to play drums."

"Anybody can play drums. Whether they can play them well, that's another matter." She picked up a pair of drumsticks and placed them in Jimmy's hands, curling the fingers around in a matched grip. She pulled him around to the other side of the drum set. "Now sit down. This will be fun."

Jimmy slowly sat, holding the drumsticks in front of him as if they were sticks of unstable dynamite.

"You don't have to hold them so tightly. Loosen up, feel the beat like you did last time."

He looked at the various surfaces around him. "But what do I do?"

She strummed the guitar. "Whatever you feel like doing. Whatever sounds and feels good to you." She played George Harrison's "Got My Mind Set on You," accenting the song's strong and clean rhythms.

Jimmy held the sticks over the snare drum.

"Anytime."

He struck the drum's surface tentatively.

"Both sticks, Jimmy . . . Come on, it's fun!"

He used both sticks to accompany her on the snare, striking with a not-entirely-unrhythmic beat.

"That's fantastic!"

He closed his eyes and nodded. He branched out to the tom-tom on his left, accenting his stylings with the lower-pitched drum.

"Good!" She pointed down to the pedal on the floor. "That's for the bass drum. Want to try it?"

He pressed the pedal and reacted with a start as the kicker struck the drum surface. He stepped on it again and again, repeating the motion until he found the rhythm she had set.

He continued on the bass drum as he struck the snare and tom-tom with increased vigor.

Kendra studied him. Could it be?

Ever so slightly, a faint smile was pulling at the corners of his mouth.

Yes.

Kendra Michaels didn't appear to be the bitch he'd thought she'd be, Adam Lynch thought, as he watched her through the one-way glass in the observation room as she interacted with the child. What he'd heard about her had been far from complimentary, but that could be due to jealousy. Her work had completely overshadowed that of the FBI agents from whom he'd received reports. Evidently, she had not done it diplomatically.

Yet every move, every expression, was warm and gentle as she taught that troubled boy. A puzzle. If he was going to use her, he had to know which buttons to push to do it. He had no doubt he'd find a way to do it. It was a skill that had earned him both applause and hatred over the years. But it was annoying that he'd been given the wrong information with which to develop a method to do it. He studied her, looking for an answer to the paradox.

Though she was of middle height and slim, she did not appear fragile at all. When she walked or moved, she had a litheness that spoke of strength and suppleness earned by frequent exercise. Her shoulder-length, pale brown hair was sun-streaked in places. Her face . . . Strength there, too. A strong chin, well-formed lips that still spoke of control and discipline, large hazel eyes that were set far apart and seemed to hold intelligence as well as humor. Not a pretty face, but for an instant, when she smiled at the boy, he had seen a flash, a beauty. It was the most dangerous form of allure, which could challenge a man to try to make that elusive beauty reappear again and again. She wouldn't appeal to everyone. She was too strong, too confident, but Lynch was drawn to that challenge.

He felt a rush of sudden eagerness at the thought of dealing with Kendra Michaels. She was interesting. He had grown so accustomed to successfully manipulating his targets that any change, any stretch, was welcome.

What was the key that he could use to make her go in the direction he wanted? Sympathy? She obviously had a warm attachment to children. But would that extend to adults? Anger? Fear? Sex? No, that last choice had popped up out of nowhere and probably had nothing to do with logical reasoning and everything to do with his physical response. The other two were possibilities, but he would have to see if they were necessary tools.

Oh well, it would come to him. He leaned back against the wall, his gaze intent on Kendra Michaels. In the meantime, he would enjoy watching her. She was like a kaleidoscope, with different shadings and settings shifting before his eyes.

Yes, Kendra Michaels was going to be an interesting project.

The hour-long session with Jimmy stretched to an hour and fifteen minutes, violating Kendra's own rule about her enforced stopping times. She wanted to leave her clients wanting more, eagerly anticipating their next session together. It was always tempting to keep going when she saw them enjoying themselves, but Jimmy had hit such a joyful groove in his drum playing that she knew he wouldn't tire of an extra quarter hour.

Kendra opened the door to the waiting room, where Jimmy's mother, Tina, had watched from behind the large one-way glass.

As Tina entered, Jimmy rushed toward her. "Mom, I played the drums!" He pounded his drumsticks into the air.

Tina laughed and hugged him. "I saw! You were amazing!" She glanced at Kendra. "I can't believe the way he lit up!"

"Yes, he did."

"I actually think . . . he's getting better."

"He could be." Kendra managed a smile. She knew that Tina wanted more confirmation than that. All the parents did. They spent their lives searching for some sign—any sign—that their children might finally be turning the corner in their afflictions, but it was rarely that clear-cut. It was a marathon, not a sprint, she liked to say, and this race could go on for the rest of their lives.

But once in a while, there could be an exception. And who was to say that exception couldn't be Jimmy?

"It was a good day," Kendra said. She gently took the drumsticks from Jimmy. "I'll see you Friday?"

"Yes!" He pounded the air again, still playing to the song in his head as his mother escorted him out.

It had been a good day, Kendra thought. Maybe she should have been more—

"So this is what you do for a living."

The voice came from behind her. She spun around to see a man strolling toward her from the waiting room. "How did you get in here?"

The man was fortyish, tall, well dressed, and his dark hair was cropped short. Ice blue eyes lit a craggy face that was as tanned as if he'd spent the winter in the Caribbean. He jerked his thumb back toward the waiting room. "The main entrance was locked, so I tapped on the door from the hallway. That nice woman let me in. She may have had the impression that I worked with you."

"Maybe because that's what you told her?"

"Not in so many words."

"It doesn't take so many words if you choose the right ones. Who are you?"

The man walked toward the piano and idly plunked a few notes on the keyboard. "If what I've heard about you is true, you already know quite a bit about me." He turned back to her. "Why don't *you* tell me who I am?"

She gazed warily at him. She had been acquiring information about him since he walked into the room, but she realized it was being submerged by the sheer impact of his personality. There weren't many people who possessed that instant magnetism, and she had an idea that he used it with the deftness and skill of long practice. Complicated. She had no need of any more complications in her life.

She checked the screen of her cell phone. "I have another appointment coming. Sorry, I don't have time for games. You should go now."

"This is no game. Humor me, Dr. Michaels." He smiled.

It was a charming smile, she thought, meant to put her at ease and draw her closer into the web. Oh yes, she had to be very careful with him.

"It's the quickest way to get me out of your hair," he continued. "Much easier than calling security. I'm curious to see—"

Kendra cut him off. "You're right, let's get to it. Who are you? Let's see. I know you have a background in law enforcement, probably the FBI." She walked around the studio, straightening it for her next client. "But I'm fairly certain you don't work for them now, though you are consulting for them in some capacity. As a matter of fact, you were at the downtown FBI branch office earlier today. And I agree with you that the third-floor conference room is quite stuffy and warm."

He stared at her for a long moment, his gaze narrowed. "Amazing. I would say that they called and tipped you off, but I didn't tell anyone that I was even considering coming here."

"No one tipped me off. I had no idea you were coming, and I'm sure they didn't either." She covered the drum kit as she continued her assessment. "When you were with the Bureau, you carried two guns, one in your left shoulder holster and the other on your right ankle. Now you're only carrying one, in the shoulder holster. I guess getting shot wasn't quite enough to put you off guns entirely, was it?"

He smiled. "Go on. I'm enjoying this."

"I'm sure everyone told you to spend more time recuperating, but you couldn't stand to sit still, could you?

That wheelchair drove you crazy, almost as much as the crutches did."

"Anybody would feel that way."

"You more than most. Is that why your wife left you?"

He raised his left hand, where a slight indention still appeared on his ring finger. "That's an easy one."

"It's all easy. That ring indention is tanned, but not nearly as tanned as the skin around it. I'd say you took it off two years ago."

"Two and a half years."

"I stand corrected. I'm assuming you don't have children. If you did, that Italian sports car you drive wouldn't be very practical."

"I know you didn't see me drive up."

She shook her head. "I didn't. Not very inconspicuous for someone in your line of work, is it?"

"I'm entitled to my indulgences. I have another, much more boring, car at home. No kids, by the way."

"You've been in this area for a while, but not always. You grew up in the Midwest. Wisconsin, I'd say. You probably even went to college there. After that, you spent a few years in the Northeast. Then you came here."

"In-freaking-credible," he said softly. "I do believe that everything I've heard about you is true."

"I'm so happy I didn't disappoint you," she said sarcastically. "Will you please leave now? I'm very busy."

"And more than a little hostile. Now why is that? Could it be because I'm FBI?"

"Possibly. If you're here, I'm sure you know I've had a few problems with the Bureau."

"I've heard rumors." He crossed his arms and leaned against a table. "But there's no way I can leave without finding out how you knew all that."

"I didn't know. There's no way I could know unless someone told me."

"But you were right on the money with everything you told me."

"It's all a matter of probability. With the information I had, the likelihood of each of the things I said was high. But I really didn't know. Will you please leave? You're taking up valuable time."

"You didn't tell me who I am. What's my name?"

"You can't have everything." She stared him in the eye. "I'd have to work on that for a while. I've given you the performance you wanted from me. You're not getting anything else." She paused. "Nothing. Don't ask."

"My name is Adam Lynch. How did you know I was with the Bureau?"

"Good afternoon, Mr. Lynch."

He studied her for an instant, then turned on his heel. "I'll go. You'll be more willing to deal with me if you don't have to worry about keeping those kids waiting. We'll continue this later."

"Make an appointment. I'll see if I can fit you in. I doubt it. The FBI isn't high on my list of priorities."

He gave a low whistle. "I understand you had a very warm relationship with one FBI agent. Jeff Stedler must have really pissed you off." He paused. "I'm curious. In the bedroom or on a case?"

She stiffened. "My God, what nerve. You'll stay curious, you nosy bastard."

"Sorry. I'm usually not that clumsy. You're having a peculiar effect on me. I'm finding there's something about you that disturbs my usual modus operandi. Forgive me." He moved toward the door. "We'll talk later."

She couldn't let him walk out of the room without asking the question.

"Wait." When he looked over his shoulder, she asked, "Did Jeff send you?"

"No, though he's the reason I'm here." He smiled.

"We'll discuss him at the same time you explain how you knew the intimate details of my life. Tit for tat." He left the studio.

Clever. Lynch had dangled that alluring tidbit of information to hook her into another meeting. He wanted something. He probably wanted her.

Kendra gazed after him with exasperation. She was tempted to just block him out of her thoughts and tell him to take a jump. But that reference to Jeff had made her curious . . . and a little worried.

It was strange that Lynch made that abrupt sexual reference to her affair with Jeff. It wasn't slick or diplomatic. For an instant, she'd seen a flicker of recklessness in his expression. Another facet of Lynch's character revealed. Another sign of the complication she'd sensed. Did she want to assuage her curiosity badly enough to deal briefly with him again?

She didn't have to make up her mind just then. She had work to do.

She went to the door to bring in Jenny Brooks, her next student.

Kendra locked up the studio and walked to her car as the late-afternoon sky softened into twilight. She had tried to block Adam Lynch from her mind all afternoon. Damn him for showing up in the middle of the day, taking her mental energy from people who needed it far more.

Forget him. She would go home and document her observations, as she usually did after a day of appointments. As much as she cared for her clients, who ranged in age from two to ninety-three years old, she knew she could make an even bigger contribution with the treatment options she had developed and was still refining with each session. With precise protocols and careful documentation, she and others were slowly pushing the discipline of music therapy away from alternative woo-woo medicine and into the mainstream of accepted scientific opinion.

If she could concentrate on what was important instead of the problem that Lynch had put before her. She still felt unsettled, and she knew that her encounter with Lynch would not be her last. She would have to consider what he'd said and decide how to handle him.

If he let her have the time to consider anything before he pounced again.

Adam Lynch was leaning against the hood of his sports car, waiting in the parking space when she drove up to her condo twenty minutes later.

She wasn't even surprised.

She got out of her Honda and strolled toward him.

He smiled. "You look a bit more mellow. Was the rest of your day successful?"

"Fairly. I think I made a few steps forward in the dance."

"Dance?"

"With my kids, learning is like a tango. Sometimes they learn the most complex steps with astonishing ease, and yet the simple ones baffle them." She turned and moved toward her front door. "You might as well come in. You'd probably camp out here if I don't get this over with."

"Possibly." He followed her. "And, besides, you want to know about Jeff Stedler."

"That's true." She unlocked the front door. "You're very perceptive."

"Which means you still care something for him."

"Does it? We were lovers for a year, but that doesn't mean it was anything more than sex."

He tilted his head. "But I don't think that you could have an extended sexual relationship with anyone unless you at least liked him."

"You have a right to your opinion." She went into the condo and turned on the lights. "But you don't really know anything about me, do you?"

"I know you were born blind due to a degenerative corneal disease in the womb. You remained blind until you were twenty." His gaze wandered around the contemporary living room decorated in rust, red, and gold shades. "Lots of color. This is charming. I can imagine how you must have embraced color when you first experienced it."

"It was as heady as a straight shot of vodka." She looked at him. "I embraced a lot of things after my operation. Everything seemed new and exciting. Including Jeff Stedler."

"Interesting. But you haven't satisfied my curiosity yet about what crystal ball you used to reveal all my secrets this afternoon."

"Secrets? It would take more than a crystal ball to learn anything about you that you didn't want me to know. But you're not going to let it go, are you? Okay, let's get it over with." She sat down on the arm of the rust armchair. "How long has it been since you were with the FBI, Adam Lynch?"

"How did you know I was FBI? You said that before I mentioned Jeff Stedler."

"Your jacket cuts a clean line, but there's still a rather distinct bulge under your left armpit."

"Many people carry guns."

"Not that many. Law enforcement and private security mostly, followed by gangsters and thugs."

He smiled. "You don't think I'm a thug?"

"Oh, you're most definitely a thug. You're just paid to be one by the FBI."

"I'm still waiting for an explanation how you knew that."

"You're obviously aware that the FBI has brought me

in to consult on a few cases. I've been in that stuffy third-floor conference room, and I've sat in those ridiculous diamond-backed chairs. When you take off your jacket and place it over the chair back, you're left with three distinct impressions: one just below the collar and two others beneath the shoulders. That's exactly what I'm seeing on that jacket of yours."

He shook his jacket lapels and brushed his shoulders. "Seriously?"

"Don't worry, it's very faint, and it goes away after a day or so."

"Okay, but how do you know I'm still not an agent? How do you know it wasn't just another day at the office?"

"In that building, agents wear their IDs around their necks. Makes it easier to swipe across sensor pads to unlock doors. But visitors wear badges that clip to their clothing." She walked up to him and pulled on his jacket's breast pocket to show a quarter-inch horizontal crease near the top. "The badge holder leaves a mark that looks like this. If you were wearing something a bit more sheer, you might see what looks like a row of tiny teeth marks."

"Fortunately, I'm not in the habit of wearing silk shirts to FBI headquarters." His gaze narrowed on her face. "But how do you know I was ever an agent at all?"

"Even though you're not wearing an ankle holster now, you still walk as if you are. You make a slight sweeping motion so your pant leg doesn't press against your phantom holster. That's law enforcement all the way."

"Really?" He looked down at his feet. "Do all FBI guys walk like that?"

"More than you'd think. Police detectives, too. It's only slightly less obvious than a Haggar slacks pant leg pressed up against the side of a nine-millimeter automatic."

"I still wear it from time to time. And you were also

right about the leg wound." His brow furrowed. "But I'm pretty sure I'm not walking with a limp."

"Not a *visible* limp."

"What's that supposed to mean?"

"To look at you, one would think you move with nothing but the utmost authority and confidence."

"I think there's a 'but' coming."

"You still slightly favor your right leg. I can't see it, but I can hear it. But what I *can* see is a pretty nasty scuff on the sole of your left shoe. It's covered with shoe polish, but I can see it's been worn down quite a bit. That might have been prevented if you hadn't been so quick to ditch your crutches."

"How do you know I didn't slip in the bathtub or have a motorcycle accident?"

"I don't. But it stands to reason that a man who has a need to carry two guns might occasionally find himself on the receiving end of some gunfire." She stood, moved across the room, and picked up her guitar, which was leaning against the stone fireplace. She started tuning it. "And you don't impress me as someone who would slip in the bathtub. You're very sure on your feet."

"And where I've lived?" Lynch asked.

"Simple linguistics."

"I'd say not so simple."

She shrugged. "Simple for me. Vocal patterns and spoken language are like music. There are many people who know a Chopin melody a mile away. Some of us are just as good with the spoken word."

"You picked up on a blend of my Midwestern and Eastern accents?

"Not only that, but exactly how the vocal patterns interact. If you had grown up on the East Coast, *then* moved to the Midwest, you would sound much different today. It's like the difference between a soup with half an onion cut into it, or a plate of sautéed onions with a couple spoon-fuls of soup ladled over them. Totally different flavor."

"And my car?"

She raised her phone and showed him the screen. There was a live video feed of the condo parking lot.

He held the phone and looked at the display. "What's this?"

"It's what it looks like. I have a Wi-Fi camera con-nected over the door. Here at home, it's a security mea-sure. I also have another one connected over the door at the studio. I like to see when my clients are coming."

"Or men in Ferraris?"

"I glanced at it just after you came into the studio. I recognized the other four cars in the lot but not that one."

"I'll be damned." He smiled and shook his head. "I have to admit, I thought everybody was exaggerating about you and your—"

"Parlor tricks?"

"I was going to say 'perceptive abilities.' I can see it was no exaggeration."

"Glad you enjoyed the show." She adjusted the tuning pegs, then looked up. "Now you talk. Why did you think it worth your while to come to see me and have me perform for you? If you want my help in an investigation, you're going to be disappointed."

"You haven't even heard what it is."

"I don't need to. I don't do that kind of thing anymore. You should have done your homework on me."

"Believe me, I did. I may not be able to write your life story based on the cut of your sweater, but I know quite a bit about you."

"Obviously not enough. Otherwise, you would have known not to waste your time coming here."

"Trust me, I won't consider it a waste of time, no mat-ter what your answer is." He added softly, "It's never a waste of time to meet fascinating people. And you're re-markable, Kendra."

"Flattery won't work with me. Cross it off your list."

"No flattery, just a statement of fact. You were blind since birth, but that didn't stop you from working your way through school and getting a Ph.D. in psychology and a masters in music theory. From a very early age, you used your remaining senses to gather amazing amounts of information about the world around you. Information that most people couldn't dream of perceiving."

She shrugged. "I used what I had."

"You used it in an extraordinary way. When you were twelve, a group of Fundamentalists accused you of being a witch, while another group in the same church said you were channeling the power of God."

She smiled. "Both explanations were much more inter-esting than the truth."

"Then, thanks to a stem-cell procedure in England, you got your sight at the age of twenty. Just seven years ago. I can't imagine what it's been like for you since."

"No, you can't." She set the guitar down. "So don't try. And I'm sure it's not important for your purpose to try to understand me."

"You're wrong; understanding is essential in what I do." He continued. "And your amazing gifts just multiplied exponentially. When you were finally able to see, you wanted to absorb everything and process every single de-tail. And so you do. You still see more than anyone else in the room, and you do it without even trying."

She shook her head. "Who says I don't have to try? It just so happens that I *like* trying. I'm greedy. I want to experience everything. I don't take anything for granted."

"If you like it so much, why don't you want to help me?"

"I've already had that experience. I'm done with it. As

I'm sure you know, I've already assisted on four investigations."

"You did more than assist. You broke those cases."

"I only did it as a favor to Jeff Stedler. He was intrigued by what I could do and asked me to do it as a favor. I agreed because I thought of it as a challenge, and it amused me." Her lips tightened. "But then he got greedy and wanted me to keep on doing it. Suddenly, it didn't amuse me any longer."

"And suddenly he didn't amuse you any longer either."

"You could say that." She met his eyes. "I don't like being used, Lynch."

"Is that a warning?" he asked softly.

"Yes."

"Accepted. But even if Stedler used you, evidently you haven't jettisoned him completely, or you wouldn't have let me into your house."

"Maybe. You said he didn't send you here?"

"No, but we've met." He added deliberately, "And I think he's a good man."

"Yes, one of the good guys. I never said he wasn't. He wants to set the world right. That's why he joined the Bureau." She added wearily, "And he wanted me to help him do it. Batman and Superwoman fighting all the bad guys. He got the idea that I could be of some help to his investigations, and I guess I was. But I just can't do it anymore."

"Perhaps you should reconsider. You can save lives."

"Don't put that on me," she said fiercely. "Jeff tried to tell me that, and I told him to go to hell. I won't be responsible for what he thinks is the right thing to do."

"It's true."

"I'm saving lives every day in that studio you visited today. It may not be as dramatic as what you and Jeff are doing, but for me, it's a hell of a lot more worthwhile."

She shook her head. "I shouldn't have decided to talk to you. Whatever your case is, I'm not interested."

"Six people, Dr. Michaels," he said quietly. "Six people have been killed in the last forty-five days."

"Starting with the man in Highland Park?"

He stiffened. "So you've been following it."

"Not really," she said. "Jeff asked for my help a couple of weeks ago, and he told me a few things. I was wondering if that was the case you were talking about. I guess that answers the question."

Lynch stared at her. "Stedler came to see you about this case?"

"I turned him down. I practically kicked him out. I told you, I'm not interested in doing this kind of thing anymore."

He muttered a curse, and his tone was suddenly urgent. "What did Stedler say to you?"

"Not much. I didn't let him get very far. About the same as you've said. Except it was five murders then, not six."

"An administrative assistant was killed in a downtown parking garage at Gold's Gym Monday night. We believe it's connected to the others. What else did he tell you?"

"Ask him yourself."

"I can't ask him myself, dammit. He's missing."

Shock rippled through her. She stared at him for a long moment. "Since when?"

"More than seventy-two hours. I think it might have something to do with this case."

She was trying to recover from the shock. "And why do you think that?"

"It's a little complex. Let's talk about it," he coaxed persuasively. "You once cared for him. You must have some lingering feeling. Help me figure this out."

"There's no evidence of foul play? He just disappeared?"

"No evidence."

"Then Jeff could be working on a case and gone undercover. He doesn't have to be in any danger."

"That's true. But a little unlikely since no one at the office knew about it. What would it hurt to assume the worst and try to make the attempt to find him? Then you could be pleasantly surprised if he showed up on his own safe and sound."

She stared at him in exasperation. This man was just like Jeff, subtly pushing her buttons to get her to do what he wanted. Only Jeff had done it because he wanted to be Galahad, and she was the lance he could use to skewer the villains. She had an idea there was nothing of the white knight about this man.

Enough.

"No," she said. "I don't even know if you're telling me the truth. You're not . . ." She searched for words. "What I would call standard-issue FBI. And the FBI has a whole organization full of people who can track Jeff down. Why do they want me for this?"

"They don't want you."

Her brows rose. "This wasn't their idea?"

"No. They have a few problems with your . . . attitude. It's all mine. Will you help me?"

His urgency had given way to something else, she thought. Could it be . . . desperation? Not likely. She'd judge it would take something almost catastrophic to cause Lynch to become desperate. Or perhaps he was just trying another button on her.

"I'll have to think about it."

"Every minute counts."

"Don't push me. I'll think about it. If you want my final answer right now, I'm afraid it's going to be—"

"Okay, fine. Just think about it. Call me."

"Do you have a card?"

He shook his head and pointed to her phone. "My information is in there. I transmitted it to your address book about thirty seconds ago."

"I don't think so." She pulled up the phone's address book and scrolled through the entrees. "You'd need my permission, and I still haven't received any—" She froze as she spotted a new name in her list of contacts.

LYNCH, ADAM. The address and phone number fields were entirely filled in.

She looked up. "How did you do that?"

He smiled. "If it runs on electricity, I can make it do pretty much anything I want. I suppose we all have our special talents, Kendra." He strode out of the room as he called over his shoulder. "I can help you better secure that thing. Sorry if I've invaded your digital space, but like I said, every minute counts."

She watched the door close behind him. He had invaded more than her digital space. Because of the intensity of the problems she faced every day, she needed serenity and a sense of order in her life away from the studio. Adam Lynch had marched in and disturbed that serenity within minutes after he'd come into her studio.

Lord, she didn't want to dive into another ugly horror like the ones Jeff had dragged her through.

Yet if Jeff was missing, then he might be in trouble . . .

And was she supposed to go to his rescue? Why, dammit? She had told him the last time he had called her that the split was permanent, and she didn't want to hear from him again. Jeff couldn't accept friendship with her without trying to bend it to suit himself, and she couldn't keep the hurt and anger from upsetting her when he did it. She had desperately wanted to keep him for a friend. She didn't let many people close to her, and there were moments when she had come close to loving Jeff Stedler. She did love his passion for justice, his dedication. Even when she was furious with him for trying to use her, she could understand that he couldn't help himself.

Okay, so she would feel guilty as hell if she didn't try to help Jeff if he was in trouble.

But how did she know that Lynch was telling the truth? What did she know about Adam Lynch?

Zilch.

Then, dammit, find out about him.

She reached for her phone. Jeff had introduced her to a few of his fellow agents on cases, and surely she could find out about Lynch from one of them.

If they'd talk to her. There were times when she'd been very impatient with them.

Jeff had said substitute "rude" for "impatient."

Well, perhaps. But they'd kept arguing with her when she'd known she was right.

She found a name in her directory. Agent Bill Santini. Yeah, she remembered him. He hadn't seemed to be too antagonistic toward her.

Maybe.

She dialed the number.

He answered the call on the second ring.

"Santini, this is Kendra Michaels. I need some information."

Silence.

"What kind of information?" he asked warily.

"Adam Lynch."

"He contacted you? I'm surprised. We told him it wasn't worth his while."

"I told him the same thing. He doesn't listen. Has Jeff really disappeared?"

"Unless he just decided to take off for the South Seas. No one has seen him for seventy-two hours. We've all been worried as hell."

"And what does Lynch have to do with it?"

"Who the hell knows? Lynch's a secretive bastard. He just showed up and started asking questions."

"And why would you answer them?"

"You must not have been around him long. People usually do what Lynch wants them to do."

"Why? He's not with the Bureau any longer, is he?"

"No, but he has friends in high places." He added impatiently, "Look, why pick on me to question? If you're so smart, why don't you work it out for yourself?"

"It would waste time." She added honestly, "And I chose you because I don't think you dislike me as much as the other guys at the Bureau do."

"Don't count on it." He sighed. "Okay, that was rude. I shouldn't have been that blunt. I didn't mean to hurt your feelings."

"You didn't. It was just an error of judgment on my part."

"Kendra, I don't really . . . You just manage to piss me off. You made me look like an idiot on the Salvatori case."

"You were wrong. And you argued with me. I had to show you how foolish that argument was."

"And you did. You have a tongue like a buzz saw. You embarrassed the hell out of me."

"Then you shouldn't have argued with me. It was so clear."

"To you." He added resignedly, "But I honestly don't think there was any malice in you. Though some of the other guys don't agree with me."

"Then I was right about your not disliking me as much as they do?"

"Aren't you always right?" He didn't wait for an answer. "Yeah, I was the right choice. What else do you want to know about Adam Lynch?"

"Everything."

"I don't know everything. I wasn't with the Bureau when he was here. I've only heard rumors."

"Rumors are good."

"Nothing much good about the rumors about Lynch. He's notorious. Or maybe it depends on your viewpoint. Some agents think of him as a legend. They call him the Puppetmaster."

"Absurd. Why?"

"He's a master manipulator. He had a dislike for the court system and didn't trust it worth a damn. When he was an agent, there were stories about how he'd manipulate criminals into situations in which they'd bring about their own deaths, forcing them into corners or tricking them into taking lethal chances." He added, "Probably his most high-profile case was when he went undercover with two different crime families in New York and Philadelphia and pitted them against each other. They crippled each other's operations and murdered many of each other's top men. It was much easier for us to step in and bring them down entirely. He was a hero for a while until he got into trouble again for disobeying orders and going his own way."

"How long did he get away with it?"

"For a long time. Until Lynch clashed with a new FBI director, and he parted company with the Bureau. He's now a black-ops strategist for U.S. Intelligence agencies."

"Lynch said he met Jeff. How?"

"That I don't know, Kendra."

Kendra was beginning to have an idea of the connection between Jeff and Lynch. Jeff would have been intrigued and enthusiastic about an agent with Lynch's capabilities just as he had been with her gifts.

"Jeff didn't mention Lynch to me when he spoke to me recently. He didn't speak to any of you about him?"

"No, I told you I don't know anything about a connection between them. Is that all?"

"What do you think of Lynch?"

"Are you asking my opinion? Will wonders never cease?"

"I don't have anyone else to ask."

"I'm glad you put me straight. I wouldn't want to get a swelled head. Lynch? I barely know him." He was silent, thinking. "I'm not sure I'd trust him, but I'd be glad to have him in my corner if I was in trouble. We were kind of glad when he showed up after Jeff disappeared." He hesitated. "Look, I know that you cared about Jeff. I want you to know we're doing everything we can."

"Thanks, Santini." He had been helpful. She should probably say something else. "You probably did better than anyone else in the Bureau could have done on the Salvatori case."

He gave a mock groan. "Condescension. That was worse than the verbal slap on the face. Good-bye, Kendra." He hung up.

She pressed the disconnect and sat there thinking. She shouldn't really have asked Santini his opinion when she'd probably discard it anyway. He was an okay agent but not particularly brilliant, and Lynch could probably manipulate him if it suited him.

Puppetmaster?

She made a face at the corny term. She could imagine Lynch being just as scornful as she felt. He was much too sophisticated to want to be labeled in any way.

Yet she admitted that she had definitely noticed him trying to pull her strings. She was glad to know where he was coming from and what she could expect.

But that didn't mean that she wanted to deal with him, even if he was trying to find Jeff. He made her uneasy. She would have to think about it.

And how she felt about being involved in the search for Jeff. If it was trouble, then she—

Her phone rang.

She tensed. Lynch?

No, her friend, Olivia Brandt.

She breathed a sigh of relief. No challenge, just warmth and affection. "Hi, Olivia, how are you doing?"

"Great. How did your day go?" Olivia asked. "Any breakthroughs?"

"A possible with Jimmy."

"I celebrate possible. Come over to my place and have a drink."

"I just got home. I need to shower and change."

"Nope. It's cocktail hour. I'll see you in ten minutes." She hung up.

Kendra shook her head. Olivia could be immovable when she wanted something. Well, maybe she needed to talk.

And maybe Kendra needed to talk instead of brood.

Why not?

Olivia was in a condo in the same complex, and Kendra could be there in five minutes. She'd have a drink and relax, and she could be back in an hour or so.

She grabbed her handbag and headed for the door. It was ridiculous that Lynch had made her this uneasy. She was in control of what she did or did not do.

Why the hell did she feel like she needed that drink?

CHAPTER 2

Olivia stepped out of the kitchen with a bottle of Chianti and poured it into two wineglasses on the living-room coffee table. She positioned her index and middle fingers on either side of the glass stems to position them as she poured.

"How was that?" Olivia said. "Did that look too 'blind'?"

"You *are* blind."

"I don't want it to show every minute of every day. Tell me, did that look too blind?"

"No. You can pour wine with the best of 'em. But I wish you would stop."

"Easy for you to say."

It wasn't easy, Kendra wanted to tell her. She and Olivia had known each other since they were small children at a school for the visually impaired. Back then, they had banded together against their challenges and discovered new ways of defying expectations.

And in the bonding had come a deep and abiding love.

Olivia had been genuinely happy for Kendra when she was suddenly given the gift of sight through an innovative new stem-cell operation, with no trace of jealousy. To the contrary, Olivia had reveled in each of the opportunities available to Kendra, and she almost seemed to live vicariously through new experiences they had only dreamed about as girls. Recently, however, Kendra noticed that her friend was concerned more and more with her outward appearance and behaviors, especially those that might reveal her as a sightless person.

"What in the hell is going on?" Kendra said. "Since when do you care about 'looking blind'?"

Olivia sat on the couch next to her and took a sip of her wine. "I've always cared about it. Even when I said I didn't."

"Not like this. Are you doing this for a guy? Because any guy who can't accept you for who you are isn't worth—"

"It's not for a guy." Olivia made a face. "Give me some credit."

"All the credit in the world." She studied Olivia as she sat there on the couch. If she could see herself as Kendra saw her, she wouldn't be this insecure, dammit. Dark sleek hair that hung in a shining curve to her shoulders, olive skin, enormous brown eyes, and lips that were almost always smiling. As usual, Olivia was dressed in the latest fashion, black velvet trousers, silk blouse, and a leopard-print vest that made her look svelte, trendy, and totally beautiful. "I'm just trying to figure this out. This isn't like you."

"I'm not one of your puzzles that you can just crack, Kendra." She grinned. "As much as you've always liked to try."

"Then don't *be* such a puzzle. Out with it."

Olivia spoke quietly. "I want people to talk to me . . . like they talk to you."

"What do you mean by that?"

"I noticed it almost from the moment you got your

sight back. The people you meet are more relaxed, more *themselves* with you now. I know that you've noticed."

"Of course. But we always knew how awkward some people could be around us. We used to laugh about it."

"Believe me, I still laugh. But if I can do a few things to make people forget that I can't see, at least for a little while, I want to try. Oh, I know it's pretty obvious in most situations, but occasionally I can pull it off. My cousin took me to a dark little bar downtown on Saturday, and I met and talked to a guy for over a half hour without his knowing. It was great."

Kendra sighed. "I knew this was about a guy."

"It isn't. I don't care about him."

"Did he freak when he found out?"

"A little. But by then the ice had been broken. Look, I don't expect you to understand."

"Of course I understand. I just don't want you to think you ever have to do that around me." She added quietly, "I know how lucky I am. I wish with all my heart that I'd been able to bring you with me out of the darkness, Olivia."

"I wasn't lucky enough to be a candidate for the operation. And someday I may come out on my own. They're making all kinds of medical strides these days." She suddenly grinned. "But in the meantime, I do the best I can with the help of my friends. Hell, no. I'm not going to pretend to be anything but what I am around you. But I'm still going to practice around you once in a while. I need constructive criticism."

"If you insist."

"I do." She took a sip of wine. "But you didn't come here to talk about my insecurities. What's bothering you? Is your mom okay?"

"Blooming. She just left on a cruise to the Caribbean

with her cousin, Jan. She told me she might bring back a sexy beachcomber from Cancún."

"That sounds like her. Then what is it?"

She should have known that Olivia would sense her disturbance. As much credit as Kendra received for her powers of observation, it was Olivia who had a way of cutting to the emotional cores of the people in her life. "A man came to see me today. He's working with the FBI on a murder case, and he wants my help."

"Another one of those. You said you were through with that bullshit."

"I know. It's the same case Jeff talked to me about a few weeks ago."

"I remember. You sent him packing."

"That's right."

"Good. You promised, no more detective work. I can't stand to go through another one of those cases with you."

"And I'll keep my promise."

"So what's the problem?"

Kendra looked away. "Something has happened to Jeff. He's disappeared."

"And that's what they want? They want your help to find Jeff?"

"They think his disappearance may be related to the case. I don't have all the details, but I don't believe he would just take off without telling anybody." She frowned. "At least, I don't think he would."

"But you're not sure." She smiled. "And that's the reason you came here, Kendra."

"Since when do I need a reason? I came here because you offered me a drink."

"You came here because you want me to tell you it's okay to do this. Maybe even that you *should* do this."

"Don't be ridiculous. I don't need anyone to tell me what to do. That's not why I'm here."

"The hell it isn't."

Shit, Olivia knows me too damned well.

"Okay. Maybe I am worried. What if he's in trouble? I'd never forgive myself if anything happened to him if I could have prevented it."

"Guilt. That's exactly what he used to rope you into the Racine kidnapping case."

"I got one of those kids back. Another few hours, and he would have been buried alive."

"But he'd already murdered the other two children, and you almost died in the process."

"You're exaggerating."

"Am I?"

Probably not, Kendra admitted to herself. The children had been abducted by a local politician's aide, and the case had totally consumed her night and day for the better part of three weeks. By the end of it, she was ill, numb with exhaustion, and her relationship with Jeff was in tatters.

"It's been over a year, and sometimes I still wonder if you've recovered," Olivia said grimly.

"This is different. This is . . . Jeff."

"Jeff . . . who you swore you never wanted to see again?"

"I still don't," she said tartly. "But I can't erase him as if he never existed. And it doesn't mean I want to see him floating facedown in the river."

"Listen, Kendra, it's not as if he was the love of your life. You came together because you wanted a little stability after those first few years of sowing your wild oats when you gained your vision. Jeff Stedler was the perfect choice, steady and yet offering you a chance to do something different and interesting. Only it didn't turn out that way. Something 'different' damn well nearly blew you apart."

"We were together almost a year. I can't just shrug that off."

Olivia shook her head. "They're using your feelings for him to draw you into this investigation." She leaned forward. "Dammit, remember how hard it was for you? You had never been in such a dark place before, Kendra. You scared the hell out of me."

"I scared the hell out of myself."

Olivia shook her head. "But that's not going to stop you, is it?"

"I haven't decided yet."

"Yes, you have. I can hear it in your voice. You've switched on the autopilot."

"You're wrong."

"It's not fun when you're the one being analyzed, is it? But I know that tone in your voice. Your mind is already working on it. We could sit here for half an hour talking about everything under the sun, and you would say all the right things. But I'd still know."

She sighed. "My damn voice. You'd think I'd learn."

"I always know when that mind of yours has kicked into high gear. I can hear the gears turning, girl." She reached out and picked up her glass. "So I'm not wasting my time." Then she put the glass down again with force. "The hell I'm not." She leaned forward, found Kendra's hand, and tightly clasped it. "You're important to me. Probably the most important person in my life. I won't lose you. Okay, do what you have to do. But don't you dare come back like that again. Do you hear me?"

"I could hardly help it." She chuckled as she reached forward and gave Olivia a quick hug. "I guess that means I've made a decision. I just had to have you tell me what it was."

"Always willing to oblige. Now, since that's settled, have another glass of wine and tell me about Jimmy's 'possible' breakthrough. You know how I adore your success stories."

An hour later, Kendra sat in her condo and stared at the phone in her hands. Was she really going to do this?

Who in the hell was she kidding?

She dragged her finger down the touch screen until she saw the uninvited listing in her phone book: LYNCH, ADAM.

Neat trick.

She pressed it to dial the number.

Lynch answered on the first ring. "I'm glad you called."

"I have a few questions for you."

"Anything."

"Do you have any suspects?"

"None."

"Does this series of murders cross-reference with any others in the database?"

"Not really."

"So Jeff was about as close to catching the killer as my mom's pug is. Assuming that the killer was even remotely aware of Jeff's existence, why would he be considered a threat?"

"You're obviously going to ask me more than a 'few' questions. Suppose you meet me at his office tomorrow morning. The Bureau will bring you up to speed. You'll be given full access to all of his materials relating to the case."

"You said they didn't want me on the case."

"They just hadn't thought of it. They have nothing but the utmost respect for you."

"Don't lie to me."

"Okay, they think you're kind of a smart-ass bitch."

"That's more like it."

"But they're willing to work with you."

"Why?"

"Because I'll insist."

"And who are you to be telling the FBI what to do? Make no mistake, I *like* it. I've had my run-ins with the Bureau."

"I understand that's an understatement."

"And I understand that you've had your run-ins with them, too."

A silence. "You've been asking questions."

"And getting answers."

"I expected that to happen, but I thought I'd have a little time to prepare the way. Did you find out anything that might turn you against me?"

"Nothing that I can't handle. But there's something I'm not getting here. You're no ordinary consultant, right?"

He paused. "Can we talk about this later?"

"No."

"I've done work for most of the federal law-enforcement agencies. In this case, I'm here at the behest of the Justice Department."

"Are you acting as some kind of profiler?"

"No. When Jeff Stedler disappeared, it became more than just a serial killer case."

"Why you?"

"Besides the fact that I used to be with the Bureau, I have a reputation for getting things done. It also didn't hurt that I live in the area. I'm familiar with the way things work around here."

"And are you up to speed on the case?"

"Totally. We can go over it tomorrow morning."

"I haven't told you I'm on board yet."

"What more do you need?"

"I want to see Jeff's condo. I'm sure his FBI buddies have already made a sweep through there."

"They have. They came up empty."

"I'm sure they did. So when can I get in there?"

"How about now? I can meet you there in ten minutes."

"You just happen to have his keys on you?"

"No."

"Right. I guess we're just going to break in?"

Silence.

"You can't be serious," she said. "You're supposed to be law-abiding."

"I'll see you there in ten minutes."

He cut the connection.

Kendra stood outside the main entrance of Jeff's six-story building, trying her damnedest not to feel nostalgic for the good times she'd had there.

There had also been plenty of bad times, she reminded herself. Arguments, both subtle and broad pressures being brought to bear, the bitter realization that she had been used. Memories that couldn't be erased no matter how much Jeff had wanted her to try.

"Thanks for doing this."

She looked over her shoulder to see Adam Lynch walking up the sidewalk toward her.

He smiled. "I wasn't sure if I'd ever hear from you again."

"But then you'd have just kept nudging me to do what you want." She stared him in the eye. "I'm not committing myself to anything more than a quick look around."

"Fair enough. From what I've seen, a quick look around from you is worth quite a bit."

"You weren't serious about breaking into his place, were you?"

" 'Breaking' is such a harsh word. It conjures up images of splintered door frames and smashed locks."

"Ahh. You're just going to gently coax our way inside?"

"I'm sure Stedler's FBI buddies wouldn't mind arranging a visit for you, but I don't want to wait that long. You would also have them breathing down your neck the entire time you were in there."

"I see. So instead, I'll just have *you* breathing down my neck."

"You could do a lot worse for yourself." He opened the building's front door. "After you."

They took the elevator to the fourth floor and made their way down the carpeted hallway to unit 432. Except for the addition of tan wallpaper on the corridor walls, nothing had changed in the year and a half since she had last been there.

Lynch gripped the doorknob and fumbled with it for a moment.

She smiled. "Is that your definition of 'coaxing'?"

Another twist, and he pushed the door wide open. "Yes, as a matter of fact."

Only then did she see that he was holding a brushed-metal picklock device in his palm. "You're fairly good with that thing."

He shrugged. "I'm glad you think so. Some women are more impressed with the sight of a man hurling himself at a locked door."

"That's a little too caveman for me. And stupid. I don't appreciate stupidity."

They stepped inside the condo, a comfortable two-bedroom unit with a large living-room area that joined an open kitchen.

She scanned the room. "Cleaner and neater than it used to be."

"Maybe he has a girlfriend who keeps it clean. I used to date someone who was a neat freak, and my place never looked better than it did when she—"

Kendra cut him off. "Possible. But it's far more likely that he's started employing the cleaning service on the refrigerator magnet." She tapped the magnet that was shaped like a vacuum cleaner. "Has anyone called them to see if he's missed any of their scheduled visits?"

Lynch smiled. "I'll ask. Anything else different?"

"Nothing but the television." She gestured toward the large flat-panel screen and pair of dark glasses on the coffee table. "I knew he wouldn't be able to resist it once the sports networks started broadcasting in 3-D."

Lynch glanced at the framed sports memorabilia on the wall. "Yeah, I didn't know he was such a sports nut."

"Then you don't know him well at all."

"Can't say that I do. I only met him once. Anything else?"

She walked around the living-room area and stopped in the vicinity of a dinette set consisting of a square table and four chairs. "Something happened here."

He tensed and took a step closer. "What, exactly?"

"I don't know. But the carpet over here has recently been replaced. Just in this area. The rest is six or seven years old, but this has been put down just recently."

He knelt to give the carpet a closer look. "Are you sure? This entire room looks like it's all of a piece."

She nodded. "Yes, it's a good job. One would think it was all laid at the same time."

"So what makes you think any differently?"

"The smells. Carpet goes through a period of outgassing to release the odors of manufacturing chemicals. It's faint, but I can pick up traces of butylated hydroxytoluene, formaldehyde, and 4-phenylcyclohexine."

His brows rose. "What's 4-phenylcyclohexine?"

"You may know it as 4-PC."

"Oh, of course." He rolled his eyes. "I don't smell a thing."

"That's because you didn't spend the first twenty years of your life depending on your sense of smell to help make your way through the world." She pointed down at the carpet. "You might have better luck if you bury your nose in the carpet fibers."

"Uh, no, I'll take your word for it. You can really identify each of those chemicals?"

"Sure. They're fairly common in most new carpets." She dropped to her knees and began pulling apart the densely packed carpet pile. "Here's the seam. See?"

Lynch slowly nodded.

She pointed to the wall behind the dinette table. "It probably goes all the way back there. Maybe seven feet by four feet."

"The pieces look exactly the same as the rest of the carpet."

She stood up. "That's what worries me. I wouldn't be disturbed if the new piece looked new. I'd *expect* it. But it looks like someone went to a lot of trouble to make this new piece look just like the six-year-old carpet in the rest of the room."

He nodded grimly. "A lot of trouble . . . and a very narrow field of expertise."

"You can start by tracing this carpet to the manufacturer. See if anyone has ordered it recently."

"I'll run it by forensics."

She stood up. "When people engage in deception, whatever it is, they usually only consider the visual. They don't think about the sounds, odors, and tactiles."

"Unfortunately, most people in law enforcement don't think about those things, either."

She turned and headed for the bedroom. "I'm finished in here. Let's look at the rest of the apartment."

They examined the bedroom, guest room, and two bathrooms. Everything was in place, exactly where it was supposed to be. There was no evidence that Jeff had been recently dating anyone, Kendra noted, unless Jeff's sleepover companion limited her stash to a year-old tube of lipstick.

"Is his car here?" Kendra asked.

"In the garage downstairs. I'll take you there."

They took the elevator down to the garage's dim lower level and walked toward Jeff's Ford Explorer. Kendra stopped a few feet short of the vehicle.

"Have the FBI guys been in there?"

"I don't think so."

She narrowed her eyes as she slowly walked around the Explorer, soaking up as much information as she could in the shadows of the garage.

"Anything?" Lynch asked.

"Jeff wasn't the last person behind the wheel."

"How do you know?"

"The driver's seat has been moved much farther back than he ever would have had it. He's five-eleven, and that seat is set for someone six-four, maybe even six-five. But the rearview mirrors are still angled for Jeff's height. As if someone else was sitting in there, maybe cleaning or looking for something. But I'm quite sure you noticed that."

"As a matter of fact, I did. The seat, not the mirrors. But I don't think anyone else caught it. Anything else?"

"The windows have been wiped clean, but if you'll look under the wipers, you'll see some pollen."

Lynch lifted the right wiper blade and looked at the thin, powdery line on the bottom edge of the windshield. "Red."

"Pink, really."

Lynch produced a small evidence envelope and scooped up some of the pollen. "The FBI lab has a guy who could identify this in no time. He'll put it under a microscope and—"

"Pineland Hibiscus."

He glanced at her. "You're sure?"

"I'm positive that's what this is. But by all means check it out."

He pocketed the envelope. "Would you like to tell me how you could possibly know that?"

"Plants with unique fragrances are very special to someone who can't see. So when I *could* see—"

"I get it, I get it. Anything else?"

She made one more circle around the car before answering. "No."

"This has been very valuable. I could really use your help, Kendra," he said quietly.

She looked away from him. "What do you think I'm doing here?"

"It's not enough. Come with me to Jeff's office tomorrow. Take a look at his desk, talk to the other agents there. They'll show you his notes."

"Are there recordings?"

"You mean his voice memos."

"Yes. He was always talking into that damned little recorder. He played his voice memos back through his car stereo whenever he was driving somewhere. He said it helped him keep case details straight. I used to tell him that he just liked hearing the sound of his own voice."

"We have most of his recordings for this case. He backed them up to his laptop just a couple days before he disappeared. I can get you a copy of the transcriptions."

"I don't want transcriptions. I want to hear them myself."

He studied her for a moment. "Does that mean you'll help me?"

Kendra cursed under her breath. Dammit, Jeff. You're not even here, and you're still dragging me back into that hellish hole . . .

"I'll pick you up at your place." Lynch's gaze was fixed on her face, reading her expression. "Eight tomorrow morning."

"One visit to his office. I'm not promising any more."

"Fine."

She turned away and strode back toward the elevator. She didn't like anything that she'd found that night. It was scaring her. The comforting premise that Jeff had gone undercover and might turn up safe and sound was fading.

"You're worried." Lynch was next to her, pushing the button of the elevator. "I don't blame you. Let me help. We can do this together."

His voice was persuasive, and that magnetism was in full effect. He was taking advantage of a moment of weakness and making the most of it.

"You're thinking I'm on the attack," he said quietly. "And I am. But it doesn't change the fact that I can help you. You're afraid I'm going to use you. Turn the tables on me. Use me."

"I might do that." She got onto the elevator. "It depends on what I find out tomorrow. He could still be alive, you know. For all I know, Jeff could have just found another way to draw me into this damn case. They call you a master manipulator? Jeff wasn't far behind you." She punched the button. "And if I help find him and discover that's the truth, I'm gonna kill him myself."

Half a block from Jeff Stedler's condo, Oscar Laird crouched low in the front seat of his Range Rover as Lynch and Kendra Michaels roared past him in their respective cars and turned the corner. The street was well illuminated by streetlights, but he had found a shady stretch under a large Dutch elm tree.

He picked up his mobile phone and dialed.

Charles Schuyler answered immediately. "Okay. What have you got?"

"Lynch and the Michaels woman just left."

"So she's working the case with him?"

"It sure sounded like it. I could hear every word they said in Agent Stedler's condo. And I've got some bad news for you . . . She knows about the carpet."

He expected Schuyler to cut loose with a string of expletives; instead there was just silence. Lethal, terrifying silence.

"Are you still there?"

"You gave me your word." Schuyler voice was quiet, each word measured.

Laird would have preferred to hear the expletives. He had worked as Schuyler's security head for many years and knew that in this mood, Schuyler was at his most vicious. "And the carpet cleaner gave me *his* word. He's the best in the business."

"How in the hell did they find out?"

"She . . . smelled it."

"*What?*"

"I recorded the whole thing. I'll let you listen for yourself. Kendra Michaels is . . . weird. She's almost creepy."

"I'm glad you're so impressed by her. What in the hell are we going to do about this? Time's running out."

"It doesn't have to be a problem. I could have her and Lynch taken care of tonight."

Silence.

"Not yet, Laird." Schuyler's voice was thoughtful. "But have your people standing by. We'll definitely keep that option on the table."

CHAPTER 3

Kendra clipped the visitor's badge to her jacket lapel and glanced around the lobby area. Déjà vu. The same guards, the same black-tiled floors, the same awful fake plants. God, she hated this place.

Lynch examined the badge clip before putting it on. "You're right. Sharp little teeth on this thing."

She turned toward Lynch. "I know there are some things you're not telling me. I haven't cared enough to press the point, but I will not even consider helping you until you tell me everything there is to know."

He nodded. "Would you believe me if I said I didn't want to influence your perceptions just yet?"

"There's not much chance of that. I trust my own judgment far too much to be so easily swayed."

The corners of his lips indented in a half smile. "I'm starting to realize that."

She heard the elevator chime and a familiar set of footsteps approaching from the other side of the guard desk. "We'll talk later . . . if I'm interested."

"Fair enough."

Agent Bill Santini appeared, a sandy-haired man of

medium height. His middle-age paunch had grown since the last time she had seen him, Kendra noticed. "Kendra, Lynch . . . Good morning." His monotone was meant to be without expression. It was not—he was definitely pissed off.

"Good to see you, Bill," Kendra said. "So *you* got picked to take us up. Does Griffin still put you in charge of the afternoon Starbucks run?"

He scowled and turned around. "Follow me."

Kendra smiled. Santini might have been helpful when she'd pumped him for information about Lynch but the truce was clearly over. And Santini was so easily annoyed by her that she just couldn't resist scoring off him.

"Can you at least *try* not antagonizing them?" Lynch murmured.

"Can't help it. Just comes naturally."

Santini escorted them to the fifth floor, where Kendra noticed that she and Lynch were attracting a lot of attention—some of it hostile, some merely curious—as they walked past the offices and cubicles. He stopped at the small conference room and motioned for them to step inside. He followed and closed the door behind them.

The head of the San Diego office, Special Agent in Charge Michael Griffin, stood and walked toward them. He was a fiftyish man with silver hair, and as far as Kendra had ever been able to tell, no sense of humor. "I was surprised when Lynch told me you would be joining him, Kendra. I'm not sure there's much you can do for us here."

"I'm not sure either, Griffin. Let's find out."

Griffin motioned toward the only other person in the room, a young blond woman with shoulder-length hair. "Kendra, this is Special Agent Sienna Deever. She's been working this case with us for the past few weeks."

Sienna stepped forward and eagerly shook her hand.

"A pleasure, Dr. Michaels. I've been reading up on the other investigations you helped along. I'm impressed."

Kendra smiled. Sienna possessed an enthusiasm that characterized many agents just out of the academy. She hadn't been beaten down. Yet. "Don't be too impressed with me, Sienna. It could make you very unpopular around here."

Sienna's face froze as she decided how to react.

Griffin brushed past her and motioned toward a series of whiteboards running down the length of the room. "Let's get started. We have a case file, of course, but this is probably a better way to get a quick grasp of what we're dealing with. These are our victims. Three women and two men. Age range from thirty-five to forty-seven."

Kendra looked at the whiteboards, which featured a driver's license photo of each victim, crime-scene shots, and vital stats. She paid particular attention to the crime-scene photos. "Serial killers don't usually mix genders like this. Were they each attacked in similar surroundings? At home?"

"Three were, two weren't."

Sienna pointed at the photographs. "Tricia Garza, Monica Sellers, and Nick Wagner were killed at home. Stephanie Marsh and Steve Conroy were killed in public places, a parking garage and a city park."

Kendra studied the crime-scene photographs. "It looks like Garza, Sellers, and Wagner lived in detached single-family homes. Correct?"

Sienna nodded. "The other two lived in apartments."

"Less private, easier to be seen coming and going," Kendra said. "Probably why these two were attacked elsewhere."

Griffin dropped down in one of the diamond-backed chairs. "That's how we see it. These people were targeted."

Kendra tried to detach herself emotionally from the horrific images on the board, but she couldn't. She never could. Others in the room could look at the splayed bodies and awful grimaces as mere puzzle pieces, but she would never have that facility.

Thank goodness.

But she was positive they would sleep better than she would that night.

She turned from the photos. "Different murder venues. Again, not typical for a serial killer. So what's the connection? There has to be one, or else you guys wouldn't be involved."

Griffin looked at Lynch. "You haven't told her?"

"I'm letting you take it, in case she has follow-up questions."

Griffin exchanged quick glances with the other two agents. "We haven't gone public with this yet. We're actually not even sure what it means."

They were clearly uncomfortable discussing it with her, Kendra realized. "Why all this buildup, guys?"

"What we're about to tell you can't leave this room."

She half smiled. "My, my, you sound like someone in a grade-B movie. It's not as if I'm going to run out and sell the story to *Rolling Stone*. You seriously overestimate my interest in this case, Griffin."

She'd done it again. Kendra could see them stiffen and draw away from her.

Sienna quickly stepped forward, as if to get between Kendra and her superiors. "Dr. Michaels, perhaps I should tell you that I was brought into this investigation because I'm a toxicology expert."

"Poisons?"

"Yes. I've published quite a few papers on the subject. I was actually an Army physician before I joined the Bureau."

"Now it's my turn to be impressed. But the bodies in these pictures don't look as if they were poisoned."

"They were, believe it or not. Every one of them."

Kendra glanced back at the photos of corpses lying in pools of their own blood.

"It obviously isn't what killed them," Sienna said. "But that's our common thread. They each had the same contaminant in their systems. It was discovered almost by accident in the first victim's autopsy."

"What contaminant?"

Sienna shook her head. "We don't know."

Kendra's brows rose. "That's your expert opinion?"

"I'm afraid so. We have half a dozen labs working on it, but so far we can't identify the substance."

"I'm not sure I understand. You say that this contaminant isn't something that killed them . . ."

"It might have, if they had lived longer. We do know that this contaminant, whatever it is, appears to be a base-altering mutagen. It invades the system and actually alters the DNA."

"That's not so rare, is it? There are insecticides that do that."

"This is no insecticide."

"Just how does it alter the DNA?"

"Hard to say without knowing exactly what we're dealing with." Sienna peeled back several pages of a flip chart on an easel until she came to a large molecular drawing. "Here's what it looks like, at least on a molecular level. We just don't know where it came from or what its purpose is."

Kendra stared at the drawing. "You're telling me this contaminant is something no one has ever seen before, except in the bodies of these five murder victims?"

"That's the way it looks."

"Interesting." Kendra scanned the vital stats written

beneath the photos of each victim. "Did they ever cross paths with each other?"

"Not as far as we can tell. They lived and worked in different parts of the city, and there's no evidence of any kind of environmental exposure that could have affected just these people."

Kendra studied the victims' photos a moment longer. "You're doing a good job keeping this under wraps from the media," she said slowly. "I'm finding that unusual. Why don't you go public with this?"

"The killer doesn't know we know about this," Griffin said. "It's the one strategic advantage we have."

"'Strategic advantage'? Shouldn't people be warned that there's a killer on the loose?"

Santini broke in, "What possible purpose could that serve? If there were a geographic pattern to the killings, we could warn people. But the killer has struck at different times and in different places. Anybody's at risk."

"Anybody, apparently, with this chemical in their systems," Kendra said. "How did you first discover this? You said it was almost an accident. Was it the medical examiner's autopsy?"

"No," Griffin said. "It's clear the examiner was obviously a moron."

Sienna shook her head. "In all fairness, nobody performing a standard autopsy on a stabbing victim would have discovered this. It's a miracle we latched on to it at all. The first victim had donated her body to UC San Diego Medical Center, where they happen to be in the midst of a major air-pollution study and the environment's effect on people of various ages. They ran a battery of tests on her organs and body tissues. That's how they discovered it, and it was unusual enough that they reported their findings back to the police department. The second body was still in the morgue, so we decided to check it out. The substance was identical, and so were the levels. The same has held true for the other victims."

Kendra nodded. "And you're positive the substance wasn't injected into the victims at the time of their murder?"

"Positive," Sienna said. "It had been in their systems for varying amounts of time but no less than a few weeks."

Kendra tried to absorb it all as she stared absently out the window. She wanted to bolt from the room, take the elevator down, and leave all this behind her.

Dammit.

"Kendra," Lynch said.

She turned around. "Let's talk about Jeff."

"He's the only reason you're here, isn't he?" Griffin's lips twisted. "To hell with the case."

Calm down. Don't let this asshole piss you off.

It didn't do any good. She was pissed and to hell with trying to hide it. "You bet it is. What do you expect? This is your case, not mine. I know you don't want me on it. If I thought you could do a decent job of finding him, I wouldn't have to be here."

"I can't tell you how much we appreciate your barging in here to show us how much more brilliant you are than the rest of us," Santini said sarcastically.

Lynch held his hands up as if to block the imminent body blows between them. "Come on, I asked for her help. She knows Agent Stedler better than any of you do, and unless I'm mistaken, she's been of considerable help to you in the past. I know that you've been told to extend every courtesy to me while I'm here, and that also goes for Dr. Michaels. Are we clear?"

Sienna was the only one who nodded.

"How far along was Jeff in his investigation? Was he getting close?" Kendra asked. "Has there been any indication that he or any of you might be in danger?"

There was no answer, but Griffin finally broke the silence. "No," he said. "Sienna here was working the medical aspect of the case, which frankly holds far more promise than anything he was doing. He was running the straight procedural angle, getting statements from family members, coworkers, the usual. He had come up with nothing."

"I want to see his desk."

"Sure, but there's nothing to see."

"I wouldn't be too sure," Lynch said. "Remember who's doing the looking." He gestured toward the door. "By all means, Kendra."

Griffin shrugged. "Whatever."

Griffin led the group out of the conference room and past the long row of cubicles they had passed on the way in. They rounded the corner, and Kendra found herself standing in front of Jeff's desk, bordered on the front and right sides with the same green partitions that marked off all of the office's cubicles.

Although she had stood in his apartment less than twelve hours before, she found herself more saddened and unsettled by the sight of his desk. Somehow, this seemed more . . . *him*. In addition to the piles of paperwork, there was the photograph of his sister and late parents, and his autographed Sammy Sosa home-run ball, which he had once confided was merely a forged duplicate—the original was secured in his safety-deposit box, protected from any after-hours cleaning crews brazen enough to rip off an agent in the heart of an FBI field office. It was where he felt most at home, more than at his condo, more than with most of his friends and family, and certainly more than he had ever been with her.

She studied the cluttered desktop as she spoke. "You have the voice memos from his pocket recorder, right?"

Santini nodded. "Lynch called and told us that you

wanted those. We transferred them all to a thumb drive. It's about thirty hours. If you'd rather have a transcription . . ."

"I'll take both, thank you." She pointed to the computer. "Have you searched his files in here?"

"Of course. The only pertinent records were already in the case file."

"How about his Internet search history?"

"We haven't taken it that far yet."

"No time like the present." She hit the space bar of his keyboard. An FBI splash screen came up with a password prompt. "What's his password?"

Griffin shook his head. "We don't know. I can have an IT guy come and give us access, but I'll have to review it before we can release that information to you. This wasn't his only case."

Bureaucracy at work. As if she gave a damn. Kendra picked up the keyboard and angled it into the light and inspected it closely as she shook it for a long moment. She spent another few seconds lightly running her fingers over the rows of keys, pausing occasionally to retry a section. She then placed it back onto the desk, quickly punched a few keys, and watched as Jeff's secure desktop appeared on the screen.

"You knew his password?" Sienna said.

"Not immediately. If you know Jeff, you know that his computer is always password-protected after five minutes of inactivity. He's constantly coming back to check e-mail without sitting down, and when he does, he uses his right index finger to enter the password with a ridiculous amount of force. It's as if he's trying to drill through to the desk. I could see that some of the password keys are loose and the others I could feel. The springs are shot to hell. His laptops at home have always been the same way."

Sienna was staring at the keyboard. "How did you figure out the order?"

"I guessed. The password is Seatbelt7. It could have been TabSteel7, BaleTest7, EastBelt7, or quite a few others, but Seatbelt7 seemed like a more obvious place to start."

"Apparently."

Kendra launched the browser and immediately drilled down to the user history.

"Stop. I told you some of this may be classified," Griffin said between clenched teeth. "Step away from that computer, Kendra. I'll get you whatever you need, but I must insist that you—"

Lynch quickly stepped protectively behind her and in front of the investigative team. "Come on, Griffin. May I suggest this isn't the time to unload a mound of red tape over us? We're trying to get your agent back."

"So are we all. But we deal with a lot of sensitive material here, and Stedler would have been the first to insist—"

Kendra closed the browser. "It's all yours. I got what I needed."

"Shit," Griffin muttered. "Glad to be of service," he said sarcastically. "Anything else?"

"Yes. Who was the last person to see him?" She turned away from the monitor. "Was it one of you?"

"No," Santini said. "As far as we can tell, it was the fiancée of Steve Conroy, victim number three. Jeff interviewed her at her workplace sometime after lunchtime last Thursday."

"I assume someone has followed up with her since."

"I did," Santini said. "According to her, it was just a routine interview. She has no idea why her fiancé was killed, and that's exactly what she told Stedler. He left her place, and no one has seen him since."

"I have her info," Lynch said quietly.

Griffin reached into his pocket and produced a small USB thumb drive. "And now you have it, too. The entire case file is here, along with those voice memos you wanted."

Lynch took the drive, examined it closely for a moment, then handed it back to Griffin. He produced his own smaller drive and held it up. "Please put that info on this one instead."

Griffin moistened his lips. "I don't understand."

"Sure you do," he said. "Your drive has a GPS chip inside it. As long as she's carrying it, you can track her to the square yard."

Kendra raised an eyebrow. "They were trying to track me?"

"Pretty good piece of gear," Lynch said. "I used ones just like it before they came out with models with more durability and better range. The online retailers have been selling that one for a steep discount lately. I guess the budget cuts have hit the Bureau pretty hard, huh?"

"We just want to keep track of our case files," Griffin said. "It's routine."

"That's pretty weak." Lynch pointed to the drive in his hand. "If you wouldn't mind."

Griffin nodded to Santini, who in turn took the drive from Lynch's hand and walked with Sienna toward another cubicle.

Griffin stared at Kendra. "Well? Any thoughts?"

"Other than on the invasion of my personal liberties?"

"As I recall, you always seemed to have had some kind of observation. Don't tell me that you've not been able to form an impression."

"It's too early for impressions."

He stared at her suspiciously for another long moment. "Are you holding back on us?"

She was suddenly angry with Griffin. She was tired of the thinly veiled antagonism and scorn she could sense behind every word. She didn't expect respect, but she resented him trying to use her at the same time that his attitude breathed derision. She had actually been fairly patient . . . for her. Screw it. Screw him. "You're the one holding back, Griffin." She paused. "At least from your wife."

He stiffened. "What in the hell are you talking about?"

She lowered her voice to malicious softness. "The pretty red-haired woman in the third cubicle from the front. Even if you weren't a married man, she's much too young for you."

His face flushed. "You're delusional."

"Am I?"

"Yes."

"You wanted my impressions."

He quickly turned on his heel. "Santini and Sienna will see you out."

Lynch was still smiling five minutes later as he and Kendra walked toward his car in the parking garage. "Was that last attack really necessary?"

"Of course not. But it sure felt good. Pompous ass. His attitude always annoys me, and I was still pissed off about his trying to plant that tracking device on me. I couldn't resist." She looked at the thumb drive in her hand. "But how do I know you're not trying to pull the same trick on me?"

"You don't. You just have to trust the fact that, if I wanted to keep tabs on you, I'd tap into another GPS device that you're much more likely to carry with you at all times."

"Like my phone?"

"It would be more logical."

"Did you already do it?"

He smiled. "Not yet. I wouldn't bother unless I thought it was necessary."

"Comforting."

He changed the subject. "Okay, out with it. How did you know about Griffin and the redhead?"

"I noticed her on our way in."

"So did I. Dark brown jacket, green eyes, very striking. Never mind her age, she's too attractive for him."

"You probably didn't notice her perfume. Angel by Thierry Mugler."

"Can't say I did."

"It's a subtle scent. I picked up a whiff of it on Griffin. He also had some of her base makeup on his neck."

"You can't tell me the brand?"

"Not with any degree of certainty. There are just too many of them out there."

"Ah, too bad."

"Though if I *had* to venture a guess, I'd say Clinique Number Three Ivory."

Lynch chuckled as he shook his head and he unlocked the car. After they climbed inside, he turned toward her. "Okay, so were you really holding back on them?"

"Not as much as I suspect they were holding back on us. You were looking at that monitor, too. Did you see what I saw?"

"Are you talking about the Google Maps page he had loaded?"

She nodded. "Jeff looked at it on 12:16 P.M. Thursday. Probably just a few minutes before he left to talk to the third victim's fiancée. Is this referenced anywhere in the case files?"

"No."

"I find it hard to believe Griffin didn't already know that."

"Trust me, it's not out of the realm of possibility. But I thought the same thing." He reached underneath his car seat, pulled out a tablet computer, and quickly typed on its glass surface.

"What are you doing?"

"Checking the Google Earth image he visited." He typed for another few seconds, then showed her his input. "This is it, isn't it?"

She studied the lengthy number he had typed in the address bar. "That's it exactly," she said in surprise.

"Are you sure?"

"Yes. I've been struggling to keep that in mind until I could write it down. I guess I needn't have bothered."

"I wouldn't say that. I'm a big believer in redundant backup systems."

She snorted. "Nice. So now I'm redundant."

"Actually, in this instance, I'm probably the redundant one." He pressed the Enter key, and the Google Maps loaded and displayed a satellite map of a remote desert area.

She looked at the screen. "Where is that?"

"It looks like the outskirts of San Diego County." He switched on the graphic map overlay. "Ocotillo Wells."

"Where?"

"About a hundred miles east. It doesn't appear that there's much in the area. Looks like an airstrip and maybe a couple of stores."

Kendra took the tablet computer and looked at the screen. "You've read the case file. Does it have anything to do with anything you've seen? Maybe a victim's family member who lives there?"

"No. That's why it stood out for me. Everything else in Jeff's browser history corresponded to this case. Then, just a little while before he goes missing, there's this."

She nodded, gazing at him thoughtfully. "What do you want to do about it?"

He took the tablet and turned it off. "I'm going there."

"When?"

"Now. If Griffin and his team hadn't already studied Stedler's search history, they will now. I'd like to get out there and take a look around before they roll into town and start flashing badges and asking questions."

"I'm going with you." The words tumbled out of her mouth before she had even decided to say them.

He looked at her. "You're a busy woman. I thought you would have an appointment."

"I do." It was with nine-year-old Bridget Finley, and she wasn't at any crucial point that would damage her if Kendra postponed the appointment. "I'll have to cancel it and rebook."

He nodded. "Good. Thank you, Kendra."

"Look, I'm still not committing to anything. If this place was somehow important to Jeff during the last hours that we can track, it's worth a shot."

He started the car. "I agree. Let's get on the road."

CHAPTER 4

Ocotillo Wells, California

Less than two hours later, Lynch and Kendra pulled off State Highway 78 and studied their arid surroundings. There were no other cars in sight, and the only sounds were from harsh winds blowing sand over the car's roofline. Other than the two-runway airstrip to their immediate left, there were only a gas station, a general store, and a small diner.

"This doesn't even qualify as a town," Kendra said, peering out the windshield. "Not a single traffic light, not a single resident. Are you sure this is right?"

Lynch nodded. "The exact coordinates point up ahead, but that looks even more deserted. This is our best bet. Let's ask around."

They climbed out of his car and walked across the gravel parking lot. "You do the talking," he said.

She wrinkled her brow. "Why me? You're the agent here. Aren't you supposed to be a master of getting people to do and say what you want?"

"Yes. Which is why I want you to do the talking. Few things tug at the heart more than a woman who can't find her missing man. If I talk, they'll think maybe I'm a cop, and he's in some kind of trouble. They won't be as quick to get involved. But with you, they'll think he might be some kind of deadbeat who skipped out on you and your four hungry kids."

She smiled. "Four kids?"

"Four *hungry* kids. Starving. And if you don't find your man, poor little Jimmy Bob won't be able to get those braces he needs."

"Is that really the image I project?"

"The first rule of persuasion . . ."

"Don't you mean manipulation?"

"You must remember that others project on you more than you ever do on them. Their assumptions, their biases, the way they look at the world . . ."

"If they see that we pulled up in that Ferrari of yours, they're going to know that little Billy Bob—"

"Jimmy Bob."

"Pardon me, Jimmy Bob, will never have a problem getting those braces."

"You're right. I should have driven my boring car today. Let's hope no one saw it." He shot her a sideways glance. "But I still want you to do the talking."

"Fine."

They stepped inside the diner and saw that the place was empty of customers. The one waitress leaned against the counter watching an episode of *The People's Court*.

She turned around. "Two for lunch?"

"No"—Kendra noticed that the waitress's name on her ID badge was Sylvia Warnot—"but I wonder if you could help me, Ms. Warnot. I think my boyfriend may have come through here a few days ago, and he's missing. We're worried sick about him." She pulled out her phone and used the touch screen to scroll through her photographs. She showed the waitress a shot of her and Jeff on

Coronado Island, then pinched the screen to enlarge his face. "Does he look familiar to you?"

Sylvia Warnot stared at the image, then finally shook her head. "I'm sorry, hon. I'm pretty sure I haven't seen him."

Kendra's expression became pleading. "Are you sure? It probably would have been last Thursday."

The waitress's eyes lit up. "I'm off on Thursdays." She pointed at Kendra's phone. "Can you use that to e-mail the picture?"

"Sure."

The waitress reached into her apron pocket and produced a pen and notepad. She scribbled an e-mail address, tore off the page, and handed it to her. "Send that picture to this address. My cousin, Patsy, was working that day, so she might have seen him."

"I'll do it right now." Kendra keyed in the e-mail address and sent the photo along with Jeff's name, the make and model of his car, and the date he might have driven through.

Lynch pointed toward the east. "What's down there? Anything?"

Sylvia Warnot shook her head. "Devil's Slide is just down the road a piece. It's an old mountain that the kids use for off-roading. Too hot for anyone this time of year, though."

"Thanks for helping," Kendra said. "It means a lot to me."

"Don't let it mean too much, hon." The waitress's expression was sympathetic but a little cynical. "Some guys just don't want to be found. They get tired of us and head for new pastures."

"I think you're wrong. Jeff wouldn't just leave me without a word." She turned toward the door. "But thanks anyway."

"You did a good job," Lynch said as they left the restaurant and walked back to the car. "Very convincing."

"I was only telling the truth. Jeff's not a man who would forget his responsibilities. He was a good guy."

"But one you decided you couldn't live with. I wonder, was it because he was such a good guy? Did he bore you, Kendra?"

She stiffened. "I told you why we parted company. Not that it's any of your business."

"You're absolutely right. Forget I asked. Just curious." Before getting in the car, Lynch pulled a pair of binoculars from the backseat and focused on the decaying mountain in the distance.

"See anything?" Kendra asked.

"No, but let's get a closer look at this Devil's Slide. The name itself is intriguing enough for me to want to go there."

They drove down the highway and turned off the pavement. Lynch steered toward the base of the mountain. Kendra could see that it was covered by dozens of crisscrossing trails carved by motorcycles and off-road vehicles.

Lynch braked to a stop. "This is the location tagged on Jeff's computer. Was he a motocross rider or an off-roader?"

"No." Kendra scanned the area. "But that woman was wrong about no one's coming out here today."

"What do you mean?"

"The tracks." Kendra pointed up at the hillside. "Looks like a jeep and at least two motorcycles have been here in the last couple hours. This wind would have already erased tracks older than that."

"Could have been kids getting their adrenaline fix."

"Possibly." She climbed out of the car and walked a few feet up the incline. Made of granite and sand, Devil's

Slide rose two hundred feet and sliced the desert for at least a mile. Its numerous slopes and contours seemed to be ready-made for the extreme vehicle sports that were obviously so popular there.

Lynch rolled up his sleeves and unfastened a shirt button. "I'm going to climb up and take a look around. Stay with the car. If I see anything, I'll—

"*You* stay with the car." Kendra pushed past him and started up the steep incline. "I didn't come all the way out here to sit in your damned Ferrari."

He smiled. "Hate me, Kendra, but don't hate my car. It would show a lack of good judgment."

They made their way up the mountainside, and Kendra soon found herself getting winded, mainly due to the loose sand's making it hard to get traction. The temperature was already well over a hundred, and that didn't help.

They finally reached the summit, and she took a deep breath as she gazed out over the arid terrain. The desert stretched toward infinity, and the only signs of life were a few cars visible on Highway 78. At least ten miles south, she guessed.

Lynch pointed ahead. "The tracks head this way."

"I see. It looks like the jeep and two cycles stayed together. They may still be out here."

"I hope so. I'd like to talk to them."

They walked along the top of the mountain, keeping to the carved-out paths that eased their way along the many slopes and curves. Many of the larger trails were marked off by rope and stakes, now half-buried in the off-season by sand and the occasional clump of vegetation. About halfway down the mountain's expanse, they found a bowl-shaped indention with hundreds of beer bottles, food wrappers, bags, and evidence of a large bonfire.

"Looks like someone had themselves a hell of a rave," Lynch said.

"Been there, done that."

He shot her a sideways glance. "When have you ever been to a rave?"

She smiled. "Believe me, I've been to way too many. Do you think just because I was once blind that I was some Goody Two-shoes?"

"So it was back when you were blind?"

"No, as a matter of fact, it was after."

"Really?"

"Why are you surprised?"

"I don't think there are many Ph.D.s dancing around a bonfire and howling at the moon until dawn."

"Not many." She looked down at the still-smoldering ashes of the bonfire as they walked past it. "My hunger for sensory stimulation hasn't always been either reasonable or productive. Just the opposite, especially in those first few years after I got my sight. I wanted to soak up every new experience I could, even the ones that weren't good for me." She shrugged. "It's a wonder I'm still alive."

"What kind of experiences?"

"If you can smoke it, drink it, chase it, or jump it, I've probably done it. It was a crazy time. I know I scared the hell out of my mom and my friends. There were even some discussions about having me committed. I can't believe the things I did."

"We all have regrets."

She looked at him. "I don't regret any of it. I certainly wouldn't do those things today, but I wouldn't be the same person now if I hadn't cut loose like that."

"So there were other affairs before Jeff?"

She laughed. "Uh, yeah. Several. But he was probably the first sane relationship I had."

"A lot of women would say it's impossible to have a sane relationship with an FBI agent."

"Women like your ex-wife?"

"We're not talking about me right now."

"Sure we are."

Lynch paused to jump over a gap in the path. After Kendra followed, he turned back. "What split the two of you up? All I know is what I read in the case files. You did good work together."

"We might still be a couple if we *hadn't* worked together. It was a big mistake."

"The Bureau doesn't think so."

"Since when has the Bureau given a damn about the success of any of our interpersonal relationships?"

"There are psychologists on staff who claim to give a damn."

"Just what I need. An FBI psychologist counseling me on my romantic life."

Lynch laughed. "If—make that *when*—we find Stedler, you don't believe you might still have a future with him?"

"Not a chance. Why are you asking me all these questions? Why the hell do you care?"

"I'm finding the workings of your mind fascinating. I want to explore it more thoroughly."

"So that you can better manipulate me."

"It's a thought. I'm wondering if your feelings toward him are softer than you think. You've let yourself be drawn into this hunt for Stedler though it's obviously against your will."

"Soft? No, my relationship with Jeff was complicated. We had good sex, a mutual respect, and there were moments when I thought we were crossing the boundaries between being best friends to happily ever after. It was a very fragile relationship, and it broke into a million pieces when he chose to try to use me. But the memories are there, and I'll probably always have feelings for him. I can't ignore what we were together even though I can't let it continue." She slanted him a cool glance. "Don't flatter yourself that you drew me into this investigation. It was my choice. Right now, a very limited choice. And, if you read the case files, you saw that I've gone to a lot more trouble for people I never even met."

"True. But it still does seem odd that—"

"Shh!" She held her finger up to silence him. "Listen!"

They stood in silence for a long moment.

"I don't hear anything," he whispered.

"Like that means anything. Be quiet."

They stood for a moment longer. Kendra finally shook her head. "Whatever it was, it's gone."

"What did you hear?"

"I'm not sure. Something metallic."

He patted his pants pocket. "My keys?"

"No. Lower in pitch. Something else."

He pointed down the ridge. "We should get to one of the lower trails. Less visible. If anyone's around, we might scare them off before we have a chance to get close."

Kendra nodded. "Good idea." As they descended, she listened for any other sounds that cut through the booming, whistling winds, but there were none.

Nothing.

But there was something else of interest up ahead.

They had already passed several large boulders. Two hundred yards away, there was an opening carved into the mountainside. It was too clean, too precise, to be a natural formation.

Lynch caught her look and turned toward the opening. "It's not the only one. Look."

She glanced around and saw half a dozen other round openings, each about ten feet in diameter, now within her line of sight. "Mine shafts?"

"Looks like it. There was a lot of granite mining in this entire area in the thirties. Let's get a closer look."

They worked their way down the trail and approached the shaft nearest them. Just beyond the shadows of the opening, she could see that the shaft was sealed off by rubble.

"The mining company might have closed this off when they abandoned it," Lynch said.

Kendra studied the rubble. "Or an earthquake might have done the job sometime since. Either way, I'd like to go look at these other—"

She stopped.

It was that metallic sound again. What in the hell . . . ?

A gunshot!

A bullet whistled past and disintegrated a rock between them.

Kendra's first instinct was to jump back, but Lynch grabbed her arm and yanked her into the mine-shaft opening.

He grabbed the gun from his holster. "Where the hell did that come from?"

"Slightly to the right, from behind three dark boulders near a clump of scrub brush."

"Are you sure?"

"Positive."

He nodded, raised his gun, and pressed himself against the inner rock wall of the mine entrance. He inched forward.

Kendra cocked her head. That metallic sound again. But not from where the gunshot was fired, it had to be—

"Stop!" she whispered.

Lynch froze.

"There's another one out there. A few yards to the left. Probably behind the rock pile."

Lynch cursed. "They've got us pinned down."

A barrage of bullets exploded against the rocks near Lynch's head. A roar erupted from behind the rock pile.

A motorcycle, Kendra realized. Blazing away to the left.

Another barrage of bullets rained on them.

Lynch threw himself back against the wall, paused, then fired toward the boulders. The shooter cut loose with another hail of gunfire.

Kendra listened. The motorcycle had turned and was racing back toward them. Shit.

It would be back in another few seconds, and after that, she and Lynch would be—

Wait. At her feet, almost entirely buried in the sand, was the severed end of a rope trail marker. She looked up. How far out did it go?

Hard to tell.

"Get back!" Lynch shouted.

She ignored him and crouched over the rope. Please, please, please let this work . . .

The motorcycle sped closer. She gripped the edge of the rope in her trembling hands and yanked it upward. Sand flew along the rope's length, revealing that it was anchored to a spike at the edge of the clearing.

The motorcycle's roar filled her ears, blending with the staccato rhythms of more gunfire . . .

The rope whipped through her fingers.

Pain. Horrible, searing pain.

She looked up from her bloody hands to see the rope catch the motorcycle rider at his chest and catapult him from the seat.

The motorcycle slid into the rock wall of the mountainside, its engine still racing. The motorcycle rider, outfitted in heavy black leather from head to toe, landed with a sickening crack just ten feet in front of them. His gun, a short-stalked automatic weapon, landed several yards behind.

The man moaned.

Kendra crouched next to Lynch and wiped her bleeding hands against her shirt.

"Are you okay?" Lynch asked.

She pointed to the motorcycle rider. "Watch him."

"He's not going anywhere."

The rider, a man in his early twenties with an acne-scarred face, coughed up a mouthful of blood. "Tommy! Tommy . . . !"

"Shut the hell up!" The voice called out from behind the boulders.

"I need help!"

Lynch aimed his gun in the rider's direction.

The man pulled off his helmet. "Please, Tommy. I can't feel my legs . . ."

"Be quiet!"

"I'm really messed up here. Help me!"

"You know I can't."

"Please . . ."

Lynch squeezed off a shot near the injured man, who recoiled.

"What was that for?" Kendra whispered.

"Just tightening the screws."

The voice from behind the boulders called out again. "I can't come out there, buddy."

"I'm gonna die, man."

"Stop talking. You know you can't talk. Just hang tight!"

The motorcyclist turned toward Kendra and Lynch. His eyes pleaded with them as two thin lines of blood ran from his nostrils.

Lynch took aim with his gun.

"Don't do it," she whispered.

Lynch shook his head. "I won't need to."

The motorcyclist's head exploded.

The gunshot had come from behind the boulders, she

realized. The man's own partner had killed him, she realized, sick.

Seconds later, she heard the familiar metallic sound again. This time she knew what it was. Zippers on a leather jacket jangling as he walked.

The next moment, the ATV started up and roared away.

"Shit!" Lynch bolted from the opening with his gun extended before him. He ran around the other side of the boulders.

Kendra ran after him.

The ATV was already halfway down to the desert floor.

Lynch pulled out his mobile phone and cursed again. "No signal up here. I was afraid of that." He walked back to the motorcyclist's corpse and rolled him over.

"What are you doing?"

"Searching his pockets. I want to know who he is."

His expression was completely without feeling. Lynch might as well have been searching an old pair of his jeans for bus fare, she thought. Cold. Very cold. "You knew that other man would kill him. What was his name? Tommy."

"I didn't know. I hoped. From the point of view of a total scumbag, it was the smartest thing to do."

"The scumbag mentality comes awful easily to you."

"With his partner down, he just wanted to get the hell out of here. But he couldn't leave the other guy alive to possibly ID him."

She looked down at what was left of the man's head. She felt sick. She had to get out of there. She turned and walked away.

Lynch's voice stopped her before she'd gone more than a few yards. "Stop running away. I need another one of those parlor tricks you're so good at."

She stared out at the desert. "What do you mean?"

"This guy has absolutely no ID on him. No receipts, no ATM statements, nothing. What can you tell me about him?"

Kendra still did not turn. "Besides the fact that he's now missing half his skull?"

"Yeah, besides that."

You don't have to look back at that monstrosity that had once been a man. Use your memory. Close your eyes. Focus.

"Kendra?"

"He's a smoker. Cigarettes."

Lynch looked at the dead man's hands. "Nicotine stains."

"It's actually from the tar. You can also see it in the corners of his mouth. And he's probably been taking tetracycline or minocycline recently. Check with dermatologists in the area. He might be a patient."

Lynch looked down at the man's pockmarked face. "It's obvious he needed it, but how do you know?"

"His teeth. They have a slight grayish blue tint. That's a giveaway, and it probably tilts the scales in favor of minocycline."

"I'll check it out."

"We didn't hear him say much, but I can tell he's probably lived on the West Coast for most of his life. Possibly some time in the Northwest, but I can't be sure of that. He's also had whiskey today, but there's no telling where he drank it."

Okay, she was better now. She had control. She turned and slowly walked back toward the corpse and knelt beside it. Now that she was in the zone, she was no longer bothered by the horrible sight in front of her. It was just a collection of stimuli to be cataloged and analyzed. She lifted the lapel of the dead man's leather jacket and placed her nose next to it.

Lynch knelt beside her. "What are you doing?"

She leaned back. "Smelling that white stuff on his jacket."

"We have forensic tests for that."

"McDonald's vanilla shake."

Lynch smiled. "Not Burger King?"

"No. Not Burger King, not Wendy's. It was McDonald's. It's still very sweet-smelling, so I'm betting he had it today. There was a McDonald's about twenty-five miles back on Highway 78. It might be a good place to start. If he was with his partner, there might be a security camera feed with both of their faces."

He nodded. "Anything else?"

"Let's look at his bike."

They stood and walked over toward the still-rumbling motorcycle. Lynch cut the ignition and lifted it upright. "A BMW GS. Good piece of machinery."

Kendra stepped around it. "The owner brought this here from somewhere else. It hasn't been ridden much in this country yet."

"It has a California plate."

"But there's much more wear on the front tire's right side. In the U.S. and other countries where we drive on the right side of the road, there's always more wear on the front tire's *left* side."

Lynch thought about it for a moment. "That makes sense. Wider turn radius, more of a lean angle . . ."

". . . and faster speed. You leave more rubber on the pavement with a wide turn. This motorcycle has been mostly ridden someplace where they drive on the left side of the road." Kendra looked at it a moment longer, then shook her head. "It's not telling me anything else."

Lynch hit the kickstand and left the bike upright. "Okay. Good. Anything else you want to see? Last chance . . ."

"No, I've seen enough."

Too much. Death. Betrayal. Murder.

All of the horrors that she had wanted to leave behind when she had told Jeff that she was through with working with him. Now that this problem had been faced, addressed, and identified, she was once more enveloped in the sheer terrible reality of it.

Stop shaking.

Don't break down.

"I'd better call and get the police and the Bureau out here. You were very helpful. I think that we—" Lynch broke off, his gaze on her expression. "Are you okay? You look a little pale."

"Wonderful. Just wonderful."

"The hell you are." He took a step closer and reached out to touch her. "I didn't think that you'd react—"

She jerked back away from him. "But you didn't stop to ask how I felt about it before you got what you wanted, did you? You just used me. Well, I gave you what you needed, and now you have time to be the good guy. It's all very familiar." Too familiar. All the bitterness and sickness she had felt when she'd broken with Jeff was flooding back to her. She turned her back to him. "I don't need your sympathy, Lynch. I'm fine." As she walked away from him, she added, "So go to hell."

The first police officers arrived in thirty-five minutes, and Griffin, Santini, and Deever arrived with an army of FBI agents an hour after that. After Kendra and Lynch had told their story and conveyed Kendra's observations no less than four times, Griffin finally pulled them both aside.

"What in the hell is going on here?"

"You don't really want to hear it again, do you?" Lynch asked.

"I thought you were working *with* us, Lynch."

"You don't find our information useful?"

"I find *her* information useful. It's your bullshit I don't appreciate."

"Basic investigative work, that's all. We're trying to find your missing agent."

"Why didn't you tell us you were coming out here?"

"I don't see the need to keep you apprised of my every move. You have access to Stedler's computer and search history. Didn't you already think to come out here?"

He was silent a moment. "It was on the list. We didn't deem it relevant."

"And it may not be. I don't know who these guys are. Anything on his license plate yet?"

"It's registered to a motorcycle in Mission Valley."

"*This* motorcycle?" Kendra asked.

"Nope. It's registered to a Kawasaki. The plate's probably stolen, and the owner just hasn't reported it yet. The cops are checking it out now." Griffin gestured to the other mine-shaft openings dotting the mountainside. "We're checking out each of those. For all we know, they were running a meth lab out of one."

"Miserably hot place to try and run a lab," Lynch said. "It's about 110 here today."

"I've seen crazier things." Griffin turned back toward them. "So tell me, why in the hell would Stedler have been interested in this place?"

"Question of the day," Lynch said. "As you say, this doesn't seem relevant to anything else he was working on."

"It's time, Lynch," Griffin said harshly.

"Time for what?"

"It's time for you to be straight with me. I need to know why the Justice Department sent you here."

"I was hired." Lynch spoke as if reading from a well-worn script. "Any questions or concerns can be directed to U.S. Associate Attorney General Frederick Jamerson. He or a member of his staff would be happy to—"

Griffin cut him off. "You know I've already spoken with Jamerson. We're as concerned about Agent Stedler's well-being as he is, but we're still at a loss as to why he sent you. If we're being kept in the dark about something, I need to know what it is."

"I don't have time to nurse bruised egos."

"This isn't about ego!" Griffin's face flushed red. "We need to know what we're dealing with here. The safety of my people depends on it. Can't you get that into your head? Jeff Stedler is the best agent I have. If something happened to him, it can happen to any one of those men and women out there."

Lynch shook his head. "I don't know any more than you do, Griffin. Sorry."

Griffin cursed and walked away.

Kendra stared at Lynch for a long moment. "If you really came without knowing why you're here, then I misjudged you."

"How so?"

"You didn't strike me as someone who would allow himself to be used like that." Her lips curled bitterly. "No, you'd be the one who'd be on the offensive. You wouldn't be sent out here by some bureaucrat without really knowing why. I don't think you're a chump, Lynch."

"If that's what I was, I'd still be working for Griffin."

"Then I guess that just makes you a liar."

Lynch laughed and stepped away, putting some distance between him and the police officers working the scene. "You're forgetting another possibility."

"Enlighten me."

"Maybe I want to know what's going on here. Maybe I want to know why one of the three highest-ranking officials in the U.S. Department of Justice has taken such a personal interest in this case. I can understand why it's driving Griffin crazy because it's making me a bit crazy.

Especially if I'm somehow being used as a pawn—or a chump, as you might say—in this game. I will find out what's going on here, but I'll do it on my own terms. That's why I came to you."

She studied him. It was the only thing he could have said that would inspire any kind of approval from her. He, of course, knew that; manipulation was his stock-in-trade. But there was something in his manner, a steely determination tinged with frustration that made her believe him.

"I need your help," he said quietly. "You may feel you've already gotten more than you bargained for, and you most definitely have. But I want to work with someone outside the Bureau on this. And not with just anyone. I want it to be you."

She shook her head. "Haven't you been listening? This isn't what I do. I've helped out on a few cases, but I'm not an investigator."

"You're better at it than almost anyone I know." He paused. "And you want to do this. You have a motivation. I'll try not to pry any more into your private affairs; but, in spite of what you went through this afternoon, you thought finding Stedler was worthwhile, or you wouldn't have done it."

He's right, damn him.

Kendra turned and stared at the mass of law-enforcement personnel swarming over the mountainside. And Olivia had also been right. There was no way Kendra couldn't help, not as long as Jeff might still be out there. He had been her friend, her lover. She might want to put a period to their relationship, but she would hate herself if she didn't at least try to help find him.

"I'll do what I can," she said slowly.

"You're in?"

"Yes, as long as I think it's worthwhile working with you. But I want to keep following Jeff's trail. If I get the sense that you and your Associate Attorney General have other priorities, I'm done. Do you understand?"

He nodded. "Of course."

"For a master manipulator, you didn't handle Griffin well just now. Please do your best not to piss off Griffin and the other FBI agents."

His brows rose in surprise. "Says the pot to the kettle."

"I don't have to be polite to them. If I stopped being rude, they'd get suspicious. But we might need them, and you might as well be the one to bite the bullet. This case could turn on the toxicology angle, and we're going to need their expertise and resources."

"I can be a team player. But I doubt if you can."

Kendra doubted it, too. She had always been a loner, and sometimes her tongue was too quick. "Then you'd better work twice as hard to make up for my lack of cooperation. It will be a challenge for you."

CHAPTER 5

Dammit, it's happening to me again.

Kendra stepped off the elevator and moved toward her condo. She was tired, but she felt a tingle of pure energy jolting through her. Her mind was racing as she jumped from possibility to possibility. She knew those familiar signs. They were always the first ones that appeared as she was drawn into the vortex.

She was already consumed by the damn case. In less than twenty-four hours, it had elbowed everything else from her mind, and the puzzles and problems of Jimmy and her other music-therapy clients seemed like a dim memory.

She mustn't let it take over. Not this time.

She pulled out her key and moved to insert it into her door. She stopped short.

Shit.

There was a quarter-inch gap between the edge of her door and the stop. The door was closed, but it looked as it did when the dead bolt wasn't engaged.

She knew she had locked it.

Someone had been in her condo.

Or was still there.

She quietly backed away from the door.

If she could just get to the stairwell . . .

Her door flew open!

She froze as she stared at the imposing figure of the person facing her.

Her mother.

"Why are you standing out there, Kendra?" She was frowning at her with an intimidating stare. "Are you really going to keep me waiting longer than you already have?"

Kendra pushed past her. "You scared the hell out of me, Mom." She dropped her keys in the bowl on the table in the foyer and turned to look at her. Her mother was almost in her sixties, but she looked twenty years younger. She was tall and shapely, with sparkling brown eyes and dark brown hair that she wore in a chignon. She had style and presence and a royal disregard for anything that she considered unimportant. "For all I knew, there could have been a murderer in here."

"You probably would have preferred that."

"No comment. Why are you here? You're supposed to be in Cancún."

"I got bored. And annoyed. The cruise line hired a young ivory-tower progressive who thought he knew everything about the history of those Mayan pyramids. He wouldn't listen to me."

"Heaven forbid."

"Don't be sarcastic. I was just trying to help him. He was wrong."

Kendra didn't doubt that he had been if her mother said it was true. "Why didn't you tell me you were coming over?"

"I need to book my visits with you in advance?"

"Of course not. But you didn't know if I'd be here."

Her mother shrugged. "I took a chance."

Kendra smiled as she came down from the adrenaline surge she had felt in the hallway. Her mother was Dr. Deanna Michaels, history professor at UC San Diego. She had never suffered fools gladly, and her tough exams and withering stares had earned her the nickname of "Deanna Doom," which had stuck for as long as Kendra could remember. She had terrified generations of young men and women, but her mother did have her fans. She was unsurpassed in her ability to weave spellbinding lectures from even the most mundane historical incidents. She was brilliant, charismatic, and could be completely fascinating . . . particularly to the young male students in her classes.

"Besides, I had a surge of maternal feeling, and you weren't in Cancún. So I came back so that I could satisfy it." Her mother beamed at her. "It was fairly overwhelming. I would have even cooked dinner for you, but you have nothing in your refrigerator or pantry."

"You can't cook."

She shrugged. "There's that, too."

"I can order in some Thai."

"I'm afraid I can't stay, honey. I've already been here for over an hour, and I promised to have drinks with some educators visiting from London."

Kendra's gaze fell to her dining-room table, where every plant in her condo had been placed, along with her garden shears and watering can. "Don't tell me you came here just to do that."

"They don't just take care of themselves. They're living things, dear."

"Mom, the one on the end is made of silk."

Her mother picked it up and proudly displayed it. "Yes, but there was no shape to it. I gave it a once-over with the shears. It looks much better this way, don't you think?"

Kendra had to admit that it did.

"But no, that's not why I'm here. I heard a nasty rumor that you were becoming involved with the FBI again. I wanted to make sure it's not true."

"A nasty rumor? Where did you hear this?"

"My sources are confidential."

"Spill it."

"Oh, all right. Your friend Olivia told me."

"Olivia? Are you serious?" Kendra tried to remember the last time Olivia and her mother had been in the same room together. Five years, maybe longer? Olivia loved Deanna but she was wary of having her life taken over by Kendra's mother. "Olivia actually looked up your number and called you to tell you—?"

"Oh, no dear. We're Facebook friends."

"*Facebook?*" Kendra was aware she must be wearing a stunned expression. She knew that, thanks to the Click-Hear Web Accessibility software, Olivia spent a good deal of time on the Internet, but this was still weird. "I'm trying to imagine you spending time on that, but I just can't make the picture in my head."

"I do it on my phone. In checkout lines, doctor's office waiting rooms . . . But we're getting off track here. Tell me you're not really being sucked back into being some kind of crime fighter."

"You make me sound like a superhero."

"You're no superhero. That was what was wrong with your relationship with that young man, Jeff. He was much too idealistic and with no practicality. I was very grateful when you decided to break with him. And the sooner you realize that though you're a brilliant woman, that doesn't necessarily translate to being some kind of superdetective, the better."

"You're lecturing me, Mom. Back off."

"Of course I'm lecturing you. It's what I do best. Now

why would you become involved again? You told me that you wouldn't—"

"It's Jeff, Mom. He's missing."

Her mother was silent. "Missing *how*?"

"As in vanished off the face of the earth."

"More." Her mother was staring at her with narrowed eyes.

And she wouldn't be giving up until she knew everything that Kendra knew. Give in. It would be easier than trying to argue or avoid. "Okay. Here's what I know. It isn't that much."

She filled her mother in on Jeff's case and her meetings with Lynch and the FBI team, taking care to leave out the part about gunshots being fired at her that afternoon. No use arousing any more of those protective feelings that were already proving difficult.

After Kendra finished, her mother slowly nodded. "I know I can't stop you from doing this. But at least allow me to get a bodyguard for you."

"A bodyguard? Are you serious?"

"You won't even know he's there."

"What makes you such an expert?"

"It doesn't take an expert to make good judgments."

Kendra froze as a thought occurred to her. "Oh, no. Don't tell me this is one of your boy toys."

"That's not nice, and it denigrates my relationship with Todd. First, he's a young man, not a boy. He's a graduate student, and I was very careful not to see him outside class until I was no longer teaching him. You make it sound as if I'm having some sleazy sexual affair with him. I never let it get that far." Her eyes were suddenly twinkling. "I wouldn't want to spoil him for lesser women. We just enjoy each other's company."

Kendra shook her head. Her mother held a strong fascination for her young male pupils despite the fact that she was definitely an older woman. "And you're telling me that the question never came up?"

"No, I won't tell you that, but it never happens. If it does, I send them regretfully on their way." She sighed. "Very regretfully. They're such great playmates."

"But, dammit, why not play with someone your own age?"

"Men my own age want permanency and lack the concept that there might be adventure right around the corner." Her lips tightened. "Your father was like that. He had a sluggish mind, and I couldn't make him move. I knew I could find a way to make you see. I *knew* it. But he wouldn't go that extra step. It scared him, and all he wanted to do was run away." She shrugged. "Usually with the first attractive woman who didn't nag him to be something he never wanted to be."

Several attractive women, Kendra remembered. Her mother had never let her be exposed to the conflict between them, but Kendra had been aware that her father had lady "friends." She had accepted it as a fact of life. After her parents' divorce, she had spent little time with her father and his current mistress. She had always felt uncomfortable, probably because she sensed he was uncomfortable. "Did you ever love him?"

"Of course I did. He was charming, sexy, smart, and I was stubborn enough to think that I could make him what I wanted him to be. But then you came along, and I realized that I didn't have the time or inclination to help him grow up when he became part of the problem." She shrugged. "So when I divorced your father, I swore off permanency for life. Most young men don't want permanency. They look on me with respect for my mind and maybe have a slight yearning for me to be their big wicked affair." Her smile was dazzling. "I'm no Mrs. Robinson, Kendra. I just like an occasional challenge."

No one should know better than Kendra how her mother embraced a challenge. Kendra herself had been the greatest challenge her mother had ever faced. She had met that challenge with strength and determination and implacable resolve. She had pushed and explored every avenue that would make life everything it could be for Kendra. She had made her self-sufficient when she was blind, then gone after the best doctors to find the medical brass ring that had given Kendra her sight. And through all the pushing, probing, and constant encouragement, there had never been a doubt in Kendra's mind of her mother's love for her. Deanna had wrapped Kendra in love even while she had forced her to develop her independence. She had been magnificent. She was still magnificent. Why the hell should Kendra judge her mother? She just wished that she'd find her present challenges in another direction.

"Todd works security at the university stadium," her mother said brusquely. "He's six-five, 230 pounds, muscular . . ." She smiled mischievously. "And I'm sure he has *lots* of stamina. You might try him. He could keep you amused as well as protected. He tells me all about his—"

"TMI, Mom. TMI."

"Todd and I are great friends. He would do anything for me. If you'd like, I can have him tag along with you wherever you—"

"No!"

"You'd rather I worry about you?"

"I'm sure Todd can keep you occupied."

"These days, I'm spending more time with David. He's not as intelligent as Todd, but he has—"

Kendra cut her off. "I don't want to hear it. We both know that you only play around with these young Adonis types because you're not tempted to make any kind of commitment. Get real. None of those guys could provide you with more than a fleeting challenge. You're too strong."

Her smile faded. "Get real? No way. Fifteen years with your father was all the reality I need."

Kendra mentally kicked herself for dampening her mother's ebullience. The woman deserved every bit of the happiness she could wring from life. "I know, Mom. You're right. But I really don't need a bodyguard."

"Fine, but if you change your mind . . ."

Kendra nodded. "I'll know that you have a piece of beefcake just waiting in the wings." She gave her a quick hug. "Now go on to your dinner, or you'll be late. I'm going to be fine."

Her mother didn't move.

Kendra sighed with frustration as she recognized that expression. She'd have to find another argument. "I'm not going to be alone. I don't need your Todd. Didn't Olivia mention that I'm working with an agent who used to be with the Bureau? I assure you that your friend, Todd, wouldn't stand a chance against Lynch."

Deanna tilted her head. "No? Tough?"

"Extremely."

Her mother was gazing at her thoughtfully. "You could be trying to throw me off the track."

"Yes, but I'm not."

"I believe you. You wouldn't lie to me." Her mother turned toward the door. "But I've lost a little faith in your opinions since you became involved with Jeff Stedler. I believe I'll have to meet this Lynch person and judge for myself."

Oh, Lord, she could see her mother confronting Lynch with her usual explosive tenacity. It would be disaster—

No, it would be funny as hell. Let Lynch try to manipulate Deanna. Kendra would enjoy sitting back and watching the fireworks.

She grinned and gave her mother another hug. "Yes, by all means. You two have got to get together."

State Route 16
11:46 P.M.

Paul Renshaw cursed as his car sputtered on the lonely stretch of road outside of Escondido. Piece of shit. Weren't Volvos supposed to be dependable?

He had been watching the Padres game at his favorite Gaslamp Quarter watering hole, and stayed to talk to the cute new bartender, a college girl who was at least fifteen years younger than he. As much as he didn't want to break down in the middle of nowhere, he really didn't relish the possibility of a police officer happening upon him and smelling the alcohol on his breath.

An array of indicators lit up the dashboard, and he realized that the engine had conked out entirely.

Great. Just great.

He pulled hard on the wheel and eased his car over to the side of the road. He cut the headlights and glanced around.

It was even darker than he had thought. The lights of San Diego cast a faint glow in the sky behind him, but ahead there was nothing but a black void. He checked his phone, and, surprisingly, there was service. He called the auto club, gave his information, and was told to wait forty-five minutes to an hour for a tow truck.

Which really meant an hour and a half, minimum.

Dammit.

He popped the hood, climbed out of the car, and walked around to the front. He raised the hood and used his phone display to illuminate the engine compartment.

Who was he kidding? Maybe he could unscrew the

carburetor lid and move the butterfly doohickey back and forth, but after that, he would have reached the absolute limit of his automotive expertise.

There would be nothing to do but sit in the car and wait for the damned—

A pair of headlights appeared. They had come from over the hill behind his car, a quarter of a mile away. At first the vehicle appeared to be racing toward him, but it soon slowed to a crawl.

Paul raised his hand to block the headlights' glare, trying to glimpse the car behind it. It was much too soon to be the tow truck, and the rounded headlights didn't seem to belong to a squad car. He soon saw that the vehicle was an SUV. It pulled alongside him and the passenger-side window lowered.

"Need help?" The driver was in shadows, but he sounded like an older man.

"Nah, I called the auto club. Thanks, though."

The man pointed to the open hood. "What's the problem?"

"No idea. It just broke down on me."

The man shifted his SUV into PARK but left the engine running. He climbed out. "Let me take a look."

"I appreciate the help, but like I said, a tow truck will be here any—"

"No problem at all. Got a flashlight?"

Paul held up his phone's illuminated screen and angled it toward the man. He had gray hair, tanned skin, and deep smile lines. It was almost as if Mr. Rogers had stopped to lend a hand. All that was missing was the cardigan.

The older man laughed at the phone. "That'll have to do. You'd do better to hold it over the engine and let me take a look."

Paul held the phone high over the engine compartment. "I can't see anything wrong, but that doesn't mean—"

Pain.

An icy shiver ran through his torso. He turned. The old man was holding a long, wet blade.

Wet with *his* blood, Paul realized.

The man was still smiling. "Relax, son."

Paul couldn't breathe. But he could move. In one quick motion, he reached up, gripped the edge of the open hood, and brought it down hard on the man's head.

"Aughh!" The man screamed, and blood spurted from his hairline. He stumbled. "You little prick!"

Paul wanted to tackle the old bastard, but his legs wouldn't cooperate. He staggered forward and fell to the ground. The asphalt felt warm against his cheek. Getting harder to keep his eyes open . . .

"Be still," the man said. "It'll be over soon."

Paul's eyes fluttered. Please, no. Don't let this be it . . .

"That's good, Paul. Rest easy."

Paul. The son of a bitch knew his name. His eyes flicked wide open.

"It's better this way," the older man said. "Believe me, I'm doing you a favor."

He tasted blood in his mouth.

He closed his eyes for the last time.

Bayfront Walk
San Diego
6:45 A.M.

Kendra plugged the earphones into her phone and scrolled through her audio library until she found the folder with Jeff's recordings. He customarily recorded them in his car after each interview or meeting, but he also spoke into his portable recorder whenever something occurred to him at any hour of the day or night.

That damned little recorder. Even now, she could remember how annoyed she'd been at how often he would cut short their most intimate conversations to start talking into the thing. Jeff would laugh his ass off if he knew she was now poring over dozens of hours of those recordings.

Lord, she hoped that would come to pass.

If he was lucky, maybe they would soon laugh together.

She glanced around the Bayfront walking path that bordered the convention center and offered a view of the two large cargo ships and the Coronado Bridge. She had gone there to do her usual run as she listened to Jeff, but she had just changed her mind. She needed to focus and absorb every nuance of what was being said, something that would be impossible if she were breathlessly pounding the pavement.

She sat on a bench and scrolled to the last date. Two entries: a four-minute recording at 6:07 A.M., another at 2:20 P.M. She pressed the first one and listened.

"Some more thoughts on my interview with Shawna Davis, fiancée of Steve Conroy, AKA victim number three . . . She gave me the names of two friends that we didn't have. She didn't seem to have a lot of affection for these people but didn't dislike them, either. It didn't sound as if she and Conroy socialized together with the friends . . ."

Kendra had braced herself for the experience of once again hearing Jeff's voice in her ears, but she was caught off guard by the tension and edginess of his tone. This wasn't his normal professional voice; she had heard him keep his cool in some of the most stressful situations imaginable, yet here, in this fairly innocuous interview recap, his inflections were clipped, and his breathing was shallow.

He continued in the same troubling manner, even as his observations bordered on the mundane. She took interest, however, as he finished: " . . . *the victim's fiancée said she didn't know a lot about his earlier life. She answered a good many of my questions with 'it didn't come up' or 'he never talked about that stuff.'* " It was a little unusual for a fiancée to know so little, but not unheard of. But it did make me think of the husband of victim number one, Tricia Garza, who also seemed to know very little of his wife's life before him. It may be nothing, but with so few commonalities between our victims, it's something to keep in mind."

Kendra looked up at the bay as the audio file ended. Vintage Jeff. Working his case twenty-four/seven, chewing over every interview and each scrap of evidence when his coworkers were still trying to decide what to eat with their breakfast cereal.

But there was something here that troubled him more than usual. Could anyone else hear it? Probably not. She felt justified for wanting more than the transcript, but even she had never suspected that his tone would be so telling.

What in the hell was going on, Jeff?

Kendra spent ninety minutes listening to more recordings, but Jeff's remarks were nowhere near as revealing as the stress in his voice.

She thoughtfully put away her phone and walked home through the Gaslamp Quarter, where the restaurant workers were starting to arrive with their seafood and fresh vegetables from the wholesale markets. There was much more to hear, but she was surprised by how much the process drained her emotionally. Memories had ambushed her at every turn and it was becoming difficult to overcome them and analyze the tapes with her usual coolness.

There was too much history there. Although the FBI work eventually drove her to split with Jeff, in the beginning, it gave her a tremendous charge to see him in his element, doing what he clearly did best. It was a side she hadn't seen before; tough, capable, and sexy as hell. He had told her that he got a similar charge from watching her on that first case, helping bring down a sports-team owner involved in murder and an international money-laundering operation. She had actually enjoyed showing off for Jeff, and he had made her believe she had a gift that should be cherished.

A gift, she thought bitterly. A "gift" that four cases later was only good enough to put her first on the scene to find two dead children who had been buried alive.

The nightmare memories were suddenly bombarding, ambushing her. Distance yourself, she told herself. It's over. She would continue listening to Jeff's recording later in the afternoon. Surely, there was no great hurry.

Bullshit. The tension in Jeff's voice had given her a sense of nagging urgency that wouldn't leave her.

As she rounded the corner onto E Street, she caught sight of Adam Lynch's Ferrari. A moment after that, she saw the man himself, leaning against the wrought-iron fence that bordered her building. He held a manila envelope.

She felt her muscles tighten with that familiar tension that seemed to be her constant response to Lynch.

He inclined his head. "Good morning."

"You could have called me, you know."

"It's early. That would have been . . . rude."

She pulled out her keys and opened the building's main door. "But showing up completely unannounced . . . I suppose that's okay?"

"There was another murder last night."

She turned toward him. "Where?"

"About forty-five minutes outside of town, on State Route 16. This one was on the side of a road."

"Same pattern as the others?"

He nodded. "It was a stabbing. Same-size blade, same toxic substance in the victim's system. This one was a Caucasian male, age thirty-three."

Kendra felt a jolt of shock. Dammit. As much as she tried to tell herself that this case was different, it was still a race. The longer it took her to reach the finish line, the more people were going to die. That realization had once almost driven her insane in other cases. "You got a toxicology report that quickly?"

"Sienna Deever has developed a blood test that gives her almost immediate results. Every time there has been a fatal stabbing in the last couple of weeks, she's gone out to the location with her kit. She knew we had another match even before she left the crime scene at four thirty this morning."

Kendra had already been impressed by Sienna during their brief meeting the day before, but she was now even more so. "Time of death?"

"Around midnight."

She pointed to the envelope in his hand. "And are those the crime-scene photos?"

He nodded. "You can look at them on the way to Route 16."

She had seen it coming, but she was still annoyed at his presumptiveness. She stepped into her building and held the door open for Lynch. "I was waiting for that shoe to drop."

"We don't have much time. The body has been removed, but the Highway Patrol is detouring traffic around the crime scene. They've promised to hold it down for us until ten thirty."

She checked her watch—9:20. "So you're telling me

we have to leave *right* now. That I can't shower or change? You want me to go to a murder scene in stretchy workout clothes."

He smiled. "It could work to our advantage. Very few women could pull off a formfitting outfit the way you do. I'm sure the cops down there will be extremely accommodating."

Her face flushed, and in the next instant, she was furious at herself for the reaction. The Puppetmaster was still at work, prodding, probing, assessing. Trying to see what buttons to push with her.

Give him nothing.

She turned and motioned back toward the front door. "We're wasting time. Let's go."

Kendra and Lynch arrived at the scene less than an hour later, after being waved through a roadblock by a young uniformed officer who was far more interested in Lynch's Ferrari than in his official ID. They parked and walked toward the Volvo S60 on the side of the road, which was surrounded by an assortment of police and FBI forensics investigators. Agents Michael Griffin and Bill Santini stood on the sidelines and turned as they approached.

Griffin tapped his watch. "Just in time to watch us tow it away. Thanks anyway."

Kendra nodded. "I don't need much time. I'm sure you've already found what there is to be seen here."

"Really? I know you don't believe that," Santini said.

Kendra pointed to the ground around the car. "Any footprints?"

"Looks like the killer swept them clean with the side of his shoe. We might be able to get a shoe size, but that's it," Griffin said. "Have you seen the crime-scene photos?"

Kendra nodded. "One puncture wound, and the victim

was facedown in front of his car. And his car hood was up when he was found?"

"Yes, and his headlights were still on," Santini said. "A passerby found him and phoned it in at about 2 A.M."

Kendra stepped closer to the car. "At first glance, it would appear to be random . . . As if he broke down and had the bad luck to be on the same road with a passing psycho."

"That's what we all thought," Griffin said. "Until Sienna ran her test. She's still with the body at the medical examiner's office."

"Then it appears that the breakdown was no accident. It's likely that the victim's car had been tampered with earlier."

"Want to take a look at the engine?" Lynch said.

"It would mean nothing to me," Kendra said. "I can identify almost every sound an engine can make, but I've never taken the time to match those sounds with what the actual components look like."

"I'm surprised," Lynch said. "You seem to have found the time to become an expert at practically everything else in the world."

"Are you being sarcastic?"

"Perish the thought."

"I will." She shrugged. "I *am* curious about the connection, but there just aren't enough hours in the day. I'll get around to it sometime."

"I have no doubt."

They walked toward the car and slowly circled it. Kendra stopped and crouched when she reached the front passenger's side. She turned and looked at the field behind her.

"What is it?" Lynch asked.

Kendra did not reply. She stood and made her way to the front of the car, where she quickly examined every

inch of the engine compartment with a speed and precision that Jeff had once told her reminded him of a laser
scanner.

"I thought you said it wouldn't be any use for you to
look there," Lynch said.

Kendra looked up. "I was wrong."

"That's a first," Griffin said, as he and Santini approached. "I should have recorded it. Kendra Michaels
just admitted that she was wrong."

Kendra ignored him. She pointed to the pool of dried
blood on the pavement. "The victim died here. One puncture wound to the chest. No other wounds, correct?"

"That's correct," Santini said.

She nodded. "Then I would say that there's a good
possibility that your killer has a gash on his head. It
might be on his forehead, but it's most likely above his
hairline."

The officers within earshot stopped what they were
doing and stared at her. Griffin asked, "And just how . . .
do you figure that?"

"I wish it was something more impressive, but it's about
as basic as you can get." Kendra pointed to the underside
edge of the hood. "Blood. It appears that the killer tried
to clean it up, but he missed a tiny stain on the underside
of the hood. And I think there are a few drops of blood
over there on the grass, too. It's hard to tell since he obviously tried to get rid of it as he did the footprints. But if
the blood under the hood checks out, you might have the
killer's DNA."

The forensics experts scrambled toward the victim's
car as Griffin peered at the tiny rust-colored smudge near
the edge of the hood's underside. He scowled. "How in
the hell were you the only one to see that when we've had
a small army combing this scene for seven hours?"

"I'm sure someone would have spotted it once you had

the car in your garage," Kendra said. "But out here, everyone had a preconceived notion what to look for. Since the victim didn't have blood on his head or hands, no one thought to look up here for it." She shrugged. "I'm not like you. Visually, it's impossible for me to take anything for granted."

Griffin glanced at the forensics tech now carefully swabbing the stain. "I wish I could say the same for some other people around here."

"I told you, it's not their fault." Kendra glanced back at the area of earth and patchy grass next to the driver's side door. "The killer obviously spent some time over there trying to sweep his footprints clean. But, if I'm right about the blood droplets on the grass over there, he may have left behind something much more valuable to us."

The forensics team was already plucking blades of grass with their tweezers and placing them into evidence vials.

"Well, I guess our work here is done," Lynch said. "Or should I say your work?"

"Maybe. What do we know about the victim?" Kendra asked. "Do we know his occupation?"

Santini consulted a pocket notebook. "Construction. He's been working for a restaurant chain lately. Retrofitting existing buildings to their specs as they expand."

"I assume he had no knowledge or relationship to any of the other victims?" Lynch asked.

"There's still a lot we don't know about him, but we haven't seen any connection yet," Griffin said.

"Does he have family?" Kendra asked.

"An ex-wife in L.A.," Santini said, still consulting his notebook. "No kids. A sister in northern California was listed as his emergency contact. She's been notified and will be coming to town later today."

A uniformed officer stepped forward. "Sorry, but I

must ask you all to clear the roadway. We need to get this road open."

Lynch turned toward Kendra. "Did you get everything you needed?"

She took one last look at the scene. "Yes. I'm through here."

Griffin waved at an enclosed-bed tow truck parked twenty yards up the road, and the vehicle immediately roared to life. He turned back to Kendra and Lynch. "We're taking the car to the FBI garage in the city. The forensics guys will go over it, and we'll let you know if they find anything interesting."

Lynch and Kendra watched as the Volvo was loaded onto the enclosed truck. The entire process took less than three minutes, and it was obvious to Kendra that the driver was accustomed to working quickly and in a way that also preserved the evidentiary value of his cargo.

She turned toward Lynch. "I want to talk to Shawna Davis."

He paused, then made the connection. "The fiancée of victim number three?"

"Yes. She was the last person to see Jeff. He interviewed her just before he disappeared."

"Santini already did a follow-up interview with her. His notes are in the supplemental section of the case file they gave you."

"I read it. I want to talk to her myself."

He motioned for her to follow him back to his car. "I thought you might say that." He checked his watch. "She should be at work now. We can visit her there."

"Where's that?"

"The Hotel Palomar. She plays piano in the lobby."

CHAPTER 6

Kendra and Lynch drove back through downtown to the Hotel Palomar, a luxurious five-star establishment that featured a popular rooftop pool and lounge at which Kendra occasionally enjoyed drinks with friends.

They parked and made their way to the main lobby, a spacious, modernistic area with dark floors and walls. Kendra immediately heard the strains of "My Heart Will Go On" wafting through the space.

Lynch pointed past the registration desk, where a woman was playing a baby grand piano. "That's Shawna Davis. The one who has on more makeup than Lady Gaga."

The small, thin woman at the piano was pasty pale, and her foundation makeup was thick, her eye makeup a little smeared. "Knock it off. She's in mourning and probably trying to hide the fact that she looks like death warmed over. A spray-on tan isn't the easiest thing to apply in the best of circumstances."

"Sorry, I didn't think. I guess you've noticed I'm not the most sensitive soul." Lynch walked closer to the woman and flashed his ID in her direction.

She nodded and continued playing the song, concluding with a flourish.

"Very nice," Kendra said quietly as she approached. "You play very well."

Shawna stared down at the keyboard. "I've already talked to the police and the FBI. I really don't have anything more to say."

"We're very sorry for your loss," Kendra said. "I know it doesn't make things easier to have people like us grilling you."

"No, it doesn't."

"We'll try not to be repetitious. We're more interested in Agent Stedler," Lynch said. "You were the last person to see him before he disappeared."

"Yeah, that FBI agent told me."

"Special Agent Santini?" Kendra asked.

The woman finally looked up, and Kendra could see that Shawna's eyes were puffed and red from weeping. "Yeah," Shawna said. "Santini was his name. I wasn't much help to him, though."

"When Agent Stedler last came to talk to you, it was for the second time, wasn't it?"

"Yes, he talked to me twice. The first time was just a couple of days after Steve was killed, and he wanted to know about his schedule, who his friends were, that kind of thing. The second time, he mostly asked a lot of questions about Steve's background, his college days, and people he grew up with."

Lynch nodded. "And you gave Agent Santini all that info, too?"

She lifted her thin shoulders in a half shrug. "What I had, which wasn't much."

"I noticed that from the notes I read," Kendra said. "But you had known your fiancé for over three years, right?"

She nodded, her eyes moistening. "He was an IT guy at a company where I was temping. It's not like he was hiding anything from me. He said he didn't like to live in the past. I met his family, but he really didn't keep in touch with old friends."

"You told this to Agent Stedler on the last day you saw him?" Lynch asked.

"Yes."

"How did he react?"

She shrugged. "He asked if I had any of Steve's old yearbooks, journals, scrapbooks, or anything like that."

"And what did you give him?"

"There was nothing to give. Steve never held on to that kind of stuff."

Kendra moved closer to her and spoke softly. "Shawna, this may seem like nothing, but I'd like you to try to remember something for me. Can you tell me how Agent Stedler's mood was on that last day? Was there anything about him that seemed odd or different compared with your first meeting with him?"

"Hell, yes," she replied without hesitation.

The immediacy of her response surprised Kendra. She had expected her to mull it over. "How so?"

"The second time, he was much more . . . intense. It was almost like he was mad at me."

"Was he?" Kendra said.

"No. At least he said he wasn't." Her lips twisted. "He apologized to me, but his mood still didn't change a whole lot after that."

Kendra wrinkled her brow. She had seen Jeff at work, and the description didn't seem at all like him, especially when interviewing a murder victim's loved one. But it matched the troubled tone she had heard in his voice on the recordings.

"How did he end the interview?" Kendra asked. "Did he discuss talking to you again?"

"No. He didn't say much of anything." Shawna thought for a moment. "He got a call, so he excused himself and left."

"On his cell phone?"

"Yeah."

Kendra shot Lynch a quick glance, and he immediately opened his tablet computer and fingered its touch-screen interface. She turned back to Shawna. "Did you tell Agent Santini about that?"

Shawna shrugged. "No, I actually didn't think about it until now. Mr. Stedler didn't act like it was a big deal or anything. I think he was finished talking to me."

"Did you happen to hear any of his telephone conversation?"

"No." She shrugged again. "Sorry."

Lynch looked up from his tablet. "Excuse me, but can you tell me what kind of phone Agent Stedler was using?"

"I really didn't notice."

"Was it a BlackBerry?" Kendra asked.

"I don't think so," Shawna said slowly, as if trying to visualize it. "Because that's what I use. I think I would have remembered that."

"Okay, good," Kendra said. "Thank you. This has been very helpful."

"Really?" Shawna said doubtfully.

"Yes."

Lynch gave her his card. "We'd appreciate it if you'd call if you come up with anything else that you think might be of interest."

Shawna nodded. "But I don't think I can help you." She blinked rapidly. "I know Agent Stedler thought it was weird that I didn't know more about my fiancé. But I knew that he was a good man and that he loved me. I'm not very smart or pretty, but he thought I was wonderful," she said unsteadily. "No one has ever loved me like that before he came along. In the end, that's all that's important, isn't it?"

Kendra nodded. "It comes pretty close," she said gently. "Do you have family with you now?"

She shook her head. "We don't get along. I'm okay. I have a temp clerical job, and I work part-time here. I'll get through this."

But she had lost the one man who had thought her wonderful, Kendra thought. "It's usually good to keep yourself busy. Maybe do something different." She said impulsively, "Why not take a couple classes at UC? My mother is a professor, and she could help you out."

Shawna gazed at her in surprise. "I told you, I'm not real smart."

"I think you may be smarter than you think you are. And you're a fine pianist." She handed her one of her own cards. "But you'll never know unless you try. Call me, and I'll put you in touch with my mother." She turned to Lynch. "Let's go."

He nodded, and he and Kendra walked toward the circular, flower-lined driveway outside the lobby. "That was a surprise," he murmured. "Do you think she'll call you?"

Kendra glanced back at the woman at the piano. Shawna was still gazing at the card she'd given her. "Maybe. I'll give her two days, then I'll turn my mother loose on her. She'll shape her up."

His eyes were narrowed on her face. "Why are you bothering? She's nothing to you."

"Okay, it was an impulse. She seemed . . . lost. Besides, my mother needs a project." She smiled slyly. "And I like serving up challenges to her. She hasn't had a decent one since the day I moved out. I guarantee that woman will have a new attitude after their first encounter."

"Suppose she doesn't decide to accept this particular challenge?"

"Then I'll find another way that doesn't involve her."

"Why? Do you need a project, too? Somehow I don't get that impression."

"You do what you choose to do, what you have to do." She frowned. "Now stop wasting time trying to probe my motives and get back to business. There were no records of incoming calls to Jeff's phone at that time, were there?"

Lynch patted his tablet. "Nope. He made a call just after he left his office on his way to see her, but that's the end of his phone activity."

"For some reason, he was using a second cell phone."

"A phone the FBI didn't know about. It doesn't appear anywhere in his file. It could have been a disposable model that came with usage minutes. If he paid cash, nobody could trace it to him."

"But why?"

Lynch handed his ticket to the parking attendant, who ran to fetch his car. After a moment's silence, he turned toward Kendra. "Beats the hell out of me. I was hoping you'd have an answer. Haven't you come up with some way to put all the pieces together yet? Santini would be very disappointed in you."

She wanted to hit him. She was feeling bewildered and frustrated and a little scared. She didn't need Lynch's mockery just then. "Go screw yourself."

His smile faded. "I was only half joking. I did hope that you might have caught something in what she told us that I didn't. You've been very . . . productive."

"And you wanted to squeeze every bit of whatever usefulness I have in this mess out of me?"

"Did you expect anything else?"

"No." The parking attendant was holding open the passenger door of Lynch's car, and she moved toward it. "I learned a long time ago that people have their own agendas and those who are willing to compromise what they want are very rare."

"But you've run across a few of those rare souls?"

"Yes." She got into the car. "And you're not one of them."

He chuckled as he started the car. "And are you, Kendra Michaels?"

"Not often. But I believe in payback."

He looked away from her. "So do I."

She was once more aware of that glint of hardness that had the texture of a machete blade. "I don't think we're talking about the same thing."

"No." He didn't glance away from the street as he pulled out of the parking lot. "I'm quite sure that we're not . . ."

Miramar Naval Hospital
4:30 P.M.

Dr. Myles Denton entered the conference room and pulled off his surgical mask. "I hope you have better news for me this time. Your handling of the details of the transfer has been atrocious."

"Hello, Denton." Charles Schuyler sat down at the head of the long table. "I feel a bit resentful. Once again, Dr. Denton, you're treating me like your employee, when it is actually the other way around."

"Interesting that you think so," Denton said. "I think it would be more accurate to say that we're partners. Each of us has his part to play in this little endeavor. And so far, I've been better about keeping my end of the bargain. I've produced the product. All you have to do is collect the last batch and get it out of the country. I think I should have my money now."

"No way. You've left me with some nasty ends to tie up. You get nothing until we get the full shipment on that plane and you hand over that disc to me."

"The shipment should be enough. It's your job to get the disc."

"You're incredible. It's your assistant who brought this mess down on us."

"And I informed on her, didn't I? So now it's your problem."

No use arguing with the asshole. Just lay down the law and change the subject. "No money until the project is safe." Schuyler pointed to the mask. "I was surprised to hear you were in surgery. I thought you were just doing research these days."

Denton shrugged. "I'm a good surgeon. One of the best, actually. Research is certainly more fulfilling in the long run, but when you've been given such a gift, it would be criminal to waste it."

"Modest as ever, Doctor."

"Let the mediocre ones wallow in modesty."

Schuyler nodded. Arrogant prick. "To answer your question, the news isn't good. The FBI is investigating the deaths."

Denton dropped down in a chair, looking much less confident than he had only seconds before, Schuyler noticed with satisfaction. "They've made the connection?"

"They've made *a* connection. We don't know what, exactly. We do know this case has the interest of someone at the highest levels of the Justice Department."

"Shit." Denton slammed his fist on the table. "It's that geriatric imbecile you insist on using. I thought you were going to make the deaths look like accidents. Isn't that what your guys do?"

"If it was just a couple deaths, and we'd had more time on our hands, yeah, maybe. But you insisted you had to have more than the one or two we agreed on. And that accidental approach isn't nearly as certain. If we try to make it look like natural causes, that opens up the possibility of a medical investigation, which none of us wants." He looked him in the eye. "Do we?"

"Of course not."

"The murders we've been doing are so obvious it was unlikely that a complete autopsy would be ordered. It's the best we could do. And, Doctor, you're the one who insisted on one hundred percent containment."

"It's essential. But why in the hell is the DOJ interested?"

"We have no idea. Even if the local police know that the deaths were somehow related, this case shouldn't interest Washington." He paused. "And we've stopped the FBI investigation in its tracks."

"Then how could this have happened?"

"We're working on finding out. The DOJ has brought in a heavy hitter, an ex–FBI agent by the name of Adam Lynch. He's working with a woman, Kendra Michaels."

"Another agent?"

"Actually, no. She's a music therapist."

"You're not serious."

"I am. She's consulted on a few cases before, but details are sparse. She's freelance, and, apparently, she's never interested in taking credit, which makes it difficult to know exactly what she's done for them in the past." His lips tightened grimly. "But I can tell you that she's extraordinary."

"Is she a threat?"

"Absolutely."

Denton shook his head emphatically. "Then stop her,

dammit. This could destroy everything. We're too close to botch it all now."

"We won't. I've taken the problem in hand. We've planned for every contingency."

"*Every* contingency?"

Denton was trying to conceal the fact that he was scared shitless. Good, that increased Schuyler's control. So much for the brilliant physician's godlike ego. Screw you, Denton.

Schuyler stood up and walked to the end of the conference table to stand beside Denton. "It could get a little messy, but you needn't be concerned with the details. How many times have you told me that you don't want to be involved?" And, when he had what he needed from Denton, he'd make sure the involvement was severed . . . permanently. He patted him soothingly on the shoulder. "I just thought you should be informed." Keep him calm, keep him doing exactly what he wanted him to do. "Another few days, and it will be all over. We'll both be on easy street. Let me worry about Kendra Michaels."

This is just what I needed, Kendra thought as she watched Jimmy playing the drums again. Lynch had tried to force a detour to the medical examiner's office to join Sienna Deever in her examination of the corpse, but she'd held firm. She wasn't putting the rest of her life on hold again, not for anyone or any reason.

The recorded tune ended, but the boy continued playing. "Jimmy, the song's over," she said over the sound of his snare.

He laughed. "But I can still hear it!"

"Of course you can. But we need to do something else right now."

His expression clouded. "No, I love to play!"

"I know, Jimmy. But now I need you to stop. Will you do that for me?"

To her surprise, he abruptly stopped.

Progress. There was a time when it would have been necessary to grab the sticks from Jimmy's hands to keep him from playing. Now he was making connections between what he heard and what he must do.

Could she be making a difference? Naturally, it was a collaboration between her, Jimmy's parents, and his teachers, but she couldn't help but think that the boy's interest in music might be helping him form connections that had once eluded him.

Don't get carried away, she told herself. As she always told the hopeful parents, it's a marathon.

She smiled. "Thank you for stopping when I asked you, Jimmy. We can play some more later, but first we're going to play some 'name that tune.'" She picked up her guitar. "You like this game, remember? I'm going to play some songs you know, one note at a time, and you can stop me when you remember it. Okay?"

He nodded. "I like it. And I'm good at it."

"Yes, you are. And getting better all the time. So, we're going to—"

A chime sounded, signaling that someone had opened the door of the outer office.

Kendra checked the screen of her phone, but the office webcam feed was a white blur. Malfunction or . . . She stared at it for a long moment.

"What's wrong?" Jimmy said.

She swiped her finger across the phone's touch screen to pull up the parking-lot webcam feed. Jimmy's mother, Tina, had left to pick up her daughter from school, but she wouldn't be back for another twenty minutes or so. And there was no trace of her gold van in the almost empty lot.

Jimmy leaned over and peered at her phone. "Two-HXW-100," he whispered.

"What?"

Her office's outer door splintered open!

A heavyset, gray-haired man in a tan sports jacket stared at her through the window of her inner studio door.

Kendra bolted toward the entrance. The man, obviously surprised to see her rushing in his direction, stepped back and raised a silver revolver.

Gotta make this count . . .

She threw herself forward and punched the knob lock.

The man aimed at her head and squeezed the trigger. Two shots rang out.

Jimmy jumped toward her. "Kendra!"

A spiderweb of cracks spread across the glass pane's surface, but the window held. The man stared at it for a moment, then barreled into it with his right shoulder. The cracks multiplied.

Kendra grabbed Jimmy's hand and ran for the other door, which would take them into the observation area behind the one-way glass. "This way, Jimmy. Hurry!"

"Two-HXW-100," he said again.

What in the hell?

No time for analysis. She pulled him into the observation room and slammed the door shut. Her first instinct was to run through the other door to the corridor, but then it would be all too easy to intercept them. No, there was only one way out.

Up.

She jumped onto a chair, grabbed another by its plastic back, and raised it above her head to push up a suspended ceiling panel. She craned her neck to see up into the ceiling. *This could work . . .*

Jimmy spun toward the one-way glass, watching as the

man repeatedly hurled himself at the door on the other side of the studio. "He's getting through!"

Mustn't panic. Stay calm for Jimmy. She dropped the chair and reached down for him. "Come here. I'm going to give you a boost. We're going up there."

He looked uncertainly through the dark opening in the ceiling.

"Now, Jimmy. *Come here*."

He snapped to attention and gave her his hands. She pulled him up to the chair and lifted him up to the opening. "See that metal beam, Jimmy? Grab on to that and pull yourself up."

"I can't!"

"You can. And I'll be right behind you. Up you go!"

She wrapped her arms around his waist and lifted him into the ceiling. He grabbed the beam and worked his way on top of it.

Thank goodness.

Jimmy wasn't the most coordinated kid. Now if he could just keep going without falling and crashing through the ceiling . . .

Glass shattered behind her. The man was in her studio.

Kendra jumped off the chair, opened the door to the hallway, then turned back around and lifted herself up.

She grabbed the beam and pushed the ceiling tile back over the opening. No time to line it up perfectly . . .

The man kicked open the door. Silence. Kendra held her breath.

Take the bait, asshole . . .

His footsteps pounded in the hallway.

He was gone. But how long did they have before he realized what happened and came back?

Fifteen seconds, maybe thirty?

"Move, Jimmy," she whispered. "We need to get to the next office."

"I can't see!"

"Shhh. Crawl forward, and be careful."

He hesitated, then moved down the beam that would take them toward the sports-medicine practice next door.

She hoped.

If there was a firewall between suites that jutted to the roofline, their journey would come to an abrupt halt. She looked ahead, trying to see in the darkness. "Hurry, Jimmy."

"I can't go any faster!"

Those footsteps again. Coming back toward her.

Shit.

"Be still, Jimmy! Be quiet."

He stopped, but she could now hear him whimpering.

After another few seconds, the footsteps stopped.

Silence.

What in the hell was he doing? If only she could steal a glance through the gap in the ceiling tile behind her . . .

Not an option.

She was depending on her vision. Stop it, she told herself.

Close your eyes.

Put yourself down in the room.

Rustling clothes. Sleeves of that cheap polyester-blend jacket being pulled taut as both arms were extended before him. Holding that gun, no doubt.

More rustling. His crisp shirt stretching from his beltline. He was turning at the waist, looking for their hiding place . . .

She heard his wiry hair bristling against the back of his shirt collar. *He was looking up.*

Another set of footsteps, from the studio. A partner?

No, she realized.

"Stop!"

Lynch!

Blam-blam-blam-blam.

Gunshots rang out from seemingly all directions, and at least three bullets pierced the ceiling just feet from where she and Jimmy were crouched. She instinctively threw her body in front of the boy.

The window shattered between the studio and the observation room.

Shit. If those shots continued, it was only a matter of time before one of the bullets tore into her, Jimmy, or both.

She was glancing around for a safe haven when, suddenly, the gunshots stopped. Footsteps pounded into the hallway.

There was a long moment of silence, then the sound of footsteps grinding against glass on the floor.

She tensed.

"Kendra?" Lynch's voice. "Kendra, are you there?"

She let her breath out. "Yes!" She turned back toward Jimmy. "Are you okay, honey?"

Jimmy angled his head away, trying to hide the tears streaming down his face. "I'm scared."

"I know. But everything is okay now. The man down there is a friend of mine, and he's not going to let anything happen to us."

"Two-HXW-100," Jimmy whispered.

Those numbers and letters again.

The ceiling tile moved aside, and Lynch's head appeared in the opening. "Kendra?"

"Where is he? Did you get him?"

"No. He took off."

"Then why are you wasting time here with us? Get him!"

"He's gone."

"What in the hell are you doing here? You could have caught him."

Lynch shook his head. "Call me crazy, but I thought it was important to see if you were all right."

"We're fine." She tried to hide the annoyance in her voice, but she knew it was a lost cause. Dammit, he should have gone after that son of a bitch.

"We?"

"Jimmy's up here with me. He's one of my students."

Lynch craned his neck to see around her. "I remember. Hey, buddy." He smiled at the boy. "You're a brave guy, you know that?"

She wanted to tell him that his words would have no effect on Jimmy, and that it took serious time for anyone to win his trust.

Jimmy hesitated, then smiled at Lynch. "Thanks."

Dammit.

She levered herself down. "Call the Bureau and the police, Lynch." She helped Jimmy out of the opening and down to the floor. "Let's you and me call your mom and make sure she's on her way. We need to give her a little preparation. We don't want to scare her."

That was closing the proverbial barn door, she thought ruefully. His mom, Tina, was going to be terrified. When you had a special kid, you had to struggle to allow him to take chances and try to become independent. It was against every maternal instinct not to protect him from the world. But this episode was over-the-top and Tina was going to have to handle it.

She glanced at Lynch, who had taken out his phone. She wanted to fire questions at him.

Smother the anger. Don't disturb Jimmy any more than he was already.

Don't show the kid that she was mad as hell and wanted to kill that bastard herself.

CHAPTER 7

"Two-HXW-100," Jimmy said again, glancing around the parking lot.

It had been over two hours since the attack, and the police and now FBI agents Bill Santini and Michael Griffin had permitted Kendra to take the lead in giving the account of the event. But after Jimmy's mother arrived, the boy was uncharacteristically verbal. Kendra was impressed with his detailed recollections about the gunman's attire and facial features. And something else, she realized.

"Two-HXW-100," Jimmy repeated.

Kendra turned toward Jimmy's mother, Tina. "Do you know what that means?"

"Probably just a license plate he saw. He calls them out all the time."

Kendra shot a quick glance at Lynch before turning back to Jimmy. "Where did you see that?"

He pointed to an empty parking spot about thirty feet away. "There."

"There was a car there?"

Jimmy nodded. "A big one."

Griffin leaned toward him. "Hey, son, are you trying to tell us—"

He was crowding the boy. Kendra swiftly cut him off. "Let me do this, Griffin."

Annoyance flashed across his face, but he nodded and moved back slightly.

Kendra knelt beside Jimmy and took a moment to choose her words. She knew from her months of working with Jimmy that he was extremely suggestible and might be quick to respond with whatever answer he thought would please them, whether it was true or not. "Jimmy, that's great you remembered the plate on that big car. What made you think of it?"

"It was him."

"Who?"

"The bad man. The man with the gun."

"What do you mean it was him?"

Jimmy looked away as if he were losing interest in the conversation. "Can I play the drums?"

"Not right now." Kendra clasped her hands over his. Make him focus. "Why do you say it was him?"

"He was in the big car. He was talking on the phone."

"Are you sure?"

"Yeah. I saw him when Mommy and I were going inside to see you."

Kendra saw that Griffin was already scribbling in his notebook. "That's 2-HXW- . . . ?"

"One hundred," Kendra finished for him. She turned to Jimmy's mother. "Did you see it?"

She shook her head. "No, but that doesn't mean anything. I was more concerned with getting Jimmy into his lesson." She thought for a moment. "But he did call out a license plate. Like I said, he's been doing that lately, so I didn't think much about it."

Kendra turned back to Jimmy. "What did the car look like?"

"It was white. And it kind of looked like that one." He pointed to a black pickup truck parked on the street. "But it was bigger."

Lynch knelt beside Kendra. "That's really good, Jimmy." His tone was the same nonpatronizing tone he'd used on Jimmy earlier. "You have a cool memory. What else can you tell us about this guy?"

"He had a phone just like Mommy's."

His mother held up an iPhone.

Jimmy nodded. "I saw the silver apple on the back."

Santini grinned and shook his head. "A license plate, the maker of his cell phone? Damn. This kid's sharper than most of the people we work with."

"Tell me about it," Kendra said.

Santini made a face. "I'm not sure if you're complimenting the boy or doing your usual scathing job of—"

Keep any additional conflict away from the boy. She cut him off. "Did you hear that, Jimmy? Agent Santini is with the FBI. You know how important and brave those people are from watching TV, don't you? It's really something that he thinks you're smart."

"Thank you . . . I think," Santini said.

"It's important that law enforcement be respected. I've set the bar," she said without looking at him. "Don't disillusion him."

He gazed at her without expression. "I'll try not to."

"Good job." Kendra patted Jimmy on the shoulder. She looked around at the other agents and police officers. "Are we finished here?"

Santini nodded.

She turned to Jimmy's mother. "I need to do something with Jimmy day after tomorrow. I'll need your permission."

Tina frowned, puzzled. "It's not his usual day for an appointment."

"No, but will you bring him anyway? It will take at least a day to get this mess cleaned up, then I'd like him back here." She turned back to Jimmy. "You know when we climbed up into the ceiling? We didn't go all the way. I was thinking that if there was a fire, we'd need to know if we could make it to the next building. Will you go up with me and help me check it out?"

He stared at her warily. "I . . . don't know."

"I won't force you. But it could save someone's life." Gently, she repeated, "We should go all the way, Jimmy."

He thought about it. "Okay, maybe I won't be scared this time."

"I don't think you will." She stared meaningfully at his mother. "We'll make it fun."

She understood and nodded slowly. "Sure, I'll bring him day after tomorrow." She turned. "Come on, Jimmy. You've been a hero long enough. Let's go home and make supper."

Lynch watched them get into their car before turning to her. "Why?"

"Jimmy lives inside himself. Sometimes he has nightmares. He'll remember what happened today, and he'll remember himself as a victim. Day after tomorrow, we'll play in that ceiling as if it were a kid's gym, and we'll go back and forth two or three times. I'll get his sister involved, but Jimmy will be in control. He'll truly be the hero. When he leaves, he won't be a victim any longer." She turned and headed for her car. "I'm going home to take a shower and change clothes. You drive. I'll take a taxi back here tomorrow and start to clean the place up. I'm tired."

"And rattled?"

She gave him a cool glance. "Maybe."

"You deserve to be rattled," he said quietly. "You handled the situation better than anyone I know could have done."

"You're damn right." Grudgingly, she added, "You helped. Though you shouldn't have dropped the ball by letting that bastard get away." She got into the passenger seat of his car. "I don't want to talk right now. I'm tired and angry, and I have to make a decision that I don't want to make. I only have one question. Do you have any idea who that bastard was? Are you keeping anything from me?"

"No, I don't know who he was." He paused. "And maybe I've not been totally open with you. I have problems with transparency. But if I have kept anything from you, it has nothing to do with what happened tonight. I had no idea you'd be targeted, Kendra. You were only supposed to be a consultant, a sort of tech."

"But you knew there might be a possibility."

"I won't lie." He got into the driver's seat. "There's always a possibility."

"That's all I wanted to know." She closed her eyes and leaned her head back on the headrest. "Take me home, Lynch."

She unlocked the door of her condo. "Come in, Lynch."

"I had no intention of doing anything else. Stay here in the foyer while I have a look around." He did a quick safety check of each room before he came back to her. "All clear."

"Nothing is clear. But it's going to get that way." She strode to the kitchen and started to make a pot of coffee. "I guarantee."

"Kendra, perhaps it's time our partnership came to an end."

"Really? I see. I'm no longer useful to your investigation?"

"You know better than that. You're extremely useful. Maybe even vital. But I'm obviously not the only one who thinks so. I'm sure that's why you were targeted today."

"I'm sure of it, too," she said sarcastically. "I generally don't have thugs attacking me on my home turf."

"I'm sorry, Kendra. When I think what could have happened to you and that little boy . . ." He shook his head. "I really didn't think this would be dangerous for you."

"Bullshit. As you said, there's always a possibility, and you disregarded the possibility because I had a skill you wanted." Jeff. He was just like Jeff. No, probably worse, because Jeff had made excuses and lied to himself on the grounds that any threat was for the greater good. Lynch had just taken what he wanted with total ruthlessness and let the chips fall where they might. "Well, I used that skill, and apparently it's extremely dangerous to be me right now."

"We can fix it. Back off. You're obviously being watched. Whoever knows you've been on the case will just as quickly realize that you're no longer a part of it. You should be okay after that."

"If they don't kill me before they make that judgment."

"Leave town for a while. Just disappear someplace and make a vacation of it. I'll keep you posted, and when things settle down—"

"That's your brilliant plan?" she said through set teeth. "Ship me off to a beach while you try to figure out what happened to Jeff? While you try to catch that scum who was taking potshots at me and a twelve-year-old kid?"

"It's for your own good."

"I'll decide what's good for me." Her hands clenched into fists at her sides. "You've seen to it that I can't do my job any longer. There's no way I'd endanger any other child the way Jimmy was threatened. Do you know what that means to me?"

"I can guess."

"No, you can't." Her eyes were blazing at him. "I make a difference, dammit. How many people can say that? When I'm with one of my kids, I'm not some freak with a weird gift. I may be only a piece of a bigger puzzle, but I can be the crucial piece. And you took that away from me." She was fighting for control. "And not only that, you risked the life of one of my kids. The life of any child is precious, but a special kid works so damn hard, fights for every step that comes easily to normal kids. Jimmy was making great strides. Now I may have to go back a few steps unless I can strike a balance. And he could have been killed just because I was an easy target while I was teaching him."

"That's all true. I've already admitted that I'm to blame. Now I'm trying to make reparations."

"Screw your reparations." She drew a shaky breath. "That son of a bitch came barging into my place and didn't care whom he killed as long as I went down. He was going to kill Jimmy, too. Do you think I'm going to let him get away with it?"

"No." His gaze was narrowed warily on her face. "I don't believe you are. But I'm not sure whether you're going to go after me or that bastard who had you treed."

"I'm not sure either. But I may need you."

"That's reassuring," he said. "Would you care to go into that in more depth? I always like to know where I stand."

"Oh, that's my intention. You want to know where you stand. Behind me, Lynch. You and Jeff and the rest of those Bureau guys have used me and had me tag along and patted me on the head when I threw you a bone."

"There's something wrong with that analogy."

"It sounds fine to me. The only thing that's not fine is that I'm tired of relying on you to keep my life and career intact while I tried to help you. No one gives a damn about me. Not you, not Jeff. But you'd better give a damn about those kids I work with, or I'll castrate you."

"I'm duly chastened, actually terrified."

"I'm not joking."

"Neither am I. I'm only pretending—to save my pride. Is there something else?"

"Yes, I'm done with your games and being your pet bloodhound. You've taken away my purpose and my job, and I'm going to get them back. I'll show those sons of bitches they can't walk in and try to hurt one of my kids." Her voice was vibrating with rage. "And I'm running my own show now. I'm not going to be used. I've been trailing along in your world. Now come and visit mine. If it doesn't scare the shit out of you. Stand aside, Lynch. Or, so help me, I'll run right over you."

He was still studying her, and a faint smile lit his face. "You know that might even be an enjoyable experience."

"Don't count on it. I'm not amused."

"I'm not counting on anything but the fact that something extraordinary is occurring, and it's interesting, very interesting." He turned to the coffee that she'd started to make. "I'll make the coffee. You go take your shower, then we'll talk." He lifted a finger as she opened her lips. "Just a suggestion, not an order. It was what you told me you wanted to do. Can't you see how obedient I'm being?"

She could see that he was intrigued and perhaps a little sexually aroused. Under some circumstances, conflict would have that effect on Lynch. What else? She would explore whatever other effect her words had made on him later. At that moment she had to take control and cool down. Anger was a danger if it interfered with thought when dealing with a man like Lynch. He would manipulate it and turn it into something—No, he wouldn't. She wouldn't let him.

She turned toward her bedroom. "I'll be back in fifteen

minutes. Then we'll go over our descriptions and impressions of that scumbag who doesn't give a damn about targeting kids."

"Kendra."

She looked at him over her shoulder.

"I really was trying to give you an out. I know how torn up you were on that last kidnap case with Jeff, when you couldn't prevent those two children from being murdered. I could see that you were making an association at that crime scene this morning. You were ready to blame yourself."

She stiffened. "What makes you think that?"

"Everything. It was in your posture, in the way your eyes narrowed, the lines that appeared on your forehead." He shrugged. "I'm not nearly as good as you, but I do have some powers of observation."

She glanced away. She hated being so easily and accurately read even though she did it to other people all the time. It made her feel vulnerable. "I don't need an out. I don't need permission from you or Jeff or anyone to walk away. And that out would only last until you decided you needed me again. Then you'd pick me up at my beach cottage in Kauai and whisk me back into the fray."

His lips twisted. "Probably. I can be a bastard."

"I noticed. And I'll watch you like a hawk."

Her bedroom door slammed behind her.

San Diego County Medical Examiner's Office Kearny Mesa

"You look exhausted, Sienna." Dr. Ross, the medical examiner, frowned at her. "Go home. I can call you with results."

Special Agent Sienna Deever shook her head as she stared at Paul Renshaw's corpse, shimmering in the reflection of the examination table's stainless-steel surface. She had been with the body since her roadside blood test at 4 A.M., and the office had kept her waiting all day until her medical examiner of choice could be flown in from a conference in Denver. She had worked with Dr. Christian Ross on the other victims in this case.

Ross was a bearded, heavyset man in his early sixties, and Sienna had been impressed with his thoroughness and powers of concentration. He had been the one to identify the DNA-altering properties in the victims' mutagens before she had even joined the investigation.

What was just as important, Sienna had a history with him.

He took a scalpel from his assistant, a rail-thin young man who had barely spoken in the several hours he had been there. Ross lowered the scalpel and made a Y-shaped incision into the corpse that began at each shoulder, met at the breastbone, and continued down to the pubic area. He peeled back the muscle and soft tissue in each direction, gently placing the chest flap over the victim's face. He looked up at Sienna. "Are you sure? I promise I'll call you with the preliminary as soon as I'm done."

She half smiled behind her surgical mask. "You think I'm squeamish, Doctor?"

"You? Nah."

"Good. Remember, I was in Iraq."

"Yeah, you've told me your war stories, Sienna. I'm thinking more about those deep dark circles under your eyes."

"I'm here for the long haul. I'll leave when you do."

"Whatever. Makes no difference to me." He used a bone cutter to clip the rib cage, then he lifted away the sternum and ribs as he sliced away the attached organ tissue. Ross studied the exposed vital organs for a long moment. "Whew," he whispered.

Sienna leaned over to look. "What is it?"

"The age of the deceased is thirty-three?"

"Thirty-three years, eight months."

Ross pulled down a magnifying glass attached to a tall stand. He looked through it, then motioned for Sienna to do the same. "Take a look."

Sienna stood over the magnifying glass. "What am I looking at?"

"Fatty brown pigmentation in the organ tissue. You see?"

She leaned over for a closer look. "Lipofuscin. This is more consistent with tissue in older subjects, isn't it?"

"*Much* older. I'm talking seventy, seventy-five." He probed near the kidneys. "Much of the connective tissue here is rigid. Stiff. Also a sign of premature aging of the organs." He looked up at her. "There were no diagnosed disease states in those records you gave me. Are you sure that's correct?"

"I'm positive. He hadn't even seen a doctor in over two years, and even then, it was just for a sprained ankle."

Ross shook his head. "I've never seen anything like it."

"Not in the other victims?"

"Never in my life. There are certain diseases that can cause certain internal organs to degenerate this way, but this appears to have been a systemwide process." He spoke to his assistant. "After extraction, I'll need you to dissect each of the organs while I go into the cranium. Document and photograph everything." He glanced back at Sienna. "We'll know more when we can look at the cell structure under the microscope."

Sienna nodded. "And then I've got a few calls to make."

"How did it go?" Lynch asked as he came into Kendra's office two days later. He had discreetly stayed out of her way since the attack, only appearing the previous night to take her home from the studio. "I saw Jimmy and his mom pulling out of the parking lot."

"Even better than I hoped. He had a good time, and if there are memories, they'll be good ones." For which she was profoundly grateful. Although she had arranged the session for Jimmy's benefit, Kendra realized that she needed it as much as he did. She had been dreading going back to the office, but seeing it cleaned up and somewhat restored gave her a much more positive outlook than she had before. Within minutes, Jimmy's only concern was playing the drums again, and that had bolstered his spirits even more.

He was clearly ready to go on with his life.

And so was Kendra. But how long would it be until she could have her own life back?

Lynch was studying her expression. "How are you doing?"

"Fine."

"Are you sure?"

She shrugged. "That attack two days ago was something of a wake-up call. It made me face a few things I'd been avoiding."

"That was pretty obvious. You blew me away. Any pertinent self-revelations?"

"I know Jeff is probably dead. I'm not stupid."

"It's a very real possibility. At this point, maybe even a probability. Which is why it should spur us to find out who and why."

"That's a good reason. But it isn't mine."

"You're still holding out hope that he's alive."

"As long as there's a chance, I need to do whatever I can." Change the subject. Don't think about Jeff. She had to focus and try to put this nightmare behind her. "Was there anything on the license plate Jimmy saw?"

"Yes, as a matter of fact. It's registered to a white Lincoln Navigator."

She smiled. "He was right about its being a truck."

"Yes. I'm impressed. The truck belongs to a private security firm in Escondido. It's a tiny office, and the place is empty. No people, no furniture, nothing. Just a working telephone line with voice mail."

"Is there a name on the business license?"

"It appears to be bogus."

"Of course."

"But we're tracking the rent and utility payments. It's hard to move money around these days without leaving a trail."

"So what's next?"

His brows rose. "You're actually letting me have a say in it? I wasn't sure that would be happening."

"I don't want you sure of me. I have to work with you, but it doesn't mean that I'll work for you. I'm done with that. I'll listen, but I'm going my own way."

"Could you be persuaded to have your way meander toward the FBI office? Actually, Sienna Deever is waiting to talk to us there."

"About what?"

"She had an enlightening evening at the medical examiner's office. She may have discovered a new pattern between our victims."

"Interesting," Kendra said as she studied the morgue photos that Sienna had plastered over every available inch of wall space in the FBI conference room where Kendra, Lynch, Griffin, and Santini had been seated. Sienna had just finished pointing out the signs of premature aging on the latest victim's vital organs. "Do we know the cause?"

"Unfortunately, no. But it might be a by-product of the mutagen we found in the victims' systems."

Griffin shook his head. "I don't buy that. Why wasn't this aging present in any of the other victims?"

"Actually, it was." Sienna turned back toward the autopsy photos. "After Dr. Ross discovered this in Paul Renshaw's organs, we took another look at the organ tissue from the other victims. All the signs of accelerated aging—the pigmentation, stiffening of connective tissue, cellular malfunction—were present, but at such low levels that he didn't take special note of them. The interesting thing is, with each victim, the signs of internal aging become more and more pronounced."

Lynch glanced at the photographs. "There's an actual progression?"

"Yes. Without exception, each victim's internal organs showed more pronounced aging effects than the victim before. I can only attribute it to the time factor between victims." Sienna moved to the conference table and flipped up the lid of her laptop. "This is still pretty rough, but I've assigned values to the various internal aging effects and averaged them for each victim. I've plotted them on this chart." She displayed a line graph and angled her laptop screen toward the others.

Kendra leaned over and traced her finger along the line, which rose only slightly along the plotted points of the first victims before sharply swooping upward for Paul Renshaw. "Is this a logarithmic progression?"

"It looks like it, doesn't it? But it's difficult to assign a precise geometric formula to anything in the health sciences. Each individual responds so differently to any given stimulus, and, of course, our sample size is very small. But whatever is happening to these people now appears to be occurring at a vastly accelerated rate. All of these victims were on the downhill slide and running out of time."

"It doesn't make sense," Santini said. "Why would

someone murder these people if they're headed for the morgue anyway?"

"Maybe they don't know," Lynch said. "We have no idea what their motive might be." He turned to Sienna. "Have you briefed San Diego P.D. on this?"

"No, but I'm sure they've been in contact with the medical examiner's office about Paul Renshaw's autopsy results."

"I'm sure," Griffin said. "From now on, let them get their info from the M.E."

"That's the cooperative spirit," Lynch said.

Griffin leaned against the table. "Excuse me if I sound a little bitter. Dammit, someone has been talking to the media. My money's on the local police."

"Talking about what?" Lynch said.

"We received a call from the *San Diego Union* newspaper this morning. The reporter knows that the murder victims are linked by this substance in their systems, and he was looking for a comment."

"Shit," Santini said.

"The story will probably break online tonight or early tomorrow. Our lives are about to get one hell of a lot more difficult. Needless to say, don't confirm or deny anything."

Kendra could sense a sudden rise in tension in the room. She was feeling the same instinctive rejection. She had once experienced firsthand how an overtalkative insider could almost derail an investigation.

"But on the positive side . . ." Griffin reached into a file folder and produced a color printout of two men in the lobby of a fast-food restaurant. "This was in the McDonald's restaurant on Highway 38. You were spot-on about the splatter on the dead motorcyclist's jacket, Kendra. McDonald's vanilla shake." He grimaced. "Though it was against my better judgment to follow such a ridiculously flimsy lead."

"But it didn't turn out to be so flimsy, did it?" Kendra asked tartly.

Griffin ignored the question. "He and his partner were there about ninety minutes before you ran into them. We still don't know who they were, but at least now we have a visual on the guy who is still out there."

"His name was Tommy . . . something." Kendra took the printout. "This is from a security camera?"

Griffin nodded.

"I guess it's too much to hope that they paid with credit cards."

"Cash. And you were also right about the victim being a minocycline user. The autopsy confirmed it. We've been working that angle, too."

"There was something else you should know," Sienna said slowly. "I can't be sure, but the autopsy indicated a minute amount of the same substance and deterioration in his body that was present in the other victims."

"What?" Griffin frowned. "That wasn't in your report."

"Because I can't be sure yet, sir. We're still testing. It was very little and was just taking hold when he was killed." She moistened her lips. "But he might have been the next victim on our charts in a few weeks."

"And not an innocent victim," Kendra murmured. "One of the bad guys . . ."

"And where did it come from?" Lynch asked.

"I'm not absolutely certain," Sienna repeated. "I'll let you know if we're right in the next few days."

Lynch took the photograph printout from Kendra and folded it. "Did your sweep of the mountain turn up anything, Griffin?"

"Like what in the hell those guys were doing out there?"

"And why Jeff was so interested in it on that last day," Kendra said.

Griffin shook his head. "No. Nothing."

"Okay," Kendra said. "Let us know if you find out anything." She glanced at Lynch. "If we're all done here . . ."

"Wait," Santini protested. "You're leaving? I thought this meeting was to share information. What's your contribution?"

"In addition to everything else we've discussed, I've also given you a physical description of the man who tried to kill me and my student, a license-plate number, and bullets in the wall of my office. I'll be in touch." She turned and smiled at Sienna. "Terrific work."

She strode out of the conference room.

Lynch smiled as he and Kendra entered the elevator, and the doors closed. "That's a major finding Sienna Deever shared. But they were probably expecting a little more from us."

"Too bad. I don't have to meet their expectations of being a team player. They've never wanted me on their team. They did their best to shut me out. I've given them enough to chew on for the time being. As I said, I'm not working for them. Or you."

"Fine. Trust me, I have no problem keeping them at arm's length. Today, I thought you and I might follow up on—"

"I've already made plans."

He looked surprised. "I see. Anything I should know about?"

"I told you I'm doing this my way now. You're welcome to come with me, but you'll have to follow my instructions to the letter."

" 'Instructions'?" He said the word as if it was bitter on his tongue.

She hadn't expected anything else. Lynch was used to giving orders, not taking them. Well, that was his decision. "The night we met, I noticed that pink pollen under Jeff's wiper blades."

"Right. The lab still hasn't gotten back to me on that."

"They don't need to. I told you, it's Pineland Hibiscus."

"What's your point?"

"I know a couple who know more about growing things than anybody I've ever met. I hung with them for a while during my wild days. They know more than your crime lab and more than any botanist, and they might be able to give us some idea where it came from."

"They grow what *kind* of things?"

Kendra shrugged. "A lot of things that aren't exactly legal. You'll have to be careful. If they think you're a fed looking to bring down their operation, you might get your head blown off."

"Suddenly I'm not so enthused about following your lead."

"Do what I say, and you'll be fine." She extended her palm. "Give me your keys. I'm driving."

"Kendra, may I point out that it's my Ferrari?"

"Don't worry," she said, deadpan. "If you get your head blown off, I'll take good care of it."

CHAPTER 8

Kendra downshifted and turned onto a dirt road outside Valley Center, an agricultural community located an hour northeast of San Diego. The road was lined by avocado trees blooming with yellow-green flowers.

Lynch flinched at the gravel kicking up from the tires. "Hey, after you're finished driving down this road, let's work my paint job over with some sandpaper. There may still be a few spots you haven't scratched all to hell."

"Stop being such a wuss." She slanted him a sly look. "Tell me, are you one of those guys who parks his precious wheels in Siberia so that no one will park nearby and possibly put a dimple in its door?"

"I don't do that. How much farther do we have to go?"

"Not far. Okay, so are you one of those guys who take up two parking spaces?"

He sighed. "Look, people in parking lots are careless."

"You are!" She chuckled. "I knew it. You are one of those jerks."

"I only do that once in a while."

She stepped harder on the accelerator, kicking up even more gravel.

"Okay, okay! Almost every time. Happy?"

She eased off the gas pedal.

He scowled. "Mature, very mature."

She smiled. "Better than being a pretentious prick. Which seems to be the prerequisite for owning a vehicle like this."

"Admit it, you love this car."

"It has its charms."

Lynch glanced ahead. "In any case, I hope these friends of yours can help us . . . and that our meeting isn't interrupted by swarms of DEA agents."

"If that happens, my friends will think you tipped them off."

"Ahh, and we're back to my head getting blown off?"

"Not likely. Charlie and Emma are good people." She thought about it. "Of course, I haven't been with them for a long time. Sometimes people change. You'll just have to take your chances."

"Comforting."

"Comfort is highly overrated." They drove for another ten minutes through ever-thickening vegetation and trees until Kendra feared that the dirt and gravel road would disappear entirely. Finally, nestled under a clump of trees against a hillside, she spotted a white RV with lime green trim. "There it is."

Lynch looked at it in surprise. "They drive that? A 1985 Winnebago?"

"They realize they might have to abandon it at any time. They know what they're doing." Kendra stopped thirty yards short of the RV. "We shouldn't drive any closer."

"So what's our play?"

She unbuckled her seat belt and opened her door. "We get out and stand next to the car until somebody realizes we're not a threat."

They climbed out of the car and stood on either side of the vehicle.

"Exactly how are we supposed to gain their trust?" Lynch asked. "This could prove boring."

"I'm hoping I'll be recognized. At this very moment, I'm guessing that someone is up on that hill looking at us through a pair of binoculars."

"Or through a rifle scope?"

"Just as likely."

After thirty seconds, the side door of the Winnebago opened. A chubby gray-haired woman in a green track-suit peered outside. "Can I help you?"

Kendra took a single step away from the car. "Hi, Emma, do you remember me?"

The woman squinted at her, then nodded. "Sure I do, child. Kendra, ain't it?"

"Yes. I need your and Charlie's help."

Emma cast a suspicious glance at Lynch. "We read about you a while back, Kendra. You're helping the police nowadays."

"Once in a while, yes. But I'm not trying to get you in any kind of trouble. You know me better than that. This has nothing to do with your operation."

"If you want us to rat somebody out, you can just leave right now. We don't do that. It's bad for business and bad for our health."

"I promise you, this has nothing to do with you or your customers. I just need your expertise. All I need is ten minutes. Please, Emma."

Emma turned back into the RV for a moment as if listening to someone inside. She turned back and motioned for Kendra and Lynch to come in.

Lynch spoke under his breath. "Are you sure you know what you're doing?"

As Kendra slammed the car door shut, she smiled at

Emma. "It will be okay," she said quietly. "Like I said, good people."

But definitely suspicious, she thought, as they reached the RV and mounted the tall first step of the trailer. Emma's stare was cold and unwelcoming.

Before Kendra's eyes could adjust to the dark interior, she picked up the strong licorice odor that had surrounded Charlie Shelton as long as she had known him. It was from a sinus-blasting hard candy, she remembered, which she could now hear rattling around against Charlie's dentures.

"Who's your friend, Kendra?"

She turned toward the rear of the RV, where Charlie sat in the shadows in a large leather recliner. He was far heavier than he had been when she last saw him, and he wore an oxygen hose beneath his nostrils.

"His name is Adam Lynch." She looked at the faded curtains covering the RV's side windows. "Do you mind if we let a little light in here? I can hardly see you, Charlie."

"Believe me, that isn't such a bad thing these days." He pointed toward the curtains on the vehicle's left side. "Go ahead and pull those open, honey."

Kendra pulled the curtains and flooded the compartment with sunlight. The kitchenette, chipped vinyl flooring, and faded seat cushions had clearly seen better days. Charlie appeared physically weak, but his blue eyes were still lit with the intense joy for life she remembered.

He motioned toward Emma, who had joined them in the RV and pulled the door closed after her. "You'll have to excuse my better half here. She's gotten very protective of me since I got sick."

"I hadn't heard, Charlie. What is it?"

He smiled. "You tell *me*. You know how much I love it when you do that."

She nodded. "Emphysema. Chronic bronchitis."

He cocked an eye at her. "Which one?"

"Both." She placed her hand on his. "And I know it hasn't been easy for you, Charlie. You have awful flare-ups, don't you? You shouldn't be out here. You should live closer to a hospital."

"That's what I keep telling him," Emma said.

"Okay, spill it," Charlie said. "Let me in on your trick."

Kendra smiled. "No trick. You have a veritable medicine chest on your end table, Charlie. I see Atrovent and corticosteroid inhalers, along with a battery of antibiotics to fight off infection. We can all hear the rattle in your chest, and your waste can is overflowing with mucus-encrusted tissues."

He chuckled. "That's the Kendra I know."

"But you should really stop smoking."

He looked startled. "Smoking?" His voice was suddenly wary. "I don't smoke anymore."

"Those awful licorice candies don't quite disguise the smell on your breath, Charlie." She pointed to a khaki jacket hanging over a chair back. "And that looks like a pack of cigarettes in the right pocket of your Windbreaker."

Emma moved toward the jacket, stepping with such force that dishes rattled in the RV's cupboards. She jammed her hand into the pocket and pulled out a pack of Marlboros. She turned back toward Charlie. "You son of a bitch!"

He raised his hands in defense. "Now, Emma . . ."

"You promised me!"

"Can we discuss this later?"

"You bet your ass we'll discuss it."

His eyes flicked back to Kendra. "Damn, I should have known better. You know, that could have been a pack of cards you were seeing in my pocket."

"I wish it had been. Anyway, not quite the same shape."

Emma, perhaps finding an ally in Kendra, suddenly softened in her attitude toward her and Lynch. "Can I get you folks some tea, or maybe some soda?"

"No thanks, Emma."

"I'd like some tea," Charlie said.

"Tough shit." Emma sat on the tattered bench seat and motioned for Kendra and Lynch to sit across from her.

Charlie shrugged. "Well, I guess that settles that."

Kendra gestured toward Lynch. "As I said, this is Adam Lynch, and I'm helping him look for a friend of mine."

"I see." Charlie looked at Lynch over the top of his spectacles. "And would you happen to be a cop?"

Lynch shook his head. "No. Former FBI, but now I pretty much work for myself."

Charlie and Emma exchanged glances.

Lynch laughed. "Look, I'm really not interested in your pot farm or that garden of exotic mushrooms against the hillside."

"Then what *are* you interested in?" Charlie asked.

"You two know more about plants than just about anyone on earth," Kendra said. "You can reel off every tree in every forest in this part of the state. And every flower in every garden."

Charlie snorted. "Close. But that's an exaggeration, little lady."

"Only slightly. Will you help me?"

"Tell me what you're looking for."

"Pineland Hibiscus. Probably someplace where there was a lot of it."

"Hmm." Charlie tilted his head back. "That's not real common around here. You see that more in states near the Gulf . . . Florida, Texas, places like that. It requires quite a bit of water."

"I know it from Florida," Kendra said. "I have an aunt who lives outside of Tampa. But I know it was pollinating somewhere around here last week. Can you zero in on it for us?"

"Well, I'd say it wasn't growing in the wild. You're looking for watered gardens or a large, maintained area. There was a major housing development in Ensenada that used them in most of their yards and medians, but they've all been pretty much replaced by now. It was probably too much of a challenge to keep them going."

"They should have hired you," Kendra said.

"They couldn't afford me. And neither could the only other place I can think of. Have you been up to Rancho Bernardo?"

Lynch nodded. "North of the city. There's some good golfing up there."

"And a lot of commercial development. It's about twenty miles northeast. I've seen that flower in a lot of the common areas, on hillsides, some of the parks, everywhere. Not very practical for our climate, but maybe a developer's wife likes 'em."

"Rancho Bernardo," Kendra repeated. "Can you think of anyplace else?"

"Nope, not in these parts. There may be an occasional backyard garden or hothouse with a few, but I don't know of any others. Of course, I haven't been so mobile lately." He waved his oxygen tube. "If someone has done some major planting in the last year or two, I might not know about it."

"You've been tremendously helpful," Lynch said. "You know, the Bureau could use a guy like you, at least on a consulting basis."

Charlie grinned. "They can't afford me, either. But if I ever get jammed up by LE, I hope you guys will step up for me."

"Come on, Charlie, I know you've made enough to re-tire," Kendra said.

"We could've retired years ago," Emma said. "We have a beautiful house tucked away on a beach in—"

"In an undisclosed location," Charlie interrupted.

"Right," Emma said. "But this fool still insists on spending eight months a year in this rat trap."

Charlie raised his hand to silence Emma. "I like to keep on the move. Am I supposed to curl up and become an old man? Not me. I've expanded the business since I last saw you, Kendra. It's kept me busier than ever."

She said warily, "I hate to even ask."

"Orchids." He smiled. "Lots and lots of orchids."

Kendra's face brightened. "Well, at least it's legal."

"Actually, it's not. The orchids I grow are on the en-dangered species list. It's quite illegal for me to sell or transport them. It's hard work, but very profitable."

Emma frowned. "It better be profitable, with all the damn time you spend on those things."

"What can I say? It's an art. You can't rush genius."

Emma rolled her eyes. "So now he's a genius."

"Ghost orchids," Charlie said. "They're endangered, but they wouldn't even exist if I didn't bring them into be-ing. I'm doing the species a huge favor. But those U.S. Fish and Wildlife Service agents are even more balls to the wall than the DEA. They'd lock me up and throw away the key."

"And you'd probably find something illegal to grow in the prison garden." Kendra stood and hugged Charlie. "You listen to your wife, Charlie. Retire and get yourself to that beach house."

He shrugged. "Maybe. But you know how many people die when they retire and start to live the good life. Lack of purpose kills you." He reached up and chucked her under the chin. "You found that out, didn't you, Kendra? You were going to taste every wine and make life this big celebration. You made a good try at it, too. We had a helluva good time when you passed our way. But that mind of yours never stopped working, and the celebration went a little stale. Right?"

"Not because of you or Emma, Charlie," she said gently. "You made my life richer. I have such good memories of those months we spent together." She smiled as she brushed her lips across his forehead. "Though you never gave me one of those forbidden orchids. What kind of friend are you?"

He threw back his head and laughed. "I didn't know they existed back then. And they're more trouble than they're worth to most people except the addicts."

"Think about that beach. Maybe you could collect exotic shells or coral."

His brow furrowed. "Coral . . . Seems I heard about some kind of coral that was on the endangered list . . ."

Emma frowned. "Charlie, you can hardly breathe, and you're thinking about going diving?"

"Just thinking, Emma . . ."

"And I think we'd better get out of here." Kendra gave Emma a hug and headed for the door. "Sorry I opened a can of worms. Bye, Charlie. Come on, Lynch."

"No can of worms, Kendra." Emma had followed them as they left the RV. She added quietly, "If you manage to get him to that beach, I can do the rest. I'm sorry I wasn't more welcoming. Charlie's right, I have to take care of him now. He's all I got." The door was closing behind her. "Thanks for coming by, honey. I'll send you our address when I get Charlie to that beach."

"Do that." She headed for the car. "I'll look forward to it."

* * *

"Interesting company you keep," Lynch said as he sped away from Charlie and Emma's farm after Kendra had reluctantly surrendered the keys. "But I could see why you would want to talk to Charlie about this. That was impressive."

"There's no one better at this kind of thing than he is. Much better than waiting for the FBI lab."

"Oh, I agree."

Kendra pulled out her phone and quickly typed a search term on the tiny keypad. "Jeff wasn't a golfer. I know he wasn't in Rancho Bernardo for *that*."

"Have you ever been up there?"

"Not since I've been able to see." She scanned the page of results. "Hmm. Charlie was right. A lot of commercial properties. Sony's U.S. headquarters are there. Eastman Kodak and Hewlett Packard also have corporate offices in the area."

"It's a nice place, but as far as I know, none of the principals in this case have any connection with it."

"Are we headed there now?"

Lynch grinned. "You know it, lady."

An hour later, they rolled into Rancho Bernardo, nestled in the rolling hills of the North County. Kendra could see signs of a wildfire that had blasted down the slopes a couple of years before, but the streets and buildings were clean and well maintained. As Charlie had said, the hillsides and medians were filled with the red and white Pineland Hibiscus flowers in full bloom.

"About as different from Devil's Slide as you can get," Kendra said. "But it looks as if he might have driven both here and there sometime in that last day or two. Yet they don't appear in any of his notes, case files, or audio transcriptions. I don't get it."

"His phone also didn't ping any of the cell towers here. Or out in Ocotillo Wells. I got the records last night."

"You mean for his company phone."

"Yes. The only one the FBI knew about."

"But we knew he was using another one, at least part of the time." She considered this as they passed a neighborhood of large homes. "He didn't want to be tracked. Not by the FBI or anyone."

Lynch nodded. "That's the way it's looking. He didn't even carry his work phone with him."

"But why wouldn't he even want his own bosses tracking him?"

"You tell me. Do you think Jeff was dirty?"

"No way in hell."

"It's either that, or maybe he thought he was working for someone who was. Take your pick."

She couldn't believe that Jeff was crooked, so the choice was easy. Someone from the Bureau? But there might be still another reason. If he was undercover, he might have thought he'd be safer with no connection to the Bureau. "Or he could have been afraid to tip his hand, which means that whoever he suspected had megapower, and he couldn't take any risks." Her lips tightened. "But it's doing us no good to make guesses. We've got to find out, dammit."

Oscar Laird tried to keep his eyes on Lynch's car as he punched in Schuyler's number.

"What's the story?" Schuyler already sounded pissed.

This wasn't going to be a good conversation, Laird thought.

"They're here."

"*Where* here?"

"Rancho Bernardo."

Schuyler cursed under his breath. "How?"

"I have no idea. I'm following Lynch and Kendra Michaels right now. They're heading north on Pomerado Road."

"How in the hell did they find their way there? Do we have a leak?"

"I don't think so. And they're pretty much just driving around. I don't think they know what they're looking for."

"You don't *think*. That's comforting. They're less than two miles away from destroying everything we've been working toward, and I'm supposed to rely on your vague hunch?"

"That's what you pay me for."

"I'm shutting down."

"Don't do it. If they knew what they were doing, they'd be there already. It wouldn't be just the two of them, and they wouldn't be aimlessly driving around like a couple of house hunters looking to get a feel for the area."

A long moment of silence. Schuyler obviously knew that Laird was right, but he hated like hell to admit it.

"Okay, Laird. We're so close to the end that I'm going to take a chance and hold out for that last shipment to be processed. Don't let them out of your sight. If this goes wrong, I'm holding you responsible."

Hollow threat.

If this went wrong, Laird wanted to tell him, they would probably both be dead.

Those bastards thought he was washed up, Steve Rusin thought. As if there were a mandatory retirement age for killers for hire. He checked his watch and leaned back in his car seat.

He was sixty-eight, and hell, it was easier now than it ever was. The years had given him the wrinkles, gray hair, and bushy eyebrows that made him appear less threatening than he had in his younger days. He now had a face that people *trusted*. He could get closer to his marks, get them to lower their guard, then pounce with the same deadly precision he'd always had. Sure, things had gone a bit awry with his last target, but he'd gotten the job done.

But he had seen the doubt in Laird's eyes. He, like Schuyler, was afraid he had lost the touch.

Idiots.

Rusin gaze narrowed on the lithe, energetic figure walking toward him on the deserted street. That would be Lesley Dunn, on her way home from the advanced Photoshop class she was taking from a local art school. She made her living as a public-relations representative at an indie record label, but she harbored dreams of becoming a graphic designer. Too bad that would never happen for her, Rusin thought.

He climbed out of the car and quickly glanced at the industrial buildings around him. It was after hours, and no one else was around. He had chosen his spot well. He unsheathed his ivory-handled blade and held the knife at his side.

He unfolded a piece of paper and did his best to look befuddled.

Lesley slowed as she approached him. There was no wariness, no fear. If anything, just a hint of concern. Perfect.

"Young lady, I'm sorry to bother you. I'm not sure if I'm in the right place . . ."

She stopped and smiled but kept about five feet between them. Smart girl. "Where do you want to be?"

He glanced pathetically at the building in front of them. "Garnet Street?"

She nodded. "That's where you are."

"I'm supposed to get my hearing aid repaired somewhere around here." He knew he was laying it on thick, but she was totally buying it.

She stepped closer. "Do you have an address?"

He squinted at the paper in his hand. "Yes. But I can't quite . . ." He angled the paper in her direction, and she stepped closer.

Yes.

As she leaned over to read the paper, in one lightning motion, he jabbed at her with the blade.

He missed.

Lesley Dunn had jumped back out of range. She moved like a cat, he thought. Impressive.

He couldn't give her time to think, to realize what was happening to her.

He lunged again. *Contact.*

But she had jumped away again, and he'd only given her a slice across the midsection. Not enough to finish the job.

Whump! Something clobbered him upside the head.

What the hell—?

Whump!

She had swung her knapsack and scored two direct hits. What was she carrying in there, rocks?

A third swing stuck his hands and sent the blade skittering across the sidewalk.

Dammit!

She sprinted down the street. He bolted after her, bending and scooping up his knife without breaking stride.

That's it, honey. Run. Do you run four miles every morning? Because I sure as hell do. Each and every day.

She doubled over slightly as she moved through the intersection. She was in pain. Her cut must have been deeper than he thought.

He could do this. He could catch her, pierce her pale skin with his blade, and it would be over. He'd be home in time for—

His breath suddenly left him. He suddenly felt . . . cold. What in the hell?

He looked down at his hand and saw that it was covered in blood. *His* blood, pouring from a wound just below his wrist. His knife had obviously sliced him after the bitch swung her knapsack into it.

No big deal. Never mind, he had a job to finish. Push through the pain. Worry about his wound later.

But she was putting even more distance between them. She'd get no help from the closed businesses, but she was nearing a more-heavily-trafficked area just a block or so ahead.

He couldn't let her get there.

He pushed himself harder, drawing on reserves that had always been there when he needed them. He felt himself moving faster, even if he didn't quite feel connected to the pavement. His legs tingled, and his stomach burned. His vision fogged. But she was feeling the same thing, he realized. It was only a matter of outlasting her. He could do this.

Keep her in your sights.

She staggered into the next intersection. She glanced back. That was always his cue to put on an extra burst of speed. But before his legs could oblige him, a pickup truck roared into the intersection.

Lesley Dunn froze in horror.

The truck struck her, and she flew over the hood and collapsed onto the street.

Rusin ducked into the shadows and watched as the truck stopped. Two men jumped out and ran to examine her.

She was alive and moving.

Shit. I'll have to eliminate all three of them.

Another car stopped. Another. Then another.

Dammit. Suddenly everyone's a Good Samaritan.

He hated the thought that there was no choice but to retreat. There was no other option.

He would have to finish Lesley Dunn off later.

Rancho Bernardo
11:30 P.M.

"Another blank," Lynch said as he gazed at the plantings beside the man-made lake that formed a part of the children's playground. "I doubt if Jeff was investigating this playground."

"So do I, but you can never tell," Kendra said. She put a question mark beside the location in her notebook. They had asked questions at the Park and Recreation Department earlier in the afternoon and been given a list of the areas where the Pineland Hibiscus had been planted in the city. They couldn't help them with any business parks or hotels, but they had decided to take what they could get. "The next planting area is just outside the city."

"If we can see it," Lynch said dryly. "It's dark, and even if a security guard doesn't go after us, there's a chance that we'll miss it anyway. Don't you ever give up?"

"No," she said absently. "Why should I? That's not the way to get anything done. You have to eliminate—"

Lynch's phone rang, and he quickly accessed the call. "Lynch." He listened for a moment before he said, "We're in Rancho Bernardo. We'll be there as quick as we can." He backed the car out of the parking spot. "Sienna. They've found another victim."

* * *

Forty minutes later, they were walking through the sliding emergency doors of Scripps Mercy Hospital. A rush of cool air hit Kendra's face, and her senses were immediately assaulted by two crying babies, a large man screaming at the admissions clerk, and an overabundance of the hospital deodorizing agent Smelleze.

Sienna Deever, talking on her cell phone, waved to them from the other side of the lobby. Sienna had called her and Lynch less than thirty minutes before but had given them little in the way of details. She finished her call before they reached her.

"So we have another stabbing victim?" Lynch asked.

"Yes. Her name is Lesley Dunn, age thirty-two. She was attacked on Garnet Street just before nine P.M."

Kendra could hear the excitement in Sienna's voice, a different tone than she had heard before. "She fits the profile of the others?"

Sienna nodded. "I came here with my kit just after they brought her in. She has the same mutagen in her system as all the rest. But there's one major difference this time."

Kendra's eyes widened as she murmured, "She's still alive?"

"Alive, but unconscious. She was hit by a car at the scene."

"Hit by our killer?" Lynch asked.

"No. Hit by someone else as she was running away from him."

"I'd say she's had a bad night," Lynch said.

"Her injuries from the car accident are relatively minor. A severely bruised hip and a dislocated shoulder. She has a knife wound on her torso, but the killer wasn't able to finish the job this time." Sienna consulted a well-worn leather-bound pocket notebook. "The details are still coming together, but it looks as if the victim is the only person actually to see the attacker. She wasn't entirely coherent, but she spoke to the driver, his passenger, and at least one other person before she lost consciousness."

"Did she give a physical description?" Lynch asked.

"Afraid not. Not according to the uniformed officer who took their statements."

"Too bad."

Kendra tried to hear herself think over the sound of the screaming babies. "Why is she unconscious? Is she in shock?"

Sienna's face suddenly became grim. "I don't think so."

"What is it?"

"I'm not sure. The doctors aren't sure. They're running tests now. It may have something to do with the chemical in her system."

Kendra nodded. "But whatever it is, it's been there for months, right? Like with the others?"

"Most likely. We'll need to do other tests to be sure."

"Is it life-threatening?"

"Again, there's no way to tell. Sorry. We're in uncharted territory here."

The triage doors swung open, and Kendra was surprised to see Agent Griffin step through them and walk into the lobby.

Lynch nodded toward him. "Keeping late hours, Griffin."

"Aren't we all?"

While the rest of them were dressed casually, Kendra noticed that Griffin had taken care to put on a nicely pressed suit, crisp white shirt, and an understated silk tie. His attitude appeared businesslike and confident. She was frequently annoyed by him, but he did know how to exude authority even after midnight in the emergency room of a big-city hospital.

"Any change?" Sienna asked.

"None," Griffin said. "But I did impress on the staff the importance of our speaking to her." He paused. "At any cost."

"She's unconscious," Kendra said. "What good would that do?"

Griffin shrugged. "She's our only witness to a mass murderer. There's a chance she could die without giving us any hint of identifying him. I merely suggested that if there's any way they can stimulate her . . ."

"Stimulate." Kendra glared at him. "My God, that's low even for you, Griffin."

Griffin leaned toward her and lowered his voice. "If it was up to her, do you think she would really want to die without helping us bring this son of a bitch down? What if it was *you* in there?"

"We don't have the right to make that decision for her. She's fighting for her life. Good God, she's been stabbed and hit by a car. We have no idea what's infecting her inside, and now you're suggesting they pump her full of stimulants to wake her up to help you with your damn investigation?" Kendra turned toward Lynch and Sienna. "I don't believe this."

They weren't returning her glance.

Kendra gazed at them, stunned. "Wait a minute. Don't tell me you agree with him?"

Lynch put his hand on her arm. "She saw the killer, Kendra. This might be your only shot at finding Jeff. Who knows if we'll get another chance like this?"

Kendra felt sick. She wanted to lash out at the three of them. She took a deep breath, then spoke in a low, even tone. "That woman deserves every chance that they can give her, without our mucking things up and maybe tipping the scales against her. I feel sorry for all of you if you really think your only hope of cracking this case is to risk her life. Screw the case." She added with sudden fierceness, "And if any of you try to do it, I'll stand over her and blow you away if you so much as touch her."

Griffin raised his hands in surrender. "Before you get too indignant, the doctors in there agree with you. They practically threw me out."

"Good."

"I want a copy of the police report," Lynch said.

"You'll get it as soon as we do. Early tomorrow."

"And around-the-clock protection for Lesley Dunn," Kendra said. "In case the killer comes back to finish the job."

"Already done. San Diego P.D. will be on her twenty-four/seven."

"Then there's no use in our sticking around, is there?" Kendra turned and strode out of the hospital.

Lynch caught up with her as she reached the parking lot.

"Kendra."

"No, Lynch." She got into the passenger seat and gazed straight ahead. "I don't want to talk right now."

He slipped into the driver's seat and sat there in silence for a long moment. "I'm sorry."

"For what?"

"For not backing you up in there."

"It has nothing to do with backing me up. It's about doing what's right. For what it's worth, Jeff probably would have been on your side. But I am surprised at Sienna. She's a doctor."

"Not anymore. Maybe the temperament of an FBI agent is more suited to her."

"Maybe, but I could tell she felt rotten about it. I hope her attitude was due to the fact that she just didn't want to contradict her boss. Though that isn't really a valid excuse."

"It's possible. I know from personal experience that Griffin doesn't like to be challenged."

"So what? I've had the exact same experience, but it never made any difference to me. I don't claim I'm perfect myself. But when you see wrong, you have to challenge it. Oh, I can ignore mistakes occasionally." She made a face. "Well, not often. But when it comes to basic human decency, how could I live with myself if I let that kind of bullshit go on?"

He studied her expression for a moment before he said softly, "You couldn't. Not you, Kendra Michaels."

She met his gaze. "And just when did you get to the point where you could do it?"

"A long time ago," he said wearily. "And the sad thing is that I don't even remember when it happened."

She was silent a moment, studying him. "Yes, you do. You just don't want to tell me. Why? Would it make you feel vulnerable? I imagine that would be a worst-case scenario for you."

"You maintain the habit of stomping in where angels fear to tread, don't you?"

"You don't have to answer me. I'm just curious. It's not as if I'm going to blackmail you." She repeated, "When?"

"A long time ago."

"How long?"

"Since I was a little kid, maybe." He shrugged. "My father was a beat cop in Milwaukee. He was one of the good guys, like your Jeff Stedler. He always tried to do the right thing. The problem is that nobody else plays by those rules. Not the bad guys, certainly not the bad cops. He spent his entire career beating his head against the wall. He had some wins, but trust me, they were few and far between."

"Still, he sounds like a good man," she said quietly.

"He was."

"What happened to him?"

"Nothing dramatic. He put in his time, retired, and just kind of faded away. All those years, all the frustration, just sapped the life out of him. No one is going to do that to me. I knew there had to be a better way, and there is. If you're smart about it and give people the results they need, they usually don't care how you accomplish what you do."

"Griffin obviously cared."

"He just hated not being in control of me. That's why I went to work for people with a much better grasp of the big picture."

"People who give you carte blanche to run roughshod over anyone who stands in your way?"

"Like I said, you just have to be smart about it." He smiled faintly. "And avoid trying to do it to the Kendra Michaelses of the world. It doesn't work." He started the car. "Now, if you're finished probing old wounds, I'll take you home, so you can get some sleep. It's been a long day."

"We're not going back to Rancho Bernardo?"

He smiled. "You're a glutton for punishment. I doubt if we're going to spot any of that Pineland Hibiscus at this hour."

She supposed he was right, but she wasn't sure if she could sleep even if she tried. Every nerve was alert, and her mind was on edge and working double time. "I'm not going to find Jeff or help that woman in the hospital if I keep bankers' hours. I want to get back to teaching my kids, and I can't do that until this is over."

He shook his head ruefully. "It's almost one in the morning. I don't believe anyone can declare that as bankers' hours. I'm going to go back to my place and get a few hours of shut-eye. We'll start again in the morning." He saw the frown on her face, and said gently but firmly, "In the morning. We may have more to work with by then. I've already put in a request for video from all the traffic cams up there. The Bureau A/V guys will hate me for it, but I'll have them scan the tapes for Jeff's car. Maybe they can give us a better idea where he went." He paused. "And see if there is any more of that Pineland Hibiscus in the area."

She gazed at him with narrowed eyes. "Are you throwing me a bone to get your way, Lynch?"

"Do you think that's what I'm doing?"

"Yes."

He chuckled. "That bit of deduction was too easy for you. I'll do better next time. I wouldn't want you to get rusty." His brows rose. "Home?"

Her adrenaline was still high, and she most certainly did not want to stop yet. But he was being disappointingly reasonable, and she knew that sometimes she was driven to the point where there was only the goal ahead, and she trampled everything else in its path.

She stared at him for a brief moment before slowly nodding. "Home."

CHAPTER 9

It was nearly one thirty when Lynch pulled into the parking space in front of Kendra's condo.

"I'll see you in the morning." Kendra reached for the handle of the door. "Unless you've changed your mind about—"

"I've not changed my mind." He got out of the car and strode around it to open her door. "But I'm not leaving you until I've checked out your apartment."

"That's not necessary. I have an alarm system, and I can take care of myself. I let you go through my condo after the attack on Jimmy and me, but I don't need you to protect me, Lynch. Jeff made sure that I knew how to defend myself in any situation."

"I hate to offend your sense of independence, but dead bodies seem to be dropping all around us. I'm going to take a look around."

"Why now? Why weren't you this worried last night?"

"Actually, I was." He took her arm and walked with her toward the condo. "I didn't want to make you nervous about the possibility, but I wanted to be sure. So I stayed in the parking lot for thirty minutes or so and watched the lights go on and off in the rooms in your condo."

"That's kind of creepy. Sort of like a Peeping Tom."

He chuckled. "Only you would think that I was creepy to try to protect you." He watched her unlock the front door. "Though I admit my imagination was working a bit overtime as I mentally followed you around that condo. I was making bets with myself what you were wearing or not wearing when you left that bathroom to go to bed."

"What did you decide?" she asked suspiciously.

"A San Diego Padres baseball nightshirt."

She went into the condo and turned on the overhead lights. "Search away."

He headed for the bedroom. "Aren't you going to tell me if I was right?"

"Nope."

He sighed. "Cruel." He disappeared into the bedroom. He came out in only a few minutes and moved toward the kitchen. "Unless the nightshirt is in the wash, I think I was wrong."

"I don't appreciate your pawing through my things." She gave him a cool glance. "Particularly since it's only to satisfy your licentious curiosity."

" 'Licentious,' that's the same as 'lustful,' right?" He opened the pantry and checked the back door. "Yes, that's definitely where I was at."

"Over a baseball jersey?"

"What can I say?" He was coming back across the room to where she was standing. "Ask any guy what turns him on the most. Sexy lingerie or a woman naked beneath a sports jersey or a crisp white man's shirt." He stood looking down at her. "I'll get out of here. You're safe now."

She didn't feel safe. She was tingling, aware of Lynch's closeness, the warmth of his body, the smell of his musk-based aftershave. Damn, where had that flood of sensation come from? One moment she had been slightly annoyed, even a little indignant and the next she was feeling this melting and thinking about how close they were to the couch across the room. She should have been more wary of Lynch. She had known from the moment she had met him that he was dangerous to her in every way. Intelligence, intuition, a boldness and power that she always found attractive in a man.

And he was reading that effect on her, she realized. His eyes were narrowed on her face, and he was smiling. "Say thank you, Lynch," he said softly. "Go on, it's easy."

Nothing was going to be easy with Lynch. Her relationship with Jeff should have taught her a lesson. He had been driven and completely ruthless about using her, but Lynch put him in the shade. Lynch was larger-than-life and would try to manipulate her in any way he could.

And she was already afraid she was letting him do it. She would be crazy to also let him have sex as a weapon over her.

She stepped back and opened the door. "Screw you, Lynch. You were only protecting an investment. Good night."

He laughed. "You're wrong, you know. I'm self-serving, but I'm not that cerebral." He went out the door and paused. "Lock it behind me. I'll pick you up at eight."

"Nine. I have calls to return from my mother and Olivia. I don't seem to have time during the day."

"Your decision. You're the one who's been keeping me hopping. Not that I'm complaining." He moved down the hallway. "In certain areas, you're very entertaining."

She opened her lips to make a scathing reply, but he had already rounded the corner.

She slammed the door and turned the lock. Block Lynch from her mind. Forget those last few disturbing minutes and get to bed. She turned out the top light in the living room and kitchen and went to the bedroom.

Suddenly, she stopped in her tracks.

"I watched the lights go out one by one."

Could he be—

She strode to the patio door overlooking the street and threw it open.

The Ferrari was still sitting in the parking spot, engine turned off.

She couldn't see his expression.

But she heard him chuckle, dammit.

She stepped out under the patio light and deliberately shot him the bird.

And his chuckle became full-bodied laughter before he started the car's engine.

She went back inside and locked the door again.

She was smiling faintly as she stood there in the dark, listening as he drove away. He was outrageous, out of control, and she should not be amused. But her responses to Lynch were never what they should be. He stirred to life the Kendra she had been during those years when she was as volatile and wild as a summer storm.

What the hell? That wasn't so bad. It was sometimes good to revisit what you were so that you could compare it to what you had become.

And what had she become? Was she heading perilously close to being her mother? Didn't they say that all daughters ended up that way? That wouldn't be so terrible. Her mother was brilliant and certainly unusual and she loved her.

But it would be terrible for Kendra. No matter how she tried, she would not have been able to stand her usual day-to-day routine if it hadn't been for the kids. In her heart, she was still that gypsy she had been all those years ago.

And Lynch had managed to resurrect that gypsy. It was only another indication of how dangerous he could be to her.

Or not. If she kept her balance and called the shots, maybe she didn't have to be careful. Maybe she could just enjoy Lynch and play his games with no harm.

She shook her head, the smile still lingering as she headed for the bedroom. She would have to think about it. In the meantime, she had to get a little sleep. She needed to check her voice mail for possible news on Jimmy, then make her personal calls as soon as she got up in the morning.

And she would not think of Lynch until she saw him tomorrow.

Oscar Laird glanced around the deserted lot as the motorcyclist pulled up alongside his car. There was no way not to draw attention when that monster machine was roaring like a sick dragon, he thought with annoyance. He'd done the best he could by choosing the lot of a sad, half-completed office complex just off the I-805 freeway, but he'd better make the meeting brief and get out of there.

Tommy Briggs dismounted from the motorcycle and walked around to Laird's passenger-side door. "Hell of a place to meet," he said as he climbed into the car. "What the hell's wrong with Rancho Bernardo?"

"I decided this was safer. The feds have been nosing around the area."

"Shit."

"We don't think they know where our lab is located, but we need to be careful with our comings and goings." Laird reached into the console and pulled out a sheet of paper with a color photo printed on it. "And you need to be careful everywhere. Those feds who almost took you down have been showing this up and down Highway 138."

Briggs's eyes widened as he stared at the photograph of himself. "You have to be kidding. Where the hell did they get this?"

"It came off a McDonald's security camera on the morning you opened fire on those two agents on Devil's Slide. Good picture of your friend, Leon, too, though I seriously doubt he'd have been eating at McDonald's if he'd known it would be his last meal."

Briggs was still staring at the photo. "How the hell . . . ?"

"You and Leon took it upon yourselves to declare war on a federal agent. They tend to take that kind of thing seriously."

"I told you that we didn't know who they were. They were heading right for our spot, and Leon panicked."

"Then you panicked and killed Leon."

"I didn't have any choice. If I'd left him there, he'd—"

"Relax. Killing him was the one thing you did right. And the feds never found your burner bench. I thought it was foolish to spend all that money on the false door to that sealed mine, but it fooled 'em. We cleared it out a couple nights ago."

"But we didn't finish the last batch."

"No, you didn't. We had to do it for you. And that will be reflected in your payment."

Briggs tossed the paper down. "That's bullshit."

"We had an agreement, Briggs. You didn't fulfill your part of it."

"I did way more than I bargained for on this job. You hired me to stay close to Leon and be the muscle to keep the project going. I didn't sign on to stand over him while he was cooking up your concoction out in the middle of freaking nowhere in 110-degree heat, fighting off scorpions and snakes every damned day while you guys worked in those air-conditioned palaces in the suburbs."

"Hardly palaces. And your working conditions were built into your payment."

"And what about killing Leon? Was that built into my payment, too?"

"Spare me." He gave him a sardonic glance. "You did that to save your own skin."

Briggs flushed with anger. "You think I liked doing that shit? I liked Leon. He made me laugh, you know?"

"Were you laughing when you blew his head off?"

"Screw you."

Laird made the effort to restrain his anger. Briggs was only a tool that had to be used. "And we both know that Leon isn't the first man you've killed. You've been lucky not to have been picked up before this."

Briggs opened his lips to deny it, but when he met Laird's eyes, he closed them without speaking.

"You'd do better to stop lying and trying to shake me down and concentrate on the fix you're in. The feds are probably going to know who Leon was in the next couple days. When that happens, will they be talking to anyone in Leon's circle who might be able to point at you?"

"Maybe." Briggs thought about it. "He's spent the last few years working at Schuyler's factory outside London, but he has a sister here, and we all went out for drinks one night. But how are they going to find him? He's never been arrested, never been fingerprinted that I know about."

"The feds have their ways, and you ran into a couple of particularly savvy agents. Could they trace you through Leon?"

"Not my home address."

"They'll find it. They'll find out everything. They won't give up until they do."

Briggs began to curse. "How in hell did they find us?"

That was the question Laird had been waiting for. "The woman. She found you. Apparently, she's exceptional."

"Should have killed her when I had the chance. Damned FBI."

"Actually, she's not FBI."

"What do you mean?"

"Her name is Dr. Kendra Michaels. She's some kind of psychologist. She consults with law enforcement but doesn't even carry a gun."

Briggs snorted. "She doesn't need one. She clothes-lined Leon right off his motorcycle. Damned bitch. And now you're telling me that because of her, I'm not going to get paid what I was promised."

"That's one way of looking at it. Or you could choose to take some personal responsibility."

"Screw that. You just told me it was her fault."

"She's definitely a threat to us . . . and to you."

Briggs's eyes were suddenly narrowed on Laird's face. "You're getting at something. I'm not stupid, Laird."

He was very stupid. But he had a basic cunning that helped him to survive, together with several lethal capabilities that made him valuable to Schuyler. "I would never suggest you're stupid, Briggs. And a solution to our mutual problem just occurred to me. You need to redeem yourself and earn the rest of the fee you forfeited. While we have to protect our security in any way we can." He smiled. "I believe I'm going to have an important position opening soon. I may have an opportunity for you to better yourself, Briggs."

"It's about time you called me back," Olivia said as soon as she picked up Kendra's call the next morning. "If I hadn't heard from you today, I was going to park myself on your doorstep and wait for you."

"You sound just like my mother. She just read me the

riot act." Kendra sighed. "Okay, I should have returned your call, but I was busy during the day, then I'd get home too late. I didn't want to wake you."

"She should have read you the riot act. You knew that neither one of us wanted you to go along with that FBI agent, then you ignore our calls."

"I didn't ignore—it just happened."

Olivia was silent. "And what else happened? I assume you haven't found Jeff yet?"

"No, but we're getting closer . . . I think."

"But you don't know?"

"It's become very . . . tangled."

Olivia muttered a curse. "That's what you said when you were looking for those kidnapped kids. Get out, Kendra. Tell this Lynch to go take a hike."

"I don't know if he'd go." She paused. "I don't know if I'd want him to go. He's very sharp, and he can help me find out what happened to Jeff. I don't want to give up now."

"I was afraid of that." She didn't speak for a moment. "Look, I want my chance to talk you out of it. I'm coming over after work, and we'll have a drink and go out to dinner."

"I don't know what time I'll be home."

"Then I'll tell you what time to be home," Olivia said brusquely. "I'll be over at seven. I'll make dinner reservations at Alfredo's for eight thirty. Don't stand me up."

"Olivia, this isn't a good time."

"Anytime is good for friends to be together." Olivia's voice was suddenly soft and persuasive. "Come on, forget about all that FBI crap and relax and have dinner with me." Olivia's tone changed back to its former crispness. "It's settled. After I have you half-inebriated and entirely mellow, we'll discuss your continuing with this FBI stuff. Bye." She hung up.

Kendra was shaking her head as she pressed the disconnect. Olivia was going to be very difficult. Kendra would have been smarter to have kept in touch with her during these days instead of making her worry. Now that worry had brought determination, and when Olivia was determined, she was a force to be reckoned with.

Of course, Kendra could skip the dinner at Alfredo's.

No, she couldn't. You didn't do that to friends you loved. She'd have to sit through dinner and let Olivia coax and persuade and amuse her as she always did. Her friend was always good to be with even when she had an agenda.

So accept, enjoy the meal, and try to convince Olivia that she was not going to end up as the basket case she'd been when the kids had been killed.

And try to convince herself at the same time.

Oscar Laird strode across the alley and approached a dilapidated twelve-unit apartment building in National City. The place was more run-down than he remembered, but it suited his purposes. Not the best neighborhood for a stroll even so early in the morning, but he was more concerned about what waited for him in apartment 206.

Laird climbed the short flight of stairs to the second story. The building's dozen units—six on each level—faced outdoor walkways and a tiny grassless plot that was a pathetic excuse for a courtyard. He warily glanced around. Most of the units were vacant, and the complex's few residents appeared to be inside sleeping.

He knocked softly and used a key to let himself inside the apartment. He closed the door, but before his eyes could even adjust to the darkness, he heard Rusin's voice.

"Hell of a place you got here," Rusin said sourly.

Laird gaze searched the room until he made out a shadowy figure sitting on the floor. "It's not the Ritz, but we can come and go without being noticed. That's more important than a mint on the pillow."

"Not only is there no mint, there's no pillow. Or a stick of furniture. Or power. Or running water. What kind of operation are you guys running here?"

"An operation that no longer has need for this apartment. At least, we didn't think we did."

Rusin stood up and moved toward him. "Until I botched a job, huh?"

"It happens."

"Not to me."

Laird stepped back and opened the dated vertical blinds that covered the front window.

"What the hell are you doing?" Rusin asked.

"Trying to get a little more light in here. I just want to take a look at your hand."

"My hand is fine. I sewed it up myself." Rusin held up his thumb and forefinger and showed him the precise, almost surgical, stitching that ran down to the back of his wrist.

"Very neat. I'm impressed."

"I take care of myself. I'm a professional."

"The Dunn job was far from professional. I'm having to arrange to have the kill completed at the hospital." He paused. "And you blundered with Kendra Michaels and the child. That's unacceptable, Rusin."

"Okay, so send me on my way. I'll find plenty of jobs and clients who appreciate me. But not until you pay me what you owe me." He added, "And tell me what shit was making those marks I killed sick. You only told me that I had to stay with them until they were dead and watch for any unusual signs of rapid disintegration immediately afterward."

"That was all you needed to know."

"Is it? I've been thinking about it, and Schuyler deals with all kinds of nasty pharmaceuticals. What if this was supernasty? What if it was contagious?"

"It's not contagious."

"So you say. What the hell is it?"

"I'm afraid that's classified information, Rusin."

"Bullshit. If there's even a chance it's contagious, and it's in my body, it better become *un*classified in the next ten seconds."

"I can tell you this. In the chemistry field, it's what is known as a catalyst."

"A catalyst for what?"

"It reacts with something specific in the bodies of each of your targets. Did you think we were so unsure of your abilities that we wanted you to stab *and* poison them?"

"It was none of my business. I once worked for a lady in Bangkok who wanted me to strangle her enemies, cut off their balls, and shove them in their mouths. As long as the customer pays, I give 'em what they want."

"That's why I brought you in, Rusin. You're good."

"For an old guy, you mean."

"For any guy. It's just unfortunate we have to part ways." Laird pulled a thin wallet from his breast pocket and opened it to reveal a syringe. "Here. If it makes you feel better, the stuff in this syringe is used to nullify the effects of the substance. Not that you'll need it." He uncapped the syringe and moved toward Rusin. "If you'll just roll up your sleeve . . ."

"Get the hell away from me with that."

"It will be fine. I've been assured this is an antidote to the—"

He tensed. "Step back, Laird."

Laird smiled. "I thought you wanted my help. Isn't that why you called and asked to meet me?"

"I'll tell you how you can help me."

"By all means."

"I have a doctor who is already on his way into town. He's on a chartered plane from Seattle, which you will be paying for. We'll meet him at the airport, and you're going to tell him exactly what I need. He'll get the medication and administer it himself."

"Aren't you being a wee bit paranoid? I told you it wasn't contagious."

"It's how I've stayed alive so long, Laird. You want to know my number one occupational hazard? Not the cops, not my marks, but my employers. Instead of thinking of me as a trusted business associate, some choose to think of me as a loose end."

"Remember who you're talking to, Rusin. When my partners wanted to go with someone younger, I told them it had to be you."

"I imagine that those partners must be having some pretty serious doubts right now. You know damned well that the cops may have my blood, maybe even a witness."

"And we have every confidence that you'll cover your own tracks. That's just another part of your job, and you do it better than anyone." Laird raised the syringe and moved toward him. "As I said, you're in no danger of contagion, but I'm perfectly willing to send you on your way with a relieved mind. We've been working together for a long—"

Rusin struck his wrist with two quick chops that sent the syringe flying across the room. Before Laird even knew what was happening, Rusin had jumped behind him and yanked his jacket down around the middle of his back, effectively pinning his arms by his sides.

"I told you how this will go down," Rusin said. He pulled the Glock automatic from Laird's shoulder holster. "If you don't mind, I'll hold on to this until our business is concluded."

"If you insist."

"You're damn right I—"

There was a tinkling of glass and the rattling of plastic vertical blinds.

Rusin grunted, his grip loosened and fell away from Laird. Then, as if his power supply had suddenly switched off, he dropped dead to the floor.

Laird peered down into the darkness and saw the hole just above Rusin's right ear. He glanced back at the window. "Helluva shot, Briggs. Helluva shot."

He fished around in his shirt pocket for the tiny Bluetooth earpiece that he'd had the entire time.

He jammed it into his ear just in time to hear Tommy Briggs laughing. "You were right," Briggs said. "He was definitely slipping. He never should have let you open those blinds. I did good, didn't I?"

Laird glanced at the building across the street, where he imagined that Briggs was already disassembling his rifle on the rooftop. "Just get your ass over here. We still need to get him into a garbage bag and into the van before it gets any lighter." Laird turned back down at the kindly-faced old man who looked as if he might have fallen asleep reading his grandchild a story. It had been a busy eight hours for Laird, first dealing with Briggs, then getting rid of this aging and too-curious bumbler. But damage control was everything, and they were on a very slippery slope and had to move fast to survive.

And that slope was getting even more perilous thanks to that bitch, Michaels. Smother the anger: they could take care of it.

They could take care of her.

Lynch pulled up in front of Kendra's building at 9 A.M. sharp, and she climbed inside to find a large Starbucks drink in her cup holder. Lynch motioned toward it. "Venti skinny vanilla latte. That's your drink, isn't it?"

She picked up the cup and let it warm her hands. "You remembered. I'm impressed."

"I doubt you're really that impressed. I heard you order on the way out to Ocotillo Wells. I'm sure you remembered what I ordered and a whole lot more."

"It's not the remembering, it's the noticing. If you take the time and care to notice something and relate it to something else that has meaning to you, whether it's a personality trait, or another observation you've made at some time, the remembering part is easy."

"And what observation did you make about what I ordered?"

She smiled. "It was a hot day, and you ordered a venti chai iced tea. You kept your straw elevated squarely in the middle of the ice cubes, I guess to make your sips as cold as possible."

He wrinkled his brow. "Really?"

"You probably don't even realize that you do it. You push your straw lower as the ice goes down in the cup."

"What possible use could that information be to you?"

"In the context of a criminal investigation? Probably no use at all. It's just a habit with me. But if I saw your half-empty cup sitting somewhere, it might give me an idea how long you had been drinking it before you stepped away. I guess that could be useful in certain circumstances."

Lynch laughed and shook his head. "In a relationship, you must be what I'd call incredibly high-maintenance."

"Only if you had something to hide."

"Even if one didn't, I think it might be a little unnerving to live under the same roof as you. Kind of like living with someone who could read your mind."

"I never heard any complaints. A man could do worse than to be with a woman who can perceive and anticipate his most intimate responses."

The words had tumbled out before she even realized what she was saying. Dammit, she had not meant to— She quickly glanced at Lynch to find his face frozen in surprise.

He was clearly embarrassed. Or disgusted. Or . . .

Aroused?

Oh, shit.

Definitely aroused.

"I'm sorry," she said.

"Sorry for what?"

Good, she thought with relief. He was going to just let it pass. "Nothing. Did you get the police report yet, or do we—"

"Wait a minute, I'm still considering the possibilities here. What you just said—"

"Was totally unprofessional. It just slipped out. And it's not a possibility. At least, not in your case."

His brows rose. "I didn't think it was."

"Can we just move on?"

"You can't dangle that out there, then just reel it in."

"I wasn't dangling anything."

"I should be the one to apologize. I had no intention of questioning your value as a bed partner." He tilted his head. "And apparently you offer some advantages that hadn't even occurred to me. Though I should have realized if I'd thought about it."

He was enjoying her slip too much. Why in the hell had she come out with that purely defensive reply? Last night, she had determined that becoming sexually involved with Lynch would be a mistake, but it was clear her subconscious was not yet on board. Did part of her actually want him to think of her that way? Or had he merely hit on an insecurity she had felt in every romantic relationship she had ever had? Either way, it bothered her that she had shown herself and revealed a possible vulnerability.

"Can we please talk about Lesley Dunn?" she said.

He didn't answer for a moment, studying her. Then he smiled, and said, "Yes. Though it's not nearly as interesting. There has been no change. She's critical but stable, and she still hasn't regained consciousness."

"There's still a guard posted, right?"

"Right. Griffin got some preliminary info from the police report this morning. It's pretty much what we were told last night, but I did get contact info for the men who helped her."

"Helped by hitting her with their car?"

"That actually may have saved her life. In any case, they're the only people who talked to her before she lost consciousness. I figured we would go see them unless you're satisfied with the police report."

"I think you know me better than that."

His smiled widened. "I certainly do."

Lynch drove down I-5 to Chula Vista, a community just a few minutes south of downtown. Within fifteen minutes, they pulled into the crowded parking lot of a body shop with a large seventies-era black Cadillac perched on the roof.

Kendra looked around at the tall wrought-iron fence, which was topped by an additional three feet of barbed wire. "I feel as if I'm in a prison yard."

Lynch pointed to the rows of pricey automobiles lining the lot. "There's over a million dollars' worth of cars over there. They need to protect their customers' wheels."

A stocky man in blue overalls stepped out from one of

the shop's four open bays. "Beautiful car, my friends. Truly magnificent," he said in a thick Russian accent, his gaze on the Ferrari. "How can I help you?"

Lynch flashed his badge. "There are two employees here we need to speak with. Caesar Williams and John Hagstrom."

The man's face clouded. "What did they do?"

"Nothing, except maybe save a woman's life. They didn't tell you?"

"Aah, they say nothing to me except a lot of excuses and whining." He turned back to one of the bays, where two men were taping off the hood of a Bentley. "C.W., John . . . Get out here and talk to these people. Since you're such heroes, I guess you don't really need to get any real work done."

The men, also wearing blue overalls, shuffled out to the parking lot. They were both in their twenties, Kendra thought, both marked with patchy stubble that would probably never become full beards.

Lynch smiled. "I'm working with the Justice Department. Sorry to take you from your work. Just a few questions, guys."

The men were obviously uncomfortable, and Kendra was fairly certain of at least one cause. She turned to the Russian in charge and waved her hand back toward the shop. "Thank you, sir. We won't keep you. I promise that it will only be five or ten minutes."

The Russian looked as if he wanted to linger, but after a moment, he slowly turned and walked back toward the office.

Kendra turned back to the two workers. "Better?"

Both men nodded, and the one with WILLIAMS on his breast patch wiped his hands with a red rag. "Are you the police?"

"I told you, Justice Department. We're actually working with the FBI," Lynch said. "We know you spoke to police officers on the scene last night, but we just wanted to follow up. You go by 'C.W.'?"

He nodded and gestured to the other man. "And this is John. I feel bad about hitting that woman last night. I couldn't help it. She just ran out in front of us."

"We know it wasn't your fault," Kendra said.

"Is she . . . okay?" John asked.

"She still hasn't regained consciousness," Lynch said. "You two were the last to talk to her, and we were hoping you could fill us in on what she had to say."

"We already told the cops everything," John said. "Is this necessary?"

"Humor us," Lynch said. "You say she ran in front of you."

C.W. nodded, still upset. "She came up Garnet Street and ran right in front of us. She kinda stumbled, then hit the pavement hard. We tried to help her, but you know, you're not supposed to move a person who has just been—"

"You did the right thing," Kendra said. "What did she say to you?"

C.W. shook his head. "She was talking kind of crazy. Like someone was after her."

"Did you see anyone?" Lynch said.

"No. At first we thought she was confused and talking about us, like she was paranoid."

"Or high," John said.

"But then she kept pointing back from where she had been running. She said a man was trying to kill her back there. She was crying, then she said some things we couldn't understand. Then she passed out."

John nodded. "Scared the hell out of us. I was sure we'd killed her."

Kendra stared at him. "You say she pointed. Which direction?"

C.W. shrugged. "Back toward the street, like I said."

"But where? Was there anywhere in particular?"

C.W. and John looked at each other. "Uh, I don't think so," John finally said. "C.W.?"

C.W. shook his head.

"I need you to do something for me," Kendra said. "Take a moment and try to remember everything that was going on around you. When she pointed back at the street, you turned and looked at *something*. Even if you thought you were looking at nothing, what did you see?"

C.W. thought for a moment. "A white building with painted bricks."

"Me, too," John said. "On the . . . south side of the street. Sorry. I actually don't remember seeing anything else."

"Something made you both look there," Kendra said. "Do you think she did? Maybe that's the way she pointed?"

C.W. nodded. "It's possible, I can't say for sure."

"Anything else you can think to tell us?" Lynch said.

"No," C.W. said. "Just that we're real, real sorry. I don't think I've been able to stop shaking since it happened. Poor woman . . ."

"Who would probably have been killed if you hadn't been there," Kendra said. "No one's blaming you. Stop blaming yourselves." She nodded. "Give C.W. your card, Lynch. If either of you think of anything more, please give us a call. Thank you for your help."

"You're done with us?" John asked, relieved.

She smiled. "See, it didn't hurt a bit." She turned and headed for the car. "Thank you again. Good day, gentlemen."

C.W. and John moved quickly toward the garage as Lynch caught up with Kendra. "You think this trip wasn't a washout?"

"Maybe. Maybe not. We'll have to explore it a little further."

"You were very gracious to those mechanics. I was a little surprised. You're usually a bit more abrupt."

"'Gracious'?" She grimaced. "That's a pretentious word. It matches your car. Why wouldn't I treat them decently? Both of those men work hard for their wages and probably have a tough time with that supervisor. They don't need anyone else giving them a hard time."

"You save that for me?"

"I figure that you're capable of protecting yourself, and no one is going to dare to lean on you." Kendra had climbed back into Lynch's car and pulled up the Google Maps street view of the accident scene on her phone. She moved her finger across the screen to rotate the image. "There it is. The white brick building. We need to go there."

"I really doubt the killer is still loitering on the premises."

She pulled the car door closed and buckled her seat belt. "Surface streets will be faster at this time of day."

Lynch smiled as he put the car into gear. "Yes, ma'am. Even if it doesn't give us anything, I will admit that it's impressive how you got them both to zero in on that building."

"It's possible that John was just influenced by C.W. But even if they didn't remember which direction she was pointing, it may be telling that they both looked at exactly the same building. Her attacker may have been there when she last saw him."

They drove north to the scene of the accident and parked a few doors down from the white building, which turned out to be a wholesale swimming-pool-supplies company. They got out of the car and glanced at the industrial buildings that lined the street.

"Did the police go over this area at all?" Kendra asked.

"Probably nothing more than a drive-through. They had no physical description of the guy who attacked her, other than it *was* a guy."

Lynch moved toward the white building's entrance, which was a small alcove framed by art deco molding.

Kendra followed him but stopped short before she reached the entrance's two front steps. "Wait."

Lynch stopped. "I see it."

They carefully moved up the steps and knelt by the front door. "Blood droplets," Kendra said. "Most of them perfectly round, meaning that the bleeder was standing in here for a while."

"So you're a blood-splatter expert, too?"

"Not at all. But I've noticed how water drops look on the floor when people come in from the rain. When they're standing still, the drops are round. When they're walking, the drops take on an elongated shape, slightly thicker in the direction of movement."

"Bizarre. Someone tracks water into my place, all I do is get pissed."

"They don't teach you guys this stuff at Quantico?"

"Maybe if you're a forensics geek." He glanced around. "So you think the attacker got himself cut and hid here for a while."

"Yes, after Lesley Dunn got hit by the car." She stepped back onto the sidewalk and looked down the street. "Give me a minute." Kendra scanned the area for more blood droplets, which were more difficult to see on the darker paved street. Finally, she locked in on one and began to move down the street, trying to picture the horrible scene that had played out the evening before.

Concentrate. Put yourself in the moment.

That poor woman. How terrified she must have been, bleeding from her midsection and running for her life . . .

Before Kendra knew it, she had walked over a block and a half. She looped around and continued her examination as she made her way back toward Lynch. She finally reached the white brick building and stood there, thinking.

"Well?" Lynch said.

"Call the FBI crime-scene guys to back me up, but it's pretty clear what happened. He confronted her down there, just past the intersection. She fought back, and he got cut by his own blade. He chased her up here until she got hit by the car. He had no choice but to duck into this entranceway when the driver stopped. He managed to get back to his car, and I even have a pretty good idea where it was parked."

Lynch pulled out his phone. "I'll get a forensics team down here, but I don't think they'll be able to tell us any more than you just did."

"They can type these blood drops and see if they match the ones we saw on the car."

"My thought exactly. And we'll see if any of these businesses have security cameras going, especially where you think the attacker's car was parked." His cell beeped, and he stared intently at his phone screen.

"What is it?"

"A text from Griffin. He wants us down at the FBI field office as soon as we can get there." He showed her the message. "It's about the carpet in Stedler's apartment. I'm gaining tremendous respect for that nose of yours, Kendra."

CHAPTER 10

In less than half an hour, they were in the eighth-floor FBI lab staring at the four-foot-by-eight-foot section of carpet that the forensics team had removed from Jeff Stedler's apartment after Kendra and Lynch's visit. Griffin and a ponytailed young forensics specialist named Dustin Freen stood with them at the long worktable.

"First of all, you were right about this being a different batch from the carpet that was in the rest of the apartment, sir," Freen told Griffin.

Griffin leaned toward the carpet. "Interesting. You're positive about that?"

"No question." Freen gestured toward a monitor on the stand behind them. "We took fibers from this piece and from samples taken from the rest of the apartment, then compared them under a microspectrophotometer. It shows us how light interacts with the fibers. It can change with time, environment, and slight differences in the manufacturing process. Even though it's the same carpet and same manufacturer, there's no doubt that this piece comes from a completely different run."

"Pretty much what Kendra's nose told us," Lynch said

dryly. "Did your people follow up with the building maintenance staff?"

Freen nodded. "They didn't replace this. They have some scraps in a utility room that they use for repairs, but we cut some samples and it's all fairly close to the carpet in the rest of his apartment." He picked up a sheet of paper. "This carpet is made by a company in Dalton, Georgia. It has a gold tint that's not all that fashionable these days, but someone did purchase forty square yards of it just last week."

"That's not much," Kendra said.

Lynch nodded. "Just about enough to cover a good-sized walk-in closet." He pointed to the sample in front of them. "Or this piece."

Freen smiled. "You're going to like this. The buyer insisted that it be sent out via overnight air freight to San Diego."

Kendra, Lynch, and Griffin exchanged glances. "Tell me we have a name and delivery address," Lynch said.

"Just a name, Bill Carthers. It was picked up here at the airport offices of the shipping company, Profit By Air. Whoever he is, he paid much more to ship it out here than he did for the carpet itself."

"Method of payment?" Griffin asked.

"Cash on delivery. We haven't gotten anywhere following up on the name. You might follow up at the shipping office for some more details."

"We'll do that," Lynch said as he turned toward the door. "Good work, Freen."

He shrugged. "Just doing my job."

"Thanks for the heads-up, Griffin," Lynch said as they left the lab and walked toward the elevator bank.

Griffin shrugged. "Least I could do. It was Kendra's catch. Besides, aren't we still sharing info with each other?"

"We are."

Griffin gave him a distinctly cool glance. "Then why have you tasked two of my agents to log traffic cams from Rancho Bernardo?"

"We have reason to believe that Jeff Stedler was there shortly before he disappeared, so I have them looking for his car. I figure with the pattern-recognition software, it won't take too long to find if it pops up."

"Two days, minimum. It's a lot of video and a lot of manpower that's desperately needed elsewhere. I know you have powerful friends, but you still don't get to make assignments in my office."

Lynch said quietly, "I could have danced around, playing nice, filling out forms, but in the end those agents would have ended up doing exactly what I told them to do. If you'd told me no, I would have made one phone call, and you would have been overridden. I thought I'd save me the time and you the embarrassment."

"Let me worry about that. I don't embarrass easily." His jaw set belligerently. "I don't know why the hell you've been given carte blanche to do whatever the hell you want, and it pisses me off. But the fact that you're here this morning is proof that I'm trying to give you all the support I can. But it's going to be my way and under my orders. I'm still running this investigation, and I need to coordinate the efforts of my team. So don't pull that crap again. Understand?"

Kendra could sense the tension and leashed anger in Lynch though his face was without expression. She was half expecting an explosion, but instead he leaned back, thought for a moment, then slowly nodded. "I can, actually. You're right. From now on, I'll run this stuff through you."

Griffin seemed almost as surprised as Kendra. Braced for a fight, his shoulders suddenly relaxed. "Well . . . Good."

Lynch nodded back toward the lab. "That was helpful. Thanks. Kendra and I will follow up, and we'll let you know what we find out."

Kendra didn't say anything as she followed Lynch back through the hallway and down the elevator. As they crossed the foyer to the elevator to the parking garage, she suddenly laughed.

"What's so funny?"

"That was unexpectedly 'gracious' of you. Even Griffin didn't quite know how to respond."

"That's why I did it."

"I had a feeling that was the reason. You completely disarmed him."

"Also, I was wrong." Lynch shrugged. "I know what it's like to lead a team, and it totally undermines your authority to have someone else come in and start giving orders to your subordinates. I was trying to be expedient, but what I did is known in the trade as a 'dick move.'"

"Not just in the trade."

He cocked an eyebrow. "Did you just call me a dick?"

"If the shoe fits . . ."

"This is why I usually work without a partner."

She gazed at him blandly. "'Cause you know you're gonna be called a dick?"

His lips turned up on one corner. "I've been called a lot worse."

"That makes two of us."

"Really? Now who—" He stopped. "I won't even go there."

"Good. Let's go to the freight office instead."

The Profit by Air branch manager's name was Diddy Riese, and he was a burly, bearded man with huge, out-of-proportion arms that Kendra could only regard as Popeye-esque. His voice's volume rose and fell in direct relation to the sounds of the jets taking off and landing from the nearby San Diego International Airport.

"After the FBI called, I pulled up everything I could find," he said, thumbing through a stack of papers on the front counter of the cramped office. "I even called the Atlanta office to see what they had."

"We appreciate that," Kendra said. "I'm sure you don't get many big rolls of carpet moving through here."

"It's expensive, but it's not unheard of. A designer suddenly realizes that he's shorted a job, or maybe someone needs to get their remodel finished in time for a party. When it happens, it almost always comes from our Atlanta office. From what I gather, Dalton, Georgia, is the carpet capital of the U.S."

"Now *there's* a claim to fame," Lynch said. "Were you here when it was picked up?"

"Yeah, I helped the guy load it into his van. He didn't say too much, but he tipped me twenty bucks."

"You wouldn't still happen to have that twenty, would you?" Lynch asked.

Riese chuckled. Then he looked at Kendra and realized that Lynch wasn't kidding. "Uh, no. Sorry. Guess you could've gotten fingerprints off it, huh?"

"Worth a shot. What kind of van was he driving?"

"It was a white-panel cargo van. A Ford Ecoline, I'm pretty sure." Riese looked back down at his papers. "Anyway, the Atlanta office said that the carpet roll was delivered by the carpet company at 11:43 A.M. on Friday the twenty-third."

"Twenty-third?" Lynch shot Kendra a meaningful glance. She had caught the significance of that date but she wished she hadn't. It scared her. The delivery was on the day after Jeff's disappearance.

Riese was looking at another paper. "And it was picked up here at 6:09 P.M. that evening."

"Good," Lynch said. "And can you describe the driver?"

"Don't need to." Riese pulled a color printout from the folder. "We have a security camera out on the loading dock."

"Oh, how I was hoping you would say that."

Lynch took the printout and held it so that Kendra could see. It showed a short, middle-aged man standing next to the van. "Does that tell you anything?"

She examined the photo for a long moment. "Well, only that they need to invest in a better security camera. I've seen forty-dollar baby monitors with sharper pictures than this."

Lynch nodded. "Believe me, this is sharper than most. Ask anyone in law enforcement, and these things have to be pretty far up the list of pet peeves. But does this tell you anything else at all?"

"Other than that man is left-handed and obviously wears a hairpiece? No."

Lynch's eyes narrowed on the photo. "Nice."

Riese nodded. "I think he was working just as hard holding down the rug on his head as he was lifting the other one into the van." He handed Lynch a DVD. "This is the video for the entire time he was here. I looked at it, and I don't think you can make out the license plate. You guys probably have some special machines to make it sharper, though."

"Not *that* special. But thanks, this could be helpful."

"This shot looks like it was taken while he was talking," Kendra said. "Did he say anything about where he was headed or where he came from?"

"Nope. He actually didn't talk a whole lot. I didn't know if the carpet was for him or if he was just making a delivery. He was kind of in a hurry, but so are a lot of our customers. Otherwise, they would just ship it ground."

Lynch pointed to the short stack of papers. "Are those for us?"

Riese handed him the stack. "All the info I have on the shipment, including the receiving documents that I had faxed from Atlanta. I just wish I knew why the FBI is interested in a guy for shipping carpet."

"Sorry," Lynch said as he held open the door for Kendra. "It's an ongoing investigation."

"Ah, I figured," Riese said, disappointed. "Maybe I'll read about it in the newspaper."

"You never can tell," Lynch said. "Thanks, Riese."

Kendra was studying the printout as she and Lynch sped away from the cargo office. "You don't think the FBI forensics team can really get any more out of the security video, do you?"

"No. In my experience, if you start with mush, no amount of zooming and sharpening is going to give you anything else."

"Still, it's not a bad shot of this guy. Don't they have some kind of facial-recognition software?"

"Sure. Only it's nowhere near as sophisticated as the stuff Facebook and Google are developing. Even if we send this to Washington, we'll have a better chance of getting results from my contacts in northern California."

"So is that our next step?"

"Actually, I want to try something else first." He cast a sideways glance at her. "You're not the only one who knows people on the fringes of society."

Her brows rose. "I have the feeling I'm about to meet one of them."

"If he's still alive."

"Is he old?"

"No, but he does have some rather self-destructive appetites. His name is Derek Carner, and he was one of the best cleaners in the business."

"And what exactly does he clean?"

"Crime scenes."

"Ah. And I'm guessing he doesn't wait until after the police are done with it."

"No. It's his job to make sure that no one knows there ever was a crime there. He worked for the MacDougal crime family until they went out of business a few years ago."

"Out of business? Victims of the recession?"

"Victims of me, if you'll excuse my immodesty. After the organization imploded, Carner went freelance. I was rather hoping that it would be him in that picture, but Carner is taller and thinner than this guy, and his face isn't nearly as round."

"Too bad."

"But Carner still might be able to identify him and tell us who he might work for."

"Or course," she said dryly. "They must know each other from the union meetings."

"They're rivals in a highly specialized field, and they're known to work in the same geographic area. I don't really think they hang out together swapping war stories, but they might know each other on sight." Lynch checked his watch. "Lunchtime. I have a pretty good idea where I'll find him. Do you want me to take you home?"

"Home? Why?"

"Carner is a seedy man, and I may have to go to some seedy places to find him."

She laughed with real amusement. "Get real. Believe me, I've done seedy. You think I'm afraid of a little grunge, Lynch?"

"Afraid, no. Revolted, maybe."

"Now that's a possibility. But I won't let it get in the way. Give me a little credit."

"Don't say I didn't warn you."

Lynch cut over to Pacific Highway, where he quickly

drove to the Under Pressure topless bar, which featured a large sign that Kendra guessed lit up in brilliant neon after dark.

Lynch pointed to the sign. "It's animated. You don't even want to know what it looks like at night."

"You sure found your way here awfully easily."

Lynch parked on the street. "Part of the job. The clubs along here attract a rough clientele. Maybe you'd better stay in the car."

She unbuckled her seat belt and opened the door. "Don't be absurd. That's not going to happen."

He shrugged. "How did I know you were going to say that?"

They climbed out of his car and walked toward the club. She looked at the shabby, weather-beaten building. "I deejayed in a place like this for a few weeks once. It was fascinating how certain types of songs, certain rhythms, certain beats would affect the tips that the women would get. It would make an interesting psychological study."

"Uh-huh. Believe me, you didn't deejay in a club like this. Clubs like this don't have DJs. More like a beer-stained old cassette deck behind the bar."

They walked around back and crossed a small parking lot to the entrance, where a beefy bald man in a tight T-shirt was seated on a stool outside. Heavy bass throbbed from within the club.

"I need to talk to Derek Carner," Lynch said.

The bouncer stared at him as he pulled out a can of Skoal tobacco, took a pinch, and placed it between his lower lip and gum. "Don't know 'im."

"Sure you do. He's a regular. Has been for years." Lynch gestured over his shoulder. "And that's his piece-of-shit truck just fifteen feet away from you. You didn't see him drive up?"

The bouncer shrugged. "Maybe I was on a coffee break."

"Maybe you're full of shit." Lynch flashed his badge.

The bouncer looked at it, then spit brown juice onto the parking lot. "Department of Justice Liaison? Are you kidding me? Look, unless your lady friend wants a job dancing, I suggest you run along. I have no idea who you're looking for."

"We'll go inside and see for ourselves." Lynch pulled a twenty from his wallet. "This should take care of the cover charge."

The bouncer stood, showing himself to be a good head taller than Lynch. "Sorry. We're all full up today."

Lynch turned and looked at the almost empty parking lot. "I can see that. Word must be getting around about your delicious lunch buffet."

"Do I need to escort you from the property?"

"After we're done here, sure. Appreciate it. I understand this neighborhood can get a bit rough."

Lynch stepped past the bouncer, but the man clamped a gigantic hand over his shoulder and pushed him back. Lynch's hands blurred as they flew toward the bouncer's chest and neck. Before Kendra could even register what had happened, the bouncer was wheezing and staggering back and forth in front of them. He dropped to his knees and clutched his neck before finally rolling over onto his back.

Lynch picked up the twenty-dollar bill, tucked it into the bouncer's shirt collar, then stepped over the choking, wheezing man. He stopped in the doorway and turned back toward Kendra. "Are you coming?"

She also stepped over the bouncer, who was now turning purple. "Now *that* was caveman," she said.

"Sometimes it's the only option. Remind me to tell you about the time that—"

Click-clock-click.

Lynch froze.

It was the sound of a pump-action shotgun being cocked. Kendra looked into the club to see a tall, tanned woman, about forty, aiming the gun at Lynch's chest. "Not another move," she said. "One of my girls is calling the cops."

"Your decision," Lynch said. "But if they come here, I'm going to help them find enough violations to shut you down for good."

"I run a good club. My licenses are in order."

Lynch nodded. "I didn't know the city was handing out gambling licenses to topless bars these days. Because I know that's what's going on next to the dressing area. And I don't think there's anyplace outside Nevada that licenses what goes on in your two VIP rooms. Do you really want to do this?"

The gun wavered slightly in her hands.

Lynch smiled at her. "You used to be a dancer here, weren't you, Sheila? Do you remember me?"

She looked at him for a long moment before lowering the gun. "Shit, you're a fed."

Lynch gestured to the bouncer, who was only now starting to catch his breath. "I tried to tell that to your friend, but he wasn't listening."

She glanced over her shoulder, where a pair of bare-breasted dancers were climbing off the stage. "What do you want?"

"I'm just here to talk to one of the guys playing cards in the back. This doesn't have to be a big deal."

She thought about it for a moment. "Okay. I'm not giving you permission, but I'm not stopping you, either. If you don't have a warrant, nothing you see will stick." She turned and stepped behind the bar with her shotgun.

"Fair enough." Lynch jerked his head toward the back, indicating that Kendra was to follow him. The bar was small and windowless, illuminated entirely by the half dozen beer signs representing brands that Kendra wasn't even sure existed anymore.

Lynch led her to a door that was almost invisible in the dark club. He tried the knob, and upon finding it locked, threw his weight against it. It splintered open, and bright fluorescent light poured into the bar.

Lynch and Kendra strode through the door to see five elderly men surrounding a poker table. They were in midgame, and one of the men leaped to his feet. "Aw, shit. A holdup!"

Lynch walked to the table, grabbed one of the other men by the collar, and pulled him to his feet. "No holdup. I just need to talk to Carner here. He'll be sitting out this round."

Carner, a stocky man with frizzy gray hair, cursed. "Come on, I'm on a hot streak. Can't this wait?"

Lynch shoved him ahead of him to the door. "Talk to me, and your karma is only going to improve."

Lynch and Kendra walked Carner through the club, where the dancers had already resumed plying their trade for the dozen or so customers. As they stepped out into the parking lot, the bouncer gave them a wide berth and pretended they weren't there.

Lynch pushed Carner against his beat-up Ford Ranger pickup truck. "I need some information."

"Ask all you want, but I ain't talking, Lynch. Confidentiality is part of my service."

"I'm not interested in your scumbag employers. I want to talk about your competition." Lynch pulled the color printout from his pocket, unfolded it, and held it in front of Carner's face. "He's another cleaner. Do you know him?"

Carner chuckled. "Where, from the union meetings?"

"I made the exact same joke. Now I feel totally unoriginal," Kendra said. She motioned toward Lynch's intense expression. "And believe me, it didn't go over any better then. He's not amused."

"You do know this guy in the picture," Lynch said. "You have a terrible poker face."

Carner's expression had told Kendra that, too, and she was impressed that Lynch had also picked up on the flash of recognition.

Carner shook his head. "I don't know who in the hell that is. First of all, it's not the clearest photo, and—"

"Don't bullshit me."

"Give me a break, will ya? I can't be talking to you about this stuff."

"You can, and you will."

Carner moistened his lips. "Okay, just saying I did know this guy. And I gave you some information that helped you track him down. What if he was working for one of the same people who I also do some work for? What do you think my life would be worth then?"

"You're forgetting about me."

"You? Are you gonna sweat me out under the hot lights? Beat it out of me? It's not even a contest. Take your best shot."

Lynch lowered his voice. "Think about it, Carner. Why would I walk in there and drag you out where everybody could see?"

"Stupidity?"

"Later this afternoon, I'm going to pay a visit to Robert Chilton and ask him some pointed questions about a man who was murdered in a game arcade in Encinitas last year. You remember that, don't you? The one that no one ever found out about. Blood and brain matter all over, but you had it all ready for the kids and their game tokens by early the next morning."

Panic gripped Carner's face. "Where did you hear this?"

"From you, of course. Just now, after I dragged you out

of that poker game. Unless I'm mistaken, at least two of the men at that table are on very good terms with Chilton. Think maybe they'll tell him that you and I had a chat today?"

Carner looked ill. "No one knows about that job."

"Exactly. How will Chilton think I know about it?"

"You son of a bitch."

Lynch held up the printout again. "Who is this man, who does he work for, and where can I find him?"

Carner cleared his throat as if trying to get rid of a sour taste in his mouth. "That's all? I guess you want me to give you a lift to his house, too."

"That won't be necessary."

Carner stared at the printout. "Shit. What do I care about him? That's John Bergen. He used to do some work for the Vietnamese syndicates. I didn't think he was actually in the business anymore. These days, I think he mostly just buys and renovates old houses and apartment buildings."

"He's gone legit?" Kendra asked.

"There's legit, then there's *legit*. Who doesn't like a bagful of cash money dropped into your lap once in a while, huh?"

Lynch folded up the printout. "Where do I find him?"

"How should I know? The phone book, Google, take your pick."

"Okay, Carner." He leaned forward, and his voice was low and fierce. "If you've been feeding me a line of bull, I'm not coming after you. I'm going to pay that visit to Chilton, and *he'll* come after you. Someone will be mopping up *your* blood someplace. Understand?"

"Yeah, you've made yourself very clear."

"Good."

"Can I get back to my game now?"

"Knock yourself out."

Kendra smiled as she watched Carner stumble back toward the door. "We saved you money, Carner. The man closest to the door was holding a straight flush. He would have clobbered your pair of nines."

It took Lynch all of three minutes to track down John Bergen's property-management business, and only another two minutes of telephone time for him to extract Bergen's current whereabouts from the company receptionist. Lynch turned the wheel and headed for Chula Vista, where Bergen was reportedly renovating his latest acquisition.

"So how did you know about the arcade cleanup?" Kendra asked. "That completely freaked Carner out."

"We had an agent working undercover in Chilton's organization. He tipped us off at the time, but we were trying to pull together a bigger case and just tabled it for a while."

"A bigger case than murder?"

"Bigger than that scumbag's murder. Sometimes you just have to look at the bigger picture. They might have nailed Robert Chilton for that one hit, but it would have blown the cover of an agent who had been working years to build a case against dozens of people."

After a few minutes, they parked in front of an older Spanish-style house with a large Dumpster in the driveway. Construction debris overflowed the Dumpster, with several lengths of molding sticking out in every direction.

They got out of the car, and Lynch walked around, opened the trunk, and flipped two switches on a black, shoebox-sized electronic device.

"What's that?" Kendra asked.

"Something that may or may not be of use to us."

"That's no answer."

Lynch slammed the trunk and turned toward a black

pickup truck parked in front of the house. He walked toward it, and without breaking stride, reached under the left-rear wheel well for a brief moment. He cleared it just as a thin gray-haired man stepped from the house with his arms full of drywall scraps.

"That's him," Kendra whispered. "The man from the security video."

The man dumped the scraps into the Dumpster. He turned toward Lynch and Kendra as they walked up the driveway to meet him.

Lynch took off his sunglasses. "Mr. Bergen, how are you today?"

Bergen regarded them warily. "Is there something I can do for you?"

"Absolutely."

"Speak up. Who are you?" Bergen wiped chalky drywall dust from his hands onto his jeans. "I'm really busy here, so I'd appreciate it if you would just get to the point."

"We know about your cleanup job in that College Grove condo last week. Is that to the point enough for you?"

Bergen stared at him blankly. "College Grove? I don't have a place over there."

"Cut the crap. I'm talking about the cleanup job you were hired for."

Still no expression, save for one of total puzzlement. "I don't know what you're talking about. I'm not a janitor. I own the houses I work on."

The guy is a damned good liar, Kendra thought. No nervous twitches, no shiftiness of the eyes, no difference in his vocal quality. He would make a perfect used-car salesman.

Lynch flashed his badge. "You're looking at felony murder, accessory after the fact. I can charge you with that right now and make it stick."

"If that's the case, why aren't I in cuffs in the back of a police car?"

"We don't give a damn about you. We need to know who you were working for. I'm guessing it wasn't one of your regular employers."

"Sorry, buddy. I still have no idea what you're talking about."

"We both know you do, and you're starting to piss me off. We're closing in on the guy who gave you the job, Bergen. If you don't give him up to me, I'm going to start dropping hints to his people that you're the one who pointed me in his direction."

Bergen smiled. "Even if I didn't."

"Especially if you didn't."

"Well, I guess that's what you're going to have to do. Because I didn't do whatever you think I did."

Lynch shrugged. "Okay. Fair warning." He nodded to Kendra, and they walked back down the driveway. Neither of them spoke until after they had climbed into his car and closed their doors.

"Your routine didn't work quite as well with him, did it?" Kendra said.

Lynch watched Bergen walk back into the house. "I wouldn't say that."

"You're chalking that up as a success?"

"The jury is still out." Lynch reached under his seat and pulled out a cable and a small remote control. He plugged the cable into his car stereo's auxiliary jack, then turned up the volume knob.

Kendra watched him punch a few buttons on the remote. "Let me guess. *The Best of Steve Lawrence and Eydie Gorme, Volume 2.*"

He cast a sideways glance at her. "No, but I'll remember to download that for next time. This is connected to that box in the trunk."

"Yes, I remember. The one you were so forthcoming about."

He pushed another button on the remote, and static spiked from the car stereo speakers, followed by a woman's voice, then a child's. Lynch used the remote to change the signal. "I didn't expect him to give up his employer so easily. All I did was light a fire under him. He's going to want to get in front of this."

Kendra considered this. "By contacting him."

"I would. Sooner than later. And he's not likely to use a landline. He'll probably use a—

The sound of a telephone ringtone blared over the speakers, as if someone had just made a call and was waiting for an answer.

"This could be him," Lynch said.

A man answered. "Yeah?"

"It's Bergen."

Lynch and Kendra exchanged a quick glance. Bergen no longer sounded so smooth; he now had a clipped, nervous tone in his voice.

"Why in the hell are you calling me?"

"This is an emergency. You really need to know what—"
The man cut in. "What phone are you using?"

"Don't worry, it's a throwaway. This is the first time I've used it. Listen, just a heads-up. The feds know about the job I did for you."

"What happened?"

"They just showed up at my doorstep. There must be a leak on your end, because I haven't told *anybody*."

"There's no leak."

"There has to be. I'm telling you—"

"You fucked up. You did shoddy work, that's what happened."

"No way. You saw that floor. It's a masterpiece. There's no way anyone could tell."

"Someone could and did tell. She *smelled* it, you idiot."

Bergen paused for a long moment. "That's impossible."

"Impossible for you, maybe. It took her all of fifteen seconds. Who exactly spoke to you?"

"A guy named Adam Lynch. He was with a woman, but I didn't get her name."

"I know who it was. She's the one who sniffed out your hack cleanup job."

"Never in all my years of doing this has anyone ever—"

The man was muttering a string of curses. "We paid a hell of a lot for your expertise. You told me you were the best."

"I am. And even if what you're saying is true, how could they have known it was me?"

"I imagine it's because you were sloppy. You were so sure no one would detect your handiwork that you didn't take appropriate measures to cover your tracks. Am I right?"

"No. You're not right. I didn't make any mistakes."

"Bullshit." The man sighed. "I need to think about this. Don't talk to anyone, do you understand me?"

"What are we going to do?"

"You're going to do absolutely nothing. Your only job now is to keep your damned mouth shut. Can you handle that?"

"What if they come back?"

"Say nothing. I'll get in touch with you in the next couple hours. Sit tight."

The call ended.

"You were right," Kendra said. "What's next? Are we going back to confront him?"

Lynch started the car. "No. We don't want to tip off whoever he was talking to."

"I thought you'd want to go all caveman on him to find out who he was working for. You do that role quite well."

"I'm flattered by your approval. I'll reserve the right to employ the caveman, but I want to try something else first." Lynch drove away from the house, raised his phone, and punched a number. Almost immediately, he started talking. "This is Lynch. I just recorded a call that I've sent your way. I need a trace. Name and location, as soon as you can get it to me. Good, I'll be waiting." He cut the connection.

"Just like that." Kendra smiled. "Cool little toy you have back there."

"Yes, I'm quite fond of it. It scans the immediate area, records mobile phone calls and carrier data. It can't trace the call, but it forwards the data to a call center that can."

"What call center?"

"One that you're better off not knowing about."

"Wonderful. It's probably in Calcutta. And does that gadget also obtain the necessary warrants to make this legal?"

He didn't answer directly. "Do you want to find Jeff Stedler or not?"

"I'll take that as a 'no.'"

"Take it however you want. Just remember that you were the one who wanted me to beat the information out of him."

She frowned. "I never actually said that."

"But you obviously had less of a problem with that than you did with—"

"With violating the Constitution?"

"Technically speaking, I think both approaches violate the Constitution."

"You have a point there." Kendra looked at Lynch as he sped toward the freeway. He had been admirably willing to let her take the lead when circumstances warranted it, but he was clearly more comfortable in the driver's seat, both figuratively and literally. He seemed to come

truly alive when stepping into a leadership role. It was
obviously where he was meant to be. His mind was sharp,
his responses right on the money, and his lethal quotient
was off the charts. She had never seen anyone as impressive and high-impact as Lynch when he threw off that
quiet, lazy façade and went into overdrive. She could see
how he had become a legend in the Bureau. She could
also see how that recklessness could make him be regarded as too volatile and hot to handle.

He glanced at her. "Something wrong?"

"No." Except that she had suddenly realized that she
was responding to both that force and recklessness in a
way that was purely sensual. *Back off.* "What about the
gadget you stuck in his wheel well?"

"Standard FBI issue, not unlike the USB drive that
Griffin tried to give you. It will ping his location to us. I'll
talk to Griffin about putting a tail on him, but in the
meantime we'll have a pretty good idea where he goes."

"You've got all the bases covered."

"You never know." He checked his watch. "The call
center should have some information later tonight, so we
can pick up on this tomorrow. I'll take you home."

She checked her watch. She still had a little time before she had to be home to meet Olivia. "Pretty soon.
Actually, there's somewhere else I'd like to go first."

CHAPTER 11

Kendra and Lynch stood in the Intensive Care Unit room staring down at Lesley Dunn. The room was dim, but it obviously would not have mattered to the unconscious woman even if the overhead fluorescents had been on at full strength. Kendra was surprised at how good the woman looked. Her delicate features caught the light in a way that a movie starlet might envy, and her serene expression suggested she was merely enjoying a peaceful slumber.

A uniformed police officer stood in the doorway, standing guard over the woman's room. The cop was a young red-haired man who, to Kendra's relief, had spent five minutes checking their IDs and calling to confirm their identities before letting them enter.

"They keep saying she's worse off than she looks," the officer said. "She may not make it."

Kendra stepped to the side of Lesley's bed and looked at the monitors. "They also say that people in comas can sometimes hear what the people around them are saying. Please remember that, Officer."

The cop shifted uncomfortably. "I didn't mean—Uh, sorry."

"We'll let you know if we need anything else," Lynch said, dismissingly.

The officer nodded and went out into the hall.

Kendra looked at the woman's face, searching for any sign of life, for any indication that Lesley Dunn was still in there, clawing to get out.

There was none. Just shallow breathing and terrifying stillness.

"She's been scrubbed clean, and her clothes were probably scissored off in the emergency room," Lynch said. "I don't know what you can tell by looking at her."

"That's not what this is about."

"Then why are we here?"

Kendra looked at Lesley for a moment longer. Did her eye just twitch? No, just wishful thinking. Kendra turned back toward Lynch. "It's about actually seeing her and remembering why we're doing this."

"I thought you were doing it all for Stedler."

"Maybe at first. But now . . . I'm not naïve enough to think that Jeff's likely to be alive. It's been days now, I get that. But if he's been killed, I know it's because he believed in what he was doing so much that he was willing to put his life on the line." Her voiced hardened. "And he did it because there is someone out there who will just keep killing if he isn't stopped. If that's not enough of a reason for me to keep pushing, then I don't know what is."

Lynch said quietly, "I don't know either, Kendra."

She stepped toward the window and looked down at the dark parking lot. "Most people hate hospitals, but I never have. Do you?"

"Yes. I've watched too many people die in rooms like this."

"I haven't. Yet. I guess that's the difference."

"You're lucky. You also had a great gift given to you in a hospital. I imagine that would give you a different perspective."

"It wasn't that dramatic. Not like the old movies, with gauze bandages being peeled away to suddenly show me a new world. Once the procedure was done, it took about eight weeks for my corneas to regenerate. I was only in the hospital for a few hours."

"It's still a miracle."

"Absolutely. But even before that, hospitals have always been places of great hope for me. You're surrounded by people who are, by and large, extremely good at what they do. And they're doing everything in their power to help you."

"Hmm. Again, you and I have obviously have had some very different experiences."

She smiled. "There are incompetent idiots everywhere, but at least here, people aspire to a higher standard. I've actually spent a lot of time working in hospitals."

"I didn't realize they offered music therapy as a treatment option."

"They don't, really. But when doctors think I can do some good, they occasionally recommend me. It's come in handy for my research. My first study focused on the effectiveness of music therapy on hospitalized infants."

"Babies?" He half smiled. "And how did that work out for you?"

"Better than your skeptical tone implies. A music therapist isn't necessarily a music teacher. We try to get our patients to engage with the music on any level. If it's not working, we try different instruments, different rhythms, different dynamics, whatever it takes. Anyway, I showed that interaction with a music therapist significantly reduced stress behaviors in those hospitalized infants. And if you lower stress, you increase their chances of healing."

Lynch motioned toward the woman in the bed. "What about her? Could you help her?"

Kendra turned toward Lesley. "I don't think so. There's been a lot of debate about the use of music to stimulate coma arousal in patients, but I haven't been convinced by the studies on the topic. I believe you might have to have some in-depth knowledge of the patient to trigger it. In any case, I'm not inclined to use her as my guinea pig. She's getting the very best care already."

She took Lesley's hand in her hand.

Cold. Still.

Kendra leaned over and whispered. "Come back, Lesley. Don't believe anything you've heard, anything they've said. In the end, it's all up to you. You can do anything, be whatever you want. Remember that, okay?" She squeezed her hand, then gently released it. "When you're ready, we'll be here for you."

"You okay?" Lynch looked sidewise at her as he pulled out of the hospital parking lot. "I'm surprised you're so upset. She's a stranger to you."

"That doesn't make any difference. I hate those scumbags who prey on the innocent. That woman probably didn't even know who attacked her. Not if it was a professional job like the others. One minute you're going about your life, making plans and looking forward to the future. The next minute, you're in the hospital, and people are wondering if you're going to die. It's not fair and it's not right and it makes me feel helpless. I *hate* to feel helpless." She shook her head wearily. "I just hope she makes it."

"She's got a bunch of doctors trying to make sure she does," he said quietly. "For more than compassionate reasons. She's got a chance."

"Yeah, I know." She moved her shoulders, trying to shrug off the depression. What else had she expected? A miraculous recovery? If Lesley fought hard enough, then that chance might be enough.

She checked her watch.

"Shit. It's seven fifteen."

"And that means?"

"I was supposed to meet Olivia at my place at seven. We're going to have drinks and go out to dinner. How long will it take to get me home in this buggy?"

He flinched. "Buggy? That's sacrilege."

"How long?"

"Twenty minutes." He stepped on the accelerator. "Or less."

"Make it less. I hate people who are late for appointments." She reached for her phone and dialed Olivia. "I'm late. God, I'm sorry. I'll be there right away." She looked at Lynch. "Fifteen minutes."

"You should be sorry," Olivia said with mock sternness. "It's just lucky that I was smart enough to realize that this might happen. You don't have to hurry. I never made the reservations at Alfredo's. I'm cooking dinner for us at your place. We'll have more time to talk. I'm browning the hamburger and onions for the spaghetti sauce right now . . . Lord, I love that smell."

"So do I. And your sauce is incredible."

"You bet your ass," Olivia said cheerfully. "And by the time you get here, it will be simmering, and we can have that drink. Hurry." She hung up.

Lynch gazed at her inquiringly. "I take it that you've been forgiven?"

She nodded. "Since it suited her convenience. Otherwise, she would have given me hell. Olivia's not shy about making her displeasure known."

"Then you must be very good friends."

"The best. We grew up blind together, and our friendship survived my getting my sight. If she'd been less giving, less loving, I'd have lost her." She smiled. "Not everyone has that generous a spirit. Until recently, she never even told me how much it chafed her that I'd left her behind." She added soberly, "But I'd never really leave her behind. I'm just waiting for her to catch up."

"Is there a chance?"

"There's always a chance. My mother is in touch with all kinds of teaching hospitals around the world. They're trying out new operations all the time. Olivia will have her turn."

"You seem very certain."

"I am certain. There *has* to be a way. I won't let her be cheated."

Lynch smiled. "Well, in the meantime, I'll keep you as much as I can out of her bad books. I'll have you there in another seven minutes."

"How precise. But I'm not in quite so much of a hurry now. She's in the middle of cooking our dinner at my condo."

He went still. "Your condo? How did she get in?"

"She has a key. I gave keys to both Olivia and my mother when I bought the condo. It was more convenient."

"I can see that it would be."

There was a cautious note in his voice that caused her eyes to narrow on his face. It was without expression, but that only made her more uneasy. "What's wrong?"

"Probably nothing. We'll be there soon."

She stiffened as his meaning hit home to her. "No! She was cooking. There was no one in that apartment but her. Okay, she's blind, but her other senses are supersharp. She would have known."

"I'm not saying that anything is wrong." His voice was soothing. "I don't know. You've noticed how suspicious I am. I just didn't like the sound of her being in your condo alone."

And neither did Kendra. It was scaring her to death. Her hand was shaking as she dialed Olivia back.

No answer.

Voice mail.

She felt as if she'd been hit in the stomach.

"Oh, God," she whispered.

She dialed again.

"Answer me, Olivia." It was almost a prayer.

Four rings.

Voice mail.

"Get me there," Kendra said between her teeth. "Fast, Lynch. Please. Fast."

"Two minutes," Lynch said. "It could still—"

"Be quiet. Don't talk to me." She didn't want to hear comforting reassurance, not when she had this terrible fear icing through her. "Just get me there."

A crowd of her neighbors were in the courtyard in front of her condo when Lynch drove into the parking area.

The door of her condo was wide open and she could see the security guard, Les Berber, who was usually at the front gate, standing there in the doorway talking on his telephone.

Talking to whom?

She jumped out of the car before it came to a full stop and ran toward the front door.

"You shouldn't go in there, Dr. Michaels." Berber, the security guard, tried to step in front of her. "It's Miss Olivia. Such a pity. Who would want to do that to such a nice lady?"

"Do what?" She pushed him aside. "Dammit, what happened to her?"

"I'll find out." Lynch held the security guard back. "Go to her, Kendra. I'll be with you in a minute."

Kendra ran into the condo.

Mrs. Jimenez from the condo next door was standing in the kitchen doorway. She turned to Kendra with relief. "I'm glad you're here. We've called the ambulance, but we didn't want to leave her like this. I was the only neighbor with first-aid experience, but I don't want to touch her. I'm afraid I'll hurt her more than help."

"She's not dead?" Kendra ran across the room. "I was afraid that she—" She inhaled sharply as she looked down at Olivia. "Dear God."

Olivia's beautiful face was a mass of cuts and bruises and was swelling rapidly. She was unconscious, and her breathing was shallow.

Mrs. Jiminez nodded. "She's been badly beaten . . . I don't know if that blood coming out of her mouth is from a cut or if she has internal injuries."

"I can't tell either until she's X-rayed." Kendra did a superficial examination. No cuts or open wounds except on the face and head, but she was lying crumpled in a weird position. There were dark imprints on the left side of her blouse. "I think she was kicked. The son of a bitch knocked her down, then kicked her in the ribs and back. She shouldn't be moved. There's no telling what kind of damage he's done to her." She wanted to cradle Olivia in her arms, and she couldn't even touch her, Kendra realized in agony. "Did they say how long it would be until they could get some help for her?"

"I checked. The EMTs should be here in another five minutes." Lynch was suddenly kneeling beside her. "Damn, he really worked her over."

"She'll be lucky if she—" She stopped and gently

stroked Olivia's hair back from that poor battered face. "No, she's going to live. Do you hear me, Olivia? We're going to get through this together." She looked at Lynch. "I was afraid that he'd killed her."

"A few more minutes, and he probably would have beaten her to death."

"Why? Did he mistake her for me?"

"Maybe. Or maybe he just surprised her and she made him angry." He looked around the kitchen. There was spaghetti sauce all over the kitchen. Floor, stove, walls. "Where's the frying pan?"

"Outside in front." Mrs. Jiminez said. "That's how we knew something was wrong. The frying pan came flying through the window, breaking the glass. My husband and I had just driven up, and he said that we should see if everything was all right with you. It's not as if you're the kind of woman who would be throwing—Anyway, Marco was getting out of the car when your front door flew open, and a man ran out. He darted around the house and disappeared."

"Would you recognize him if we can show you a photo? Maybe the security cameras got a shot of him."

She shook her head. "It was too dark, and we only got a quick glimpse. I'm sorry, Kendra." She looked toward the door. "I hear a siren. I'll go out and meet them."

"She fought him," Kendra said. "And when she found out he was too strong for her, she threw that pan out the window to try to attract attention." She looked at Lynch. "He kicked her, Lynch. And he kept on kicking her. Look at those boot prints on her shirt."

"Easy."

"Easy? She could die. And it's my fault."

"For giving her your house key? How would you know that—"

"No, for getting involved, for dragging her into this—"

The EMTs were coming through the front door. "I'm going to ride to the hospital with her. Find out who did this, Lynch. He's not going to get off scot-free."

He nodded grimly. "I'll ask questions and check the video cameras. I'll catch you later at the hospital."

She nodded as she stood up and let Olivia be surrounded by the medical team. "I'll be there."

He hesitated. "Will you be all right? Would you like me to come with you?"

"No, I want you to find out the name of the man who shoved his boot into Olivia's ribs. That's all I need from you."

He looked down at Olivia's slim, crumpled body. They were preparing to lift her onto the gurney, but she was still deeply unconscious. "I'll call you later." He turned and left the condo.

He thinks Olivia is going to die, Kendra thought dully. He thinks I'm going to need someone when my best friend passes.

But it wasn't going to happen. She wouldn't let Olivia be killed by a random attack by a beast who would do this to her. She'd keep her alive and with her by sheer will.

And by prayer.

Olivia had been cheated of so much all her life, but she had fought back and reclaimed as much as she could. Surely, God wouldn't take away her chance to make that life even richer.

"You're coming with us?" one of the EMTs asked over his shoulder as they carried Olivia out of the kitchen toward the front door. "We're taking her to St. Anthony's. It's closest, and we've got to get her there right away."

Because he, too, probably thought there was a good chance that Olivia was going to die. They were wrong, they had to be wrong.

"I'm coming." She jumped to her feet. "Let's get out of here."

St. Anthony's Hospital

"How is she?" Her mother breezed into the hospital waiting room with her usual bold confidence, but her expression showed grave concern as she studied Kendra's face. "Not good. How bad?"

"I don't know. She's still in surgery. Severe concussion. One broken rib pierced her lung, and she has kidney damage. Internal bleeding. They won't know if there's anything else until they get in and start trying to put her back together."

"That's more than enough." Deanna sat down in the chair next to her. "My God. Olivia. You always think things like this happen to other people, not to women like Olivia. Have you called her father?"

"Not yet. I thought I'd wait until she was out of surgery. He's in Stockholm at some conference. He can't do anything with an ocean between them."

"I'd want to know if it was you. I'd be on the phone with your doctors and make sure that they were doing what I wanted them to do."

"We have a different kind of relationship. Olivia's mother died when she was only six, in the accident that blinded Olivia. Her father has always been overprotective and resents the fact that Olivia won't live with him and let him take care of her."

"It doesn't change the fact that he loves her. I remember when you were kids, he'd pick her up after the two of you had been playing together. He adored her."

"But he couldn't let her go." She leaned wearily back in her chair. "So she had to break with him. It hurt her."

"It's not easy to let go of a child. Particularly one with . . . problems."

"You mean blind as a bat," Kendra said ruefully. "But you managed. You let me be as free as I could be. Then you made sure that I had that operation."

"I'm remarkable. What can I say?" She reached out and covered Kendra's hand on the arm of the chair. "And I had a remarkable daughter." She squeezed her hand, then released it. "But I think I'll be the one to call Olivia's father. We share a problem and a search for a solution."

"Whatever." She was too tense and raw to argue. If her mother had made up her mind, she would prove an irresistible force, and Kendra wasn't up to struggling against her at the moment. Something else suddenly occurred to her. "How did you know about Olivia?"

"Not from you," her mother said tartly. "I would have thought you'd have called me. I care about Olivia, too. She was in and out of my house from the time she was eight years old."

"I wasn't thinking."

"No, you were only feeling. It didn't occur to you that I'd want to be there for you?"

"Mom, drop it, okay?" She repeated, "How did you know?"

"Lynch told me."

Kendra's eyes widened. "Lynch?"

"He drove by the campus. I was teaching a night class, and he came in and introduced himself." She tilted her head. "He's . . . very unusual. Very different from Jeff. I'm not sure I approve of him, but he's interesting."

"That's for sure," Kendra said dryly. "And you don't have to approve of him. I don't approve of him either, but he's excellent at what he does. So he told you about Olivia's injury?"

"Yes, then he whisked me out of the class, canceled my coffee date with Todd, and drove me here."

"Whisked? Canceled? And you permitted it? That's not like you, Mom."

"I didn't think so either. It just kind of happened—and then it seemed very reasonable in retrospect. That's why I'm not sure I approve of him. Was I manipulated?"

"Probably. You'll have to decide that for yourself. Lynch has that reputation. Where is he?"

"He dropped me off at the front entrance. He said he had something to do for you."

"Yes, the video cameras at the condo." But he had decided that picking up her mother and bringing her to the hospital had first priority. He'd wanted her to have someone she loved with her during this time of pain.

And she was suddenly passionately grateful to Lynch for bringing her mother to her. There were only two people in the world that she loved, and one of them was in that operating room fighting for her life. The other one was sitting there in silent support, ready to wade in and fight any battle Kendra had to wage. It didn't stop the pain or the worry but it made her feel less alone.

She reached out and grasped her mother's hand tightly. "I'm glad you came, Mom. I should have called you myself."

"Yes, you should. I'm glad you're willing to confess to a fault that I admit I was responsible for fostering. I wanted desperately to make you independent . . . even from me." She added brusquely, "But you can stop it now. I believe you've learned the lesson. A little leaning is not a bad thing and can make the one leaned upon feel a sense of value."

She smiled shakily. "I'll try to moderate."

Her mother looked away from her. "But one lesson I wish you'd take to heart. I love Olivia, but I love you more. I don't want you to end up in surgery or the cemetery because some cheap criminal decides your life has no worth. You are a unique human being, and you must not let men like Lynch put you in a position where you're at risk. I've worked far too hard for that." She smiled. "Of course, I can't claim that I'm solely responsible for that uniqueness. You did have a little to do with it. However, I definitely have a stake in the final result."

As usual, she was not willing to give Kendra's father even a little credit. Kendra's lips twisted. "But one of the things you taught me was that no result is final. The more you learn, the more the result alters. What starts out to be one thing can become something else entirely as you uncover new information." She squeezed her hand again. "That's why you taught me that I had to keep on learning, that I could never stop."

"I do wish you'd stop throwing my past lessons at me. You're making me most uncomfortable. I deserve to change my mind if I want to pursue another path. Look at all the politicians who do it." She grimaced. "No, never mind. I refuse to compare myself to a politician. I believe I'll just be quiet and think about Olivia and try a Buddhist meditation technique that one of my students taught me."

"Todd?"

"Heavens, no. Todd is much more physical than cerebral." She leaned back and closed her eyes. "It's going to be fine, Kendra. Those doctors are very good, and we'll supply the spiritual support. Olivia will have it all. Now relax and think wonderful thoughts."

Relax? Not likely. Maybe she should try her mother's meditation technique.

Or think about the childhood magic that she and Olivia had woven in that darkness that had bound them together. Surely that would be both meditation and prayer.

Start at the beginning, eight years old, the day when

she had met Olivia at the school for the blind. Let it flow, let the memories come alive.

She closed her eyes.

Woodward Academy for the Physically Impaired
Oceanside, California

The surf was wild that day.

Kendra could hear it crash on the rocks below her. She was alone there behind the rocks, but she could hear the other students who were picknicking out on the cliff talking and laughing and playing games. She heard Miss Woodward warning them to stay away from the high safety fence near the cliff edge. Not that the warning was needed when they were all afraid and always obeyed the rules. Miss Woodward was busy at the moment but she would notice that Kendra wasn't with the other students soon, and she'd have to leave and go back to them. Mama had told Kendra that she wanted her to try to be friends with people at the new school, and she would do as her mother asked. She didn't want to tell her that things always seemed to go wrong when she talked to anyone, but Mama and she usually ended up alone anyway. Maybe this school would be different from those last two schools. And, if it wasn't, at least Kendra liked the fact that the school was located near the ocean, and the sounds and scents were always changing and interesting. Even now, she heard the seagulls coming close to the shore to eat the bread crumbs the other kids were throwing to them.

Kendra automatically cataloged each sound, identified it, then closed them all out to concentrate on another sense.

She lifted her head and felt the warmth of the sun on her cheeks.

Not that she really knew what the sun looked like. Some things were hard for Mama to tell her about. Though she did try, she always tried. She would sit down every night after class and ask Kendra questions about what she didn't understand.

But even when Kendra had asked her about the sun and how a round ball high in the sky could feel warm on her skin, she had not understood her answer.

And Mama had known that she hadn't understood, and Kendra could feel her sadness. She had wanted to hug her and tell her that it didn't matter, but everything mattered to Mama.

"Hi, I'm Olivia. You're the new girl, Kendra, aren't you?" One of the students had come around the huge boulder, and she plopped down on the ground beside Kendra. "Would you like to share my peanut butter and jelly? I heard Miss Woodward tell another teacher that she couldn't get you to eat lunch. She said it was because you were . . ." She stopped to remember the word. "Difficult. Though that's a funny thing to call not liking chicken salad. I don't like it either. That's why my daddy makes me a sandwich every morning. I'm almost eight. How old are you?"

She wished the girl would go away. She didn't want to listen to her. She wanted to listen to the surf and the wind. She had heard a new sound beyond that crashing surf. A dolphin? Mama had taken her to the aquarium and let her listen to the sea creatures. Kendra was almost sure it was a dolphin. "I'm already eight, and I don't want your sandwich."

"It's grape jelly. That's specially good." Kendra could hear the sounds of the girl settling more comfortably against the boulder. "You climbed over the safety fence to get here, didn't you? I don't think Miss Woodward

would like it that you're this close to the edge of the cliff. We're not allowed to go behind these big rocks."

"You climbed over it, too, or you wouldn't be here."

"I was curious. I heard you climb the fence, and I wanted to know where you were going."

"Heard? You didn't see me?"

"No, I heard you go past me, and I knew this place was here." She paused. "I can't see anymore. I'm blind, like you. But Miss Woodward is right, I can hear that we're close to the edge, and you might fall over."

"I wouldn't fall over," she said impatiently. "You might be that stupid, but I wouldn't. I'm five steps away from the edge here and three steps away from where it narrows near where you came around the boulder."

"How do you know?"

"I paced it. Mama says I always have to know where I am and what to expect. I liked the sound of the sea, and I wanted to get closer."

"But you weren't scared?"

"Because it was new to me? Don't be silly. I'd be scared all the time. Everything is new at first."

Silence. "I've never been on the real edge of the cliff. I've thought about what it would feel like but . . . Will you show me?"

"Do it yourself. Five steps."

Olivia didn't move.

"Scaredy-cat." Kendra jumped up and held out her hand. "Take my hand."

"I'm not scared . . . much." Olivia got to her feet and reached out until she grasped Kendra's hand. "I just don't like . . . new stuff."

"Then why do you want to get close to the edge? Yes or no?"

"Yes."

"Little steps," Kendra said as she pulled her toward the cliff edge. "One, two, three, four—stop."

"You said five steps."

"The last one takes you off the edge. Want to feel? Put the sole of your shoe down against the cliff wall. Go ahead, I'll hold your hand."

"I don't think—" She took a deep breath, and her foot probed the edge, extending out off the cliff. "Hold tight." Then she jerked her foot back and stood beside Kendra. "It's not so scary." She added immediately, "Yes, it is. But I like it. It feels . . . different." She started to turn away. "But I'm ready to—"

"Stop!" Kendra's hand tightened. "You're all turned around. Step straight back."

Olivia froze and took a step back. "I'm ready to eat my sandwich now. Let's go sit down."

Kendra led her back to the boulder and let go of her hand. "You're back where you started." She dropped down where she'd been before. "You can either sit down or go back around the rocks to Miss Woodward and everyone else. You should probably go back."

"No." Olivia sat down beside her. "Well, do you want half my sandwich or not?"

Kendra didn't want the food, but she suddenly knew she didn't want Olivia to go away, either. It wasn't often that she felt this way with anyone but Mama. She had liked the feeling of taking care of this girl who was nothing like her. It had made the loneliness go away for a little while. "Yes, please." She slowly held out her hand, but Olivia was already touching her arm, then her hand. An instant later, a moist and slightly sandy piece of bread was thrust into her palm. "Thank you."

"Tell your mom to make your lunch tomorrow. Then we'll trade half and half," she said. "How long have you been blind?"

"Since I was born."

"I don't know how that would feel. It must be strange not to have ever seen anything." She was silent. "I was in a car accident two years ago, and after that, they told me I'd never see again. I hate it."

"Do you? I can't see, but everyone else seems to be pretty dumb about what's going on around them. So I don't know whether I hate being blind or not. I suppose I should. It makes Mama so sad."

"You should hate it," Olivia said firmly. "It's much better the other way."

"How can I . . ." She shook her head. "I won't hate anything just because you tell me I should. Why don't you just go away?"

"I don't want to go away." Olivia was silent. "Though they'll probably come looking for us and make us go inside in a few minutes. I think the sun's gone behind the clouds, and it feels . . . wet. We're going to have a storm."

Kendra could also feel that dampness that usually preceded the storm. "It won't be right away. We have at least thirty minutes."

"You sure?"

She nodded emphatically. "Yes, I'm always right."

Olivia giggled. "Daddy would say that you shouldn't say things like that. People won't like you."

"For telling the truth?" She frowned. "Mama likes me, and I don't care about anyone else."

"My mama died in the accident. Daddy says she's in heaven, where there's lots of stars and golden gates."

"I guess that sounds okay," Kendra said doubtfully.

"It's wonderful, Daddy says so."

"I don't know anything about golden gates. Mama told me that the sun is supposed to be golden, too. I don't know about that either."

"You don't know much, do you?"

"I know things that you don't," Kendra said, stung.
"You thought we were going to have to run back inside
just because it got cloudy. So you're not so smart. Who
cares about what the sun looks like anyway? I don't need
to know stuff like that."

Olivia was silent, then took her hand. "I'll show you.
Put your finger out and we'll draw the sun in the sand
together. It's a circle . . ."

The sandy earth was warm under the pad of Kendra's forefinger.

Warmth in the darkness.

"That's the way it is, round and round and round, and
so bright and warm. The rays make patterns . . ." Olivia
said. "I sometimes lie in bed and remember how everything looked, so I'll never forget it. If I forgot, then I'd be
like you, wouldn't I? I wouldn't like that. Can you see the
sun now?"

Warmth and a faint lifting of the darkness. But she
wasn't alone in the darkness, Kendra realized with surprise. Olivia's hand holding her own. Round and round.
The rough sand and the sun surrounding them with light.
Strange that she felt as if she at last knew what Mama
had been trying to describe to her. Was she seeing it or
just imagining what Olivia wanted her to see?

"I think . . . I don't know. Maybe."

"Sure you do." Olivia's hand closed desperately
around hers. "You've got to help me remember. I don't
like this darkness. I want it to go away. It scares me."

"There's nothing to be scared of. That's silly."

"Aren't you scared of anything?"

"Not of anything on the outside." Only of being alone
in the darkness. Only of making Mama sad. "And I don't
have anything I have to remember."

"But you should know about stuff." Olivia dropped
her hand and got to her knees. "That's okay. I'll make

you see it. I'll tell you all about everything. Everything in the whole world."

Because by telling Kendra, she would not lose her own mind pictures and memories. How did she know that? Kendra wondered. Maybe it had something to do with that moment of shared darkness. "Mama tells me everything that I—"

"Oh, but I can do it better. You said that you could see it."

"I said . . ." What had she said? "Maybe."

"It will be fun." Olivia jumped to her feet, her voice vibrating with excitement. "We'll be best friends. We'll be together forever. You need me."

Kendra suddenly believed her. She did need this girl who had come into the darkness of her life and shown her the sun.

And Olivia needed Kendra.

And neither one of them would ever be alone again . . .

"She's still alive."

Kendra looked up as Lynch joined her at Olivia's bedside in the ICU. "So far." Don't be negative. "She's still in a coma. She's got a long way to go, but she's going to make it."

Lynch came forward. "Is that what the doctors said?"

"It doesn't matter what they said." Her glance shifted back to Olivia. "She looks like a mummy with all those bandages on. She'd laugh and make a joke if she could see herself."

"Would she?" He came closer and looked down at Olivia. "She sounds like a person I'd like to know. A sense of humor is a jewel beyond price. May I ask what the doctors found during surgery?"

"Bad stuff." She tried to keep her voice steady. "The worst is the kidney. They had to operate, and they're not sure—" She threw back her head. "But I'm sure. It will take time, but she'll be fine. I *know* it."

"Then I'm sure you're right." His voice was very gentle—for Lynch. "Where is your mother?"

"I sent her home. She had a class to teach today, and there wasn't any sense in both of us being here. I told her I'd call her as soon as Olivia woke up."

If she woke up.

No, think positive. Those damn doctors didn't know everything. They didn't know how strong Olivia could be, how determined. She changed the subject. "My mother's not sure she approves of you. She doesn't like anyone to try to manipulate her. And she hates it when they succeed."

"I just took her off guard. I wouldn't have had a chance if she hadn't been worried about both of you."

"If she decides that's true, then she may let you off the hook. If the decision goes against you, then you're toast."

"I suspected that would be the way of it." He smiled faintly. "She's a lot like you, isn't she?"

"Not one bit. Well, we're both stubborn. We both care about each other. That's about all the similarity." She met his gaze. "But I don't want her hurt. She may not realize what a powerhouse you are. If she goes after you, then you take it and smile."

"Whatever you say. I don't usually attack aging professors."

"Aging? My mother? You didn't take her measure at all, did you?"

"I wasn't paying much attention to her. I was worried about her daughter."

She was silent. "Thank you for bringing her here. It . . . helped."

"I hoped it would. You looked vulnerable. It shook me a little. I've never seen you like that."

"When you're blind, you hide vulnerability at all costs. Just the handicap is vulnerable without any added show of weakness." She looked back down at Olivia. "But I never had to hide it from Olivia. She knew what I was feeling. We could sense each other's pain and joy." She took Olivia's hand. Was it colder, or was that Kendra's imagination? "I was blind from birth, but Olivia had six years of sight before she lost her vision in an accident. I was terribly confused as a child. I could use my other senses, but I didn't know . . . I couldn't imagine. I had no frame of reference. But Olivia would tell me how it *looked,* she'd help me to build a picture in my mind through touch and hearing. Do you realize what a miracle that was? She gave me all that she had left, and we shared it." She added musingly, "And, do you know, that world we built in the darkness was pretty damn wonderful. It was like reading a book where every description and character becomes your character, your world. I doesn't matter how the author sees it. Your imagination makes it belong to you to accept or change as you like. When we were little, we'd make it a fairy story. Later, it became less fun and more work. But that's how it is whether you have special problems or not, isn't it?"

"I think perhaps the two of you might have had it a little more difficult than the rest of us." He cleared his throat. "May I get you anything? A cup of coffee?"

She shook her head. "No, thank you. You can go now. There's nothing you can do. It's not as if Olivia and I aren't used to being alone together. Sometimes it felt as if there were no one else in the universe." She tried to steady her voice. "I just have to stay here and try to get through to her and tell her she can't let go. I think I can reach her. There have been a few moments today that I've thought she was aware of me. I just have to go deeper into the darkness. This time, she's the one alone in the dark, and

I'm the one who has to make her see that she doesn't want to stay there."

"I'm feeling kind of . . . helpless." He added with barely repressed violence, "I don't like it. I want to *do* something."

She looked numbly at him. Strange, he *was* upset. Lynch was so tough and calloused that it was odd to see him so frustrated. She would like to help him, but it was hard to think about anything but Olivia. "The video cameras at the condo . . ."

"They caught an image but it was badly distorted," he said curtly. "I gave it to Griffin to process and try to give us something to work with. They extracted skin from under Olivia's fingernails when she got to the hospital. They're checking it for DNA."

"That's good." She wished he would just go away. She wanted to concentrate on trying to pierce the wall that was keeping Olivia in that deep coma. She couldn't do it if she had to think about him. She had to concentrate and go back to that time when she and Olivia were one in their darkness. "Lesley Dunn. Why don't you go check on Lesley Dunn?"

"In other words, stop bothering you." He nodded curtly and headed for the door. "Why not? It's clear I'm not able to do anything here. Call me if you need me. I'll stop in later." His lips twisted. "Whether you want me or not."

She didn't answer, and, the next moment, the door closed behind him. She was barely aware that he was no longer there. Oh God, Olivia's hand was losing what little warmth it still possessed. Her hand tightened on Olivia's. "No, you don't," she said fiercely. "Neither one of us ever did things the easy way. You're not going to do it now. I won't let you. You come back to me."

No movement.

Her breathing was shallow.

Would it stop entirely?

"No, you can't do it. You come *back*."

She closed her eyes and let the darkness flow over her.

He wanted to smash something, anything.

Lynch strode down the corridor, not looking to the right or left.

Not exactly the right mood or philosophy to experience in a hospital.

And completely at odds with his usual cynical coolness. How long had it been since he had felt the urge to tilt at windmills and find a holy grail?

Not that a holy grail would help Olivia. She was dying, and it was stupid even to hope. She would die and Kendra would lose her best friend and her heart would break. Death and the pain it brought were facts of life. It happened all the time. Kendra would survive it just like everyone else. No big deal.

Except this time it was a big deal to Lynch.

"I was looking for you, Lynch." Griffin had gotten off the elevator and was walking toward him down the corridor. "And for Kendra Michaels. She's at ICU?"

"Leave her alone." Lynch didn't bother to try to keep the savage anger from his tone. He stepped in front of Griffin, and his lips were tight, his eyes glittering. "No questions. You can get a statement from her later. You bother her now, and I'll break your neck."

For an instant, Griffin was intimidated. He took an involuntary step back before he caught himself. "The hell you will," he said. "I've had enough from you, Lynch. Are you crazy? I've always thought that you were a little unstable. Sometimes it works for the Bureau that you can be just as violent as the scum you're stalking. But you don't turn that crap on me. If I wanted to question Kendra Michaels, I'd do it. Now get out of my way."

"No way. She's upset, and there's no reason for you to make it any worse."

Griffin's eyes widened. "Shit, I believe I see a hint of softening in that croc hide of yours. Amazing." He tried to brush him aside. "But it doesn't mean I won't—" His gaze narrowed on Lynch's expression. "Back off, Lynch. I can see you want to hurt someone, but it's not going to be me." He hesitated, then sighed resignedly. "This bullshit isn't worth risking my neck when I have three kids to raise. I wasn't going to question her."

"Then why the hell are you here?"

"Lesley Dunn. I got a call two hours ago. She's dead."

Lynch stiffened with shock. "How?"

"Cardiac arrest. I just came from Scripps Hospital. She seemed to be rallying this afternoon, but she coded, and they couldn't save her." He paused. "It could be a result of the previous attack, but we're checking the IV and the meds."

"She had a guard."

"Who would not have known if the meds were tampered with or not. You know bribes can be far more subtle and effective than a direct assault." He shrugged. "Or maybe she couldn't fight any longer and just succumbed. It happens."

It happens. That's what Lynch had been telling himself about Olivia. Just accept it. Life could be dirty and unfair, and you just had to turn away and go on. "Find out," he said harshly. "This one isn't just going to 'happen.' We're going to know everything there is to know."

"Too bad Kendra isn't available," Griffin said speculatively. "She might be able to examine Dunn's room and tell us—"

"Don't even think about it." He punched the button for the elevator. "And don't tell Kendra about Lesley Dunn. Not a syllable. I won't have her any more upset than she is right now. She was hoping Lesley Dunn would make it. I'll go over to Scripps and see what I can find out."

"Do that." He smiled maliciously. "Though you're not nearly as good as Kendra."

"At last you admit she's unique? My, how the mighty have fallen."

"I always knew she was good. She just makes me uncomfortable." He added, "And I was never sure if she wasn't still in touch with Stedler. If he's dirty, she could be, too."

"You're nuts," Lynch said flatly. "She doesn't know where Stedler is, and she's not dirty. So find another excuse for feeling inferior when she shows you up." The doors opened, and he got on the elevator. "Or get used to it, get used to *her,* dammit. So she has a few prickles. You don't have any idea what made her the way she is."

Griffin's brows rose. "And do you, Lynch?"

This time, she's the one alone in the dark.

A little girl alone in an eternal darkness and forced to fight the panic and the bewilderment.

He punched the button for the lobby. "Yeah, maybe. I'll call you if I find out anything at Scripps."

CHAPTER 12

"You'll have to leave the room now," the brunette ICU nurse said gently to Kendra. "Dr. Rawlins needs to examine her. You may be able to come back later."

"No." Kendra's hand tightened desperately on Olivia's. "I can't go. Not for a minute." She hurriedly glanced at the nurse's name tag: N. BRANDOW. "Tell him that she'll die if I leave her, Nurse Brandow."

The nurse shook her head. "That's not true. We'll be right here with her. If there's an emergency, then we'll—"

"She'll die," Kendra said. God, make them believe her. "I'm holding her back. Something happened when he hurt her so badly. It scared her, and she doesn't want to come back. No one ever hurt Olivia like that before. It was a terrible shock. She thinks it's safer to stay in the dark. But it's not, and she'll slip away. I can't let her—"

"I'm sorry, but we'll have to call security if you—"

"I'll handle this, Nancy." A man in teal scrubs with a young face but receding hairline was coming toward the bed. "No security." He smiled at Kendra. "I'm Elden Rawlins, and I really do have to examine your friend. I promise I won't hurt her if you'll just step outside."

She shook her head. "She'll die. She wants to go deeper. She's only waiting for me to leave."

"Perhaps I should get Dr. Michaels a sedative?" the nurse suggested tentatively. "She's been here all day and most of the night. She's a little distraught."

Don't scream at her or this doctor. Doctors were gods in hospitals, and they could keep Kendra out of ICU. Her gaze clung to Rawlins. "I'm not hysterical, but I am determined. I know what I'm talking about. I can pull her through this if you don't get in my way." She gestured to Olivia. "She's not in a deep coma. She can hear me. I know it. She just doesn't want to hear me. She needs time to heal, then she'll come back. But I have to be here. She has to know that I won't let her go."

Dr. Rawlins tilted his head. "And how do you know she can hear you?"

She wished she could give him a clever, incisive explanation based on fact and logic. But she couldn't do it. Now, when it was more important than anytime in her life, she couldn't do it. "I've been there in the dark with her. I know what she's thinking, what she's feeling." She moistened her lips. "Please. Believe me. Let me stay."

He studied her face. "It's not good for you. You're under severe stress. And you're not being logical about this."

She repeated, enunciating every word with slow precision. "Let-me-stay."

"Doctor?" the nurse murmured.

He hesitated, then turned toward Olivia. "Let her stay." He heard an exclamation from the nurse and glanced at her with a smile. "I've heard of stranger things in the years I've treated patients in ICU, Nancy. Astral projection, the power of prayer . . . When death is so near, you never discount anything. Screw rules and protocol. As long as she doesn't do anything that could hurt the patient, permit her nonstop access." He took the chart from the bed. "Now let's see if we see any signs of . . ."

"I brought your guitar." Her mother took it out of the case and handed it to Kendra. "Though I can't see how it will help. You're sure Olivia can hear you?"

"I'm sure." She tuned the strings. "Though the nurse believes I'm crazy. That's okay; Olivia is getting used to the idea that I'm not going to let her go. I think some of the shock is dissipating." She made a face. "At least, I've felt safe going to the bathroom for a few minutes and throwing water in my face."

"What does the doctor say?"

"That she could pass at any minute." She looked down at the guitar. "Or not. That I mustn't get my hopes up, that she's still on the edge. He's not offering much hope. But he lets me stay, and that's all I want from him. I'll do the rest." She glanced at Olivia, and said to her, "No, *we'll* do the rest. It's time you did your share. So get ready."

"May I ask what the guitar is for?"

"Olivia loves true country but hates what she calls twangy, whiny hillbilly. So I'm going to occasionally play the whiniest hillbilly tunes I can find for her." She said to Olivia. "Do you hear me? If you want me to stop, you've got to open your eyes and tell me to do it."

"That's a most unusual application of your therapy skills," Deanna said doubtfully. "Are you sure that it won't drive her the other way?"

"I'll play some of the stuff she likes, too. I have to strike a balance. But she's very intolerant when it comes to music, so I'm hoping that constant exposure to whine will spark something."

"Are you going to sing to her?"

"I hope she breaks before that. I'm no good at the nasal whining required. They fired me from a bar in Fort

Worth." She said sternly to Olivia, "But I might if I don't get the right response." She started to play "Scarborough Fair," and she immediately felt the rush of serenity that the music always brought her. "Don't get used to this. I know you like it, but we're going to move on."

Her mother stood looking at her for a moment, then moved forward and touched the dark circles beneath Kendra's eyes. "You look like hell. If you don't get some sleep, they're going to be treating *you* in ICU."

"When she comes back to me." Kendra's gaze was searching Olivia's face for some response. All those damn bandages . . . "I can't leave her."

"I know that." Deanna dropped down into the chair across the bed. "And you shouldn't pay any attention to those doctors. If I'd given up on you, then you'd still be blind." She was silent. "A good friend is worth anything, just like a good daughter. Do what you need for Olivia. And then we'll worry about you." She leaned back in the chair. "I have to teach a class in an hour, and I have to leave soon. So please don't start your hillbilly repertoire immediately. Perhaps a little Debussy?"

"I guess we can manage that." She changed to "Claire de Lune." "Though it's much too soothing."

2:40 A.M.

There was someone next to the bed.

The doctor, Kendra thought hazily. No, he'd been here only an hour ago. She liked Dr. Rawlins. He never gave up even though he couldn't see that—

It was Lynch, looking down at her.

"Hello," he said quietly. "How is she doing?"

She shook her head. "Why ask me? I'm sure you've talked to the nurses at the station."

"I don't want to hear it from them." He smiled faintly. "I didn't expect to see her still alive after twenty-four hours. You two must have something going for you."

"You bet we do." She looked down at her hand clasping Olivia's, and said unsteadily, "She's being very stubborn. But we'll get there. What are you doing here?"

"Is it too much to believe that I was concerned about you?"

"No, you're not as hard as you pretend to be." She grimaced. "No, that's not true. You're every bit as hard, but you're still very human. But it's the middle of the night, and that indicates urgency."

"I told you I'd be back."

Her gaze was on his face, and even in the dimness, she could see something that made her uneasy. "Why are you here?"

"Lesley Dunn is dead."

She stiffened with shock. "When?"

"Right before I left you yesterday. I met Griffin in the hall on the way to give us the word."

"But he didn't tell me. Why?"

"For God's sake, you were contending with enough," he said roughly. "I wasn't going to let Griffin pile anything else on you. I saw you with the Dunn woman. I knew it was going to tear you up."

She reached up and rubbed her temple. "So unfair . . . She fought so hard. I thought she had a chance." She could feel her eyes sting. Strange that she had not yet cried for Olivia, but Lesley Dunn was bringing tears . . .

Not so strange. It was over for Lesley, and Kendra was still fighting for Olivia. She would not let it be over for Olivia.

"She did have a chance," Lynch said. "She had rallied a few hours earlier." He was silent. "Someone slipped poison into her IV. We just got the results back."

"Shit."

"And the media got hold of the story. They don't know all the details, but they know about the poison. That's why I'm here. It's going to be all over the cable channels. I didn't want you to hear it from anyone else."

"Do we have any idea who did it?"

"Not yet. It could be the male nurse who changed the IV or any one of a half dozen hospital personnel." He shrugged. "Or the invisible man who managed to slip onto that floor and do the deed. I'm leaning toward the male nurse. I've been checking up on him, and he's a gambler who's often low on funds. We're trying to check on phone calls, etc. before we gather him in."

"He might give us a lead?"

"Maybe bring us one step closer." He started to turn away. "That's all. I just wanted you to know."

"Thank you."

He suddenly turned and strode back to her. "Listen." His hands grasped her shoulders. "I'll do anything you want me to do. Anything." He gave her a quick, hard kiss, then let her go and strode toward the door. "Call me, dammit."

She stared after him. What had that been about? Not passion. Maybe frustration? It didn't matter. It was a night for emotional explosions, and Lynch was evidently feeling his share. It could be that he was trying to comfort her in a time of need and didn't know quite how to do it.

And this was a time of need, she thought wearily. She was sick of death and the good being taken down. Olivia, Lesley . . . who would be next?

But Olivia was not going to die.

She leaned forward and put her cheek on Olivia's hand. "She shouldn't have died, Olivia. It's all wrong. And I'm tired to my soul of worrying about you. That's not right, either. I need you to stop this. It's hurting me. I wouldn't do it to you. You're scaring me. We've been together since the beginning. You can't leave me now. I want you to—"

"You're . . . getting . . . my hand . . . wet."

Kendra froze.

It had been the faintest whisper, but it was not her imagination.

She slowly lifted her head to stare at Olivia's face.

Her eyes were mere slits, but they were open.

Oh, God, thank you.

"Always complaining," she said unevenly as she wiped her eyes "When it's all your fault. You stay here with me. No going back. Do you hear me?"

"I hear . . . you. How could I help but hear you? You wouldn't . . . shut up."

"Because you were being stupid. You couldn't stay there in the dark alone. You would have . . . you couldn't stay there."

"That's what you kept saying. I . . . decided maybe you were right." Her eyes were closing. "Besides, it wouldn't have been any fun . . . without you. I don't like . . . being alone."

"Don't shut your eyes. Not yet." She jumped to her feet and pressed the bell for the nurse. "I'm going to the door to make sure someone is coming. There may be something they have to do for you, and I don't know if they'll believe that you're awake. They think I'm some kind of weirdo."

"And your . . . point is?"

"That you owe me. So don't shut your eyes for a little while. I want to show you off."

"I'm tired. And you're just scared."

"Yes." She was motioning frantically at the nurse who was hurrying down the corridor. "So indulge me. Stay awake, okay?"

"On one . . . condition."

"Name it."

"That you never play 'There's a Tear in My Beer' again. It . . . was cruel and unusual punishment."

"You deserved it. Did you like 'Does My Ring Hurt Your Finger' better?"

"No, that was the next condition."

The nurse was in the room and moving toward Olivia's bed.

It was out of Kendra's hands. "We can negotiate." She went back and sat down in the chair. "Let's see how you cooperate with the medical staff here. I want you well and out of this hospital, dammit."

"She's awake," Kendra told Lynch when he picked up the phone two hours later. "I don't know the full extent of the damage or the healing time yet, but that's a major breakthrough." She drew a deep breath. "She's going to live, Lynch. I know it." She paused. "And, what's more important, she knows it."

"That's great, Kendra." His voice was completely sincere. "I couldn't be happier."

"Neither could I." She added, "I haven't been able to question her about the attack yet. I'm going to have to play that by ear. It scared her, and I won't be responsible for causing any lasting trauma. If I have to ignore it, I will. I'm not sure how much she'd remember anyway." She paused. "And I won't let you question her either."

"Don't be too protective. It might be a catharsis for her."

She stiffened. "And give you what you want."

"What we both want. Think about it. Do you want to let that creep get away?"

"Of course I don't. I want them all to go down. That's why you have to do your job and bring them—"

"Wait a minute. *My* job? I thought we were working on this together."

"We were, and look what happened." Her hands tightened on the phone. "If I hadn't been involved, Olivia would never have been hurt. She almost died, and I still don't know what permanent damage there will be. And it's not the first time. There's always cause and effect when I try to help. Last time, it was those children in the kidnap case. If I hadn't brought Jeff so close that the kidnapper felt threatened, he might never have murdered them. I should have stayed out of it. I do more harm than good. Chasing around after scum was never what I wanted to do."

"Not even to find Jeff Stedler?"

"You find him. Maybe that way, he won't turn up dead, too."

He was silent a moment. "Do you really mean that?"

"Of course I mean it. My job is to stay with Olivia and help her through this."

"Your job is to use that unique skill to stop those scumbags out there in their tracks and maybe save a few lives. I'm sure Stedler didn't blame you for the death of those kids."

"No, he just wanted to use me again. I blamed myself." Nightmares, weeks of trauma, memories that would never leave her. "Just as I blame myself for Olivia. She was going to try to talk me into stopping my work with you. She wouldn't have even been at my condo if she hadn't been worried about me."

"So you're going to give her what she wants. Guilt, again? Why don't you ask her if she wants you to feel guilty, if that's going to enrich your relationship?"

"Be quiet. You don't know anything about our relationship."

"Only what you told me. But an outsider sometimes sees things that others don't."

"Or invents things to help him manipulate the situation."

"I'm not above that, but I have a peculiar reluctance to do it in your case."

"Peculiar, indeed. Forget it, Lynch."

"Oh, I won't forget it. But I'll let it go for now. You're angry and defensive and frightened, and I won't—"

"Frightened?"

"You're damn right. Maybe if I'd realized how scared you were of the fallout from what you're able to do, I might not have pulled you into this case." He paused. "Nah, I would still have done it. You're too valuable a weapon to ignore. And, if I feel any guilt, I don't let it bother me. You should work on having that same attitude."

"Screw you, Lynch." She hung up.

She drew a deep breath and tried to tamp down the sudden rage that had flared. Why be angry with Lynch? He was in her life only because she permitted it. Now she was going to close herself away from him, and that would be the end of their association.

Or would it? Lynch might not give up so easily if she was as valuable to him as he said. He was so clever that there was no way of knowing how or where he would strike. She had actually begun to anticipate how he would handle situations and pull the strings. It was stimulating and exciting working with him.

And annoying and bewildering and a complete tightrope walk on the edge of everything she knew and believed.

All the more reason to back away from him.

He was wrong. She wasn't afraid, she was just wary. Couldn't he see that she wasn't the one who was being hurt?

But she was also being hurt. She couldn't lie to herself and say she was only thinking of others. She didn't want the pain . . . or the guilt. She wanted to hide away in the life with the children she loved and could help.

And yet Lynch had managed to give her another guilt trip because she was refusing to work with him.

Damn him.

Jeff had never succeeded in making her feel this terrible burden about not using her ability. He usually just ended by making her angry. It was only another indication how much more dangerous Lynch was to her.

All the more dangerous because she was drawn to him in ways that were more sensual and powerful than she wanted to admit to herself. He possessed a basic, primitive masculinity that was in sharp contrast to that keen, cynical intelligence. That ability to stir and intrigue might be his most potent weapon.

Avoid him. She had enough to deal with helping Olivia get back to normal. She didn't have a chance in hell of Lynch's leaving her alone if he thought he might possibly get what he wanted from her. But he might give her a short respite if he thought it smarter to wait until she was less upset.

And she'd make every minute count until she had to deal with him again.

She walked quickly back down the hall toward the ICU.

Forget it, Lynch thought, as he downshifted while driving up a steep stretch of Torrence Street. Forget her. She was taking too much of his time and effort. It wasn't as if he wasn't used to working solo. He preferred it in most cases. He rated check-minus in the plays well with others box. That was why he and the FBI had been such a bad fit. He was much more at home working alone on the special tasks he performed for the intelligence community.

So why had he been so upset when Kendra had opted out? It's true, she stimulated him both mentally and physically. Like a good tennis partner who challenged him to elevate his game, Kendra made him want to bring all of his skills to bear. If only to keep himself from being outclassed by a reluctant amateur.

And face it, that challenge included a strong thread of sexuality that was becoming stronger the longer he was with her. It was all the more titillating because he knew he had to keep that sexuality burning low, or she would step back. There was no way she would want to become involved with another law-enforcement type. She had been stung too deeply by Stedler.

Besides, he shouldn't dwell on that side of their relationship. Her value was primarily as a partner working through the unusual permutations of this case. Concentrate on that aspect alone.

Yeah, sure.

Sex was too damn important to him to leave it out of any equation. After his divorce, he had been careful to limit relationships to physical satisfaction. It was safer, and no one would get hurt if he turned his back and walked away.

But he hadn't wanted to walk away from Kendra. He had wanted to go closer, to warm his hands at the flame that flickered, then was gone. What would it take to make that flame flare and burn? The temptation to experiment and find out was almost irresistible. He was tending to forget what was smart and what lessons he'd learned.

Get straight, get back on track. Accept the value Kendra offered him that had nothing to do with sex. When she was willing to offer him anything at all.

He had been tempted to apply more pressure, but any attempt to push her buttons would only enrage her and erase any chance of her helping later. No one liked being played, and Kendra was more sensitive to it than anyone he had ever known.

Of course, she was more sensitive to just about everything, and that facet was arousing a variety of emotions in him. He was becoming attuned to that acute emotional vulnerability in Kendra and found himself mirroring that emotion and trying to find a way to protect her from it. It had shocked him that he felt that protectiveness with such savage intensity. It was just as well that he was distancing himself from her for a while.

Go about the investigation, do what you always do before you brought her onto the case.

Forget about Kendra Michaels.

Ten minutes later, Lynch stood in the dark side yard of a house where the "cleaner," John Bergen, had spent the previous night. Lynch had taken a calculated risk in not confronting Bergen sooner, but as long as the tracking device was still working on the car, he knew he could keep tabs on him. A mapping app on Lynch's phone told him that Bergen was on his way back to the house, which was empty except for a sleeping bag in one of the back bedrooms.

Lynch crouched low as Bergen's car approached, and the headlight beams crossed the front of the house. Bergen killed the engine, climbed out of the car, and moved across the overgrown front yard.

Lynch silently moved from behind him and grabbed his arm. "Hello, Bergen."

Bergen emitted a sound that was half gasp, half scream. He clutched his chest. "Jeez, you scared the hell out of me. What's the matter with you?"

"You lied to me, that's what's the matter. And now I need some answers."

Bergen tried to wrench free, but Lynch's grip was too strong. "I already told you, buddy. I have no idea what—"

"You're lying again." Lynch raised a small dictation device and played him a few seconds of the phone call he and Kendra had heard and recorded after their first meeting with him "You're a damned good liar, Bergen, but not good enough to explain your way out of this."

Bergen relaxed his tensed arm, admitting defeat. "Okay, fine. Shit. But I'm not talking until I get my lawyer."

"You don't understand. You're not under arrest. No one even knows I'm here. You're going to tell me what I need to know, then I'll decide what to do with you. Lawyers will have nothing to do with it."

Bergen wrinkled his brow. "What kind of cop are you?"

"I'm one who doesn't give a damn about the rules," he said softly. "Someone tried to kill the young woman who was with me when I came to see you, and I'm a little annoyed about it. And I'm even more annoyed that he put another innocent young woman in the hospital. I believe you can help me find who did it."

Bergen chuckled. "I think you're going to be disappointed."

Lynch wrenched the man's arm behind his back and pushed him toward the street. "We'll see, won't we?"

Bergen half slid, half stumbled across the yard. "Wait a minute. I need to get something out of my car."

"The handgun under your front seat?"

Bergen looked over his shoulder at him. "How did you know?"

"One, we're in Southern California. Two, if I had a client list like yours, I'd sure as hell keep some protection in my car."

Bergen shrugged. "Makes sense."

"Not precisely difficult to guess. My associate would do a lot better than me if she were here. She's very good at that sort of thing." He smiled. "But I'm not too bummed about it. I have my own way of getting information that's completely out of her realm."

Lynch cuffed Bergen's hands behind him and shoved him into the passenger seat of his Ferrari. A moment later, he was speeding down the road.

"Where are we going?" Bergen asked.

"Away from where anyone would think to look for you. I don't think you were hiding from me at that house, were you?"

Bergen didn't reply.

"All those houses and condos you own, and you hole up in a place that doesn't even belong to you. I know because I checked. Does it belong to a girlfriend? A family member?"

"I used to own it, but not anymore. Nobody has actually lived there since I sold it. I guess the new owner is just waiting for the market to improve before he sells. Anyway, I figured it was someplace I could crash without anybody's finding me." He shot him a sour glance. "Anybody, that is, except you."

"If I found you, somebody else could, too."

"Maybe, maybe not. I'm just not taking any chances."

"Chances?"

"You seem like a smart guy. I'm sure you have it figured out."

"Your employer. You told him that we're onto you, and now you're afraid he might make you disappear to keep you from talking."

"Very good. You get a gold star. The kind of people who hire me wouldn't think twice about snuffing me out. Kind of goes with the territory, you know?"

"You didn't have to tell him at all. He would have no idea we found out about you."

Bergen shrugged. "Professional courtesy. He needed to be prepared to cover his ass, just as I needed to cover mine. Besides, he paid well and could use me again. But you heard that call between us. He blames me for this. Some bullshit about that woman smelling my work."

"That's exactly how it went down, Bergen. It's entirely your fault that we found you. And I really don't mind if everyone knows it."

"Ah, shit." With his hands still cuffed behind him, Bergen slumped forward in his seat. "So where are you taking me?"

"Ever been to Sunset Cliffs?"

"Yeah."

"Beautiful spot, isn't it? You know, I once went to three weddings in one year there. At one of them, the groom was afraid of heights. He kind of freaked out."

"Yeah, my daughter got hitched up there." He moistened his lips. "It's a little windy. And it will be pitch-black up there."

"Really? I guess I'll see for myself. We'll be there in a few minutes."

A glaze of perspiration now covered Bergen's face. "Come on, man. This isn't necessary."

"Where's your sense of adventure?"

"I've already had enough adventure in my life. Let's work this out."

"You're the one who will have to do the working. You can start by telling me who hired you to clean the mess in Jeff Stedler's apartment."

"I don't know."

Lynch shook his head. "Okay, we're not off to a good start here."

"I'm telling the truth."

Lynch shot him a skeptical glance. "You work for people with absolutely no idea who they are?"

"Sometimes. My regulars were always my bread and butter, but there are jobs from people I've never met and will never meet. And you can understand if many of them are less than forthcoming with their personal information. To tell the truth, I'd rather not know who they are. It's more comfortable that way."

"I can almost believe that. Okay, tell me who you saw at Stedler's apartment that night."

"Nobody."

"Ah, Sunset Cliffs State Park, just ahead." Lynch pointed to the freeway sign. "Just another couple minutes."

"I'm telling you there was nobody. I got a call at one in the morning telling me that there was a mess to be cleaned up in this apartment dining room. And that my work needed to be flawless. No one could ever know that anything funny had happened there even if somebody went there looking for it."

"The guy didn't give you a name?"

"No, but a caller ID number came up on my phone. I figured the guy was using a throwaway. He said I could call it if I needed to get in touch."

Lynch drove to the end of I-8 and sped up Sunset Cliffs Boulevard to Ladera Street. He did not speak, letting Bergen have a chance to stew as they drew closer to the sound of the ocean crashing on the rocks. Lynch parked on the street and killed the engine.

"What do you know?" he murmured. "Pitch-black, just as you said." The car rocked from the strong ocean breezes. "Windy, too. You were right on the money."

Bergen said nothing.

Lynch climbed out of his car and walked around it and pulled Bergen from the passenger-side door. He steered him up the road alongside a white wooden fence until they reached an opening. Lynch guided him onto the cliff's damp and slippery upper plateau, which was even darker than the roadway behind them.

"Can't see a damned thing," Bergen said, his voice cracking. "If you're not careful, you're gonna walk us both right over the edge."

Lynch stopped and gripped the handcuff links behind Bergen's back. "Stop here for now. Invigorating, isn't it?"

"Go to hell."

"Is that any way to talk? I'm expanding your horizons. But now I need you to do the same for me." He added softly. "Give me something I can use."

"I'm telling you, I don't know who hired me."

"What happened to Jeff Stedler?"

"Who?"

Lynch pushed him closer to the cliff's edge. "Don't play dumb. The guy who lived in the apartment."

The waves crashed against the rocks beneath them, driven by the ferocity of the wind. "I—I didn't know his name." Bergen's voice trembled. "I came over that night, cleaned up what I could, then left. There was ten thousand dollars for me on the dining-room table."

"Your fee?"

Bergen nodded. "The guy told me I'd get another ten thousand once the job was done."

"Tell me what you know about the man who lived there. What happened to him?"

"I'm telling you, I didn't see or talk to anybody else."

Lynch pushed him even closer to the ledge. "Then how did you get in?"

The winds howled around the rock structures below that they could not see in the darkness.

"Two keys in a little black plastic bag," Bergen said quickly. "They were jammed between the sidewalk and the grass near the front door. The guy told me to let myself in, then take the keys with me when I left. I never saw anybody."

"Bullshit."

Lynch shoved him harder toward the cliff. Bergen's foot caught a rock sticking out of the ground, and he fell headlong into the void.

Until, at the last instant, Lynch pulled back on the handcuff links. Bergen teetered over the cliff's edge as a fine mist sprayed him from the rocks below.

"You're crazy!" he screamed. "You're gonna kill us both!"

"It's a distinct possibility. These rocks are slippery." Lynch raised his voice to be heard above the wind. "So how about you stop jerking me around so that we can go home? Tell me what happened in that apartment. And tell me exactly what happened to Jeff Stedler."

Bergen threw his shoulder back for balance. "I don't know!"

"You cleaned up his blood, didn't you?"

"No!"

"What?"

"I said no. No blood."

Lynch pulled him back a couple of feet. "Don't bullshit me."

"I'm not. There wasn't a drop of blood in that apartment, I swear. No splatter marks, no bullet holes anywhere . . . Believe me, I know what I'm talking about. I've cleaned and patched a lot of 'em."

"Then why were you brought in?"

"There was something else there on the carpet. Something yellow."

"Piss?"

"No. Brighter, almost fluorescent. I don't know what it was."

Lynch pulled him back farther still. "Keep talking."

"It wasn't on the wall or anywhere else. Just the dining-room carpet. I rush-ordered a carpet piece and replaced it the next night."

"Kudos, by the way. It was a perfect match for the rest of the carpet in there."

"If it was so perfect, we wouldn't be having this conversation."

"Well, it looked perfect."

"Look, I don't consider myself an artist or anything like that, but I know my job." Bergen no longer sounded quite so breathless. "I know what needs to be done to make a carpet look lived on for two, five, or twenty years. But is it true this woman could really smell the difference?"

"It's true."

"Damn."

"Did you ask what the yellow stuff was?"

"Yeah, I tried cleaning it first, and it helps to know what you're dealing with, you know? Anyway, the guy didn't tell me shit. I was on my own. It wouldn't come out, so that's why I had to rush-order another piece."

"What did you do with the stained carpet you pulled out?"

"Aah, I tossed it in a Dumpster someplace."

Lynch thought about it. "Okay, you're going to show me that Dumpster and tell me exactly the day and hour that you tossed it."

"Hey, I don't remember exactly where it was. How am I supposed to—"

Lynch spun Bergen around and once again pushed him toward the ledge.

"Wait!" Bergen yelled. "Dammit, wait!"

Lynch stopped. "Yes?"

Bergen paused, trying to catch his breath. "Okay, maybe I do know where the Dumpster is."

"I thought you might. Now tell me something else that will keep me from considering you expendable."

"What if . . . I told you that the carpet scrap is still in there?"

Lynch slowly turned him around. "After all this time?"

Bergen nodded. "Because that Dumpster is the one in the driveway of the house I'm renovating. You stood eighteen inches away from it."

"It hasn't been emptied?"

"Not since that night. I'm telling you, it's still there."

Lynch leaned closer. "You'd better not be lying."

"I'm not. I swear I'm not."

"We'll soon see." Lynch pushed him toward the path that would take them back to his car. "Okay, we've seen enough up here. Sometimes it's fun to take a little time and just be a tourist in your own town once in a while, isn't it?"

CHAPTER 13

Twenty minutes later, Lynch stood in the driveway at the one-story fixer-upper while Bergen waded through piles of construction debris in the twenty-yard Dumpster.

Bergen popped up and gestured with his flashlight. "This might go faster if you helped, you know."

"I'm standing watch."

"Is that what you call it? Look like screwing around to me."

"The last thing I need is to get stuck in that metal mausoleum if your employer comes to silence you. You were right to go into hiding. Once it was known that we'd found you, you became a liability."

"That's how I figured it. I've been in tough spots before, but I've learned if I drop out of sight for a while, it usually blows over."

"This one might be different. You might think about leaving town."

"You'd really let me do that?"

"Just keep looking."

Lynch glanced up and down the residential street. No sign of trouble, but he'd be happier when could get away from anyplace where Bergen might be expected. On the other hand, any attempt on the man's life would prove invaluable if he could manage to grab the killer in the act.

Very cold. Kendra would not be pleased at that thought. Nor would she approve of his dangling Bergen over the rocks at Sunset Cliffs. Oh well, he missed Kendra, but working alone did have its advantages.

"I found it!" Bergen's voice echoed in the Dumpster. "I've got it."

Lynch heard broken glass and boards knocking each other. Then a large piece of carpet, almost identical to the one he had seen at the FBI lab, snaked over the edge of the Dumpster and fell to the driveway. Lynch picked it up and angled the surface toward a streetlight. There was a brighter-than-bright yellow stain about eight inches in diameter.

Bergen climbed out of the Dumpster and pointed to the stain. "What did I tell you?"

"Just like you said, Bergen. Lucky for me that you got lazy on this job. Seriously, your own driveway?"

Bergen sighed. "I was tired, okay? I really didn't think anybody would know. And believe me, it would be far from a slam-dunk to dump this behind a restaurant or something. If someone happens to see a rolled-up carpet being dumped in the middle of the night, the first thing they think is, ooh, dead body. At least here it blends in with the other stuff I've been tossing."

"I can't argue with that." Lynch carefully rolled up the carpet with the fiber side in. "And you definitely helped your cause by turning this over to me."

"Wasn't a hard choice to make. Either this or the rocks at the bottom of Sunset Cliffs." Bergen chuckled. "You weren't really going to throw me down there, were you?"

Lynch didn't answer.

Bergen's smile vanished as he studied Lynch's expression. "I . . . see."

"Do you? What's better is that you saw and understood up on those cliffs." Lynch picked up the carpet and hoisted it onto his shoulder. "May I give you a lift someplace?"

"Back to my car, I guess. In the morning, I'll swing by my place, gather a few things—"

"Wrong. You're going to get in that car tonight and drive."

"Where?"

"Out of town, out of the state, preferably somewhere you've never been before. Follow your own advice and lie low until things cool off. You're not going home to pack up a few things, you're not going to stop at your favorite bar for a good-bye drink, and you're not going to make one last booty call to whomever you've been seeing. You're just going to drive." He paused. "Feel free to call me if you get into a jam."

"You have a business card?"

"My number is now in your cell-phone directory. Adam Lynch."

Lynch walked toward his car with the carpet roll on his shoulder. "Oh, and there are six different ways I'll be able to find you it if becomes necessary. If you're lucky, you might think of three or four of them. Hide yourself from everyone else. But don't try to hide from me, Bergen."

The Following Morning
7:45 A.M.

Kendra's cell phone rang as she came out of the showers at the hospital.

Lynch.

She felt a mixture of curiosity and annoyance as she accessed the call. "Why are you calling me? Did you find out something important about Jeff?"

"Not yet. Maybe I just wanted to hear the sound of your voice. I haven't had anyone barking at me lately. I think I'm beginning to miss it. Neurotic, right? Where are you?"

"I'm still at the hospital. They gave me a bed so that I could stay close to Olivia."

"What about your kids?"

"I'm updating my reports and having phone conferences with the parents. They'll let me know if there's a problem."

"I wouldn't think that would be enough for you. Aren't you a little bored?"

"Why? Olivia is my best friend. She never bores me. Particularly when she needs me."

"But you've avoided the crisis. Does she really still need you?"

"I'm staying with Olivia, Lynch. Drop it."

"Consider it dropped. I just want you to know that she may not be the only one who needs you. I've become very attached to you."

"Because I'm the only one who barks at you?"

"Among other things. You tend to escalate matters in all kinds of directions. There were moments during the action last night when I thought about you at the most unlikely times."

She stiffened. "What action?"

"But you're not interested, are you? You left it all in my court."

"You want me to ask you again? Screw you, Lynch. You'll tell me anyway. Why else did you call?"

He chuckled. "You're right. Out of the generosity of

my heart, I didn't want to leave you completely out of the loop. I wouldn't do that to you when you've worked so hard to find the answers."

She wanted to slap him. "And did you find one of those answers last night?"

"I found one of the question marks. I located the piece of carpet that was cut out of Stedler's apartment."

She tensed. "And?"

"No blood. Another kind of stain."

"What kind of—"

"I've got to hang up now. I'm at the FBI Forensic Lab, and Sienna Deever just came in with the report on the carpet." He hung up.

Kendra felt a surge of sheer frustration as she pressed the disconnect. It was exactly what Lynch wanted her to feel, she realized. He knew exactly how to tease and manipulate her. In the last few days, they had grown to know each other better than some people did who had been together for years. There were still blank pages in their association, but what they did know made for a complex and edgy relationship. He had realized that she would want to know everything there was to know about that carpet, then left her hanging.

She should have been at that lab to hear that report herself instead of having to rely on Lynch, dammit.

And that was precisely what Lynch had wanted her to think.

He had figured that she wouldn't be able to stand being shut out of a crucial piece of the investigation. His instinct had been totally accurate, and that was another reason for her to try to separate herself from him.

And why was she standing here letting him do this to her? Lynch could be a Pied Piper, and he was trying to lead her down the path he wanted her to take.

And he was making her want to take that path, too.

She couldn't listen to that siren call. She was doing the right thing. She had a duty to Olivia.

Go to hell, Lynch.

She started down the hall toward Olivia's room.

Or was she blaming Lynch for her own intense drive and curiosity? She had always hated leaving anything unfinished. Maybe that siren call was deep within herself . . .

FBI Forensic Lab

"Déjà vu," Lynch said, looking at the carpet scrap on the same bench where he'd seen its twin only a couple days before. FBI forensics specialist, Dustin Freen, once again addressed the assembled agents, which that morning included Lynch, Griffin, and Sienna Deever.

Freen showed a spectrometer image on the monitor overhead. "No surprise here, but the piece that Lynch provided is most definitely from the same batch as the rest of the carpet in Agent Stedler's apartment."

"Good work," Griffin said to Lynch. "But I'd feel better if we had a statement on the record by the man who replaced it."

"He's currently unavailable. But he gave me his statement," Lynch said. "Eagerly."

"And, I'm sure, under no duress."

"Guilty conscience, I guess."

Griffin pointed to the yellow stain, and asked Freen, "Any idea what this is yet?"

Freen turned to Sienna. "Do you want to take this one?"

She nodded and turned to the other two agents. "We're not finished yet, but we've already run the stain through several tests. Electron microscope analysis, Raman Spectral Comparator, and we're sending out for others." She glanced at Lynch and Griffin. "It's very . . . exciting. It's the same substance we've been finding in the murder victims' systems."

"Holy shit," Griffin said. "Are you sure?"

"Positive." Her eyes were glittering in her taut face. "At least *a* substance that we've been finding. It may be interacting with something else, but this is essentially what we've been finding in the victims' organ tissues."

"That's incredible," Lynch said. "But you still haven't answered the million-dollar question. What the hell is this stuff?"

She shook her head. "We still don't know."

"When will you know?" Griffin asked.

"Difficult to say. We've sent it out to the labs we think will have the best chance at identifying it quickly. This is like nothing we've seen. Even though we can break down most of the elements, we still don't know the reason or purpose of the formula."

"Can't you even make a guess what we're dealing with?" Griffin asked.

"We agree that it does seem to possess some cortico-steroid properties, but even that is preliminary. And your guess is as good as ours as to how so much of it ended up on the floor of Agent Stedler's apartment."

Lynch stared at the large yellow splotch, which was now reminding him of a figure from a disturbing Rorschach figure. The stain looked like a pair of hideously thin lips, twisted into a maniacal grin, taunting him, baiting him.

Hmm, better keep that one from the agency shrinks.

He turned to Sienna. "Is this toxic? Could it cause the premature aging we've been seeing in the victim's internal organs?"

She grimaced. "Sorry. We need to wait for the lab

results. Our preliminary lab results don't suggest it, but right now, I can't absolutely say what effect this stuff would have on the human body."

"But maybe with a little more time . . ." Freen offered.

"With a little more time, someone else may be dead," Griffin bit out. "I just spent half an hour talking to Lesley Dunn's father about why his little girl is in a metal drawer in the hospital basement. And I didn't have any answers for him." He glanced at Sienna. "Agent Deever, I appreciate your quarterbacking the medical aspect of this case. Your background made you a good choice to interface with the labs and medical community. But we may need to make a change."

She stared at him in disbelief. "Sir?"

"It may be time to bring in someone else with a bit more hands-on laboratory experience. I'm going to talk to Washington about it."

"Sir, you can't. This is my case. The time it would take for someone else to get up to speed would—"

"You'll stay on the case, of course. I'm just saying that we might benefit from a new perspective."

Sienna flushed. "Sir, with all due respect. I don't see how you can justify—"

"Agent Deever, I don't have to justify it at all. At least, not to you. Are we clear?"

Lynch watched Sienna's face as she fought the anger and outrage she was feeling. David against Goliath. He knew exactly how she felt. He also knew that what she said or did in the next fifteen seconds could have an irrevocable impact on her career.

Freen stared uncomfortably at the floor, probably wishing he was somewhere, anywhere else.

Sienna finally drew a deep breath and nodded jerkily. "Yes, sir. Of course."

"Good. We'll discuss this later."

"Yes, sir."

Good girl, Lynch thought. It will only gnaw at your soul for a little while.

Griffin turned toward the door. "Has Lesley Dunn's autopsy been performed yet?"

"Not yet," Sienna said. "It's going to be done later this morning. I'd like to be there . . . if you don't mind, sir."

"Of course." Griffin headed for the door. "Call me as soon as you're finished." He disappeared down the hall toward his office.

Lynch watched Sienna rush past him as he went down the corridor toward the elevators. She was heading toward the bathroom as soon as Griffin was out of sight. She was probably going to either cry or punch a wall. He figured Sienna to be a wall puncher.

He'd meant to give her a word of support and encouragement, but she was clearly not in a mood to appreciate the fact that her humiliation had been witnessed. She'd have to cope with it herself.

The incident had brought back bad memories of his own days of working with Griffin. The man ran his own little kingdom and did not like to be challenged or in any way questioned even if it was to clarify his directives.

Rather like another arrogant bureaucrat he knew.

And it was time to give that man a call.

As he reached his car in the parking lot, he pulled out his phone and punched in a number. After a few seconds U.S. Associate Attorney General Frederick Jamerson answered.

"Jamerson."

"Adam Lynch."

"Lynch . . . Where in the hell did you get this number? I never give this number out to any—"

"Your cell phone gave it to me. It's scary to think how many state secrets you entrust to that thing. Anyway, sorry for the privacy invasion. I didn't want to wait half a day to talk to you."

"I know that tone. This isn't going to be a pleasant chat, is it?"

"How well you read me, Jamerson."

"I like to think I do, but your daily written reports have been a bit, shall we say, brief and uninformative. It's hard to grasp how you're really feeling about the situation there."

"I'm feeling a little pissed off. I hate going into a case blind, and I've had time to mull over that resentment. You didn't tell me the truth. You just pointed me in the right direction and told me to chase down what happened to Stedler. If Stedler is dead, he wasn't killed by some psycho who was afraid of being caught. You know damned well there was more to it than that."

"We didn't know. We have suspected. And I think you may have suspected something of that nature also. You were just intrigued by the assignment. You wanted to probe deeper."

"I guess you also knew that Stedler wasn't being entirely forthcoming with his FBI superiors in this investigation. He chose to hide things from them. Is there any special reason you didn't choose to share those very important tidbits with me?"

Jamerson didn't answer for a long moment. "We live in a political world, Lynch."

"Yes, we do," Lynch said softly. "And sometimes it makes me want to throw up. You're playing games, and I don't know if you're straight, or you're trying to maneuver what's happening to protect your department from some kind of fallout."

"You're being very disrespectful, Lynch."

"And you're taking it, which means that you don't want to have me walk away from this case. Why?"

Another silence. "You're exceptional. And I can deal with you if necessary."

"I'm not dirty, Jamerson."

"I never said you were. But you're willing to take a chance if the situation warrants and, if it's called for, you can be discreet. We've been led to believe that the situation may become toxic in nature."

" 'Toxic'? Odd that you should use that word. I just came from a lab where we discussed the possibility of toxic elements. Coincidence?"

"I'm sure that you'll explain that question in your next report. I'm going to hang up now."

"We're not finished. Tell me what's going on."

"What's going on is that you're doing an investigation that has serious implications that may affect my department. You accepted the assignment, and we've been very pleased with your work."

"Don't bullshit me. Details, dammit."

"Let's see, I don't want to be totally uncooperative. Will it help if I tell you that it was Stedler who contacted us for help, that he didn't want to go through the Bureau?"

"It helps, but it's not enough. I'd already guessed that. More."

"That's all you're getting. It's your job to supply me with the details."

Lynch held on to his temper by a thread. He wasn't getting anywhere with Jamerson. Hell, he hadn't really expected to get him to talk.

"Then that's what I'll do," Lynch said. "You bet I'll find out what the hell is going on. I'll dig and I'll hunt and I'll find every nasty secret that you or any other of your political cohorts wants me to be discreet about. And when I do, I may or may not report to you."

"My, my, insubordination, Lynch?"

"What do you think? You'll have to wait and see, won't you?" He hung up.

He took a deep breath, and, in the next moment, he had regained control. He started to dial Kendra when another call came in.

Griffin.

He accessed it quickly. "Any more autopsy results?"

"No, but something a good deal more interesting . . ."

Five minutes later, he was dialing Kendra's phone.

"I'm not going to be manipulated, Lynch," she said when she picked up the phone.

"And you're not at all interested in anything that happened at the meeting this morning."

"Not unless it's about Olivia."

"I don't know if it's about Olivia. I don't think so. I don't even know if it's about Stedler. It's all vague as hell." His words were sharp with impatience. "But you're going to listen to me. I'm feeling a little used by all the powers that be, and I'm getting irritated. I'm going to go after those bastards full steam ahead. Sorry your heart's bleeding for your friend, but you can help me move faster, and I'm not going to let you go. I'm going to give you a report every single day. Because you *are* interested, Kendra. I've watched you, studied you. That brain of yours can't help but start ticking. You want to know. And one day soon, you're going to admit it and come back to work." He quickly told her of the meeting and his talk with Jamerson. "There it is in a nutshell. Now I'm on my way to the FBI office to check reports on that biker who was killed at Ocotillo Wells. The Bureau agents and local police officers showing that McDonald's photo around haven't come up with any other leads yet. The biker's autopsy backs up your own observation. He was taking minocycline. So our guys are also hitting every dermatologist from Irvine down to the Mexican border."

"They waited for the autopsy? I knew that by just looking at him."

"Apparently there were other possible causes for his dental discoloration."

"None as likely."

"I'm not defending them, but they didn't want to allocate the manpower until they were sure."

"Idiots."

"In any case, they're trying to make up for lost time." He paused. "See, you are interested."

She didn't speak for a moment. "Slightly."

"Well, I believe I have a little information that will move that interest up a few notches on the scale. I just took a call from Griffin. Last night, San Diego P.D. located an abandoned car in an alley in National City." He paused. "The license plate was 2-HXW-100."

She inhaled sharply, instantly making the connection. "The number Jimmy kept repeating. Were they able to trace it?"

"It was a Lincoln Navigator off a local impound lot."

"Damn."

"But there were fingerprints. There had been an attempt to wipe the car clean, but there were prints on a tool in the trunk. They ran them through the FBI database and struck gold."

"Who is he?"

"Frank Rusin. Hit man. He matches the description of the man who attacked you and Jimmy. Griffin has told the police to put out an APB to pick him up. He says it's only logical that he's the same man who attacked Olivia, too."

"You're damn right it's logical. So is Griffin putting his agents on it, too? I want him caught. No, I want him in that same horrible, pitiful condition he left Olivia. But catching him will be a start. Find him, Lynch."

"Griffin isn't dragging his heels. He's committed to catching Rusin. I'll be on it, too." He paused. "Care to join us? Aren't you tempted?"

"Yes, I'm tempted. But Olivia needs me. You're trying to draw me over to the dark side. It's not going to work."

"Yes, it will. Because you're the one who will talk yourself into it. I totally discount my own influence. All I'll have to do is get a lead on where I can locate Rusin, and you won't be able to resist. You want to nail that bastard so bad, you can taste it." He went on before she could reply. "But it's time for me to back away now. I don't want to push too hard. I'll call you when I have something else interesting to tell you."

"Or dangle?"

" 'Dangle' is a fine word. Have a good day, Kendra."

He was smiling as he hung up. Not a bad result. Nothing accomplished, but he'd established a beachhead and routine, and a gradual assault was sometimes more effective.

And any assault on Kendra was both fascinating and a challenge . . .

One Day Later
1:50 P.M.

"Go *away*," Olivia said distinctly. "You're driving me crazy, Kendra."

Kendra gazed at her indignantly. "What are you saying? I'm not doing anything but sitting here talking to you."

"And watching them bring my food and trying to feed me. And doing a thousand other little piddling services that make me feel as if I'm wrapped in cotton wool. Get out of here."

"I'm not going anywhere. You almost died. You're still going to take a long time to mend. Maybe months."

"And you're going to sit there and keep on trying to coddle me? That's a great way to end a wonderful friendship."

"I'll try to stay out of your way."

"As if you could," Olivia said. "I know you. You'll try to run things, you'll try to run *me*. You're too much like your mother to just let me handle my own recovery. Look, I have at least one more operation on this kidney before it's going to be okay. I have plastic surgery on my lip and rhinoplasty on this broken nose. I'm going to hate being an invalid and I'll be bad-tempered and say things I don't mean and in general be a total bitch. But I figure that I'll be entitled, and I have no intention of feeling guilty." She paused. "Since you already have the monopoly on that."

Kendra stiffened. "And that means?"

"You know what it means. I shook you up when I got hurt, and you can't get over it. Well, straighten up and get your brain working instead of your emotions. Why should you be blaming yourself instead of that asshole?"

"Because none of it would have happened if I'd taken your advice and just walked away from Lynch."

"I could have been run over by a truck on the way to meet you. Would that have been your fault, too?" She tapped her chin with her index finger. "Oh, yes, I was coming to see you. Naturally, that would make it entirely your responsibility."

"He hurt you. He hurt you so much that you went into shock and almost didn't come out," she said fiercely. "Do you know how that made me feel?"

"Not as bad as it did me," Olivia said dryly. "But you're making me feel worse." She made a face. "No, that's not

true. You're annoying me, but he still gets the prize."
Her expression was suddenly tight. "He was . . . evil."

"Was he?" Kendra asked. "You've never said a word
about him or the attack. Do you want to talk about it?"

"No." She shrugged. "But I suppose I should. I was
wondering why Lynch or Agent Griffin weren't in here
asking me questions."

"I told them to stay away from you." She paused.
"There's been a break in the case, but I didn't tell you about
it. They may have a lead on the man who attacked you. I
figured you could deal with it later."

She smiled. "Protecting me again?"

"Yes, and stop acting as if you wouldn't do the same
if it were me."

"Of course, I would." She was silent a moment. "Do
you know that in a way I'm glad that I went through this
horror."

"Don't even think that. Why?"

"Because it brought back those days when we were
growing up, and the dark became our friend. We were
so close . . ."

"We're still close." Her hand grasped Olivia. "We'll
always be close. I love you. You're my best friend in the
world."

She nodded. "But things are different now. You moved
a giant step away from me when you had that operation. It
wasn't your fault, and I'm happy for you. I'm trying to
keep pace and make a life of my own. Most of the time I
have a hell of a good time, but sometimes I miss what we
had."

"Oh, shit."

She chuckled. "I'm not trying to make you feel guilty.
That's what I'm steering you away from. I just had to tell
you how I feel. And the reason I'm telling you is that the
fringe benefit from this attack is that I realize that we'll

always be together. No matter what happens to us, what we have is going to go on." She added simply, "I was lost, and you came after me. And it made me feel as if I'll never be lost again."

Kendra's throat was tight. What was she supposed to say?

Olivia suddenly smiled impishly. "Too bad you couldn't leave it at that instead of spoiling everything by trying to act like Mother Teresa."

"How ungrateful can you be?"

"Grateful? When you were torturing me with those hillbilly songs?"

"By very respected artists." She was managing to smile. "But I'd just as soon not to have to do it again. I think we'll keep you from getting hurt like that in the future." She paused. "Would you tell me what happened? Maybe there's something that would help us catch him. We think we know who he is, but other than that, we've been coming up with zilch."

She shrugged. "I don't remember too much. It happened so quickly."

"You were talking to me on the phone and telling me you were making your world-famous spaghetti sauce. It must have happened in the kitchen. Right?"

She nodded. "I'd just turned on my iPod and was listening to Rihanna while I turned on the oven. I started to unwrap the garlic bread, and I heard him. He was trying to be quiet, but I heard his steps. He was crossing the living room and coming toward the kitchen. He was walking on the balls of his feet, but he was wearing boots. I knew it wasn't you because I'd just talked to you. And why should he be trying to be quiet if he had any business in the condo?"

"You should have run like hell."

"I was planning on it. But he was moving fast, and he

was right behind me. I grabbed the handle of the skillet and turned to face him. He said, 'Now that's a mistake.' I didn't know what he meant. What was a mistake? Maybe he thought I could see and would be able to recognize him. Maybe he was talking about the skillet in my hand. I didn't have time to worry about it because he was on me, and he was choking me. I swung the skillet and hit him in the head." She moistened her lips. "And that really pissed him off."

"I can imagine. Do you want to go on?"

"There's not much more. He just began beating me. I tried to fight back, but he was much stronger. He . . . liked what he was doing. He was laughing." She whispered. "He was hurting me. I could feel my ribs breaking. I knew he was going to kill me, but all I wanted was for the pain to stop. I got away once and managed to toss the skillet through the window. But he still didn't stop. It only made him more angry. He threw me down and began kicking me in the side and back." She shook her head. "And that's all I remember."

Kendra leaned forward and gently brushed Olivia's hair away from her face. "That's enough. Just a few more questions. Sound. You said he was wearing boots. Anything else?"

"A leather jacket with zippers. Three or four zippers. I heard them jingle and pull when I was fighting him."

"A leather jacket?" Rusin had worn a suit when he'd attacked Jimmy and her at the studio. That didn't mean a great deal, but she was having trouble picturing the man she had seen in boots and a leather jacket. "I know he only said a few words, but was there anything distinctive about his voice or the way he spoke?"

"I don't think so." She added ruefully, "But I'm not like you. I was scared, and I couldn't pay attention."

"Take a minute. Think. Don't turn away from it because you were afraid."

She smiled wryly. "I'm not turning away. I'm hiding my head under the blankets." She was silent. "Maybe . . ."

"Maybe what?"

"Do you remember Denise Harrell from Miss Woodland's school? She had that stud earring in her tongue that so grossed you out. Even though we couldn't see it, the idea turned you off. He talked a little . . . no, a lot like her. The placement of his tongue in his mouth was . . . different."

"That's good, Olivia."

"I'm trying."

Olivia's expression was controlled, but Kendra noticed that Olivia's hand was trembling beneath Kendra's. Kendra hated doing this to her.

But she had to get it over with so that Olivia could forget it.

As if that would ever happen.

"He was on top of you. You were touching him, you felt his weight. Was he big? Small?"

She thought about it. "Small, I think. But strong, wiry."

Rusin had been big, muscular.

"Any identifiable scent?"

Olivia shook her head. "Just the usual stuff. Aftershave, soap, sweat."

"You touched his face. How did it feel? A beard? Was it lined or smooth? Young . . . or older."

"Smooth. A slight stubble. Not many lines. Twenties, maybe."

"Twenties?"

"Yes, is something wrong?"

"No." Except that Rusin was in his sixties and had the lines to prove it. "They were able to get skin from underneath the four fingers on your right hand. Did you scratch him?"

"Yes, the left side of his neck. But it didn't stop him. Nothing stopped him."

"We'll stop him," Kendra said grimly. "Can you think of anything else?"

"I didn't give you much to go on. I can tell there was some problem. I'm sorry."

"Don't be. You did great. There are a few discrepancies, but Lynch will just have to work around it."

"Lynch? Why don't *you* work around it?"

"I'm not leaving you."

"The hell you're not. Now we're back to square one."

"No, we're not. We never got to square one." She frowned. "And why are you so eager to have me going back to working with Lynch? You're not making sense. That's the last thing you wanted."

"I don't want it now." She paused. "But I don't want that man out on the streets and hurting anyone else. It was terrible, and I can still hear myself whimper every time he hit me. I hated being that helpless." She added soberly, "And I won't be that helpless again. When I get well again, I want you to ask one of your law-enforcement contacts to teach me to protect myself. I'll never feel entirely safe again, but that will help."

"I can teach you. I had karate lessons when I was working with Jeff."

"No." Olivia's voice was firm. "You'd be too easy on me. Let me go, Kendra." She added quietly, "And I'll let you go."

"Why? It's not as if you're keeping me from doing something I want to do."

"No, but maybe it's something you should do." She smiled crookedly. "Do you know how much I'd like to hold you back? But I've been lying here remembering how you were right after your operation. You wanted to gobble up the entire world. For a few years, you tried to do it. You were testing yourself, exploring everything you were and could be. I could see you were doing the same thing when you were working with Jeff. You liked it. It stretched your mind and every sense." She said softly, "But you got scared when those children were killed. You didn't quite go down into that same darkness I did, but you were close. So you stopped doing those investigations and drew into yourself. I let you do it. Hell, I encouraged it so that I wouldn't have to worry about you. But that's a cheat, and I won't do it any longer. You go out and gobble up some more of the world and live life to the max. And if you can put down that son of a bitch who hurt me, that's definitely a plus. I feel very uneasy about his still being out there." She closed her eyes. "Now go away, Kendra. I want to take a nap without you hovering over me."

Kendra got to her feet. "This isn't all about you. It's my decision what I want to do."

"Not if I tell the nurses you're not a welcome visitor. In this hospital room, it is all about me. Just go away and have lunch and think about what I said. Then call Lynch and tell him you're going to give me a going-away present when I leave the hospital." Her lips tightened. "I really would like that bastard who did this to me thrown into jail for the next hundred years or so."

"I was thinking of something more immediate and lethal."

"That would work, too. One more thing." She didn't open her eyes. "Don't you dare get hurt. I plan on being busy learning karate, and I don't want to bother with sitting around holding your hand as you did mine."

"I'll keep that in mind."

"And I wouldn't object to a phone call now and then."

"It can be arranged." She stood at the door, gazing

back at her. Olivia looked incredibly wounded and fragile in the crisp white bed. She might be wounded, but there was nothing fragile about her, Kendra thought. "You're sure you don't want me to hang around a little longer?"

"Go." Olivia turned on her side. "You're very persistent. Next you'll reach for your guitar. And then I'll have to ask them to throw you out."

"No appreciation." She hesitated and turned away. "You'll get your going-home present, Olivia. I promise you."

Olivia smiled. "I'll hold you to that."

Kendra walked out of the hospital room and down the hall. She felt oddly unsettled and uneasy. She had been so determined to stay and see Olivia through her convalescence, and she had been thrown out and told to go about her business.

And should she do it? Olivia's words had struck a chord of truth within her. Olivia, who knew her better than anyone, had said that it was fear that had kept her from working with Jeff after the death of those children. Fear that had caused her to stop exploring life and cling to a career she loved but that was infinitely safer.

She would have to think long and hard about it.

But in the meantime, she had promised Olivia a present.

She took out her phone and called Lynch. "Come and pick me up at the hospital. I want to go back to the condo and look around. And then we have to check out a few things. Olivia just gave me a blow-by-blow description of her attack. What a son of a bitch."

Silence. "Does that mean you're going to stop playing Florence Nightingale and come back on the job?"

"I said so, didn't I?" She paused. "Olivia threw me out."

"Bless her. Any reason?"

"She wants us to give her the man who put her in that hospital. I told her that it would be no problem."

"It may be a problem, but it can be done."

"It *will* be done."

"I'm not arguing." He hesitated. "Though I do have a few other leads we need to pursue."

"Not until we find the man who attacked Olivia. That has to come first. I've been thinking about her description and a few things are making me damned uneasy. I'll meet you outside in front of the hospital in fifteen minutes." She hung up.

CHAPTER 14

Lynch drew up before the hospital in his usual dazzling and spectacular manner, attracting the attention of three nurses and a teenager in a yellow nylon jacket.

She had missed that damn Ferrari, she realized as she got into the car. And she had missed Lynch. He had become such a part of her life that it left her with a strange feeling of emptiness not to be with him. In a way, he was like his car, bold, high-speed, and totally memorable.

His brows rose. "Why are you smiling?"

"I was thinking that you were as showy as this car."

"No one has ever called me showy," he said dryly. "It's not recommended behavior for FBI agents."

She shrugged. "People remember you, and you wouldn't drive this car if you wanted to be understated." Few people she had met were as memorable as Adam Lynch. Even when he was low-key or silent, you wanted to watch and see what he was thinking, what he was going to do next. "So it's good that you're no longer connected with them, isn't it?"

"That's their viewpoint anyway." He drove out of the hospital parking lot. "Your condo, you said. You think you'll find something there?"

"Maybe, but while I was waiting for you, I changed my mind. I can check out the condo later. It may not be necessary. I want to go see Griffin right away. I want him to double the agents working to find that dermatologist."

"Why?"

"Because that doctor may lead us to the man who killed the dead man from Ocotillo Wells." Her lips tightened grimly. "I think our Tommy scumbag was the one who attacked Olivia."

"Rusin attacked Olivia."

"So we assumed. I believe we were wrong."

"Why?"

She briefly described her conversation with Olivia about her attacker. "Black leather jacket, boots, in his twenties. It could be him, Lynch."

He nodded slowly. "Maybe. But Griffin has zeroed in on Rusin. You'll have a tough time shifting him."

"You said the condo photo wasn't very good. May I see it?"

He reached in his pocket and pulled out a photo. "Only a partial profile and blurry as hell."

Kendra was disappointed. Lynch was right, the condo security photo was atrocious. She couldn't tell anything, certainly not the age of the man. "I can see the problem. The video on my personal alarm system didn't show anything at all. It's focused on the parking area, and he went directly around the condo and took off toward the back. But we may have another one that's better. Do you have any more of the photos of that motorcycle creep from Ocotillo Wells?"

"In the glove box." He watched as she rummaged through the glove box. "You really think he's the one who beat up Olivia?"

She was closely examining the photo. "This one isn't great, but I think it's recognizable," she muttered. "There's a good chance it might be him. Olivia said her attacker was wearing a leather jacket with zippers, boots, and had a small frame. Both of those check out."

"Not much to go on."

"Enough to start," she said grimly. "Olivia also said his speech might have been slightly changed by a tongue stud. But I can't recall if the man at Ocotillo Wells had any difference in speech. The roar of that motorcycle drowned out any nuances I might have picked up." She added impatiently, "But what are the chances of someone else's wearing boots and a leather jacket going to my condo to attack me? It's just too coincidental. It's not as if I've offended any of the Hells Angels . . . lately."

"Lately?"

She ignored the question. That was another time, another place. "But this condo photo isn't clear enough to confirm that it wasn't Rusin who was there."

"So what do you want Griffin to do?"

"I told you, I want him to take the heat off Rusin and concentrate on finding that dermatologist. He's our only lead to finding the man who attacked Olivia."

"If he was the man," Lynch added dryly, "Griffin may give you trouble. He's prickly about having his toes stomped on. He regards the manpower he has going after that dermatologist as entirely adequate."

"But that was before we knew Olivia's description matches the killer we saw at Ocotillo Wells." Her hands clenched on the photo. "We've got to find him and find him fast. What if he leaves town?"

"Do I detect a hint of obsessiveness?"

"He hurt Olivia. He almost killed her. Hell yes, I'm obsessive."

He smiled. "Then I'll let you go in without me and lay your case before Griffin. He might be resistant to any pressure from my direction. I was a little contentious with him the few last times we had encounters." His smile faded. "Don't worry. If we have to go around Griffin, we'll do it. I'm tempted to do it anyway. But it could be simpler if you could persuade him. At any rate, I admire your determination. Let's hope Griffin will be equally receptive."

Griffin was not receptive.

"I've got more than enough agents tracking down the doctor who prescribed those meds for the guy in the morgue. I've set Santini on it, and he's moving smooth and fast. I'm expecting word from him anytime now. And, as far as we know, Leon Sanders's partner took off and may be in Mexico by now." He looked at the McDonald's security photo and tossed it back down on the desk. "Besides, Rusin is the logical suspect. He was the one who attacked you before."

"I tell you, it wasn't Rusin. He didn't fit Olivia's description. By all means, find Rusin, but bring your big guns down on that man from Ocotillo Wells," Kendra said. "I'm almost certain it was he."

"From a description given by a blind woman."

"Yes." She leaned forward and put her hands on his desk. "Dammit, don't you dare be condescending. You got a hell of a lot of information from that blind woman. She told you what he was wearing, that he had a small frame, that he might have a tongue stud. A woman who wasn't blind might have had trouble giving you a better description when she was being beaten to the point of death. And besides that description, she scratched him and furnished you with DNA evidence and a way to connect him to the crime."

Griffin was silent a moment. "You're right. I've had eyewitnesses who couldn't remember anything under similar circumstances. But how do I know she was accurate? She's not you, Kendra."

"And that's your reason for not trusting her? Half the time, you don't believe what I tell you either. *I* trust her."

"But you say you're *almost* certain it's the same man. I'm stretched thin in manpower as it is."

"I won't lie. I can't be completely certain, but it's worth a shot."

His brows rose. "You're usually more sure of yourself."

"And you resent me for it."

"Sometimes. I don't like to be shown up." He paused. "Sometimes I've just been glad someone around knew a few answers."

The answer surprised her. But then Griffin had surprised her a few times since she'd come on the case with Lynch. "You could have fooled me."

"What did you expect?" His voice was cool. "You're a wild card. I've climbed the ladder and made a success of this office by operating strictly on logic and keeping to recommended practice. I'm responsible for what goes on under my watch. I've made a success by relying on solid investigative procedure. I don't trust hunches."

"It's not as if I'm trying to convince you that I've had some psychic vision or something. I don't have proof, but I have a witness's description." She put up her hand as she saw him open his lips. "Okay, she's blind, but you've already said that you've had less-credible witnesses."

He smiled slightly. "I admit there have been times when I thought you had a psychic flash. Disconcerting."

"Do it, Griffin." Her voice vibrated with intensity. "Go along with me just this one time. Put more agents on this search. Lesley Dunn was just killed. There could be others going down. You're wrong about Rusin. This son of a bitch may be able to lead us to where we want to go."

He gazed at her without expression. "And you'll get revenge for what happened to your friend?"

"Yes." She met his eyes. "I won't deny that's highest on my list right now. I want to find out what's happened to Jeff, and I want to punish that asshole for what he did to Olivia. But what difference does it make if my motives are personal? We're on the same page as far as ending this as soon as possible."

He looked down at the photo on the desk. "I'll think about it."

"That's not good enough."

His expression hardened. "Don't tell me what to do, Kendra. I said I'll think about it. Now get out of my office. I've got work to do."

She didn't move, her fists knotting in frustration.

"If you're as clever as I think you are, you'll not push me," he said softly. "It would be a mistake."

She whirled on her heel and strode across the office. The next moment, the door was slamming behind her.

Lynch strolled toward her from across the squad room. "That slam nearly tore that door off its hinges. Does that mean we have to work around Griffin?"

"Probably. I don't know." She moved toward the elevator. "He wouldn't commit." She gave a glowering glance back at the door. "He doesn't like wild cards."

Lynch chuckled. "I could have told you that. Why do you think I'm treated as a pariah around here?"

"That's different. I'm not undisciplined."

"Aren't you?" He tilted his head. "Why do you think that I came to you when I needed a little help? I knew I could work with you. You are definitely a wild card, Kendra."

"You're wrong. I take responsibility, I'm logical, and I'm rarely impulsive." Her thumb jabbed the elevator button. "I just think people should listen to me when I know I'm right."

"I won't argue. Think about it." He stood aside to let her enter the elevator. "So there's a chance Griffin will go along?"

"There's a chance. We'll give him a little time to see if he comes through." She turned to him. "But we're not going to wait around twiddling our thumbs while we're doing that. You said that you had a few other leads that we could follow. Where do we go from here?"

"Our old friend, Bergen. We may be able to track that call he made. He gave me the number, and it was a pre-paid cell phone, but we might be able to track the tower. We should have had the info a long time ago. I made a follow-up request while you were in with Griffin, and I'm expecting a call back."

"Bergen. I'd almost forgotten him." She shook her head in wonder. "How could I do that?"

"You were a little preoccupied with harassing Griffin. Just as well. He wouldn't have been a particularly pleasant memory." He took her elbow as the elevator door opened. "But now we have to deal with it. I'll check and see if I've had a return call as soon as we get to the car."

But when they got to the car, Lynch didn't check his phone. He sat there for a moment, staring thoughtfully at the FBI building several yards away.

Kendra frowned. "What is it?"

"I was just wondering if this was the appropriate time to give you my present."

"Present?"

"Considering your combative mood, I believe it's exactly the right time." He reached under his seat and pulled out a metal lockbox. He opened it to expose a sleek, gray, nine-millimeter Beretta and a loaded ammo magazine. He took the gun out of the box and handed it to her. "Just a little token of my affection. Do you know how to use it?"

"Yes, Jeff taught me." She took the weapon gingerly. "But I don't like guns, and I'm not great with them."

"You should spend some time familiarizing yourself with it. You'll find it can become your best friend."

"Why are you giving this to me now?"

"I decided that you should have it while you were away from me with Olivia. You refused the guard Griffin offered you though you're clearly a target. I'd like to be with you twenty-four hours a day, but that's not happening. This little baby can take my place."

She gazed down at the gun. It looked lethal, but she doubted if it would be a tenth as dangerous as Lynch.

"Don't refuse it," Lynch said quietly.

"I have no intention of refusing it. I said I didn't like them; I didn't say they couldn't be useful." She pounded the ammo magazine into the gun. "And sometimes necessary."

Lynch smiled. "Practical, as always. I should have—" His phone rang and he answered. "Yes?" Kendra watched as he listened intently for the better part of a minute. "Good. Let me know when you get anything else." He cut the connection.

"What was that?"

"They finally got a fix on that number Bergen called a few days ago." He made a face. "It took them long enough."

"It was lucky that it wasn't an emergency."

"Your tax dollars at work. Pure bureaucracy. It went to an undocumented mobile phone, probably a disposable. But it pinged a tower on North Coronado Island."

"*North* Coronado? Are they sure?"

"Positive." He checked his phone. "They've already e-mailed me a map with the tower's exact location."

Kendra glanced at the map. "That's where the Navy base is."

Lynch nodded. "But there's also a country club and residences nearby. The call center will work up a more precise footprint of the area served by the tower."

"That will take them what, another two days?"

"Don't be sarcastic. It's not a matter of national security, so it might take them that long." He glanced at her. "Got anyplace you have to be?"

"Besides North Coronado Island?" She shook her head.

"Then we're on our way."

Within minutes, they were on Interstate 5, and five minutes after that, Lynch paid the toll and drove onto the massive Coronado Bridge, a two-mile-long structure that swooped across San Diego Bay, in a graceful curve, to the island.

"You're very quiet." Lynch glanced sideways at her. "What are you thinking?"

"I was thinking about what Jamerson told you about Jeff's contacting them. Why would he do that? Can you trust this Jamerson to tell you the truth?"

"On occasion. Do I trust him?" He shook his head. "But, then, I'm sadly lacking in trust. It must have been left out of my DNA."

"I've noticed. You've said very little about Jamerson to me since this all began."

He shrugged. "It wasn't necessary. I told you I was doing a job for the Justice Department."

"And you didn't want to elaborate in case I might learn something about you that you didn't want me to know." She tilted her head and studied him. "I don't know much about you at all, Lynch. I think I'm beginning to resent that. There's a lack of balance. You know too damn much about me."

He looked away from her. "What do you want to know?"

"I've never seen where you live. Do you have an apartment? A house?"

"A house."

"You've gone through my condo. May I come over to your place?"

"Sometime maybe."

"You don't want me to come."

"Not until I decide how much I want to reveal to you."

"You never let acquaintances or coworkers see your home?"

"Sure I do. I'm really not all that secretive."

Kendra gave him a skeptical look.

"Well, at least as far as my own personal space goes," he clarified. "When I invite most people into my house, they may get a sense of my hobbies, maybe a few of my interests, and that's it. With you, I suspect it would be like throwing the doors open wide to my soul." He grimaced. "God, that sounded melodramatic. It just came out that way."

"Sickeningly melodramatic. Not like you at all. Why?"

"Because it's not entirely inaccurate. It took hours to figure out how I felt when you sized me up on our first meeting. It was a definite mixture. First and foremost, I was impressed. And, I don't know why exactly, but part of me was even flattered."

"Flattered?"

"I guess we all like it when someone pays attention to us. And no one pays attention like you do, Kendra. We've gotten used to people becoming less and less connected with each other, so it's nice to run across someone who is the exact opposite of that." He drove in silence for a moment longer. "Anyway, as I was grappling with those emotions, part of me also felt . . . violated."

"I didn't say anything that a lot of other people didn't already know about you."

"I know that. The difference was that I hadn't made the choice to share those things with you."

She lifted her chin with a hint of defiance. "It sounds like someone has control issues."

"You're correct as usual." He looked into her eyes. "But I have an idea you've run into this before, haven't you? How many people have closed you out because they can't stand the thought of invasion?"

She didn't speak for a moment. "Enough. But I thought you'd have the confidence to make the adjustment."

"Give me a little time. I'll get there. But you can see why I'm not so anxious for you to come over and laser-scan my home."

She could understand it, but it was still causing a slight feeling of the usual alienation. "It's not as if it's important to me. Besides, you're being silly. I've ridden in your car. Do you want to hear what your car has told me about you? First of all, that you're—"

"I don't want to hear it."

"I just want to show you that discovery isn't necessarily connected with—" She stopped as she saw his expression. "Seriously?"

"Seriously. Why don't we concentrate on the case right now? I believe we've both revealed a little more than we're comfortable with."

"I'm perfectly comfortable with—" But she wasn't going to lie. She thought she had become accustomed to all the emotional side effects of being the oddity everyone considered her to be. But for some reason, Lynch had managed to jump over the barriers she had erected. "That's a good idea." Kendra watched an oil tanker leaving port. "But it's a little difficult concentrating on anything with all this bumping on this bridge. It's a real—"

Suddenly she tensed and leaned forward in her seat.

"Are you okay?" Lynch asked.

She nodded. "That sound . . ."

"The ship?"

"No." Kendra leaned forward even more.

Close your eyes.

Listen to what the car is telling you.

Clack-clack . . . Brrrump.

Clack-clack . . . Brrrump.

Her eyes opened. "Hear that? The sound that the tires are making on the roadway."

Clack-clack . . . Brrrump.

Lynch nodded. "What about it?"

She pointed ahead. "What are those metal plates stretching across the road? They almost look like teeth."

Clack-clack . . . Clack clack . . .

"Expansion joints. They allow the bridge to give a little in high winds, earthquakes, whatever."

"And there are places between those where the road looks rough, like the pavement is uneven."

Brrrump . . . Brrrump . . .

"Some kind of construction project. Maybe a resurfacing." He watched as she focused on the road ahead. "Does this mean something to you?"

"Yes. Pull over as soon as you can."

At the end of the bridge, Lynch drove to a U-shaped lot at the edge of Tidelands Park, which offered a spectacular view of the bay they had just crossed.

Kendra had already begun searching her phone's directory of audio files, furiously swiping her finger across the touch screen. She selected one and used the scrubber to skip through one of Jeff's dictations. She held up the phone between her and Lynch. There, faint in the background, was that familiar sound:

Clack-clack . . . Brrrump.

Clack-clack . . . Brrrump.

Lynch looked up. "He came here."

"And not just once. I'm pretty sure I heard this in several of the recordings." Kendra lowered the phone. "Did he have any official reason to come here?"

"No reason that I know about. We can check the case files, but I don't think any of the victims or their friends or families lived over here. And I know he didn't mention Coronado in any of his daily logs."

"And he didn't mention it in his recordings even while he was driving across that bridge. Jeff was coming here in those last few days, and for some reason, he wanted to keep it quiet."

She raised the phone and listened for another moment. "Okay, here's where he left the bridge. You can hear where the sound of the pavement changes." She touched the ten-second-replay button and played it for him again, this time turning up the volume so that he could clearly hear the sounds above Jeff's dictation.

Lynch glanced up as the slight, airy whistle of tires on the bridge suddenly gave way to a lower-pitched droning. "I hear it. That's what it sounded like back there?"

"Exactly. Let's get back on that main road and see where this takes us."

As Lynch drove back to Pomona Avenue and transitioned to Third, Kendra tried to focus on the audio recording's background sounds. After less than two minutes, her hand tightened on the recorder. "He stopped! And he turned somewhere near here. I can hear his blinker."

"Turned which way?"

"There's no way I can tell that. Dammit."

Close your eyes.

Put yourself in Jeff's car.

"I hear a trolley. I think it just crossed in front of him."

"There's no rail service here."

"Not that kind. One of those orange-and-green Old Town tour trolleys you see driving around."

Lynch hit his left turn signal. "Orange Avenue is just ahead. It's the largest cross street near here. If you're really hearing a tour bus go by, it probably happened there."

Kendra continued to listen as Lynch completed the left turn. "Why this direction?"

"Just a guess. A right turn would take us to the water. This leads us to the heart of the island."

She listened for another moment. "I think you guessed right. It now sounds like he's behind the trolley, with more and more traffic around."

Lynch nodded. "Just like it is here."

"There's another sound . . ." She placed the device closer against her ear. "I could hear the tour guide on the trolley's PA system, but only for a second. It might have stopped somewhere along here, and Jeff passed it."

Lynch pointed to a group of tourists adorned with cameras, baseball caps, and fanny packs, all seated on sidewalk benches in front of a pub. "I'd say that's the trolley-tour stop."

"Good." She didn't speak for an instant. "Now it sounds like he went through a busy intersection . . ."

"We're crossing it now," Lynch said. "Loma Street."

Her eyes widened. "He just put on his turn signal."

Lynch swerved to the right without putting on his own blinker. "It has to be here. Churchill Place." He looked ahead. "I hope you hear ocean soon, because that's where we're headed."

After less than a block, they passed a gateway of palm

trees and continued on to Ocean Boulevard, which ran alongside the island's west side. Kendra struggled to separate the pounding surf on her left from the sounds emanating from her phone.

She finally nodded. "Yes!"

"Yes, what?"

She said impatiently, "Yes, he was here."

Two minutes later, they found themselves on a large cul-de-sac that ended at a guard gate for the sprawling North Island Naval Complex.

Lynch spun around the cul-de-sac and stopped. "Did he go in there?"

Kendra shook her head. "No."

"Then what did he do?"

She listened for a moment longer. "He turned around just like you did. And he parked here on the street and continued his dictation." She stared thoughtfully at the guard gate. "He just sat here."

"As if he was staking it out, maybe waiting for somebody to come or go?"

She shook her head. "I don't know. All I can tell you is what he did. Anything else is pure guesswork."

"Well, this location matches up with the cell-tower hit from Bergen's call. Whoever hired him to clean Jeff's apartment was probably behind those gates when he took Bergen's call."

Kendra looked at the entrance for a moment longer. "And exactly how many people are behind those gates?"

"Thousands. It's a veritable city."

"All naval personnel?"

"No. A fair number of civilian employees, too."

She picked up his binoculars and scanned the tightly clustered buildings visible on the other side. "I'd love to find out what in the hell Jeff thought he could find out by sitting here."

Lynch motioned toward the beach. "I could think of worse places for a stakeout. Put down the car top, slather on the suntan oil . . ."

Kendra adjusted the binoculars' focus wheel and studied a two-story building with bold lettering on its side. She suddenly stiffened. "That's . . . interesting. The Thatcher Center for Naval Medical Research." She handed him the binoculars. "The white building with gray trim."

Lynch took the binoculars and examined it. "So what?"

"Stephanie Marsh. One of the victims, the one who was killed in a parking garage. She worked for a surgeon who was a Navy physician. She was his administrative assistant."

"I remember." He frowned thoughtfully. "But I can't recall the place she worked."

"But Jeff was staking out an area that had a medical research center. Do you think it means anything?"

Lynch shrugged. "Remember where we are. San Diego is a big Navy town. There may be hundreds of medical doctors out there with Navy contracts. But it's worth verifying her place of employment." He pulled out his phone, punched a number, and put it on speaker so that Kendra could hear.

Griffin answered on the first ring. "Griffin."

"Lynch here. Kendra is with me. She's managed to put us outside Gate 5 of the North Island Naval Complex."

"And why would she do a thing like that?"

"Because Agent Stedler was staking out this spot not long before he disappeared," Lynch said. "Any idea why he would be doing that?"

He was silent. "Can't say that I do. You're sure about this?"

"Positive," Kendra said. "Well, as positive as I can be considering the—"

Lynch cut in. "We need some information on the

employer of one of the victims. The name of the doctor who Stephanie Marsh worked for and her address of employment."

"I see where you're headed. Let me check records." Griffin paused. "Here it is. He's a well-known naval surgeon. Dr. Myles Denton."

"And why did he need an administrative assistant?"

"It's not that unusual. He's an important man. He's retired from active service, but they still call him in for difficult surgical cases since he's in the Reserves. He's evidently a superb surgeon."

"And what does he do when he's not being a superb surgeon?" Kendra asked.

Another silence while Griffin checked. "Research. Underwater pulmonary research. Several years ago, he came up with two medicines that expand lung capacity. It says that the SEALs use them on occasion."

"And he did this while he was in the Navy?"

"The first medicine he developed while he was still active, the second he created as a researcher for Thatcher Pharmaceuticals, which has a naval research center in San Diego."

"Bingo," Lynch murmured. "And that research center is within a stone's throw of Gate 5 at the base where we're sitting right now. And I'll bet Stephanie Marsh's employment address is Thatcher Medical Research Center."

"Right," Griffin said. "Holy shit. Do we have something?"

"See if you can find any connection with any of the other victims to either Thatcher Pharmaceuticals or that surgeon. Can you shoot me a photo of Denton right away?"

"What about Charles Schuyler, the Thatcher CEO? There are several shots of the two of them all buddy-buddy at various conferences."

"Really? Interesting. Yeah, give us a photo of Schuyler, too."

"And check and see if they've been involved in anything together other than pulmonary research," Kendra was frowning thoughtfully. "Research. Pharmaceuticals. Deadly unknown substance. A link appears to be emerging."

"Are you going to go on the base and check them out?" Griffin asked.

"Not until we get a little more info from you," Lynch said. "I want to know what questions to ask. Just send us those photos, then—"

"Wait a minute. Santini is here trying to tell me something." There was the sound of voices in the background, then Griffin came back on the line, his voice triumphant. "I told you I had enough agents checking out that dermatologist, Kendra. We've got him."

"When? Who is it?" Kendra sat up straight in her seat. "What did he tell you?"

"Two hours ago Santini located Dr. Joseph Powell, who has a dermatologist practice on the south side of town. He recognized the victim as his patient, Leon Sanders, and gave us an address where he lived with his sister." He paused. "Are you ready for this? Santini got an ID from Leon Sanders's sister on the guy who shot at you at Ocotillo Wells and beat up your friend, Olivia. His name is Thomas Briggs."

"Tommy Briggs," Kendra said. "What did the sister say about Briggs?"

"Just that he was some kind of paid muscle who was supposed to protect her brother. She was pretty bitter when we told her Briggs had shot Leon."

"Paid by whom?" Lynch asked.

"She wasn't sure. She said Leon never talked about his work at Ocotillo Wells to her. She just got the impression it was drugs or something else pretty nasty. She said when he got back from London six months ago, he was boasting that this one risky job might set him up for life. He said it was so important, they'd assigned him Briggs to guard him while he was working."

She asked the million-dollar question. "Does she know where Briggs lives?"

"Yes."

She inhaled sharply. "Where?"

"He has a Residence Inn suite where he stays when they're not in the desert. It's about ten miles from where Leon and his sister live. We have it under surveillance now."

"Is he there?"

"We think so. Santini left two agents to stake out the motel. There's a rental car in front of the unit. He's not going to leave without our knowing it."

"Unless he slips away."

"He's not going to do that, Kendra. We know what we're doing."

She was silent a moment. "I know you do."

"Good God, what an admission."

"It's just that this is so important. Briggs almost killed Olivia. He mustn't get away, Griffin."

"This case is more to than revenge for your friend," he said quietly. "He may be the key, and I won't let him get away until I find what doors he can open."

"A favor," Lynch said. "Let us open those doors first."

"What?"

"Let me and Kendra be the first to talk to him. Alone."

Total silence. If Kendra hadn't heard Griffin's slow, measured breathing, she might have thought that he had hung up.

Griffin finally spoke. "You have a gargantuan pair of cojones, Lynch."

"They're absolutely magnificent."

He was silent again. "I'll let you in the room with him during questioning, but that's the best I can do."

"Come on, you wouldn't even be close to having him if it wasn't for Kendra."

"He's not ours yet."

"He will be, and it will all be because of her. Just give us forty-five minutes alone with him."

"You're asking? Not demanding? Not threatening to sic the Justice Department on me?"

"I'm asking. You want answers. I'll get you answers. It may not be according to the rule book, but it will be quick, and it might save lives."

Another silence. "The Residence Inn on El Miro Boulevard. Suite 42. You go in before we take official custody. I don't want to know how you plan on handling the interrogation. I did not give you permission to barge in and take over my case. I may even complain to the Justice Department about your actions. Everyone knows that you have no discipline and would be completely out of control in a situation like this."

"A wild card?" he asked softly. "Wild cards can be useful, can't they?"

Griffin didn't answer the question. "Forty-five minutes." He hung up.

Kendra let out the breath she'd been holding. "I didn't think he'd do it."

"Griffin isn't always predictable. I thought it was worth a shot." He put the car in gear. "He wants this case wrapped up and is willing to sacrifice us to nudge it along. Why not? His ass won't be on the line."

"It could be. He's still taking a chance. Jeff was one of his agents. Maybe taking a chance is worth it to him." Kendra looked back at the naval base and suddenly tensed. "Or maybe . . ."

"What's wrong?"

"Nothing, I guess. It's just that . . . Jeff was here. His recording brought us to the base. And Jeff was out there in the desert with Sanders and Briggs. It's getting to be all about Jeff, isn't it?"

"It always was about Jeff."

"No, I mean . . ." It was hard to explain. "Things are moving so fast. Everything seems to be closing in around us. It was remote before, a hunt, a puzzle, but it's changing. It's as if he's showing us the way."

"Are you going mystic on me?"

"No." She met his gaze. "I'm telling you how I feel. Take it any way you want to take it. Imagination. Fate. Jeff."

"I'll take it with a grain of salt." He added gravely, "And gratitude that you're willing to share your feelings with me. I value that privilege, Kendra." He had driven onto Coronado Bridge. "Let's hope you're right and that Stedler or Fate or the powers that be show us the way to break Briggs and make him talk."

CHAPTER 15

The Residence Inn on El Miro Boulevard was one of the older cedar structures that looked more like a two-story condo than a motel.

Kendra couldn't see any sign of a stakeout as they parked some distance down from Suite 42. But then she didn't expect to see any obvious surveillance. As she'd told Griffin, she knew that the FBI knew what they were doing.

"I'll go around back and climb up to the window at the penthouse level," Lynch said. "I'll let you in the front door when I've secured the place."

"You're going in by yourself?" Her lips tightened. "What's my part in this, Lynch? I'm supposed to stand by and wonder if that bastard is going to kill you?"

"Something like that." He got out of the car. "Stop going ballistic. There are some things that you do well and there are some things that I'm qualified to do better. That's why Griffin felt confident to leave Briggs in my hands when I told him I'd get answers. We only have forty-five minutes, and I don't have time to set up an attack that would make you feel needed." He got out of the car. "I'm going in to take Briggs down, and by the time I let you in that front door, Briggs will be intimidated and on the way to giving us what we want to know." He moved toward the motel unit. "And you won't get in my way."

"I wouldn't get in your way. I'm not—" She was talking to air. Lynch had already disappeared behind the motel unit.

Arrogant bastard.

And that arrogant bastard was going to risk his stupid neck collaring a murderer who was more brutal than anyone she'd ever met.

And she was scared to death.

He had tied her hands. By moving so quickly, he had assured that she couldn't follow him or run the risk of getting in his way as he'd told her she might.

She got out of the car and moved close to the motel so that she couldn't be seen from inside the unit.

Wait.

Hope.

And curse the arrogant bastard who was making her stand outside twiddling her thumbs.

Three minutes.

Five minutes.

Seven minutes.

Surely, she should have heard something from the—

The front door swung open.

Briggs?

"Kendra."

Not Briggs. Lynch stood in the doorway.

She was there beside him in seconds. "What did—"

Then she saw Briggs.

He was lying on the second step leading to the bedroom penthouse. His face was a bloody mess, his lips and nose bleeding. His left arm was twisted at an odd angle.

And his eyes were gazing warily at Lynch. No, not warily, fearfully.

Lynch had promised her intimidation. He had delivered.

"Come in. We need to get busy. I wasted a little extra time on him." He pulled her inside the room and slammed the door. "That's Briggs. Poor guy fell down the stairs."

"I see," Kendra said. "On his face?"

"I kind of remembered how Olivia's face looked when we took her to the hospital. That's why I spent a little extra time." He strode over to Briggs and threaded his fingers through his hair and jerked his head back. "But I didn't finish. I thought you'd like to be here to watch. Kendra Michaels, Tommy Briggs."

"I know who she is," Briggs said sullenly. "They told me all about her. She's the one who's freaky. She's caused the—" He screamed as Lynch's fingers skillfully pressed on a nerve center on his neck. "Shit."

"Don't be impolite to the lady," Lynch said. "I'm already a bit pissed at you."

"Stop already. I didn't touch her."

"No, but you tried. And ended up hurting another woman instead." Lynch ran his knuckles down a reddish purple burn on Brigg's face. "But she left you with this souvenir of your visit. Scalding-hot frying pan?"

Briggs winced in pain. "She wasn't supposed to be there. I was told that Michaels lived alone."

Lynch grabbed him by his jacket collar and knocked his head back against the stairs. "And who told you?" He punctuated his words with further head jabs against the stairs. "Who? Who? Who?"

"Laird!" Briggs finally screamed out.

Lynch stopped and loosened his grip on Briggs's collar.

"Good," Kendra said. "Let's discuss Laird, Briggs."

His expression was suddenly cautious. "I ain't talking about him. I don't care what you do to me. I've seen what he does to guys who don't do what he wants."

"But this Laird wanted you to hurt me, and you failed," Kendra said. "What do you think he'll do to you for that?"

"He'll get me out of this, that's what. He was giving me another chance."

"And you thought he was telling you the truth? My God, you're dumb."

"I ain't dumb," he bristled. "Everyone thinks I'm dumb, even Laird thinks I'm stupid. But I watch, I listen, I know more than he thinks I do."

"Good, then you may come out of this alive," Lynch said.

"You're the law, ain't you? You're not going to kill me."

"Don't be too sure. Law officers don't usually assist scum like you to 'fall down the stairs' either." Lynch's hands closed into fists. "I'd suggest you talk, Briggs."

His eyes darted to Kendra. "She's a doctor. She won't let you hurt me."

"Don't count on it," Kendra said. "If you're counting on my Hippocratic oath to save you, I'm not that kind of doctor. Who is Laird to you?"

Briggs was silent.

Lynch took a step closer to him.

"No," Kendra said sharply.

Briggs's smile was almost a sneer. "I told you. She's a doctor. A woman doctor. She's soft."

"Am I?" She took a step closer, her eyes narrowed on his face. "Let's see how soft, Briggs." She reached out and touched the blood flowing from his cheek. "You're bleeding. I want you to bleed, Briggs. You made a mistake when you hurt my friend. When I was sitting in that hospital, I was thinking of all the things that I wanted to do to you." She wiped her fingers on his shirt. "I was angry when Lynch got to you first. But it's not too late. I can do—"

"You're bluffing."

She ignored his interruption. "Look at my face, Briggs. What does it tell you? I love my friend, Olivia. Do I want to make you suffer?"

He stared at her, then moistened his lips. "Maybe."

"But there's only one thing I want more, and that's to find out what you know about another friend." She took out her phone and showed him a photo of Jeff. "Jeff Stedler. Have you seen him?"

He looked away and shook his head.

"I believe you're lying. You don't lie well. He was at Ocotillo Wells. You must have seen him."

"I didn't see him in the desert."

"Okay, I'll drop it for now. Let's go back to the original question. Laird. Is he your boss?"

"I ain't got no boss. I run my own show." He scowled. "And I told you, I won't tell you anything. Go ahead, tell that Lynch to beat me up. I'll take you to court. You'll lose your license."

"Why don't you go take a walk, Kendra?" Lynch suggested. "Five minutes should do it."

She was tempted. Briggs was ugly and weasel-like and proving more stubborn than she thought. It would take a long time to break him. There should be another way to—

There *was* another way.

"I'm tired of dealing with him, Lynch," Kendra said tersely. "Let's just let the poison rot him." She turned away. "We'll find Jeff on our own." She looked back over her shoulder at Briggs. "The FBI will be taking you into custody as soon as we leave here. You'll be held in jail, and you might last thirty days before your insides rot away. And I'll enjoy every minute of it. Come on, Lynch."

"If you insist." Lynch sighed. "But I was hoping for another trip down the stairs."

"He may not know enough to make it worth our time." She had reached the door. "And being with him makes me want to throw up. We're out of—"

"Rot?" Briggs repeated. "What do you mean rot? What poison?"

"You tell us," Kendra said. "All we know is that Leon Sanders would probably have died of that substance in his body if you hadn't blown his head off first. Whatever you were doing out in the desert was toxic."

He moistened his lips. "You're lying. You're trying to scare me."

"Am I?" She pulled out her phone and strode back to him. "Here are the victims murdered by Frank Rusin, you may know him. They all had the same toxic substance in their bodies as Leon." She flipped the photos one by one in front of his face. "Leon was the last one to prove positive."

"That doesn't mean I have that stuff inside me. Leon was the one burning that shit."

"I take it you're not talking about meth," Lynch said.

"Don't be an asshole," Briggs said. "This wasn't no penny-ante job." His lips tightened. "And that's all I'm saying."

"How do you know you don't have it?" Kendra asked. "If Sanders was working on this substance, and he contracted the disease, then it's probably airborne." She paused. "And whoever hired you knew that the two of you might be dead men before the job was over. They didn't give a damn whether you lived or died. They probably preferred that you die and get rid of any witnesses against them."

Briggs cursed viciously. "That son of a bitch." He regained control. "Not that I believe you. It could just be contagious, and I ain't been around any of those marks in those photos. You could be lying about Leon. You ain't got no proof I've got that crud."

Kendra shrugged. "There's a test to prove whether you have it or not."

"Then give it to me. You're a doctor."

"I'm a psychologist. And I don't give a damn if you have that poison in your system. I hope you do have it."

"Then somebody else can test me. Have them do it."

"Why? We don't *care,* Briggs."

"You want to know stuff. I might tell you a little if you get me tested." He added, "Only a little, understand?"

"And when we confirm, you'll spill your guts," Kendra said. "Because the only way we're going to be able to cure you is to find out exactly what you were cooking in that desert and find a remedy."

"But I don't know that I have it." He was sweating. "And I'm not going to let you bluff me."

"Then let's verify." She dialed Griffin. When he picked up, she said, "I need Agent Deevers here at the motel. Where is she? How quickly can she get here with her test kit?"

"About ten minutes. Your time is running out, Kendra. Another twenty minutes, and you have to turn him over to us."

"I know. Tell her to get here as quickly as possible and bring her bag." She hung up and turned back to Briggs. "Ten minutes. If you tell me enough in that ten minutes before she gets here, I'll let her run the test. If you don't, I'll tell them to take you into custody."

"I ain't telling you everything."

"You will," Lynch said. "But we'll start with names. Laird? Oscar Laird? Security head at Thatcher Pharmaceuticals?"

Briggs eyes widened. "You know about Thatcher?"

"What's Laird's connection to you?" Lynch repeated.

Briggs didn't answer at once. "I guess if you know about Thatcher, it won't be telling you too much. Yeah, Oscar Laird is with Thatcher."

"That's not telling us anything we don't know. More. You answer to him?"

"Sort of."

"What's the stuff you were dealing with in the desert?" Kendra asked. "You said you knew more than Laird thought you did. What do you know about that substance?"

Briggs eyes sidled away from hers. "I've said enough for now."

"You've not said anywhere near enough," Lynch said with soft venom. "We haven't been convinced that your miserable hide is worth saving. Talk. What do you know about that chemical?"

Briggs finally shrugged. "Not much. They told us that there was a big hurry for us to do the final finish. It was set to be flown out of the country two days from now."

"Flown where?"

"The Middle East. Iraq or Iran or somewhere else like that."

"Well, that's precise."

"What do I care? Leon was set to do the finishing. He had to combine the final ingredients of the formula, then cook them like you do crystal meth. I was just supposed to guard him and the stuff." His lips twisted. "It was working out fine until you stuck your nose into our business."

"What is this 'stuff'?"

He shrugged. "They called it Pegasus 2. They said that they had to do the final finishing procedure outdoors instead of the lab, and that's why they set us up at Ocotillo Wells." He made a face. "It stunk big-time."

"The formula was called Pegasus 2? What was it supposed to do?"

"They didn't tell me." He smirked. "I told you, they tried to keep us from finding out anything. But I snooped around a little . . . just for my own protection. I saw sealed cans of some other formula at a warehouse when we made a delivery. It was marked Pegasus 1. It was in an old box labeled with some address in Panama City, Florida."

Kendra frowned. "It was the same substance?"

"I didn't say that," Briggs said. "I said it looked like the same kind of packaging. Only those cans and boxes looked old, and October 2004 was printed on the outside." He frowned. "Look, I've told you enough. When do I get that test?"

Lynch ignored the question. "So you and Leon were out there working on a formula called Pegasus 2. And you saw old crates labeled Pegasus 1, which might or might not be the same formula. You really expect us to believe you don't know what the substance is capable of doing?"

"Laird never told Leon or me nothing. We were just grunts to them." He smiled slyly. "But that kind of changed after old man Rusin started fouling up on the hits. Rusin was real scared that it might be contagious. I heard Laird tell Rusin that the stuff was like a catalyst."

"A catalyst," Kendra murmured. "An activator. But to activate what?"

"How do I know?" Briggs said. "But it better not be activating anything inside me, or I'll go after Laird and cut his nuts off."

"And you don't know anything about Jeff Stedler. Is he dead? Did you or Rusin kill him?"

"I ain't talking no more. Now get me that—"

There was a knock on the door.

"Sienna." Lynch strode across the room and threw open the door. "Come in. You must have been close."

"I was on my way here." She smiled. "Santini was a little too smug about locating the bastard. I wanted to at least be in on the collar." Her brows rose as she saw Briggs. "He's a little worse for wear, isn't he?"

"He fell down the steps," Lynch repeated.

"And you brought me here to give first aid?"

"Not exactly. You said you had a kit that could test for that foreign substance. Can you test Briggs for it?"

"Sure." She opened her black bag. "But couldn't it wait until after he's in custody?"

"No," Kendra said. "We made a bargain. How long will it take?"

"A few minutes. I just need to swab his mouth and compare results to the other victims'."

"I ain't got it." Briggs was glaring balefully at her. "I feel strong as a horse."

"I'm sure you do," Sienna said. "None of the victims had any symptoms even though some were advanced." She glanced at Kendra. "Well, what am I supposed to do?"

"He wants it done. He's giving you bull." She looked at Briggs. "Yes or no? Last chance. Once they put you away, I'll do everything I can to keep you from being tested. I want you dead, Briggs."

Her sincerity must have been clear to him.

He scowled. "Do it," he said harshly.

"Open your mouth." Sienna picked up two toothbrush-sized swabs and carefully scraped the inside of each cheek. "That should do it." She turned and placed one of the swabs in a clear glass tube. "Okay, this will only take a minute or so. The liquid will turn a bright blue if he's been infected."

"I ain't got it," Briggs said. "I wasn't around that stuff much at all. Just a couple times when—" He broke off, then stared at the tube. "It's not changing. See?"

"She said it would take a minute," Kendra said. "Shut up, Briggs."

"I ain't going to shut—"

He was staring at the liquid, which suddenly darkened into an opaline blue.

"Positive." Sienna looked up from the tube. "And strongly advanced. Being so close to the source must have increased the—"

"You're lying." Briggs was pale. "I ain't gonna die. Not because of some crap like this."

"You will unless we can find an antidote," Kendra said. "And since we don't know what the hell we're dealing with, that may take some time. Talk, Briggs."

"I'm not telling you anything else," he said hoarsely. "This could all be a trick. I want to see a lawyer."

"By all means," Lynch said. "Sienna, tell the agents outside to come in and take Briggs into custody. Let him sit in a cell for a night and think about how his buddy Laird let him breathe that poison without even warning him." He gazed into Briggs's eyes. "We'll be there first thing in the morning, and if you tell us more of what we need to know, we might work on getting that antidote and keeping you alive."

"It's a trick. I'm going to live. I don't have that crap inside me."

"How much time does he have, Sienna?" Kendra asked.

She shrugged. "I have no idea. I've been dealing with dead bodies and one survivor who was almost dead. It's advanced. It could be a week or two. Or it could be sooner." She looked at Briggs. "You'd be smart to tell us what we want to know so that we can get to the bottom of this illness."

"I'm okay. I want my own doctor. Not some FBI—" He was breathing hard. "You're all lying."

"Whatever." Sienna moved toward the front door. "I'll call in the guys on stakeout."

"Do that." Kendra followed Sienna to the door. "Were you just trying to help us pressure him?" she asked in a low voice. "Lies or truth?"

"Truth," Sienna said as she started down the steps. "He's probably a dead man."

Kendra turned back to Briggs as she closed the door behind Sienna. "You're sure you don't want to talk to us? We need addresses, names, anything to do with that substance." She paused. "Anything to do with Jeff Stedler."

"Screw you." He was breathing hard, as if he were running. "I don't have to tell you anything more. Do you know what Laird would do to me? I'll get my lawyer to make you get me that antidote. I've got rights."

And the sad thing was that the justice system would bend over backward to give this murderer his constitutional rights, Kendra thought. Even if it meant he would eventually walk out of that courtroom a free man. "That will take time. You may not have time. We'll be visiting you tomorrow morning. If you're smart, you'll reconsider. Lawyers are good at stalling but not—" She broke off as Sienna and four FBI agents streamed into the room.

Sienna glanced at her inquiringly as the agents surrounded Briggs and fired questions at Lynch. "Any luck?"

She shook her head. "He's shut up tight now, but we may be able to use some of the info he gave us before."

"What info? Griffin will—"

"We're not going to leave Griffin out in the cold," Lynch said as he joined them. "Though Briggs didn't give us enough to wrap anything up. Maybe Griffin will have better luck with him."

"He gave us one thing," Kendra said. "The warehouse."

Lynch nodded and turned on his heel. "Let's go find it."

"You should inform Agent Griffin," Sienna called after

them as Kendra joined Lynch as he went out the door. "He won't like your going off on your own. This is an official investigation, and—"

"Keep us informed on Briggs," Kendra tossed back over her shoulder. The next moment, she was hurrying after Lynch as he headed for the car. "And how are we to find this warehouse?" she asked as she got into the passenger seat. "Briggs clammed up before we got details."

"But we have the name of the substance. Pegasus. We know that Charles Schuyler, the CEO of Thatcher Pharmaceuticals, is up to his neck in this mess." He pulled out his phone. "And we should have the photos of Schuyler and Denton we requested from Griffin earlier. There they are. Griffin marked the photos with a letter over each of their heads to identify them. Look happy, don't they?"

The two men were sitting at a banquet table and smiling into the camera. They both appeared to be in their fifties or early sixties. The surgeon, Denton, was tall, a little lanky, with dark hair that was receding slightly. His eyes were light, blue or gray, and his smile was bright and confident. Schuyler was heavier, with a shock of gray-threaded dark hair and an olive complexion. He was also smiling, but there was a tinge of cynicism in the curve of his lips. "They seem . . . close."

"Bound by a mutual lust for the long green?" He glanced down at the phone. "And here's the shot of Oscar Laird, whom Briggs was telling us about."

Laird was a powerfully built fortyish man with a dirty blond crew cut and handsome, craggy features.

"Griffin's being very cooperative," Kendra said dryly. "He's evidently trying to give us everything we might want or need."

"I'll take it." He was driving down the boulevard toward the freeway. "At any rate, we need to ask all of them a good many questions. Schuyler, first. Let's head for the

Thatcher offices at Rancho Bernardo." Then he suddenly slowed and pulled off the street onto a supermarket parking lot. "But I need to get some other answers before I chat with Schuyler." He was dialing his phone. "My old friend, Jamerson. It's time you met the gentleman. I'm putting the call on speaker."

"Not yet." Kendra stopped him and started to dial. "I want to make another call first. It's more important."

"To whom?"

But her call had already been picked up. "Olivia, we've got him. His name is Tommy Briggs, and he's in FBI custody."

"You're sure it's the right man?"

She chuckled. "You're damn right. He even had the burn mark from your skillet on his face. That will do until the DNA evidence comes in. I thought you'd rest better knowing that the bastard is off the streets. But since we gave you your going-home present a little ahead of time, you'd better concentrate on getting out of that hospital."

"I'll work on it." She paused. "Thank you, Kendra."

"My pleasure. Believe me, truly my pleasure." She hung up. She turned to Lynch. "Sorry. Now you can make your call."

He was dialing. "No problem. I agree that calling Olivia was more important."

"Really?"

"Really."

The call at the Justice Department was answered on the third ring. "Jamerson. What the hell is happening, Lynch?"

"That's what we want to know. Kendra Michaels is on speaker, Jamerson. You'll remember she figured prominently in my reports."

Silence. "Call me back later."

"No way. She's entitled." He paused. "And we're entitled to know why you were so interested in what Jeff Stedler was doing here."

"It's confidential."

"Really? And was what was being concocted at Panama City, Florida, in October of 2004 also confidential?"

He repeated warily, "Panama City?"

"Let me help you. Pegasus 1?"

He inhaled sharply. "Where did you hear that name?"

"I sincerely wish it had been from you, Jamerson. Instead, you let me stumble around in the dark."

"That's because Pegasus 1 no longer exists. The last of it was destroyed in 2005."

"It does exist. It's here in San Diego getting ready to be shipped to the Middle East."

"That's not possible."

"It's real, and I think you knew about it. Who told you? Stedler?"

"He told me something, not enough. He never mentioned the Pegasus Project. You're positive you're not mistaken?"

"I'm sure we're on the right track. I won't be positive about anything until you tell me what we're dealing with here, Jamerson. Stop tying my hands. Talk to me."

Jamerson hesitated. "Stedler said he had a confidential source who tipped him off about a lethal project under way. He was extremely protective of this source, and he refused to give his—or her—name even to me. He said it might be a job for Homeland Security."

"Then how did you become involved?"

"Well, I suppose he trusted me. At the time, he didn't know what the project was. He speculated it might even be materials for some kind of explosive device. He said he was working with this source to get a sample of whatever it was that they were producing."

"Well, he got it," Lynch said. "It somehow ended up all

over the floor of his apartment when they grabbed him."
He added grimly, "And he hasn't been seen since."

"Shit. He was in way over his head. If this is truly the
Pegasus Project, then it's more dangerous than Stedler
could have imagined."

"I'm still waiting for you to tell me what it is."

Jamerson was silent.

"Oh, for God's sake, Jamerson. Maybe you'd rather sit
on your ass and let that nasty brew be shipped out of the
country? We just may be able to stop it."

"I think it's time we brought in Griffin and the FBI."

"So that you don't get stung and brought up before
Congress for mishandling a national emergency? I've every intention of bringing Griffin into this, but not before I
know what I'm doing. Tell me about the Pegasus Project."

Jamerson hesitated, then started to speak quickly and
concisely. "It was a highly speculative project, one of
those pie-in-the-sky things that no one thought had a real
chance of succeeding. The idea is that a population center
could be infected with an airborne contaminant that, on
its own, would be harmless. Those infected could live for
the rest of their lives with no ill effects. Then, at any time,
be it days or even years later, a second airborne formula
could be dropped, and it would kill those people instantly.
But anyone who had not been exposed to the first substance would be unharmed."

Lynch nodded. "So a whole town could be wiped out
in minutes, but invading troops on the ground would still
be fine."

Kendra shook her head. "That's monstrous."

"A large portion of the population would agree with
you," Jamerson said. "But aside from the obvious public-
relations problems, the formulas never worked properly.
The two formulas, Pegasus 1 and Pegasus 2 as they were
called, were tested extensively on animals. Pegasus 2 was

supposed to be harmless to anyone who hadn't already been exposed to Pegasus 1, but it always made a certain portion of the test population seriously ill, and even killed some."

"What does Panama City have to do with it?" Kendra asked.

"That's where the lab was set up during those first years between 2003 and 2005."

"And Denton was in charge?"

"No, they set up a complete dummy operation. Denton was the big cheese, the creative mind, and they didn't want anyone to know he was connected with the project. He worked off by himself and was brought into town at crucial points in the experiment."

"How was Thatcher Pharmaceuticals involved?"

"It wasn't. It was purely a military project."

"And what was Denton's reaction when the military canceled his project?"

"Rage. Accusations. He's pretty much of an egomaniac. He liked being the fair-haired boy, the genius behind the scenes. Only according to Hal Spander at Homeland Security, it was pretty obvious that he would have preferred to be center stage."

"So how did they control him?"

"He quieted down after a while. He had some other pulmonary scuba meds on the fire that were bringing him favorable attention. He got a lot of public ego stroking and finally stopped brooding and dropped his protests."

"He might have dropped the protests, but I think the brooding continued," Lynch said. "Homeland Security wasn't keeping an eye on him?"

"Of course, they were. But as I said, Pegasus was extremely sensitive and complex to create even if you had the formulas. It took years of skilled, knowledgeable scientists to produce the supply we had at the lab in Panama

City. After it was destroyed, we didn't have much to worry about. We just checked on Denton occasionally to make sure he wasn't doing anything questionable."

"It didn't occur to you that when he teamed up with Thatcher Pharmaceuticals, that might be questionable?" Lynch asked sarcastically.

"I wasn't involved. It was a Homeland Security problem." He paused. "Until I got the call from Jeff Stedler. He said there was something ugly going on down there in San Diego that I should look into. I didn't know until this moment that it was the Pegasus Project."

"And he never called you back," Kendra said quietly. "So you sent in Lynch."

"Blind," Lynch added bitterly.

"I told you, I didn't realize that Stedler was investigating Denton. He just said there was something ugly going on."

"Well, I told you I'd find out what the dirty little secrets were all about," Lynch said bitterly. "You could have helped more, dammit."

"I'm telling you now, aren't I?"

"Because that Pegasus Project scared you shitless."

"This could all be a false alarm," Jamerson said. "I don't see how Denton could have reproduced those formulas. He did the basic work, but there were several scientists who had input in the finished product. Remember, he could never get them to work correctly."

"Maybe, with the resources of a multinational corporation, he was able to lick it."

"Still, it would be a logistical nightmare to develop it in secret and perform the clinical trials with all the trial and error that entails."

"But it sounds like he already has the first formula," Kendra said. "Briggs said the containers he saw looked old, and the boxes were from Panama City, Florida. The most logical scenario would be that Dr. Denton found a way to prevent the finished product of Pegasus 1 from being destroyed. Or at least a good portion of it. He kept it hidden away until he had found a partner to help him continue refining the second formula."

"Pegasus 2, which they could never get to work correctly during the official project," Lynch added.

"So Schuyler with Thatcher Pharmaceuticals showed up on the scene and they became a team." She made a face. "Or should I say a Deadly Duo? They obviously found a buyer for their weapon of mass destruction. The only thing I'm wondering is how those murder victims were infected with the substance."

"They still needed to run tests as they developed it," Lynch said. "It would have been relatively easy to pick random victims and expose them to an airborne mist. In fact, it would have been safer for them if the victims were chosen at random."

Random, in the same way they had planned to unleash that contaminant on millions of unsuspecting people. Kendra shuddered. "Hideous."

"And they realized that some of their subjects were infected with a version of the formula that still didn't work," Lynch said suddenly. "At least not the way it was supposed to. Remember, the goal was for the second formula, Pegasus 2, to be harmless by itself. But Denton, Schuyler, and company realized that those unknowing test subjects were going to get sick. So those people were murdered before they could manifest symptoms."

Kendra nodded. "Unusual symptoms, like premature aging of the organs and who knows what else that might be recognized by a savvy medical examining team."

"Or it could have been an accidental exposure like what happened to Leon Sanders," Lynch said. "And Stephanie Marsh might not have been random since she worked for Denton. I'm leaning toward a combination of both motivations."

"This conjecture is all very well," Jamerson said coldly. "But it's not stopping the situation from becoming critical. When I hang up, I'm calling Homeland Security and Griffin myself and telling them everything. I'd suggest you get moving and try to stop Denton in his tracks. That Pegasus mutagen mustn't leave the country."

"From your description, I wouldn't say Dr. Denton is the principal problem," Lynch said. "He may have started the ball rolling, but Schuyler is the heavy hitter. He's the one who hires the big guns."

"Stop them. Both of them." Jamerson hung up.

"You heard him," Lynch said sarcastically. "The great man said that we should take care of them. Too bad he didn't give us a hint how to do that."

"Rancho Bernardo," Kendra said. "Nothing's changed except we know more about what's going on. Let's go see Schuyler."

He glanced at her as he started the car and drove out of the parking lot. "You look . . . charged. I didn't expect that reaction."

"Charged? Are you crazy? Do you think I'm enjoying this? How could I? It's too serious. It scares me. The idea of that horrible substance killing people without them even knowing they're targeted. And the sheer callousness of selling that stuff to a country that wants only to kill us." She shivered. "I can't understand it. I can't understand them. Do you wonder that I want to stay as far away as I can from men like Denton and Schuyler?"

"No, but someone has to deal with them," he said quietly. "Stedler knew that." He paused. "And you know it, too. You may hate it, but it won't stop you. I don't see you backing away."

Her lips tightened. "I can't. Not now. I'm caught."

"And maybe a little charged?"

"Maybe." She was feeling a zinging, an excitement that a challenge always brought her but it was mixed with a heavy heart and a sense of impending—what? The depression and urgency that she'd begun to experience earlier was back and growing stronger every moment. But she didn't want to think about that strange emotional cloud hovering over her now. "This isn't the time to analyze. It doesn't matter what I'm feeling. Let's just get moving."

"Get moving," Schuyler said, as soon as Denton picked up the call. "I just heard from Laird that he had a call that the FBI has picked up Briggs. I don't know how much he's already told them or if he'll spill his guts before we can stop him. I told Laird to get that last batch of Project Pegasus loaded on the plane. I'm heading for the airport right now."

"You've ruined everything." Denton's voice was a shrill squeal. "You kept telling me that you'd take care of everything, and all I had to worry about was making sure that the project would work. Now you're telling me that the FBI may know everything?"

"I didn't say that. I said that we should cut our losses and head for Tehran. The FBI is close on the trail."

"And you couldn't even get rid of that woman who was causing all the trouble. What good are you?" he said. "I may not go anywhere. Why should I? You're the one they'll blame for everything. The government values my brain and my skill. You're just a crooked pill pusher." He added with malice, "And when they find out your fine company is nearly bankrupt and going down the tubes, and you bought that palace in Tehran, they'll be sure that you have terrorist leanings. They may even send one of those drones after you."

Schuyler controlled his anger. It would only be for a little while longer. "And you think that I'm the only one who is in trouble? What about that disc you stole from Homeland Security files at Panama City? How are you going to talk yourself out of that?"

Denton was silent. "You haven't found the disc yet. They won't know about it."

"Unless we leave a loose end who can tell them about it. I'm through with protecting you. You can go with me on that plane to Tehran or stay here. I don't care which you do." He paused. "I'm leaving for the airport in the next three minutes. I'll take off within the hour."

"I have to have that disc. It's evidence against me."

"Then go to the warehouse and make a last try at getting it." He added deliberately, "Or tie up that loose end."

"Have Laird do it."

"No, you're going to get your hands dirty. I'm not going to let you weasel your way out of this and leave me in the lurch. I'll see you at the airport." He hung up.

CHAPTER 16

"Schuyler's not here," Lynch said as he came back to the car after going to the executive suite. "His secretary said he had an emergency appointment and wouldn't be back for the rest of the day."

"Did you believe her?"

"No, but I went to the executive garage, and the CEO parking spot was empty. The word 'emergency' struck me, though. She might have used it because Schuyler's demeanor was tense or hurried."

"Because he might know that Briggs has been picked up?" Kendra said. "It just happened."

"It could be that he was being watched. At any rate, Schuyler has flown the coop. Did you locate any nearby warehouses?"

She shook her head. "I Googled it and didn't find anything. Then I walked around the immediate area and didn't see anything but plush office complexes. It's a very well-to-do little town. I can't see Briggs or Sanders making deliveries here without attracting attention. The local police would definitely be interested in someone who looked like a Hells Angel." She frowned thoughtfully.

"Let's try Ocotillo Wells. It's out of the way. There's a small airport nearby. It would have been convenient for Sanders and Briggs to make their deliveries. I don't remember seeing a warehouse, but it's worth a shot to see if there's one there."

He nodded as he started the car. "Ocotillo Wells it is. From here, it will probably take us over an hour."

His phone rang after they'd been on the road about forty-five minutes. He made a face. "Griffin. He's probably going to give me hell for not calling him personally instead of leaving it up to Jamerson." He accessed the call. "Jamerson told you everything Kendra and I know, Griffin. Maybe you'll be able to get more out of Briggs than we—"

"Briggs is dead."

He stiffened. "What?"

"You heard me. He collapsed in the interrogation room while we were questioning him. One minute, he was sitting there spitting out curses and swearing that he was going to sue us all, the next minute his eyes glazed over, and he stopped breathing."

Kendra's eyes were wide with shock. "Did you try to revive him?"

"Of course," he said curtly. "Though none of us were eager to get close to that scumbag. Particularly after Agent Deevers diagnosed him as having the same substance in his body as Sanders. He couldn't be saved."

"What happened?"

"How the hell do we know? Heart attack? He was scared shitless. The presence of that substance in his body was an advanced case. It could have been that."

"What does Sienna say?"

"The same thing I am. She doesn't know. She said she couldn't tell until the medical examiner got through with Briggs's body. When they took him to the morgue, she trailed along with them. She said she'd call me with the results."

"Weird," Kendra murmured. "The whole thing is bizarre."

"You think it's weird," Griffin said. "I think it's big trouble. He died under interrogation. There's bound to be an investigation. They'll probably accuse us of waterboarding or something. We've got to clean this mess up quick. It won't look so bad if we've saved the nation from biological catastrophe. Jamerson said that Charles Schuyler is involved. Have you questioned him yet?"

"No, he wasn't at the main office."

"Find him," Griffin said. "I checked him out after I talked to Jamerson, and his company is going bust. Desperate men do desperate things. And I sent a couple agents to pick up Denton for questioning."

"Let me know when you have him," Lynch said. "I think it will all be going down very fast from now on. We're heading for Ocotillo Wells to check out the airport and any warehouses in the vicinity."

"Schuyler's there?"

"We don't know, but we're going to find out. Rancho Bernardo didn't look promising, so we're going to try the desert. It might be a good spot from which to make a quick getaway."

"Nothing like being positive," Griffin said sourly. "Do you need backup?"

"I have no idea, but it wouldn't hurt to send them."

"I'll have a team on their way within five minutes," Griffin said curtly. "And I'll yank Sienna off that autopsy and send her with them in case you find any of that substance out there."

"I'll be in touch." He hung up, and said to Kendra, "We'll have help, for what it's worth. You heard Griffin. They'll be leaving San Diego in five minutes."

"We may not need help. Ocotillo Wells is only guess-work." She frowned. "Briggs . . ."

"You're right, it's weird."

"Dammit, I want to know how he died."

He studied her face. "It's really bothering you."

"It may have something to do with that escalation of the effect of the substance. It could be there is a conta-gious factor involved, it might be—" She shook her head. "I'm guessing. I just want to know." She reached for her phone. "I'm calling Sienna."

"She may not know anything yet."

She dialed Sienna's number. "Then she'll tell me that she doesn't." She made a face. "Voice mail." She hung up. "I'll call her later."

"Griffin may have already pulled her away from the examination and sent her our way. Or maybe she's still in the exam room. I'm sure she'll get back to you."

She nodded. "That sounded both patronizing and soothing, Lynch. Knock it off."

"Yes, ma'am. I'll watch it in future." His smile faded. "I wasn't patronizing, but I was trying to soothe you. Briggs's death seems to have upset you. I don't like to see you upset. So accept it. My instinct is to try to make your pain go away. That seems to be how it is."

She felt a surge of warmth move through her. "No pain. Just curiosity and puzzlement. And it wouldn't be your business anyway." She was silent, and added, "But it's kind . . . and surprising . . . of you to care." Her gaze shifted to the scenery flying by outside her window, and her brow once more knitted in a frown. "I just don't . . . it's weird . . ."

There were three warehouses a short distance down the slope from the Ocotillo Wells airstrip. As Lynch drove over the hill, they saw that all of the vinyl-tiled warehouses appeared to be deserted. But then so did the rest of the airport, Kendra noticed. There were several small aircraft parked in an adjoining holding area but there was no one servicing them.

However, no one could say the same for the Gulfstream jet parked in a hangar set off from the runway. There was an aura of luxury, urgency, and speed surrounding the plane. The doors of the hangar were thrown wide. The plane was already being fueled for takeoff. The cargo bay was open, and there were two gray-uniformed men loading boxes from a hand truck. Another man with a blond crew cut, wearing a brown leather jacket, was obviously calling out orders to the men.

"Oscar Laird?" Kendra asked, her gaze on the man with the crew cut. It was difficult to see his face from that distance, but he resembled the photo of the security head.

"Good chance. What do you bet some of those boxes have Panama City labels?" Lynch said softly as he pulled the Ferrari out of sight behind the bank of warehouses. "I think we've struck pay dirt."

"It looks like they're in a big hurry," Kendra said. "Tehran express? It's terrifying. If these formulas work the way they're intended, entire cities could be infected with Pegasus 1 without the population's even realizing it."

"Making those people susceptible to being murdered with just a whiff of the second formula," Lynch said soberly. "The idea pisses me off. What do you say we cheat those bastards out of making their delivery?"

"How?" Her eyes narrowed on the three warehouses. "Which one? It could take us hours to search all of them for those boxes."

"Watch the trucks and see which warehouse they go back to after they load the boxes from the hand truck on the plane." He glanced around the field. "I don't see any vehicles except that beat-up gray truck over by the fence.

Either Schuyler hasn't shown yet, or we could be wrong about their leaving immediately."

"It wouldn't make sense for them to load those boxes if they hadn't scheduled an immediate departure," Kendra said. "They couldn't keep—They're coming back."

The small truck was speeding back toward the ware-house area. The truck pulled into the loading dock of the middle warehouse and the uniformed men jumped out of the cab. The next moment, they had disappeared inside the building.

"Let's go." Lynch jumped out of the car. "See those metal fire-escape balconies that line the second-floor rear of each of those warehouses? We'll go to the building on the right, climb to the rear balcony, then swing over to the balcony of the center warehouse. When we get inside, we'll verify that those boxes are Pegasus Project, then see about disabling that jet."

"When we get inside? They're bound to be locked, right?"

"I'm not worried about that part of it."

"I am. And hadn't we better tell Griffin to get a move on it?" She was hurrying after him up the four flights of stairs of the warehouse. "Or have your Jamerson stop that plane from taking off?"

"Griffin already has agents on the way. If he said they'd be out of the office in five minutes, he'll see that they are. If we get a chance, we'll try to escalate. And we can't have Homeland Security scrambling jets to take down a plane until we verify that it's a national threat."

"How sensible and discreet. Not like you at all, Lynch." She had reached the second-floor balcony and was gaug-ing the open distance between that warehouse and the balcony of the center warehouse. "It's at least ten feet." She looked down at the ground at least thirty feet below. "No rope. No ladder. How do we get across?"

"Jump." He positioned himself outside the iron railing surrounding the balcony, then turned to face the center warehouse. "I'm six-four. I'll launch myself and grab the rails."

"And how do I—"

He was already in motion, pushing off with the balls of his feet and flying through space.

He missed!

No, he'd grasped one of the rails with one hand and was hanging, swinging, by that grip.

"Lynch!"

He didn't answer as he reached up with the other hand and grabbed the rail. "It's—okay." He pulled himself up to the floor of the balcony and lifted himself over the rail. "Piece of cake."

"Yeah, sure." Her heart was beating so hard, she could scarcely breathe. "You're an idiot."

"I only misjudged by a little." He took off his jacket, shirt, and gun holster. He tied the arms of the two garments together. "I'm going to swing this jacket over to you. Try to grab the arm of the jacket, and I'll pull you across. You'll have to get on the other side of the railing."

She was already climbing over the railing. "And what if that shirt tears away from the jacket?"

"I won't answer that. You seriously object to soothing. Well, maybe a little soothing. You have a good chance. I don't buy cheap clothing, and the material is good." He swung the jacket.

She reached out.

She missed it.

He swung the jacket again.

She lunged and grabbed a bit of the material. The weight of the jacket pulled it out of her hand.

"Again," she said.

This time, she grabbed it and held on tight with both hands.

"Are you ready for me?" she asked.

"Most of the time. But you've been known to surprise me."

"Lynch," she said through her teeth. "If you drop me, I'll not be pleased with you. I'll be so displeased that you'll be in grave danger of extinction."

He smiled. "Come ahead. You're safe with me."

"Like hell." But she took a deep breath and jumped into space.

Her palms were burning with friction.

She was dangling, her arms almost jerked from their sockets.

Hold on tight.

He was pulling hand over hand.

She was moving upward.

"Got you!" He released the jacket and grabbed her arms and pulled her over the railing. He held her close for an instant and then released her. "I did that rather well. You may compliment me now, Kendra."

She could scarcely breathe, and her knees were weak. "You may still be in danger even though you didn't drop me." She took a step back. "See if you can get us inside this warehouse."

He nodded as he fastened the holster with his .44 Magnum back on over his white T-shirt and moved along down the balcony. He checked two windows and stopped at a narrow door. "The security system is probably off since those guards are going in and out packing and loading . . ." His gaze narrowed on the lock at the door, and he bent above it. "We'll know in a minute . . ."

He swung the door open.

No alarm.

"Come on," he whispered. "Let's find those boxes. Quiet."

It was hard to be quiet as she moved through the halls of the building, which seemed to squeak at every other step. Though Lynch seemed to move with catlike litheness as he led her down the staircase from the second floor to the first. The place was like a rabbit warren, with the huge area divided up into crude wooden-walled compartments of various sizes, demarked by a series of mazelike corridors.

She froze as she saw daylight pierce the dimness across the huge room as the massive doors were thrown open.

Sounds suddenly assaulted her.

Curses.

The creak of wheels on the loading dock.

Then the light disappeared as the guards slammed the door shut. The next minute, she heard the roar of the truck.

Lynch held up his hand, listening.

No sound.

"I think we're okay," Lynch whispered. "You take the compartments on the left. I'll take the ones on the right. Call if you run across the stash. Now's the time to take the safety off the gun I gave you. Be careful."

As if she needed him to caution her. She was wound as tightly as a violin string. She only wanted this to be done. She took the safety off her gun and shoved it back into her jacket pocket. She moved toward the first compartment.

Trash.

A few magazines.

An ashtray overflowing with cigarette butts.

The second compartment.

An old Domino's pizza container.

She tensed, her eyes widening.

And a surgeon's scalpel stained with dried blood lying on the floor.

She moved slowly toward the third compartment.

Even in the dimness, she could see the bloodstains on the rough wood floor.

She could smell sweat and blood and pain.

It was all pain.

She could hear the sound of it in the breathing that came from the figure huddled in the corner of the compartment.

She came slowly toward that corner.

It was too dim to see clearly.

But she knew. Oh, God, she *knew*.

"Jeff?"

She fell to her knees beside him. His clothes were ripped to shreds.

He was ripped to shreds.

That surgeon's scalpel in the other room . . .

"Jeff, it's Kendra. Tell me how I can—" He couldn't tell her anything. There was duct tape over his mouth.

She tore it off.

"Kendra . . ."

She pulled the tape from his wrists and gently slid her arms around him. "I thought you were dead."

"Close." He reached up and touched her cheek. "Beautiful . . . always so beautiful. Inside . . . and out. I never told you that, did I?"

"No." She turned her head and kissed his fingers. Her voice was shaking. "Because you're an honest man, and I'm not beautiful. It's going to be okay, Jeff. I'm here. I'll take care of you. Can you walk?"

"I'll try. I'll do anything . . . you want me to do." He leaned forward, then fell back against the wall. "I'm sorry. I can't do it. Too weak. Get out of here, Kendra."

"Shut up. I won't leave you."

"They'll be back. They always come back. Laird would have been here now except he's been loading the plane."

"Let them come. I'll make them wish they'd never been born," she said fiercely. "Who did it?"

"You must know, or you wouldn't be here."

"Schuyler?"

"And Denton. He was the one who offered his scalpel. He knew a lot about how to . . . hurt. When they took out my eye, he told them how to do it so it wouldn't kill me."

"Your eye." Her eyes strained in the dimness to look at his face. She felt like throwing up as she saw the gaping hole where his right eye had been. "Why? Why would they do that?"

"You always told me I was stubborn. They . . . thought so, too."

"Dear God, Jeff."

"Get out of here."

"I can't leave you. I'll get Lynch, and we'll carry you out of here."

"Adam Lynch . . . He's here?"

"We've been looking for you." Her voice was anguished. "I wish we'd found you sooner. Why did they do this to you?"

"They wanted the disc. Denton stole the disc with all the information about the Pegasus Project from the Homeland Security files. It wasn't only his work but the compilation of . . . several other scientists. He couldn't reproduce it alone, and they needed the disc to . . . seal the deal with Iran."

"And you had it?"

"Stephanie Marsh stole it and gave it to me. She was Denton's assistant. She found out what—they were doing and couldn't stomach it. They killed her."

"Yes."

"She died because she tried to do something . . . right for the world. How could I give that damn disc to them?"

Jeff would find it impossible even at this horrendous cost. Justice was the creed he lived by. How many times had she told him that he was obsessed? She had been part of that obsession but without that bright true light that had burned within him. "No, I can see how you would be . . . stubborn." Tears were running down her cheeks. "But you can stop now. We're going to get you out of here." She started to get up. "I'm going to go get Lynch. I'll be right back, and we'll—"

"Kendra Michaels?" The man standing in the doorway was smiling at her, but there was a Glock pistol in his hand. "Oh, don't go away. I've been looking forward to our first and last encounter. You've been a thorn in my flesh since you came on the scene."

She had seen a photo of that olive skin, thick dark hair, and powerful body only hours earlier today. "You're Charles Schuyler." She drew a shaky breath. "You son of a bitch. You did this to Jeff?"

"I was only a participant. It was a joint project. That disc is important to both Denton and me. However, it seems we'll have to do without it. I debated whether to take him with us on the plane, but I decided that some men just can't be broken. We did try, didn't we, Stedler?"

"Go to hell," Jeff said.

"You see?" Schuyler said. "I would have given up a long time ago if Denton hadn't been so determined. I have enough money to survive and live the good life in Oriental splendor. The Iranians will have to be satisfied with the finished weapon. They can have their own scientists work on reproducing it."

"Then why didn't you tell them to stop? Why did you do this to him?"

He shrugged. "He didn't matter, and it was a way to

control Denton." He checked his watch. "Who should be here within a few minutes." A door opened and slammed. "I believe that's him. Always punctual."

Kendra had been trying to figure how she was to get to the gun in her jacket without alerting Schuyler. Denton might be a distraction.

But where was Lynch? Kendra wondered. He must have heard that door open. Stay away, Lynch. Don't be gathered into the net.

Denton was suddenly bursting into the cubicle. "You changed your mind, Schuyler? You're going to take care of him for me. It's only right when you—" He stopped in shock as he saw Kendra. "Who is she? What is she doing here?"

"Dr. Kendra Michaels, Denton. Surely you remember our discussing her?"

"She's with the FBI. Get rid of her, and let's get out of here."

"I believe we have a little time. My information is that she works with a single agent from the Justice Department. He's probably around somewhere and will have to be taken care of. But you're right, we should definitely start the ball rolling."

He lifted the Glock. "It's been an interesting association, Denton. Good-bye."

And shot him in the forehead.

Schuyler watched dispassionately as the doctor fell to the floor. "He looks shocked, doesn't he? Denton was always so sure that he was more brilliant than anyone else in the universe. You'd think he would have seen it coming. I was through with him. Why should I let him live?" He turned to Jeff Stedler. "That should have made you happy. He was the enemy, and now he's dead."

"You're all the enemy," Jeff said. "But you're dirtier than the others, Schuyler. You're scum."

"And you're now officially a dead man." He lifted the gun again, then suddenly swiveled it to point at Kendra. "No, I think we'll take out the bitch first. One final torture for you, Stedler."

"No!" Jeff threw himself in front of Kendra.

Panic raced through her as she tried to push him away and pull the gun out of her jacket. "Jeff, don't do—" Then she felt Jeff's body jerk as the bullet tore through him. "Oh, God. No."

"Yes," Schuyler said. "Now let's take care of—"

"Roll into the shadows, Kendra. Now!" Lynch's voice. Lynch at the door behind Schuyler. Lynch's bullet striking Schuyler in the shoulder and spinning him away from the door.

But Schuyler was turning, shooting, and Lynch was falling against the wall.

Kendra had her Beretta out. "Drop the weapon, Schuyler. You're not going—"

"Bitch." Schuyler gave her a malevolent glance and fired over his shoulder as he ran out of the compartment. The bullet plowed into the wall next to Kendra's head.

Lynch was struggling to get to his feet. Blood was running down his cheek from a surface wound on his temple. "Are you all right?"

"Am I all right? You're the one who almost got his head blown off." She crawled back across the room to Jeff. "He's hurt. I have to help—" She looked at Lynch over her shoulder. "Go get that bastard. Don't let him get on that plane and go off to Al Qaeda paradise. I want him dead and on his way to hell."

Lynch turned away and was heading for the door. "Call Griffin and tell him to get help to take down that plane if it gets airborne."

He was gone.

Was Jeff gone, too?

There was no time to call Griffin. Not with Jeff lying there wounded, maybe dying.

She was holding that poor, tortured body in her arms, her hand frantically searching to find his wound. "You have to live, Jeff. You've fought them so hard. You did such a good job. But now you have to beat them."

Her fingers touched blood pouring from a wound in his chest. "I'm going to lay you down and apply pressure to stop the wound." Her voice was uneven. "Hold on, Jeff. You can't let them win."

"Don't—lay me down. Keep holding me. It's not going to matter." He reached up and touched her lips with his fingers. "And I've already won. Lynch won't . . . let them get away. And I have you here to make things right. Have—to tell you . . . I always loved you. You have to know that, Kendra. It's just that things got in the way— they seemed—more important."

"Hush, you did what you had to do. I should have helped you."

"You came into my life." His voice was fading. "That—helped me. Hold me tighter."

Her arms tightened around him. "Don't you die on me, Jeff." Her voice broke. "We can make this work. Just don't leave me. Life can be good."

"Life was—always good with you. You made me better than I ever—could have been alone." His eyes were closing. "Every day was a . . . World Series, and I was the MVP who hit the home run to win . . . the game. Remember that, Kendra." His breathing was shallow. "Home run . . ."

His head fell against her arm. His breathing had stopped.

Dead.

He was dead.

"Dammit." Tears were flowing down her cheeks as she rocked him in her arms. Her friend, her lover, the man who had led her down paths both painful and full of joy. This shouldn't have happened. A good man should not have been torn apart and had his life taken away. There should have been something she could do.

And now there was still nothing she could do except sit there, holding him.

Close your eyes.

This time to say good-bye and pray for the soul of her beloved friend.

The huge doors flew open, flooding light into the dimness of the warehouse.

Kendra, jarred, quickly straightened away from Jeff. She reached for her gun.

Three shots echoed through the warehouse.

A low cry, then silence.

Kendra carefully put Jeff down and got to her knees.

"Kendra? Are you there? It's Sienna."

Relief surged through her. "Here, Sienna." She got to her feet. "To your right aisle from the door. Who's with you?"

"Santini and Brockman." Kendra could hear Sienna's swift footsteps crossing the warehouse. "But they're running out to the plane to intercept Schuyler. I told them I'd see if I could locate you. God, I was so worried when we saw Oscar Laird go into this warehouse. Are you all right?"

"Yes, I didn't even see Laird."

"He came running from the plane. You won't see him alive again. He pulled a gun, and Santini shot him." Sienna stopped in shock at the doorway of the compartment, her gaze on Denton's crumpled body. "What the hell happened here?"

"Denton. Schuyler just killed him." Her gaze went down to Jeff on the floor at her feet. "And Jeff."

"Jeff Stedler?" Sienna moved toward him, going into

combat medic mode, tearing off her jacket. "Are you sure? I can try to administer—"

"No, he's dead." Kendra drew a long shaky breath. "I'm very sure."

Sienna looked at Jeff's body for a long moment. "I'm sorry, Kendra," she said quietly. "I only met him a few times, but everyone said he was a good man. The best. I know how upset you must be."

"Yes." Her lips tightened with anger. "You could say that I'm upset. But that's an indulgence I can't afford right now. Jeff's dead. I can't just sit here and mourn him. Lynch is out there somewhere trying to do something, trying to stop Schuyler. I have to go help him."

"Right." Sienna nodded, her gaze on Jeff. "Poor guy, they really worked him over. Why?"

"They wanted information. He didn't give it to them."

"Good for him. He must have been brave as hell. Did he tell you all about it?"

Kendra shook her head, and said unsteadily, "Those last moments weren't about anything but what we were together." She moved toward the compartment doorway. "But I have to put that aside. Come on. Santini and Brockman may not be enough help for Lynch."

"I'm with you there." Sienna was keeping pace with Kendra as she half ran down the corridor past the compartments that led toward the door at the loading docks. "Santini is always sure that I have more medical than practical know-how. It's time I showed him that I have both, dammit." She threw open the huge double doors. "The plane is still there, but the cargo bay is closed."

Kendra had stopped to look at the body of Oscar Laird, who was lying next to the door. His eyes were staring up at the ceiling, and his mouth was open in a silent scream. Three bloody holes gaped in his chest.

"Kendra."

"I'm coming." She turned away and moved toward the door where Sienna stood. She stood staring out at the blazing hot tarmac, simmering in the midafternoon heat.

She stiffened, her gaze narrowing. But she was no longer seeing the concrete tarmac or the jet.

Close your eyes. Put it together.

No, don't close your eyes. Not this time.

"I don't see Santini and Brockman," Sienna said. "But there's Lynch at the end of the runway." She gestured with her Colt Python. "You go help him, and I'll cover you from here."

Kendra didn't move.

"Hurry," Sienna said impatiently. "Someone could pick Lynch off from that jet. We don't know how many of his men Schuyler has on that plane with him."

"We?" Kendra repeated softly. "*I* don't know, but I'd be surprised if you didn't, Sienna. And if I went running out to Lynch, we'd both be easy targets for you, wouldn't we?"

Sienna went still, then swung around to face Kendra. "What on earth are you talking about?"

"You're dirty, Sienna. So dirty it makes me sick. And so clever. You almost got away with it."

Sienna stared at Kendra as if she had begun speaking an undecipherable language. "You're not making sense."

"Santini didn't shoot Laird. You did. I heard the gunshots. Three bullets, straight to his chest. But not from Santini's gun."

Sienna's brows rose. "And the exceptional Kendra Michaels knows exactly what every gun sounds like?"

"This time it's about what I didn't hear." Kendra leveled her gun at her. "Santini never carries anything except an automatic. His spent shell casings would have been pinging on this concrete floor like bell chimes." Kendra gestured to the floor without looking down. "No bell chimes, no shell casings. Which would be the case if he was shot with a revolver, like the one you're holding. It's not even FBI-issue, is it? No, of course not, you'd want a gun that couldn't be traced."

Sienna did not reply.

"And Santini and Brockman aren't even here yet, are they? There hasn't been time since Griffin sent them from the office in San Diego. Lynch and I have driven it, and the time factor is off. It should have taken another twenty minutes. Yet here you are with guns blazing. Because you had a head start. You left Briggs's body at the medical examiner's lab and took off before Griffin even called you. Did Schuyler promise you a seat on his plane? Or are you here just to clean up his loose ends, like Laird?"

"Guesswork. This means nothing."

"Doesn't it? You've just given me a prism through which a lot of things are looking pretty damn clear. Jeff believed there was someone working inside the FBI, which was why he was so secretive in those last days. You passed yourself off as the star agent, but everything you did or observed was something someone else would have told us anyway. But I'm sure you did everything you could to hide the fact that those murder victims were unknowing test subjects. If their reactions had been allowed to progress, someone eventually would have recognized the symptoms, and that would have ended Schuyler's big payday real quick, wouldn't it?"

"I had nothing to do with this."

"Sure you did. I'm quite sure you visited Lesley Dunn alone in the hospital sometime during the day she died, with access to her IV line. We can look it up. And trust me, we'll find out what you swabbed in Tommy Briggs's cheeks before he died this afternoon. You swabbed his mouth twice. One swab gave you the results you needed, and I assumed the other was for another test. But there was no other test, was there? The other swab was for you to poison him. Quick enough to keep him from making an official statement, but slow enough to avoid suspicion. What was the poison?"

Sienna slowly shook her head.

"We'll find out. It's just my nature to be curious. I can never tell when I might need to know something. By the way, I need you to drop your gun now."

Sienna's grip on her gun tightened. "You think you know all the answers."

"Not all of them. I don't know how long you've worked for Schuyler, or how long you were helping him pave the way for his Pegasus Project. But I'm sure you were much more valuable to him when Jeff Stedler got on his trail."

Sienna looked away for a long moment, and she suddenly smiled faintly. "You know, Kendra, I felt a kinship with you from the moment we met. All those *muy macho* agents looked down on me, too. We were both smarter than they were, and they resented it." Her smile deepened. "I was wondering how long it would take you to work your way to me. I almost made it, didn't I?"

"Because I liked you," Kendra said. "I wanted to believe in you. Drop the gun."

"Even though I knew you were going to cause me trouble, I really hoped we wouldn't have to kill you."

Kendra was startled by the frank admission. "Just tell me one thing . . . Did you know what they were doing to Jeff in this warehouse?"

"He was a fool. He wouldn't talk." Her words were icy cold. Completely without conscience or compassion.

"And you're the one who told them he was getting close, and they had to take him out?"

She shrugged. "But, Kendra, that's what they paid me for."

Kendra drew a deep, harsh breath. Sienna was trying

to rattle her, get under her skin, and make her lose focus. "Damn you to hell."

"Not nice. I won't wish the same for you." Sienna whirled with a lightning movement and dropped to the floor of the loading dock as she lifted her gun. "Though I'll be the one to send you there."

A bullet plowed into the door next to Kendra as she dodged to the left behind a post.

Remember what Jeff taught you. Make every movement, every bullet count.

But Sienna was moving, rolling, and it was almost impossible to get a bead on her. She was a trained agent and had the advantage.

Another bullet splintered the wooden dock only inches from Kendra's face.

Help me, Jeff.

What had he told her?

Don't think about what's happening now. Think about what's happening next.

Sienna was rolling to the left. Aim at the spot where she'd be in another second.

Now!

The bullet tore through the air and blasted into Sienna's neck as she rolled into the shot.

Sienna screamed. She dropped her gun and clutched her throat. Blood was gushing, pouring, through her fingers.

Kendra got to her feet and walked over to where Sienna lay.

Sienna was gasping, gurgling, her gaze fixed desperately, pleadingly, on Kendra.

Pleading for what? Mercy? Life? After what she'd done?

Kendra stared down at her, feeling nothing but cold antipathy. "It seems you were wrong about sending me to the nether regions. You'd know better than I do, but I believe my bullet blasted your jugular. You probably have a minute or two before you bleed out. But you're not worth my staying around to bid you farewell." She picked up Sienna's gun and shoved it in her pocket. "You'll have to find your way to hell alone."

She turned and ran down the ramp and out on the tarmac.

The next minute, she was running across the runway toward Lynch.

CHAPTER 17

The air was suddenly heavy with a low rumble, accompanied by the high-pitched whine of a jet engine.

Lynch's head lifted at the sound.

The hangar's tall doors were opening, and the Gulfstream 550 jet rolled toward the airstrip.

Schuyler.

Another few seconds, and the man and his deadly Pegasus cargo would be gone. Minutes after that, his plane would be over the airspace of a foreign country and out of reach of U.S authorities.

No way, Lynch thought.

He'd be damned if he was just going to stand on the runway openmouthed as the plane disappeared into the sky.

He looked around and assessed his options. Not many. And certainly nothing that would do the job of the shoulder-mounted missile launcher he needed. Nothing there but a few cars, a pair of tumbleweeds, and—

His eyes narrowed as he saw a group of large canisters toward the end of the runway. There, on a flatbed loading cart, were twenty black-and-gold fifty-five-gallon drums.

Water? Or could it be . . .

Lynch sprinted toward the runway.

Schuyler moved through the jet's narrow single aisle and thrust his head into the cockpit. "What's taking so long?"

The pilot didn't look up from the instrument panel. "In case you hadn't noticed, those were real bullets back there. I didn't bargain for this."

"Sure you did. You quoted me four times your normal rate. You knew you were taking a risk."

"Risking my license, maybe. Not my life."

"Stop whining and get us in the air."

"I want double."

"We'll discuss it later."

"Now. Or I stop this plane and tell anyone who inquires that I didn't know what the hell was going on. I want double our agreed-upon amount."

Schuyler cursed, but he knew this was no time for a negotiation. He—or more likely, his new friends—would take care of this opportunist later. "Fine! Just get us out of here."

The pilot flipped an illuminated switch on the panel above him. "Buckle yourself in. Next stop, Tehran."

JP-8 JET FUEL 220 LITERS

It was exactly what Lynch had hoped to see stenciled on each of the twenty drums stacked on the tarmac, probably readied for transport to an oil rig or to a remote ranch. He pulled out his pocketknife and cut the nylon cargo straps on several of the drums.

"What the hell are you doing?" Kendra was running toward him.

Lynch glanced at the jet turning onto the runway and turning its nose toward him. "I'm asking myself the same question. I'm hoping this will be an answer." He handed Kendra the knife. "Cut the rest of these straps."

She sawed at a nylon strap as he swiveled one of the drums onto its side and kicked it onto the runway.

Then another. Then another.

The jet drew closer and picked up speed.

Kendra hacked through another strap.

Lynch hurled the remaining barrels into the runway, grabbed Kendra's hand, and pulled her back toward the warehouses.

He kneeled, pulled out his gun, and took aim at the barrels as the plane approached them.

BLAM!

BLAM!

BLAM!

Nothing.

"You missed?" Kendra was incredulous.

"No way. Either those barrels are impenetrable, or that fuel isn't as combustible as I thought it was." He fired again.

BLAM!

BLAM!

Lynch cursed. He had been aiming for the drums' midsections, but maybe if he tried the ends . . . He kicked more barrels toward the runway.

The plane picked up even more speed as it took off. It struck the barrels and scattered them as if they were no more than Wiffle balls in the path of a Mack truck.

Kendra stiffened and pointed to the plane as it lifted into the sky. "Look!"

One of the cargo straps, still attached to a barrel by a holding clasp, had caught the jet's landing gear. The barrel dangled below the plane, knocking against its underside.

"*Yes.*" Lynch raised his gun, bracing his wrist over his

left forearm. This time he aimed for the barrel's top rim. "Make it count," he whispered to himself. "Don't blow it. For God's sake, don't blow it."

He squeezed the trigger.

BOOM!

Get Kendra down and away from that exploding plane.

Lynch whirled around and knocked her flat against the tarmac. They lay facedown as the roar filled their ears, and the heat blazed from the sky above. Debris rained down around them for what seemed like a full minute though it could only have been a matter of seconds.

Kendra could scarcely breathe under Lynch's weight. He was protecting her with his body.

She could feel the heat from the burning plane, but she couldn't see it.

She *had* to see it. She had to know that Schuyler and that foul substance he was peddling were destroyed. She had to know that Jeff's suffering and death had not been for nothing. She pushed against Lynch. "Get off me."

"In just a minute. I have to make sure that the debris—"

"Get *off* me," she repeated fiercely. "I won't have this. What makes my life so important? One man has already died to save me today. A good man who was probably worth a hell of a lot more than I'll ever be. You're not going to be the second." She shoved him aside and sat up.

The plane was a flaming ruin. It had crashed into the warehouse complex, and the entire area was a blazing inferno. The smell of jet fuel and acrid smoke was overwhelming.

"No one could live through that, right?" Her hands clenched into fists. "Schuyler's dead? That damn Pegasus Project is dead?"

"Nothing could survive that fire," Lynch said quietly. "That heat is so intense that there's no question. It's destroyed, Kendra." He sat up, and his hand gently brushed a strand of hair back from her forehead. "You look . . . very fragile. Tell me you're okay."

She wasn't okay. She didn't know how or when she would be okay. There had been too much pain and death and an ugliness that had seemed to take over the world.

"Kendra?"

She saw a car screech to a halt some distance away and Santini and Brockman jump out of the vehicle. They were staring at the burning plane, and Santini was already on the phone. "You'd better call Griffin," she said dully. "Or he'll be calling you, Lynch."

"Screw Griffin," he said roughly. "Are you okay?"

"No." She got slowly to her feet. "But there's no way I'm going to let this break me. It won't happen. They didn't break Jeff. He didn't survive them, but he wasn't broken." She started across the tarmac toward Santini. "But I'm not going to let them look back from hell and have even a minor victory. I'm going to survive, Lynch."

EPILOGUE

"You've been here all morning. You didn't have to come to visit me today, you know," Olivia said quietly. "What made you think that I'd want you here on the day of Jeff's funeral? There are priorities, Kendra."

"And you're alive and my best friend and therefore high on my list. I'm not cheating Jeff of his good-bye. The service isn't until two. I think he'd like the idea of sharing this day with you."

"I liked him, you know," Olivia said. "I was scared to death after you almost had that breakdown. And I was worried that he wasn't good for you, but I did respect him. He was that rare specimen—an honorable man."

"Yes, he was. And you shouldn't have blamed Jeff. I was responsible for my own decisions." She gave her the ghost of a smile. "You've always told me that I take things too much to heart."

"And there's nothing wrong with that." Olivia's hand reached out and grasped Kendra's "It's a gift I value. I wouldn't want you any other way." She paused. "And I'm not worried about your having a breakdown any longer. You've gone beyond that and come out on the other side."

Kendra chuckled. "You mean I'm getting callous?"

"No, I mean that you have scar tissue now that will help you get through the pain. You'll need it."

"No more than any other teacher with special kids." Her smile had faded. "What are you trying to say, Olivia?"

"I'm saying that once you get over this trauma, you'll start thinking and making decisions about what's important to you."

"I've made those decisions a long time ago."

"But we all change, don't we? I changed when I ended up here in this hospital. I had to reevaluate my life and my safety and how I wanted to live my life. You'll do the same."

Kendra shook her head. "All I want to do is go back to my old life and heal." She squeezed Olivia's hand. "And see my friend and my mother very often and remember that there's kindness and people in this world who only want to do good."

"That won't last," Olivia said softly. "Because you'll know you can change some of that bad to good. Not many people can say that. You won't be able to resist doing it."

"You're wrong." She stood up and kissed Olivia's forehead. "Watch me." She headed for the door. "I'll be back tomorrow. I have to stop at FBI headquarters before I go to the funeral."

"Why?"

"Not because you're right about anything you've been saying." She smiled crookedly. "I only have to tie up the last loose end."

She met Griffin as she got off the elevator.

"I didn't expect to see you here." Griffin's voice was awkward. "I meant to call you, but somehow I didn't get around to it. I thought I'd talk to you at the funeral."

"And now you don't have to bother." She gazed beyond him at the empty office. "Where is everyone?"

"I gave them the day off, so they could all go to the funeral." His voice was low and sincere. "They would have gone anyway. They all liked Jeff. *I* liked Jeff. He was a great guy and the finest agent I've ever run across. You may think I'm a son of a bitch, but I don't lie."

She stared him in the eye. "I don't think you're a son of a bitch. You just have your own code, and it's not mine." She changed the subject. "Have they cleared Jeff's desk yet?"

He shook his head. "I thought I'd do it myself after the funeral. He has a sister, doesn't he?"

She nodded. "Nicole. She'll be at the funeral. I'll pack his stuff up and bring it to her. Is that okay?"

"Sure. If you're positive that's the way you want it."

"That's the way I want it." She started making her way across the office toward Jeff's desk. "I'll see you at the funeral."

She could feel his gaze on her back, then heard the sound of the elevator.

She stopped in front of Jeff's desk, bracing herself for the pain as she looked at all the familiar things that had made Jeff who he was. The photo of his sister, Nicole. The replica of the Sammy Sosa autographed baseball. His parents' photo, faded by time . . .

The pain came, then became bearable.

Scar tissue, Olivia?

She went to the copy room and got a box and began to pack away the mementos. She had to stop a few times, but she made it through.

"Was this necessary?" Lynch asked roughly from behind her. "I'd say this was cruel and unusual punishment."

She turned to look at him. "I didn't hear the elevator."

"You were occupied." He came closer to the desk. "Someone else should have done this. I would have done it if you'd asked me. But you didn't ask me. You've been ignoring my existence since Ocotillo Wells."

"It was over. I needed time to myself." She studied him. "You look very formal and conventional in that dark suit. Not like you at all."

"I can put up with it. I'm going to the funeral of an exceptional man, and I wanted to honor him."

"That's nice." She rubbed her temple. "Why are you here?"

"I stopped by the hospital, and Olivia told me where you'd gone. I was going to take you to the funeral. Are you through? May we go now?"

"You don't have to take me anywhere."

"May we go now?"

Stubborn. Always stubborn. She was too delicately balanced on the edge to fight him.

"I'm almost finished. There are only a few more things." She put the picture of Jeff's parents in the box and reached for the baseball on its stand. She opened her handbag and took out a small knife that she'd taken from the condo kitchen that morning.

She took the baseball and began carefully slicing the threading.

"What are you doing?" Lynch's gaze was narrowed on her face. "You said that Stedler worshipped that ball."

"He worshipped the one he kept in the safety-deposit box. This copy wasn't as important to him. It just brought back memories."

"So you're chopping it up?" he asked warily.

"You think I've gone off the deep end?"

"It occurred to me that you might need a little rest."

She put down the knife and began pulling the hide of the baseball apart. "Maybe you're right. But while I was lying in bed last night, I began to think of Jeff and those last moments with him."

"And that made you tear up his baseball?"

"He was talking about a home run. He said life with me was like being the MVP at a World Series and hitting the winning home run." Her voice was unsteady. "He said, 'Remember that, Kendra. A home run.'"

"That meant something to you besides a personal tribute?"

"Not at the time." Her eyes were stinging. "But later it did. Jeff wouldn't have told me where that disc was because it would have been a danger to me in the position we were in at the time. But he wouldn't have wanted it to fall into anyone else's hands after all he'd gone through. He knew me. He knew it would eventually occur to me what he meant." She carefully separated the folds of leather of the baseball.

She began gently to probe the interior.

Did I understand, Jeff? Is this what you wanted?

Yes.

The next moment, she drew out the two-inch disc.

"I'll be damned," Lynch murmured.

"That's all I needed to do." She put the disc in an envelope and put it in her handbag. "I'm not sure what I'm going to do with it yet. I'm leaning toward burning it ceremonially in my fireplace over drinks with Olivia when she gets out of the hospital."

"Am I invited?"

"Maybe." She studied him. "You're not tempted to grab it and turn it over to Jamerson?"

"Not even a little bit." He took the torn baseball from her. "I know a shop where we can have this repaired. I'll get it back to you in a few days." He closed the box of mementoes. "It's time we left for the funeral. I'll carry this. Are you going to keep that ball yourself or give it to his sister?"

"I'll keep it. She'll have the original." She stood up and moved toward the elevator. "I think he'd want me to have it."

"I think he would, too." He pressed the elevator button. "Besides his personal feelings, you were his partner. Even in that final moment, he trusted you. He knew you'd come through for him." He smiled, then said softly, "As you'll always come through for me, Kendra."

She stiffened, and her eyes flew to his face. "What are you talking about? I'm done, Lynch."

"For the moment. You're hurting, and you want to heal. We have time."

"No."

"Yes. I've watched you, studied you, seen your excitement and the adrenaline flowing." He added, "And I'm afraid that I'd miss you far too much if I walked away. So I believe that I'll have to bring to bear all my powers of persuasion to keep you from drifting too far from me."

And those powers of persuasion were very strong indeed. She could feel the waves of magnetism that always surrounded him flow toward her, threatening to pull her in the direction he wanted her to go even in this moment. "No way, Lynch."

"I'll be very gentle. No force, no pushing." He took her elbow and nudged her into the elevator. "But I'll always be there offering you the chance to expand your horizons. And someday you'll say to me, 'Okay, Lynch. Pick me up at the condo. But just for this one case.' "

"You're dreaming."

"Am I?"

She met his eyes, and for that moment, she could almost believe that the scenario he had built would come true.

"Don't worry about it," Lynch said gently. "I wouldn't do anything to hurt you. It will always be your choice."

"Dammit, you're soothing me again." She jerked her gaze away as the elevator started to descend. "And you're damn right it will be my choice. How arrogant can you get?"

He threw back his head and laughed. "You'll have to see, won't you? At the least, I promise I'll be the ultimate challenge for you." His eyes were suddenly glittering with sly mischief. "And you know you can never resist a challenge, Kendra."

"There was blood . . . Blood everywhere. But now the police are trying to cover it up."

Kendra Michaels stared at Janet Sanders in the parking lot outside her office. The woman was carrying on like a paranoid lunatic, but Kendra knew better. She had known Janet too long.

"Slow down, Janet. Where was the blood?"

Janet took a deep breath. "My fiancé's house. I saw it three nights ago. I went over there and saw it. He was gone, but there was blood all over his kitchen floor and walls!" She shuddered. "It scared me, Kendra."

"Understandable." Kendra was attempting to process the disturbing information Janet was hurling at her. She hadn't even known her old friend had a fiancé. She certainly hadn't expected to see Janet waiting for her outside the medical office building where Kendra based her music therapy practice. She had just seen her last client of the day and was heading to her car when Janet suddenly approached her.

Kendra tried to remember how long it had been since she had seen Janet. A year? Maybe two?

Janet Sanders had been her teacher at the Woodland Institute for the Vision Impaired more than a decade before, during Kendra's teenage years. A lifetime ago, Kendra thought, when she was still blind and living in the darkness. Janet had helped her learn how to live in that world.

No, not just to live there; Janet had shown her how to *flourish* as a sightless person, to feel beautiful and worthy at an age when she might have felt strange and awkward.

Then, just a few years later, when Kendra gained her sight via a revolutionary stem cell procedure, Janet had been one of her first visitors, doing everything in her power to help her adjust to an exciting yet bewildering new world.

Now, however, Janet was anything but the calm and reassuring presence Kendra had always known her to be. Her clothes were disheveled, and her mop of blond hair was falling over her eyes. Her hands were jammed into the pockets of her oversized sweater. She looked as if she hadn't slept in days.

"Calm down." Kendra motioned toward a large bench just a few feet down the sidewalk. "Let's sit down, okay?"

"I don't need to sit down, Kendra, I just—"

"You *do* need to sit down. You're starting to hyperventilate." Kendra took Janet by the arm, guided her to the bench, and sat with her. "I need you to slow down. Tell me exactly what happened."

Janet nodded and took a moment to catch her breath. "Okay. I've been dating this guy for a year. His name is Dale Baylor, and we met in the Sierra Club." She moistened her lips. "He's pretty special, Kendra. I never thought I could feel this way about anyone. You know my job was my whole life."

"And there were a lot of us who were grateful you felt that way. You're a great teacher, Janet."

"I love my students. I love my job. It makes me feel

worthwhile. But Dale . . . He made me feel beautiful. He told me that inside and out I was wonderful. I know I'm not pretty, but when he tells me I am I believe him."

"You should believe him. You are wonderful, Janet."

"That's not important." She gestured impatiently. "What's happened to Dale is the only thing that matters right now. I spend pretty much every weekend at his place. But when I went over last Friday night, the door had been busted open. . . . And there was blood." Tears welled in Janet's eyes. "So much blood, Kendra."

"Where?" Kendra asked.

"Everywhere, like I said. All over the kitchen floor, some splattered on the walls and even the cabinets. And Dale was gone. But his wallet, keys, and cell phone were on the counter."

"What about his car?"

"Still in the driveway. I can't tell you how scared I was. I got out of there and called the police. They met me back there and took my statement. The forensics team went over the place, and they took pictures and video. There was a detective in charge, his name was Sutker, and he seemed like a nice guy. He said he would be in touch."

"Has he called you?"

"Hell, no. I called them about a hundred times over the weekend. No one was ever available to take my call, so I left messages. No one called me back."

"That would not be unheard of, especially on a weekend and if the police hadn't made any progress."

"Well, I went back to Dale's house Sunday—last night—to get a few things of mine. I brought some friends with me. My key didn't work on the front door. The lock had been replaced and the broken door frame had been repaired and painted. So I tried my key on the back door, and it opened. All of Dale's things were gone, and so were mine." She shook her head in bewilderment. "It was as if he'd never lived there. And there was no trace of the blood."

"It had been cleaned?"

"More like cleaned out. No furniture, no car, no food in the refrigerator. I mean, it was empty. My friends probably thought I had made the whole thing up. If they hadn't already met Dale, they might have thought I'd made *him* up."

"Maybe a family member of his cleared it."

"He *had* no family. Anyway, I staked out the police station this morning and waited for Detective Sutker. While I waited, I called him a few times. They kept saying he was busy and that he would call me back. Same old runaround. Finally I spotted him, and I blocked his car with mine."

"Not a good idea, Janet."

"Yeah, for a second I thought he was going to shoot me. But I wasn't going to let him get away without answering a few questions."

"And did he?"

"He practically called me a liar."

"What?"

"He said I was being hysterical and that I was exaggerating. That there was no sign of a break-in, and that what little blood may have been on the scene could have been from a carving accident or maybe from a tincan lid. He said there was nothing unusual about the scene."

"What? He said that with a straight face?"

"Absolutely. He told me that I just needed to get on with my life and get used to the fact that Dale had left me. He said it wasn't unusual for women to manufacture stories like this when faced with romantic rejection. He said it makes it easier for women to deal with."

Kendra bit her lip. "Hmm. Charming guy."

"That's why I came here. I didn't know what else to do."

Kendra leaned closer to her friend. "You know I'm always happy to see you, Janet, but what made you come to me?"

"I need help. Dale needs help." Janet glanced around and lowered her voice. "And I've heard things about you."

"What things?" Kendra asked warily.

"That you sometimes help the police."

She had been afraid this was where Janet was heading. It was a side of her life she didn't often discuss, even with her friends and family. "And where did you hear this?"

"From Lynne, our school administrator. I think she speaks to your mother fairly often."

Kendra nodded. Her mother. Of course.

"The teachers at the school still talk about you all the time, and not just because you can see now. You were amazing even when you were just fourteen years old. The first time I met you, you knew that I was wearing glasses, what kind of shoes I was wearing, what I had eaten for breakfast, and that I had spent the previous night with my boyfriend. Even when you were blind, you saw the world more clearly than anyone."

Kendra shrugged. "I used what I had."

"You used it like no one I've ever seen. And I've seen thousands over the years. And you're even more amazing now that you have your sight."

"I don't take anything I see for granted, that's all. After all those years of seeing nothing, I just want to absorb every detail and know what things mean."

Janet nodded. "And what details have you used to figure me out today, Kendra?"

"What are you talking about?"

"Don't play dumb. I've known you too long. I could sit here and tell you what I've been doing, but you probably already knew in the first twenty seconds. Tell me."

"Janet, I don't see why I should waste your time—"

"I need to know I didn't come here for nothing. *Tell me.*"

Kendra sighed. "You're still volunteering at the ballet, but for some reason you've been focusing on the American Ballet Theatre instead of the San Diego Ballet Company, even though it meant driving all the way down to Costa Mesa every night when they were in town last week. And you did drive down there five nights in a row when they were performing *Giselle,* didn't you?"

Janet stared at her for a long moment. "Okay, that's amazing, even for you."

"And even though you were upset and spent the morning staking out the police station, you didn't come right here, did you? You still pulled it together enough to go to work and teach a swimming class this afternoon."

"There was no one else qualified to fill in. The kids would have been disappointed."

"Of course they would. I would have been when I was your student. And you're still fond of those overpriced coffee drinks. You had one on your way over here."

Janet brushed her lapel. "Don't tell me I spilled some on myself."

"Not a drop. But it's possible you may have spilled some on the seat of your new Volkswagen Bug." Kendra pointed to a yellow VW parked just a few feet away. "That one. Nice car. It suits you."

Janet smiled for the first time since confronting Kendra. "There must be fifty cars in this lot. How did you know it was mine?"

"Modern-day VW's have a unique fob that swings out the ignition key with the press of a button, kind of like a switchblade knife."

"But you couldn't see it. It's been in my sweater pocket the whole time."

"Along with your hand. You've opened and closed it a few times since we've been sitting here. Nervous habit? I couldn't see it, but I could hear it. It's a very distinctive sound. There's only one Volkswagen in this entire lot, so that has to be yours." Kendra pointed to the car. "I see five parking stubs on your dashboard with Segerstrom Center for the Arts clearly printed at the top of each. None show a great deal of sun fading, meaning that they were put there recently, no more than a week or so, and probably on consecutive days, since there is some variation, but not a lot, in the fading between the various tickets. I happen to know that ABT's production of *Giselle* played there Tuesday through Saturday last week, so it wasn't a great leap to figure that your volunteer work has recently been centered in Costa Mesa."

"And the swimming class? My hair is dry."

"It is. But I can still smell the chlorine. It's kind of hard to miss even after you've shampooed. I have fond memories of that school's over-chlorinated pool."

"What about my iced coffee? Was that just a guess?"

"They're all guesses. I work the odds based on my observations." Kendra pointed back to the trash can next to the building entrance. "There's a clear coffee drink cup in the trash over half full of ice with no trace of any melting, meaning that the last of the liquid had been slurped up just seconds earlier. I didn't see anyone entering the building or leaving the parking lot, so I'm thinking it was yours."

Janet nodded. "You never disappoint, Kendra. It doesn't surprise me that the police come to you for help."

"But I'm not a cop. I've helped the FBI on a few cases, but my work is in this building, helping people and doing academic research. I don't want to be anything but a music therapist."

"I know, and believe me, I wouldn't be here if I had any idea where else to go. If the police won't help me, what else can I do?"

Kendra stared at Janet for a long moment. She resented the intrusion that her occasional investigative work made in her life, but this was different. Janet was a friend, and she was clearly distraught. And what's more, Kendra *owed* her. When would she ever get another chance to repay Janet for all the wonderful things she had done for her?

"I'm really not sure what I can do for you, Janet."

"Okay. Okay," Janet said jerkily and jumped to her feet. "I knew it was a long shot when I came here. I'm sorry I bothered you with this, Kendra."

Kendra took her arm. "But I'm willing to try. Of course I'll help you any way I can." Kendra stood up. "Normally I might like to see his house, but if it's been cleaned out like you say, that might not do us much good."

Janet breathed a sigh of relief. "You're going to do it? So where do we start?"

Kendra thought for a moment. "Go back to your place and gather every piece of information you have on Dale. Every photo, every vacation video, and everything that belonged to him. I'd also like the name of every friend he has. Is he on any of the social networking sites?"

"No. He says he doesn't believe in that stuff. And he says he doesn't keep in touch with anyone from his past. He says he'd rather look forward than back."

"Where did he work?"

"He ran a business out of his house. Computer support for local businesses."

"Interesting. And he doesn't believe in using computers to promote his business?"

"He said that his business only makes him aware how insecure our personal information is on the Internet."

"Well, I'm not going to argue with that."

"I'll pull his stuff together. Do you want to meet tomorrow?"

"No. Tonight. The sooner I get started, the better chance I'll have of helping you." Kendra walked toward her car. "I'll be at your place in an hour."

* * *

An hour later Kendra stood in the kitchen of Janet's modest Escondido home staring at a mound of photographs and personal mementos on the glass dinette table.

"Are you sure you only dated him for a year?" Kendra said. "There's enough stuff here for twenty years of marriage."

"You said you wanted everything. And I'm too sentimental to throw anything away. I still have the ticket stubs for every movie and concert we saw together."

"I can see that." Kendra picked up a stub. "Who's the polka enthusiast?"

"Neither of us, but we both like beer."

"Ah."

Kendra held up a photograph and studied it. "Is this him?"

Janet looked. "Yes. It's not a great shot, though. Here, let me find a better one." Janet pulled several more photos from the pile, but in each one her fiancé's face was turned away or partially obscured.

"He wasn't crazy about having his picture taken, was he?" Kendra said.

Janet continued looking through the pile. "Not really. Almost every time I was about to snap a shot of him someplace, he asked to take my picture instead." She finally pulled another photo out. "Here's a good one. I guess I surprised him."

Kendra took the photo from her and looked at the handsome fiftyish man seated at the back of a catamaran. Dark hair, tanned skin, and a warm, inviting smile. "Good-looking guy. Where was this?"

"Catalina. It was just a couple of months ago."

"Do you have any video?"

"He gave me an iPhone for my birthday, and we shot

some video on it at his house. It's not of him, though. He was doing the shooting."

"I'd like to see it. Is it still on your phone?"

"No, it's on my computer now." Janet flipped up the lid on her laptop, clicked open the file, and played a ninety-second video in which Janet spoke to her unseen fiancé as he demonstrated her new phone's capabilities.

After the video ended, Kendra thought for a moment. "This was in his house?"

"Yes, his living room."

"Where was he from?"

"He was born in Dallas. He lived there all his life until he moved here to San Diego just a couple years ago."

"Hmm. Interesting."

"Why?"

"Show it again."

Kendra watched the video three more times, trying to focus on the myriad details in Dale Baylor's home. Was there anything there that could give her some insight?

She scanned the living room. A typical bachelor's home, heavy on consumer electronics and light on decorative touches. Dale Baylor was left-handed, probably a non-smoker, had expensive taste in wines, and was a fan of seventies rock and spy novels.

Kendra turned back to the pile on the table and picked up a small, framed art print of a woman seated on a Victorian armchair. "What's this?"

"A gift from Dale. He said she reminded him of me."

"I can see why." Kendra angled it into the light. "Have you shown this to anyone else?"

"I don't think so. I keep it in my bedroom. Why do you ask?"

"I'm going to take this with me, okay?"

"Sure, but why?"

"I'll tell you later. Just wait for my call, Janet." Kendra

pulled on her jacket as she walked to the door and opened it. "It shouldn't be more than a couple hours."

Kendra knocked on Janet's door two and a half hours later.

When Janet answered, Kendra did not step inside. "I need you to come with me. Grab your sweater, it's very cool out."

"Why?"

"There's no time to explain."

Janet stared at her. "You're scaring me."

"Don't be scared. Just come with me. I'll drive."

Kendra led Janet to her car. They climbed in, backed out of the narrow driveway, and started down the dark street.

Janet turned toward her. "Are you going to tell me what we're doing?"

"I took that picture to the FBI."

"What?"

"They owe me a few favors, and I know they want to keep me happy. I saw your fiancé's thumbprint on the upper left corner of the glass."

"Seriously? How did you even know it was his?"

"He has a large callus at his thumb's knuckle line. Maybe from holding ropes while boating. I saw it in several of the pictures you showed me. Even when I couldn't see his face, I could still see that."

Janet shook her head. "I–I'm speechless. No. I'm not. The FBI. That's big stuff. I'm not sure I like the idea you'd do this without even asking me."

"You wanted my help, Janet. And I found out something very—" Kendra's eyes flicked to her rearview mirror. "Oh, shit."

"What is it?"

"Get down in your seat. We're being followed."

Janet instinctively whirled around to look.

Kendra pushed her down by her shoulder. *"Get down."*

She pushed the speakerphone button on her steering wheel, and a man immediately answered. "Sutker."

Kendra was aware of Janet stiffening at the name. "Sutker? What the—"

Kendra raised her hand to silence her. "Not now." She spoke into the speakerphone. "It's what I thought. He's on our tail. I'm on Fifth about to turn north onto Quince Street."

"Okay," Sutker said. "We're ready for you, Kendra."

Kendra cut the connection.

"Who's on our tail?" Janet said.

"Someone has been watching your house. I couldn't see him, but that Ford Explorer was the only car on the street with the windows fogged over. They were still fogged when I came back two hours later, so I knew someone was staking you out. Either that, or your street has become a prime make-out spot."

Kendra turned right onto Quince Street without signaling. Behind them, the Explorer's tires squealed as it took the unexpected turn.

"He's getting closer," Kendra said. "Just stay down."

She gunned the engine just as the street behind them lit up with police flashers. Sirens wailed and more tires squealed as four unmarked cars surrounded the Explorer. Kendra drove another half a block before slowing to a stop.

"What in the hell is going on?" Janet asked.

"Shh." Kendra cocked her head to hear the amplified voice blaring from one of the police cruisers.

"What are they saying?" Janet asked.

"I couldn't make it out. If I had to guess, probably some variation of 'step outside the vehicle with your hands up.'"

Janet threw open her car door. "What if it's Dale?"

Kendra tried to grab her arm, but Janet had already jumped out of the car. "Janet, no!"

Kendra climbed out after her just in time to see a man in a dark shirt and trousers sliding out of the Explorer's passenger-side door. Angling the door as he would a shield, he raised a handgun toward the police cars.

The street exploded with half a dozen guns firing at once. The muzzles flashed white in the darkness.

The man flew backwards and landed sprawled on the sidewalk.

Janet screamed and lunged forward.

Kendra held her back. "No, it's not him, I promise."

The police emerged from their cars and cautiously stepped toward the lifeless figure on the pavement. One man turned to another and shook his head. "Deader than hell."

A thirtyish detective in a tan jacket left the other police and ran toward Kendra and Janet. "Are you all right?"

Janet gazed at him in surprise. "Detective Sutker?"

"Yes. You're not hurt?"

"No, who was that man?"

"We'll find out soon enough when we run the ID." Sutker turned to Kendra. "Sorry for all this, Dr. Michaels. When you called, we had to make sure he was really tailing her."

"I guess I would have had an easier time convincing you if he had pulled his gun on Janet," she said sarcastically.

"You know that wasn't going to happen. He was just waiting to see if she made contact."

Janet looked from Kendra to Sutker. "Contact with whom?"

Sutker glanced away, obviously not wanting to answer the question.

Kendra took her arm. "With Dale. He thought you might know where Dale was."

"Why would he think that?"

"Because Dale was in the Federal Witness Protection Program."

"What?" Janet glanced at Sutker for confirmation, but his face was without expression. She turned back to Kendra. "Are you sure?"

Kendra nodded. "I had a pretty good idea back at your apartment. You know I'm good with dialects, and I was positive Dale was lying about being born and bred in Dallas. I'm guessing he was raised somewhere along the Georgia or South Carolina coast, with his accent flattened by a Midwestern influence from one or both of his parents."

Sutker's eyes widened. "How the hell did you—"

"That doesn't matter now." Janet appeared stunned. "You're saying he didn't tell me the truth?"

Kendra nodded. "He obviously lied to you about where he was from, he claims to have no family, and he has no contact with friends or anyone from his past. He is also unusually averse to having his face photographed. That suggests a man hiding from something, perhaps even the law, but the fact that the police would engage in some kind of cover-up and encourage you to stop asking questions led me to think in a different direction, maybe in terms of witness protection. So I had my friends at the FBI run the thumbprint."

"Why?" Janet asked.

"I knew that if he was in Witness Protection the match request would be immediately flagged and an alert would go to the agency responsible for him. I hung around long enough for the FBI field office to get an urgent call from the U.S. Marshals Service, wondering what in the hell they were doing tracking their protected witness."

"I'm sure your FBI buddies loved that," Sutker said. "Having to explain why they were running a fingerprint for a nonagent?"

Kendra shrugged. "I have a history of annoying them."

Janet leaned back against Kendra's car. "I just can't believe it. So Dale . . . He's okay?"

Sutker nodded. "He's fine. If it means anything, I'm sorry about the way I spoke to you earlier today. When you called us, we treated it like any other crime scene. But then we got a call from the Marshals Service, and they explained everything. Someone broke into your fiancé's house and tried to kill him. Turns out he's pretty handy with a kitchen knife and he killed his attacker. He called his handler and they pulled him out of there and removed the body. But you showed up before their team could clean the rest of the scene. Believe me, the only reason we behaved the way we did is for his protection."

"His protection? What did he do?"

Kendra looked at Sutker. "We had an agreement, Detective."

"Your agreement was with the Marshals Service, not me." He hesitated and then shrugged. "But I told them I would give you a ride. Least I could do." He motioned toward his car. "Please come with me. It's only a short trip."

Short, indeed. Just three blocks away Sutker parked on a dark residential street.

"Why are we here?" Janet said.

As if in answer to her question, the rear door opened on a car parked across the street. A man climbed out and closed the door behind him.

Janet stiffened and then gasped as she recognized him. "Dale."

She jumped out of the car and ran across the street toward him. He moved toward her, but they stopped short of each other in the middle of the deserted street.

Kendra and Sutker climbed out of his car and stood several feet away.

Tears welled in Janet's eyes. "You didn't trust me? Why didn't you tell me?"

Dale shook his head. "Janet . . . It wasn't that at all." He moved closer to her. "God, I thought I would never see you again."

"Answer me. Why didn't you tell me?"

"I wanted to, Janet," he said hoarsely. "But I was afraid. Afraid I'd lose you."

She wiped tears from her cheeks. "That could never happen."

"Not even if you found out that I had lied to you about who I am?"

Another man climbed out of the car that Dale had come from. He flashed his U.S. Marshals Service badge at them. "Henry Samuels, ma'am. Whatever he may have told you, he's a good man. He did the right thing."

"You don't have to tell me he's a good man." Janet's gaze never left Dale's face. "What happened?"

Dale looked away. "I worked for a company in Savannah, and I found out some things about my employers that I wished I didn't know. They were mixed up in a lot of bad, scary stuff from drugs to Mafia-controlled vice. I thought about just ignoring it, but I couldn't. I ended up testifying against them. The next thing I knew there was a price on my head, so I entered witness protection. I moved here, and I was really hating life . . . until I met you. After that, I didn't regret anything that had happened."

"Then why were you just going to leave without telling me?"

"It was for your own good, Janet. After that man tried to kill me the other night, I knew that I couldn't stay. I had to leave you. I had to start all over." He added simply, "It broke my heart."

"Did it?" Janet thought for a long moment. "Then take me with you."

"What?"

"I mean it. Take me with you. I'll start over with you."

She met his gaze. "You said you loved me, that you wanted to spend your life with me. Unless you've changed your mind."

His eyes widened. "Are you kidding? I'd love to have you with me. But I could never ask you to—"

"You didn't ask. I volunteered."

"But it's your entire life. It would mean leaving behind everybody and everything you've ever known."

"I know, Dale. But I'll have you." She smiled. "And I'm quite capable of creating a dandy new life for myself wherever we go. I won't depend on you for anything but what we have together. Deal?"

"Deal. I'm not sure it's a great bargain for you." He drew her into his arms. "But I'm going to be selfish and take it anyway." He kissed her. "I want you to know, if you change your mind, I'll let you go."

"Oh, shut up. You're not going to get rid of me. I've made my mind and Kendra will tell you that I can be very determined when I— But you don't know Kendra." Janet pulled away and gestured toward Kendra. "Dale, this is my friend Kendra Michaels." She added huskily, "My very, very good friend."

"I've already heard about her." Dale shook Kendra's hand. "I understand you threatened to go to the media and scream bloody murder unless the Marshals Service arranged this meeting."

Kendra smiled. "You understand correctly."

Marshal Samuels scowled at Kendra. "And the U.S. Marshals Service doesn't appreciate being blackmailed, Dr. Michaels."

"Too bad," Janet said. "I sure appreciate it. When do we leave?"

"Immediately," the marshal said. "The sooner we get you both out of town, the better. Don't you want to think about it? Are you sure you want to do this, ma'am?"

Janet looked at Dale. "I'm sure."

"Okay. It's your decision." He shrugged. "After tonight, Janet Sanders won't exist."

Even in the darkness, Kendra could see color drain from Janet's face.

"Then I guess this is goodbye." Janet forced a smile as she turned toward Kendra. "You know I can't thank you enough."

"Are you scared?"

"Maybe a little. It's kind of a shock to realize that all my past and experiences don't exist."

Kendra hugged her. "Janet Sanders will always exist for me. And for the thousands of other kids you helped over the years. None of us will ever forget you. You know that, right?"

Janet's smile became warm with feeling. "I do now. Thank you, Kendra."

Dale put his arm around Janet and walked with her back to the marshal's car. The marshal climbed behind the wheel and started the engine while they settled into the back seat.

As they pulled away, Kendra waved, but Janet's attention was focused solely on the man beside her.

As it should be, Kendra thought. She was looking forward not back. But Kendra wasn't at that point yet. She had too many treasured memories of her years with Janet. It would take time to let her go.

She lifted her hand in a final farewell that was more for her own sake than for her friend.

Then she watched as their car moved down the long street, until it became one with the lights of the city.

Read on for an excerpt from the next book

by Iris Johansen

TAKING EVE

Coming soon in hardcover from
St. Martin's Press

CHAPTER ONE

He was ready.

Jim Doane drew a deep breath as he locked the front door of the small cedar house behind him. All the searching and planning was at an end and now it was time to put the plan into action.

Soon, Kevin. I know it's been a long time, but I had to be sure before I moved forward. Everything has to be in place.

He threw his suitcase into the trunk of the car and then carried his metal toolbox and shoved it on the passenger seat. Then he climbed into the driver's seat and started the car.

"Doane, wait." His neighbor, Ralph Hodder, was running toward him across the postage-stamp-sized lawn that separated their houses. "Did you think you were going to get away before I saw you?" He was breathing heavily as he stopped beside Doane's car. He was overweight and even the short run had robbed him of breath. "No way, man."

"Yeah?" He tensed and then deliberately forced himself to relax. Hodder was no threat. He was overreacting. "Do you need something, Ralph?"

"Yeah, I need to thank you. My son said that you were going to be gone for quite a while and I just wanted you to know I'd keep an eye on your place." He clapped Jim on the back. "We'll miss you. You've been a good friend to Matt, a real role model, and Leah and I appreciate it. Raising a teenage kid is always a headache but having you next door, helping him work on that old car, and letting him talk to you has made it easier."

"No problem. Matt's a fine boy and I was glad to help. In the end the most precious things we have are our children."

"You're right there." His smile faded. "Matt said you were leaving because you had family trouble. I hope that everything will be okay."

"It will be fine. But it may take a little while so I'm grateful that you're going to watch the place." He'd better pretend to be concerned. It wouldn't do to let Hodder know he'd been tempted to burn the place to the ground. "I'll call you now and then and check on it if that's alright."

"We'll be glad to hear from you. I'll have Matt cut your grass until you get back." He stepped back from the car. "You've been a great neighbor, Doane. I'll try to be one, too. Thanks for being good to my son."

"Take care of that boy," Doane said as he backed down the driveway. "You never realize how much you love them until you lose them. Believe me, I know."

But that wasn't true; he had known how much he loved his son from the moment he had been born. It hadn't taken loss to drive that truth home. His Kevin had been extraordinary in every way and being his father had dominated his life.

Until that bastard had taken away his son.

He controlled the flare of rage that went through him. He could not afford anger now that the game had begun. Everything must go according to plan. All the sorrow and rage must be put away until he had the weapon he needed to satisfy it.

He checked his GPS that was already set for Atlanta, Georgia, and pulled out his address book. He hesitated and then carefully looked around him before he reached over and unfastened the large tool chest on the passenger seat and flipped open the lid.

He needed to share this first moment of the journey with his son. They had both waited far too long. He drew back the velvet cover he had draped over the silk nest built in the interior of the tool chest. "We're on our way, Kevin. I'm keeping my promise."

The empty eyeholes of the burnt and blackened skull gazed up at him.

Pain shot through him. After all these years, he would have thought he'd become accustomed to the horror, but there were still moments like this when it hit home. He remembered what a handsome boy Kevin had been and his sweet smile and the way he . . . Tears stung his eyes. He reached out and deliberately touched the skull. "Forgive me. I still love you. I'll always love you." His gaze lifted to the photo of the woman taped to the lid of the tool chest. "She'll give you back to me the way you were." His lips tightened. "And then she'll give us the son of a bitch who did this to you." He gave one last look at the skull before he closed the lid. "She can do it all, Kevin. We'll see that she makes it happen."

He reached forward to the GPS and typed in Eve Duncan's address.